Praise for **LORD OF THE SILENT**
and other AMELIA PEABODY novels by
New York Times bestselling author

ELIZABETH PETERS

"Between Amelia Peabody and Indiana Jones,
it's Amelia—in wit and daring—
by a landslide."
New York Times Book Review

"Another thrilling episode of crime
solving. . . . Readers will find all the delicious
trappings of a vintage Peters extravaganza—
lost tombs, kidnappings, deadly attacks,
mummies, and sinister villains."
Publishers Weekly (* Starred Review *)

"Picking up the latest Elizabeth Peters
mystery . . . is like hearing from old friends
and learning of their latest adventures."
Chicago Tribune

"The appearance of a new Amelia Peabody
Emerson adventure is always joyous news."
Omaha World-Herald

"The hype is true. This is Peters' best book."
Toronto Globe and Mail

"Peters has created a marvelously complex
world of characters the reader comes to care
about quite a bit."
Topeka Capital-Journal

"[Peters] kicks up a desert storm."
People

Books by Elizabeth Peters

The Amelia Peabody Series
A River in the Sky • Tomb of the Golden Bird
The Serpent on the Crown
Guardian of the Horizon • Children of the Storm
The Golden One • Lord of the Silent
He Shall Thunder in the Sky
The Falcon at the Portal
The Ape Who Guards the Balance
Seeing a Large Cat • The Hippopotamus Pool
The Snake, the Crocodile and the Dog
The Last Camel Died at Noon
The Deeds of the Disturber • Lion in the Valley
The Mummy Case • The Curse of the Pharaohs
Crocodile on the Sandbank
and
Amelia's Peabody's Egypt *(Edited with Kristen Whitbread)*

The Vicky Bliss Series
The Laughter of Dead Kings
Night Train to Memphis • Trojan Gold
Silhouette in Scarlet • Street of the Five Moons
Borrower of the Night

The Jacqueline Kirby Series
Naked Once More • Die for Love
The Murders of Richard III • The Seventh Sinner

and
The Copenhagen Connection • The Love Talker
Summer of the Dragon • Devil-May-Care
Legend in Green Velvet
The Night of Four Hundred Rabbits
The Dead Sea Cipher • The Camelot Caper
The Jackal's Head

LORD
OF THE
SILENT

ELIZABETH
PETERS

HARPER

An Imprint of HarperCollinsPublishers

This is a work of fiction. Names, characters, places, and incidents are products of the author's imagination or are used fictitiously and are not to be construed as real. Any resemblance to actual events, locales, organizations, or persons, living or dead, is entirely coincidental.

HARPER

An Imprint of HarperCollins*Publishers*
10 East 53rd Street
New York, New York 10022-5299

First Harper paperback printing: March 2010
First Avon Books paperback printing: April 2002
First William Morrow hardcover printing: June 2001

10   9   8   7   6   5   4   3   2   1

To Tim

Amon, King of the Gods, Lord of the Silent
who comes at the voice of the poor . . .
who gives bread to him who has none . . .
father of the orphan, husband of the widow . . .
though the servant offends him, he is merciful.

*Epithets and attributes of Amon-Re,
a composite from various prayers*

FOREWORD

The Editor feels it necessary to state that she is not in need of any additional Emerson papers. In recent months she has received documents purporting to answer this description. A cursory examination proved that they were unconvincing forgeries. She has, not to belabor the point, enough material to occupy her for several years, and she is presently on the track . . . But she will say no more. The persons who have the documents she needs know who they are. No others need apply.

As for the material contained in this volume, a few words of explanation may be in order.

Though textual evidence indicates that Nefret Forth, as she then was, occasionally interpolated material into earlier parts of Manuscript H, she clearly played a more active role in the composition of this document after her marriage. Manuscript H becomes, in short, a collaboration. This was only to be expected of a lady of such forceful character.

Her marriage, and the distractions attendant thereon, also affected her correspondence with Lia

Todros. There are fewer letters, and they contain information of little narrative value. The Editor has therefore omitted them, believing that the Reader is not much interested in comments about babies and rapturous descriptions of the married state. (I assure the Reader that these are repetitive, unoriginal, and boringly proper. He or she is not missing a thing.)

The material from a file the Editor has labeled "M" is in part self-explanatory. There is no explanation of how certain sections came into Mrs. Emerson's hands. The Editor has her own opinions on that point. The intuitive Reader will no doubt draw his or her own conclusions.

ACKNOWLEDGMENTS

I am indebted to my granddaughter, Jennifer Shea, for adding another corpse to the story, and to Kristen Whitbread, my invaluable assistant, for several useful suggestions. Horus owes his survival to her. Professor Peter Dorman of the Oriental Institute found a particularly obscure tomb for me, and George B. Johnson checked my Ladysmith. Special thanks to Dennis Forbes, editor of *KMT, A Modern Journal of Ancient Egypt*, and a walking encyclopedia of everything pertaining to Egyptology, not only for finding us various ram-headed sphinxes but for reading the entire manuscript in its earlier, messy stage. Thanks also to my editor, Trish Grader, the best in the business.

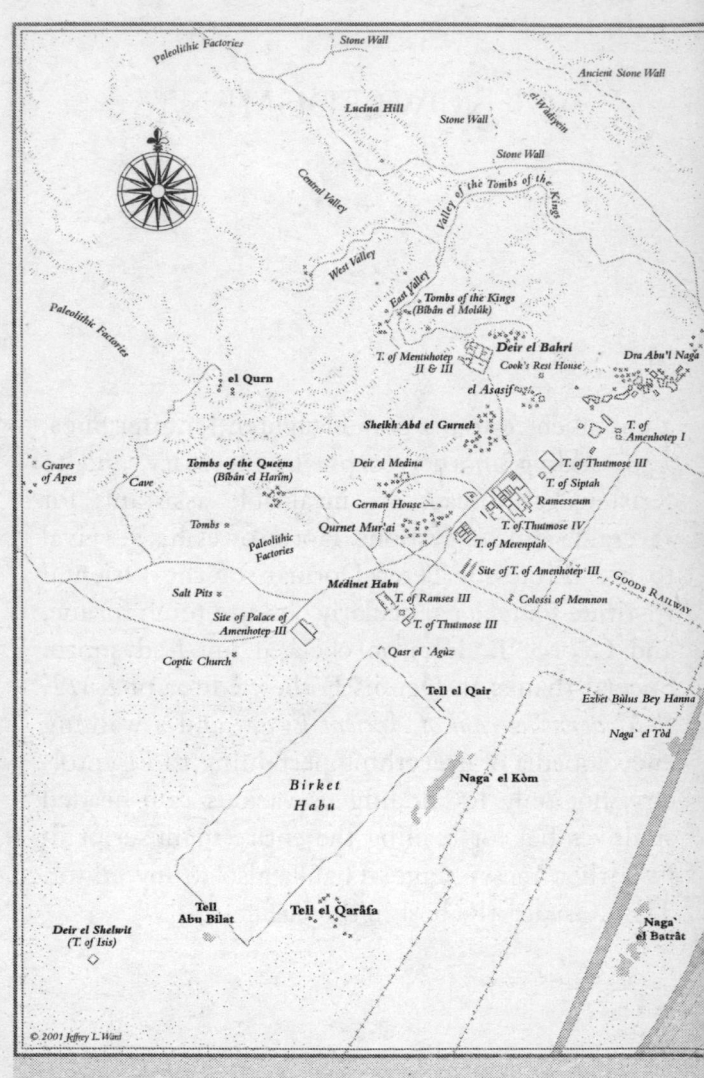

Paleolithic Factories

Stone Wall

Ancient Stone Wall

Lucina Hill

Stone Wall

el Wadiyein

Stone Wall

Central Valley

Stone Wall

Valley of the Tombs of the Kings

West Valley

East Valley

Tombs of the Kings
(Bibân el Molûk)

Paleolithic Factories

T. of Mentuhotep
II & III

Deir el Bahri

Dra Abu'l Naga

el Qurn

Cook's Rest House

el Asasif

Sheikh Abd el Gurneh

T. of
Amenhotep I

Graves
of Apes

Tombs of the Queens
(Bibân el Harûm)

Deir el Medina

T. of Thutmose III

Cave

T. of Siptah

German House

Ramesseum

Tombs

T. of Thutmose IV

Paleolithic
Factories

Qurnet Mur'ai

T. of Merenptah

Salt Pits

Medinet Habu

Site of T. of Amenhotep III

GOODS RAILWAY

T. of Ramses III

Colossi of Memnon

Site of Palace of
Amenhotep III

T. of Thutmose III

Coptic Church

Qasr el `Agûz

Tell el Qair

Ezbet Bûlus Bey Hanna

Naga' el Tôd

Birket
Habu

Naga' el Kôm

Tell
Abu Bilat

Tell el Qarâfa

Deir el Shelwit
(T. of Isis)

Naga'
el Batrât

© 2001 Jeffrey L. Ward

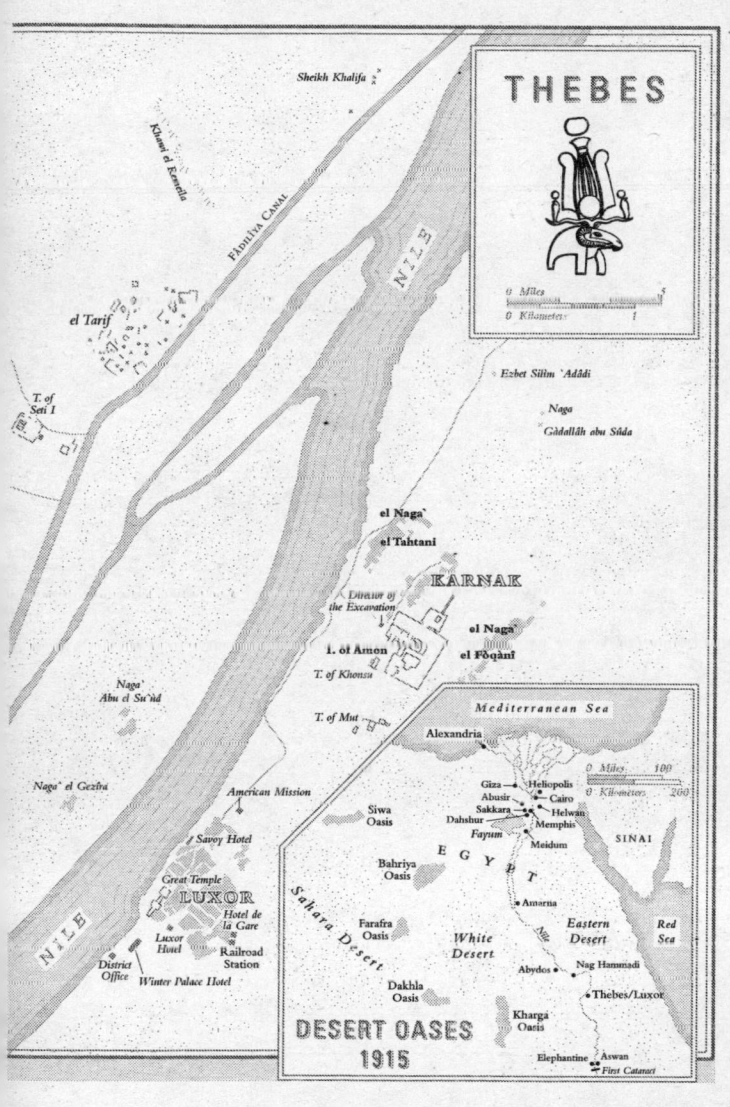

ONE

I challenge even you, Peabody, to find a silver lining in this situation," Emerson remarked.

We were in the library at Amarna House, our home in Kent. As usual, Emerson's desk resembled an archaeological tell, piled high with books and papers and dusty with ashes from his pipe. The servants were strictly forbidden to touch his work, so the ashes were only disturbed when Emerson rooted around in one pile or another, looking for something. Leaning back in his chair, he stared morosely at the bust of Plato on the opposite bookshelf. Plato stared morosely back. He had replaced the bust of Socrates, which had been shattered by a bullet a few years ago, and his expression was not nearly so pleasant.

The October morn was overcast and cool, a portent of the winter weather that would soon be upon us, and a reflection of the somber mood that affected most persons; and I was bound to confess that these were indeed times to try men's souls. When the war began in August of 1914, people were saying it would be over by Christmas. By the autumn of 1915, even the sturdiest optimists had resigned themselves to a long, bloody conflict. After appalling casualties, the opposing armies on the western front had settled into the stalemate of trench warfare, and the casualties continued to mount. The attempt to force the Straits of the Dardanelles and capture Constantinople had been a failure. A hundred thousand men were pinned down on the beaches of Gallipoli, unable to advance because of the enemy's control of the terrain, unable to withdraw because the War Office refused to admit it had made a catastrophic mistake. Serbia was about to fall to the enemy. The Russian armies were in disarray. Italy had entered the war on our side, but her armies were stalled on the Austrian frontier. Attack from the air and from under the sea had added a new and hideous dimension to warfare.

There was a bright spot, though, and I was quick to point it out. After a summer spent in England we were about to leave for Egypt and another season of the archaeological endeavors for which we have become famous. My distinguished husband would not have abandoned his excavations for anything less than Armageddon (and only if that final battle were being fought in his immediate vicinity). Though acutely conscious of the tragedy of world war, he was sometimes inclined to regard it as a personal inconvenience—"a confounded nuisance," to quote Emerson himself. It had certainly complicated our plans for that season. With overland travel to the Italian ports now cut off, there was only one way for us to reach Egypt, and German submarines prowled the English coast.

Not that Emerson was concerned for himself; he fears nothing in this world or the next. It was concern for the others who were accustomed to join us in our yearly excavations that made him hesitate: for me; for our son Ramses and his wife, Nefret; for Ramses's friend David and his wife Lia, Emerson's niece; for her parents, Emerson's brother Walter and my dear friend Evelyn; and for Sennia, the little girl we had taken into our hearts and home after she was abandoned by her English father.

"It only remains," I went on, "to decide how many of us will be going out this year. I had never supposed Lia would join us; the baby is only six months old and although he is a healthy little chap, one would not want to risk his falling ill. Medical services in Cairo have improved enormously since our early days there, but one cannot deny that they are not—"

"Damn it, Amelia, don't lecture!" Emerson exclaimed.

Emerson's temper has become the stuff of legend in Egypt; he is not called the Father of Curses for nothing. Sapphirine orbs blazing, heavy brows drawn together, he reached for his pipe.

Emerson seldom calls me Amelia. Peabody, my maiden name, is the one he employs as a term of approbation and affection. Pleased to have stirred him out of his melancholy mood, I waited until his stalwart form relaxed and his handsome face took on a sheepish smile.

"I beg your pardon, my love."

"Granted," I replied magnanimously.

The library door opened and Gargery, our butler, poked his head in. "Did you call, Professor?"

"I didn't call *you*," Emerson replied. "And you know it. Go away, Gargery."

Gargery's snub-nosed countenance took on a look of stubborn determination. "Would you and the madam care for coffee, sir?"

"We just now finished breakfast," Emerson reminded him. "If I want something I will ask for it."

"Shall I switch on the electric lights, sir? I believe we are due for a rainstorm. My rheumatism—"

"Curse your rheumatism!" Emerson shouted. "Get out of here, Gargery."

The door closed with something of a slam. Emerson chuckled. "He's as transparent as a child, isn't he?"

"Has he been nagging you about taking him to Egypt this year?"

"Well, he does it every year, doesn't he? Now he is claiming the damp winter climate gives him the rheumatics."

"I wonder how old he is. He hasn't changed a great deal since we first met him. Hair of that sandy shade does not show gray, and he is still thin and wiry."

"He's younger than we are," said Emerson with a chuckle. "It is not his age that concerns me, Peabody, my dear. We made a bad mistake when we allowed our butler to take a hand in our criminal investigations. It has given him ideas below his station."

"You must admit he was useful," I said, recalling certain of those earlier investigations. "That year we left Nefret and Ramses here in England, one or both of them might have been abducted by Schlange's henchmen if it hadn't been for Gargery and his cudgel."

"I don't know about that. Nefret defended herself admirably, and Ramses as well." Emerson puffed at his pipe. He claims tobacco calms his nerves. Certainly his voice was more affable when he went on. "However, I admit he was of considerable assistance the time we were locked in the dungeon under Mauldy Manor with the water rising and the house on fire and . . . What are you laughing about?"

"Fond memories, my dear, fond memories. We really have led interesting lives, have we not?"

"Too damned interesting. I would rather not go through another season like the last one." His voice grew gruff with an emotion his reticent British nature would not allow him to express.

I knew what emotion it was, though, for I shared it. He was thinking of our son and how close we had come to losing him.

Ramses had been in trouble of one sort or another as soon as he could crawl. In his younger days he had been kidnapped by master criminals and antiquities thieves, fallen into tombs and off cliffs . . . but a complete catalog would fill too many pages of this narrative. He had reached his mid-twenties alive and relatively unscathed; but maturity had not tempered his reckless nature, and he had never faced greater dangers than the ones he had encountered the winter of 1914–15.

Everyone knew that the Turks were planning to attack the Suez Canal. What was not generally known was that they hoped to inspire a bloody uprising in Cairo to coincide with their attack, and divert troops from the Canal defenses. They found willing allies in a group of Egyptian nationalists, who were bitterly and justifiably resentful of Britain's refusal to consider their demands for independence. Kamil el-Wardani, the charismatic young leader of this group, was the most dangerous of the nationalists, but there were others who were ready and willing to cooperate with the enemy; so when Wardani was taken into custody, the authorities determined to keep his arrest a secret and have someone else replace him—someone loyal to England who would report on the enemy's plans, including the location of the arms the Turks were secretly supplying.

There was only one man who could have carried off such a masquerade. Ramses's resemblance to the Egyptians among whom he had spent most of his life, his fluency in Arabic and several other languages, and his expertise in the dubious art of disguise made him the perfect candidate. It would be impossible to overstate the peril of his position: Wardani's men would have murdered him if they had learned his true identity; the Germans and Turks would have murdered him if they suspected he was betraying their plans; and since "Wardani" had a price on his head, every police officer in Cairo was looking for him. Ramses and David, who had insisted on sharing the danger, had succeeded in preventing the uprising and had given the War Office a nice little bonus by exposing the traitor who had been selling information to the Central Powers; but each had suffered serious injuries and for several unfortunately unforgettable hours I had been afraid we were going to lose both of them.

".What about David?" I asked.

"Yes, there's another thing," Emerson grumbled. "He's become absolutely indispensable to me; there's not a finer artist or epigrapher in the business. But how can I ask him to leave his wife and child?"

"You can't. The difficulty will be in preventing him from leaving *them*. He and Ramses are as close as brothers, and he feels he is the only person who can control Ramses's recklessness."

"No one can do that," Emerson muttered. "I had hoped he'd settle down once he was married, but Nefret is almost as bad as—"

He broke off with a grunt as the door opened again. This time it was Nefret herself who entered.

"Did I hear my name mentioned?" she inquired innocently.

Ramses was with her. He usually was. I speak quite impartially, without maternal prejudice of any kind, when I state that they were a very handsome couple. His aquiline features, bronzed complexion, and wavy black hair formed a striking contrast to her fairness. At six feet and a bit, he was considerably taller than she. The top of her golden-red head barely reached his chin—a particularly convenient height, as I had once overheard him remark in a suspiciously muffled voice, when I happened to be passing the half-open door of their room one afternoon. Naturally I did not pause or look in.

I deduced that they had just returned from a morning ride, since both were suitably attired for that activity. Like Ramses, Nefret wore breeches and boots and a well-cut tweed coat. Fresh air and exercise had brought a pretty color to her cheeks, and loosened tendrils of hair curled over her temples.

"Ah," said Emerson, self-consciously. "Er. Come in. We were just discussing our plans for the coming season."

"I trust you had intended to consult us," said Nefret. "Father, you know we agreed that we wouldn't ever again keep secrets from one another."

Though she had joined our family at the age of thirteen, after we rescued her from the remote oasis in the Western Desert where she had lived from birth, she had not used that affectionate form of address to Emerson, or called me Mother, until after she and Ramses had become one. Emerson had always loved her as dearly as a daughter; to hear that word from her lips reduced him to jelly.

"Yes, yes, of course," he exclaimed.

The young people seated themselves on the sofa, where Nefret proceeded to make herself comfortable, tucking her feet up and leaning against Ramses. He put his arm around her and gave me a sidelong smile. It was very pleasant to see the change in him since his marriage. As a child he had been perniciously verbose. As an adult he had employed speech to hide his feelings instead of expressing them, and he had schooled his countenance to such an extent that Nefret often teased him about his stone pharaoh face. I had given him several motherly lectures on the inadvisability of concealing emotions that were deep and warm, but Nefret's loving, impulsive nature had had a more profound effect. It is difficult for a man to remain aloof with a woman who worships the ground he walks on, particularly when he feels the same about her.

"So," said Nefret briskly, "what was it you were saying, Father? I am as bad as . . . shall I guess who?"

"I only meant . . ." Emerson began.

"We know what you meant," Ramses said. "Stop teasing him, Nefret. If you are worried about me, Father, you needn't be. I've no intention of getting involved with that lot again. This is going to be a purely archaeological season, with no distractions of any kind."

"I've heard that before," Emerson said darkly. "We can only hope, I suppose. So you two were planning to come out with us?"

"Of course," Nefret said "We never considered anything else."

Emerson shook his head. "You must weigh the danger, Nefret. Do you know how many ships we've lost to German submarines since the beginning of the year?"

"No, and neither do you," Ramses said. "The Admiralty is trying to keep that information under wraps. I'm not arguing with you, Father, I'm only considering the alternatives logically. Are you planning to spend the rest of the war here in England?" He didn't wait for an answer, there was no need. "The Germans have agreed to spare passenger liners, especially neutrals—"

"That's what they agreed before the *Lusitania*," I murmured.

"If you are waiting for a guarantee, you won't get it," my son said, in a hard flat voice. I saw the fingers that rested on Nefret's shoulder tighten, and I knew they had argued this same issue before. It had been a waste of breath, as I could have told him. Ramses was as dedicated to Egyptology as was his father, and he knew how much Emerson depended on him. As for leaving her behind, safe in England, she wouldn't have stood for that, any more than I would.

"Ah, well," I said cheerfully. "Looking at the situation logically, as you proposed, it is not as if we are strangers to danger. I expect the risk of being torpedoed is less than other risks we have faced, and if it should occur—"

"We'll get out of it some way," Nefret said with a grin. "We always do."

"That is the spirit," I exclaimed. "So it is agreed? The four of us and—who else? You will have to do without Seshat this year; the kittens are not due for several more weeks. What about David?"

"He's staying here," Ramses said.

"Have you talked with him?" Emerson asked.

"Yes." His lips closed on the word, but Emerson's piercing look forced him to elaborate. "In the eyes of all but a few people in Cairo, David is still under suspicion as a rabid nationalist and a member of Wardani's former organization. He'd be subject to arrest and imprisonment if he returned, and the War Office wouldn't lift a finger to save him. That's the chance you take when you play the Great Game," he added, giving the last two words the ironic inflection with which he always pronounced them. "If anything goes wrong, you are expendable."

Nefret's blue eyes were troubled. "I'm glad he realizes that. He has other responsibilities now. Lia and the baby couldn't come out this year anyhow. Aunt Evelyn and Uncle Walter won't want to leave their first grandchild, or be away from England while Willy is in France."

"No, of course not," I said. Evelyn and Walter had already lost one son, Willy's twin, a loss still keenly felt by all of us who had known and loved the lad. So far Willy had led a charmed life, but if he were wounded and sent home to recuperate, his mother would want to nurse him. "What about Sennia?"

Emerson groaned. He adored the little girl, and had missed her desperately the previous year, but the dead children of the *Lusitania* still haunted him.

"She'll be better off here," Ramses said.

Nefret turned her head and looked up at him. "You will have to be the one to tell her, then. I simply suggested the possibility last week and she went into one of her tantrums."

"The way you women let that child bully you is a disgrace." Ramses's heavy dark brows drew together. "She can control her temper perfectly well when she wants to. She only uses it to get her own way."

"Are you volunteering to break the news?" his wife inquired sweetly.

"I'd as soon face a charging lion," Ramses said with considerable feeling.

Nefret laughed, and I said, "I trust, Ramses, you do not include *me* in your blanket condemnation of female ineptitude."

"Good Lord, no. You're the only one in the family who can handle her. I'm afraid it's up to you, Mother."

"Oh, dear," I murmured. "I would really rather not."

Nefret let out another of her rich chuckles. "It is comical to see the two of you confronting one another. The resemblance is strong in any case, but when you are both in a temper it's like seeing two Aunt Amelias, one grown up and the other six years old."

Though Nefret usually called me Mother, sometimes she slipped and referred to me by the name she had used for so many years. I didn't mind. What I did mind was the assumption—shared, it was clear, by all parties—that it was up to me to reason with Sennia. She seldom tried her tricks on me, but if anything could throw her into a tantrum, it would be the threat of being separated from Ramses. She loved all of us, but he was her idol—foster father, elder brother, playmate, rescuer.

"Oh, very well," I said. "I am accustomed to having all the unpleasant tasks left to me. I will speak with her tomorrow. Or the next day."

"Or the day after?" Ramses suggested.

I gave him a hard look and Nefret gave him a pinch—little reminders that if he continued to amuse himself at my expense he might find himself saddled with the job after all. The lines at the corners of his mouth deepened, but he said meekly, "Thank you, Mother."

"Hmph," I said. "That is settled, then. I will begin making my usual lists, and you, Emerson, will find out about sailings. I trust you have not forgotten that we are dining out this evening."

None of us enjoys formal dinner parties, and visits to London were not pleasant these days. However, this had been an invitation we could not easily decline. The Cecils were one of the oldest and most prominent of the English noble families. They had served their country as soldiers and parliamentarians; the father of the present marquess had been Prime Minister and Foreign Secretary.

Social snobbery is a weakness from which I do not suffer. The first overture from Lord Salisbury had been for a weekend at Hatfield—an invitation for which many would have unhesitatingly sold their souls to Old Nick—but even if I had been inclined to accept, Emerson had put his foot down flatly on that. "Good Gad, Amelia, have you taken leave of your senses? Three days with a mixed bag of vapid women and hunting squires and bleating politicians? I would run amok after three hours."

"You know what he wants, don't you?"

"Yes," said Emerson, through his teeth. "And he is not going to get it."

Salisbury did not give up so easily. A second invitation, to dinner at the family mansion in London, followed soon after my declining the first. I knew perfectly well that he was not moved by a desire to make our acquaintance; he was under pressure from other persons who were not inclined to give up easily either. I pointed this out to my grumbling husband, and he finally agreed that we might as well face his lordship down and put an end to the matter once and for all.

He began grumbling again as we dressed, for Emerson hates formal attire. It took the combined efforts of myself and Rose, our devoted housekeeper, to get him into his evening clothes and locate his studs and cuff links, and he might have backed out if I had not agreed to his demand that he drive the motorcar instead of letting the chauffeur do so. Such little concessions are necessary if the marital state is to flourish. It was a concession on my part, for Emerson drives with a panache that keeps one in a constant state of trepidation.

There was less traffic than usual, however; since the zeppelin raids had begun, a blackout was in effect and most people endeavored to get indoors before darkness fell. To be honest, I had forgotten about this or I would not have allowed Emerson to drive. We reached Berkeley Square without incident, however, the only damage being to my nerves.

The party was small and intimate—our four selves, Salisbury and his lady, and another gentleman, fair-haired, languidly graceful, smiling, and supercilious. After the other introductions had been performed, Salisbury said, "You know my brother, I believe?"

We did. It is impossible not to know other members of the Anglo-Egyptian community in Cairo. Lord Edward Cecil was the Financial Adviser to the Sultan (in other words, he and Englishmen like him ran the government). Our acquaintance with him was slight, since the social set of which he was a prominent member was composed of boring officials and their even more boring ladies. One would have supposed, however, from the warmth of his greeting, that he was among our closest friends. He was particularly gracious to Ramses, whom he and his circle had snubbed the year before because of Ramses's outspoken opposition to the war. If I had had any doubts about the purpose of the evening's entertainment, Lord Edward's behavior would have dispelled them.

No one was ill-bred enough to refer to the matter then, or during dinner. The seating arrangements were awkward, owing to the uneven number of guests, but Lady Salisbury had done the best she could, placing me between Salisbury and his brother, and Nefret across the table with Ramses and Emerson. When the butler brought in the decanters, Lady Salisbury rose and caught my eye. I smiled pleasantly at her and remained seated.

"You will excuse me, I hope, Lady Salisbury. Since I have a personal interest in the subject the gentlemen intend to discuss, I prefer to join in."

Lord Edward's eyes moved from me to Nefret, who looked as if she had taken root on her chair. His elegantly shaped brows lifted. "I told you so, Jimmy."

"You needn't rub it in." Like the other gentlemen, Salisbury had risen to his feet. "My dear . . ."

Breeding shows. The poor woman had been

thrown completely off her stride by my unorthodox behavior, but she was quick to recover. She swept elegantly out of the room and the men resumed their chairs.

For a few moments no one spoke. I was waiting, as seemed proper, for Salisbury or Lord Edward to introduce the subject, and they also seemed to be waiting. Emerson, who has not my gift of patience, was about to burst into speech when the door opened and a man entered.

He was of medium height and build, with shining black hair slicked back from his forehead, and a face like a wedge. His sharp nose and pointed chin appeared to have squeezed his lips between them. His stretched skin and the fine lines that covered it, especially around the eyes, were unmistakable signs of long years spent in the tropics—not in Egypt, or I would have known him—possibly in India. He took the chair Lady Salisbury had vacated and fixed a cold stare on me.

His attempt to disconcert me was of course a failure. I stared back at him. "If this gentleman—I use the term loosely, since he was obviously listening at the door—if he is to join in our discussion, perhaps he will be good enough to mention his name."

The thin lips opened a crack. "Smith."

"Dear me, how unoriginal," I remarked.

"Will you take a glass of port, Mrs. Emerson?" Salisbury inquired. He sounded a trifle rattled.

"No, thank you, nor a cigar. Feel free to smoke, if you like; far be it from me to mar the atmosphere of masculine congeniality."

"You've already done that," said Emerson approvingly. "Let's get down to business, shall we? We have wasted enough time already, and I want to get home. The answer is no."

He pushed his chair back. "Don't be so precipitate, Emerson," I said. "The answer is no, but there are several questions I would like to have answered. First—"

"You are both being precipitate," Nefret said. "And patronizing. He can speak for himself."

She had dressed in her finest. Her blue frock was a Worth original and she wore a parure of Persian turquoises set in gold and diamonds. Not that she needed such adornments to set off her youthful beauty and her aristocratic bearing. She had done it for him—to make him proud of her. Indignation had brought bright spots of temper to her cheeks and made her blue eyes flash; even the enigmatic Mr. Smith paid her the compliment of a quick, indrawn breath. I realized she was absolutely furious with everyone—including me and Emerson.

All eyes turned toward Ramses. Long fingers wrapped round the stem of his glass, he had been staring fixedly at the ruby liquid that filled it. Now he looked up.

"No."

"But my dear chap, you haven't even heard the proposal," Lord Edward said smoothly.

"Make it, then," Ramses said pleasantly.

Brows raised, Lord Edward glanced at the man who sat at the other end of the table. Smith had not spoken except to give a name that was certainly not his own. Now he said, "I cannot and will not discuss important business while women are present. If they insist on remaining we will have to arrange a meeting for another time and place."

Ramses raised his eyebrows. They were very thick and very black, and they tilted up at the corners in a way that gave his face a decidedly skeptical expression. "There would be no point in such a meeting. I was prepared to listen to your proposition as a matter of courtesy, but I cannot conceive of anything that would induce me to take on another assignment."

"I'm afraid we can't accept that without an attempt, at least, to make you change your mind," Salisbury said in his calm, well-bred voice. "Your duty to your country—"

"Duty," Nefret repeated. Her voice was unsteady and the pretty color had faded from her cheeks. Her eyes moved to Lord Edward. "You would know about that, wouldn't you? You were a soldier, leading your men into battle, sword in hand, with flags flying and bugles sounding the charge. I've been told it's quite exciting while it lasts, and when it's over you can bask in the admiration of the ladies and discuss the brilliance of your strategy with your fellow officers over a glass of port."

Lord Edward was no fool. He didn't try to stop her.

"Not at all the same," said Nefret, "as walking a sword's edge, instead of carrying one, not for a few glorious hours but for month after dragging month. No bugles, no flags; dark alleys and dirty little back rooms, never knowing, when you enter one of them, whether you'll get a knife in the ribs from someone who has found out who you are. No praise, no admiration, only white feathers from stupid women and insults from men like your friends, Lord Edward. And you."

He was staring at his clasped hands, and his cheeks were a trifle flushed. "I had to do that, Miss—Mrs. Emerson. It was for his own protection."

"And now you want him to do it again. Hell and damnation, you all know what happened to him when he went after the traitor your pompous lot never even suspected. How dare you speak of duty to him?"

"His Majesty's government is well aware of his contribution," Lord Salisbury said stiffly.

Ramses had listened without comment, his eyes on Nefret's face. Now they moved to Salisbury. "And that of David Todros? He risked far more than I, and he did it for a country that insults him and denies him social and political equality. My wife . . ." His voice lingered on the word. "My wife gives me too much credit. I just happened to have the right qualifications for that particular job. I took it on because I hoped to save lives, including the lives of the Egyptians who thought they were fighting for the independence of their country. I was, and am, in complete sympathy with their aims. I don't like violence and I'm sick to death of role-playing and deception, and of putting my friends and family at risk."

"Not to mention yourself," said Emerson, who had controlled himself longer than I had expected.

"Your part in that business and your real identity are known to a number of unpleasant individuals, including the chief of the Turkish secret service. If they so much as suspect you are back in the game, they'll be down on you like a pack of pariah dogs. Anyhow, I can't spare you. I need you on the dig."

"Is Egyptology more important than fighting this war?" Mr. Smith demanded.

Emerson's sapphire-blue eyes widened in surprise. "Of course."

It was deliberate aggravation, at which Emerson excels; but when Mr. Smith's lips curled in a sneer—an expression for which they were well-suited—Emerson abandoned irony for blunt and passionate speech.

"This war has been a monumental blunder from the start! Britain is not solely responsible, but by God, gentlemen, she must share the blame, and she will pay a heavy price: the best of her young men, future scholars and scientists and statesmen, and ordinary, decent men who might have led ordinary, decent lives. And how will it end, when you tire of your game of soldiers? A few boundaries redrawn, a few transitory political advantages, in exchange for an entire continent laid waste and a million graves! What I do may be of minor importance in the total accumulation of knowledge, but at least I don't have blood on my hands." He drew a long breath and, having expressed his feelings to his satisfaction, went on in a calmer voice. "Well, that's settled. Good night, gentlemen. Thank you for a most entertaining evening."

We emerged from the civilized luxury of the

house into bedlam. I had been vaguely aware of sounds from outside the thick walls and heavily curtained windows, but had been too preoccupied to pay much attention. They were clearly audible now—loud popping sounds, like a series of corks being removed from champagne bottles. The sky overhead was patterned with moving strips of light.

"Dear me," I said, drawing my evening wrap closer around my throat. "It appears to be an air raid. That must have been what Lord Salisbury was trying to tell us. Perhaps we ought to have listened to him instead of rushing away."

"Do you want to take cover?" Emerson inquired. "There is a tube station down the street."

"What would be the point of that? Bombs fall at random. I want to go home."

In the lull between the guns I heard another sound—a distant humming. "Look," Nefret whispered. "Up there."

They looked very pretty and harmless, floating like great silvery fish in a sea of black. The searchlights stabbed at them, and another series of explosions rattled the air.

"Those aren't bombs, they are our guns," Ramses said. "From the batteries in Hyde Park. Father, will you allow me to drive? I hope you won't mind my suggesting that my night vision—"

"This is no time for courteous debate," I exclaimed. "Where is the motorcar? Ramses, you drive."

Emerson took my arm. "Yes, we may as well go on. There are only three of the confounded things and they seem to be well north of here. Once the

Germans start getting their aeroplanes across in force it will be a different matter."

"Emerson, will you please stop making pessimistic remarks and hurry?"

The sky over the East End was red with reflected flames. They were aiming at the docks, and hitting them too, if I was any judge. I couldn't take my eyes off those pretty silvery shapes. Why the devil couldn't our guns bring them down? Guns in Hyde Park and on the Embankment . . . What would be next, aerial duels over Buckingham Palace? Inside my gloves my palms were sticky with perspiration. I despised myself for cowardice, but this was my first air raid and I hated it—not only the feeling of helplessness, but the remoteness of the business. If someone is going to kill me I want him to take a personal interest.

Ramses drove with what seemed to me excessive slowness—until he came to a sudden stop just in time to avoid a dark form that wandered out into the roadway directly in front of him.

"Drunk," he said, as the individual proceeded on his wavering path.

"It takes some people that way," Emerson remarked. He turned, his arm over the back of the seat. "Sorry you didn't have that port, Peabody?"

"No. But I will be ready for a stiff whiskey and soda when we get home."

"So will we all. Cheer up, my love, it's almost over. They can't keep this up all night."

I could no longer see the zeppelins and the guns were not sounding so often. I couldn't tell where we were; Ramses had taken a roundabout path. The neighborhood seemed to be one of small shops and warehouses. I was beginning to relax when there was a shout from Emerson and a weird whistling noise. Ramses's shoulders twisted and the car shuddered and spun and jolted over the curb. It came to a jarring stop, but the sound of the impact was drowned out by a violent explosion. I found myself on the floor of the vehicle, with Nefret on top of me trying to cover my head with her arms.

"Nefret?" Ramses wrenched the door open and lifted her up. He added, rather as an afterthought, "Mother?"

"Quite all right," I croaked. "What the devil was that?"

Emerson's large hands untangled me and raised me to my feet. "Don't sit down yet, the seat is covered with debris, including broken glass. Steady, my dear. Any damage?"

"Not to me. Nefret pushed me down and shielded my body with hers. Is she hurt?"

"A few cuts on her arms," Ramses said. There was blood on his face and on Emerson's. The windscreen had shattered, spraying them both with glass.

For a time we stood staring blankly at one another. Except for the gaping hole in the street and the crumpled bonnet of the motorcar, the entire incident might have been a horrible dream. The night was still, and only a tranquil half-moon lit the dark sky. The car was jammed up against a brick wall next to what appeared to be a factory. The moonlight was bright enough to enable me to read the sign. It stuck in my mind, as inconsequential facts do at such times: BRUBAKER'S BEST PATENTED BRACES.

"Well, well," said Emerson. "Let's see if we can get the confounded thing to start, shall we? That was inspired driving, my boy."

"Pure luck. If there hadn't been a brick wall handy . . ." He was still holding Nefret by the shoulders. "It was one of our own shells."

We did not get home until two in the morning. One of the tires had to be changed, and although the engine had started at Emerson's first vigorous turn of the handle, it jerked and coughed whenever Ramses changed gears. Gargery, who had been waiting up for us, turned pale at the sight of the blood-streaked, disheveled crew and wanted to ring the doctor at once.

"You see wot 'appens when you go off on your own," he exclaimed indignantly.

Nefret reminded him that *she* was a doctor and Emerson shouted, "Hell and damnation, Gargery, not even you could protect us from an exploding shell. Serve the whiskey, and then go to bed."

Soon thereafter, Nefret took Ramses off to their room, and I did the same with Emerson. He objected violently when I tried to apply iodine to his cuts, but I did it anyhow. Thanks to Nefret, I had got off without a scratch.

"I have not had a chance to say this," I remarked, over Emerson's mumbled curses, "but that was a very eloquent speech, Emerson. Well done, my dear."

"Bah," said Emerson. "It relieved my feelings, but it had not the slightest effect. People like Cecil and Salisbury are so swathed in self-conceit, common sense cannot penetrate."

"Not to mention Mr. Smith. Obviously that is not his real name."

"Obviously." Emerson swiped irritably at the iodine that was running down into his mouth. "We know *what* he is, at any rate. Curse these people, they so enjoy mystification and subterfuge."

"I can't help being a little curious as to what he had in mind."

"I am not at all curious," Emerson said. "And I hope to heaven Ramses isn't either. He meant it, didn't he? He has done his part. He wouldn't change his mind—would he?"

"No, my dear," I said firmly. "But they may not give up so easily. Smith is an underling, a go-between. I feel certain he was sent by someone higher up. Perhaps Kitchener himself."

"I don't care if he was sent by the King or the Prime Minister or God Almighty. They cannot force Ramses to take on another assignment and he knows as well as I do that it would be foolhardy in the extreme. If he doesn't," Emerson added, with a snap of his teeth, "I will have Nefret point it out to him in terms he can't ignore."

FROM MANUSCRIPT H

The voices came floating out of the darkness.

"Tie his arms and feet and let's get out of here."

"Leave him alive? Are you mad? He knows who I am."

"Kill him, then. Or shall I cut his throat for you?"

"Oh, no. I've looked forward to killing him for a long time. Take him downstairs."

Down to the filthy little room in the cellar, where the greasy coils of the whip hung from a hook on the wall and old bloodstains darkened the floor. Suddenly he was there, sight and feeling restored: the air clammy against his bare back, the ropes tight around his wrists. Once he had believed he feared the kurbash more than death itself. Now, watching his enemy lift the heavy length of hippopotamus hide, he knew he'd been wrong. He was sweating with terror, but he didn't want to die, not yet, not like this, without a chance of fighting back. He closed his eyes and turned his face away . . . and felt against his cheek, not the rough stone of the wall, but a surface rounded and warm and gently yielding.

"It's all right," she said softly. "I'm here. Wake up, my love. It was only a dream."

He had reached out to her in his sleep and she had moved instantly to meet his need, drawing his head to her breast. Ramses let his breath out and relaxed the arm that had gripped her. There would be bruises on her fair skin the next day, where his fingers had closed over her side.

"Sorry. I didn't mean to wake you. Go back to sleep."

"Don't be an idiot," said his wife. "It's my fault. I shouldn't have brought the subject up tonight."

"How did you know that was what—"

"You talked."

"Oh." He knew he was being even more of an idiot when he pulled away and turned onto his back. They had been married a little over six months, and he still hadn't got over the wonder of winning her, of a closeness of mind and body and spirit greater than he'd ever dared imagine. He no longer minded admitting his weaknesses—not to her . . . not much—but whimpering like a frightened child with a nightmare . . .

Nefret got out of bed. Surefooted and silent in the dark, she found the candle that was standard equipment in case the electricity failed. Ramses wondered what unfailing instinct had told her he couldn't have endured the abrupt glare of electric bulbs. The gentle candlelight left his face in shadow and sent shimmers of gold through the tumbled masses of her hair. She had left it to hang loose, as he loved to see it and touch it.

"You're still shutting me out," she said, sitting down on the side of the bed. "I know why. You want to spare me. You can't. I saw what he'd done to you. Do you suppose *I* don't think of it, dream of it? I wish he were still alive so I could do the same to him."

She meant it. Her face had the remote, inhuman calm of a goddess delivering judgment. Sometimes he forgot that his sophisticated, beautiful English wife had been High Priestess of Isis in an isolated region where the old gods of Egypt were still worshiped.

"At least you had the satisfaction of killing him," he said, and then wished he had bitten his tongue off before he spoke. "Oh, God, I'm sorry. Of all the filthy things to say!"

"Why? It's true. That's what has been preying on your mind, isn't it? After all those years of being tormented by him, hating him as much as he hated you, you never got the chance to pay him back. You wouldn't be human if you didn't resent me just a little."

"That's bloody nonsense. Resent you for saving my life?"

"Thereby adding insult to injury." She was smiling, but her lips were tremulous. "I'm glad we can talk about it now. Dear heart, don't you realize you couldn't have punished him as he deserved, even if he had been in your power, with no one to see and no one to stop you? You're too damned decent even to gloat over a fallen enemy."

"You make me sound like the most ghastly prig," Ramses muttered. He could feel his taut muscles relaxing, though. Maybe she was right. As she frequently reminded him, she knew him better than he knew himself.

Nefret leaned over him and took his face between her hands. "You do have a few faults."

"Thank you. That makes me feel a great deal better."

"And one of them," said Nefret, turning her head as he raised his, so that his lips came to rest on her cheek instead of her mouth, "is being too hard on yourself. Don't do that, I haven't finished."

He took her by the shoulders and pulled her down till she was lying across him. She was laughing or crying—he couldn't tell which, he only felt the tremors that shook her body. "Sweetheart, don't cry. What's the matter?"

She raised herself, planting her elbows painfully on his chest. Two tears, one from each eye, slid with exquisite slowness over the curve of her cheeks. "I didn't mean to," she said with a gulp. "I was determined not to. But I'm too frightened to play fair. Promise me—"

"Anything, my dearest. What are you afraid of?"

"You! Promise me you won't give in to Smith and Salisbury and the rest of them."

"You heard me refuse. I hated the whole bloody business, Nefret—the deceit and the lies, the betrayal of people who trusted me, the worry I caused Mother and Father. You can't suppose I'd do it again."

She shook her head vehemently. "I know you too well, Ramses. If they convinced you that there was a job only you could do, and that innocent people would be injured or killed if you didn't do it, you'd agree. I won't let you. I couldn't stand it. Not now, when we've only had a few months together. Swear to me—"

"Please don't cry," Ramses said desperately. "*I* can't stand *that*. I'll swear by anything you like."

"Thank you." She brushed a last tear from her face and leaned closer. "Have you ever wondered why I'm so desperately in love with you? Not because you're tall and handsome and—ooh." She let out a breathless giggle as his wandering hands settled into place. "Well, *that* has a little something to do with it. Darling, I know I can't keep you safe and out of trouble. I love your courage and your strength and your maddening habit of taking unnecessary risks, and the way you champion the underdog. All I'm asking is the right to share the danger. If you won't let me fight for you as you would for me—"

The sentence ended in a gasp of expelled breath as he caught her to him. "Do you have the faintest idea how much I love you?"

"Tell me. Show me."

The air raid had been an enlightening experience. It was by no means the first of the war—there had been a number of attacks, on London and various towns on the east coast—but it was the first for me, and it had reminded me of a truth I knew well, but sometimes forgot: that perfect safety is not to be found in this imperfect world and that facing danger is sometimes less dangerous than trying to avoid it. Or, to put it as Emerson did: God has a peculiar sense of humor. It would be just like Him to drop a bomb on our house in Kent after we had decided to avoid the perils of travel by sea.

The incident had not changed my opinion about Sennia's coming with us, however. After the earlier raids, Evelyn had suggested we send her to them in Yorkshire, and this seemed to me the most sensible solution. I feared Sennia would not see it in that light. Since I am not in the habit of postponing unpleasant duties, I decided to speak to her next morning.

Sennia was in the day nursery, so busy with some

private game that she did not hear me approach. I stood in the doorway watching for a while. The room was cheery and bright; toys and books filled the shelves, pretty rugs covered the floors, and a fire burned on the hearth. The day was not cold, but Basima, Sennia's Egyptian nursemaid, found our English weather chilly. There was even a cat stretched out on the hearth rug.

Horus did not resemble an amiable domestic puss even when he was asleep. Like all our cats, he was the descendant of a pair of Egyptian felines; his brindled coat and large ears were reminiscent of the large hunting cats shown in Egyptian wall paintings. He opened one eye, identified me as (relatively) harmless, and closed it again. There was another thing, I thought; if Sennia came with us, Horus would have to come too. He behaved like a fiend with everyone in the family except the child and Nefret, who had been his former one could hardly say owner, not with Horus—associate until he abruptly transferred his loyalties to Sennia.

Sennia was building with her blocks. The towering structure was obviously intended to represent a pyramid, and I was not left long in doubt as to the identities of the small doll shapes she moved up and down the slopes.

"Uncle David and the Professor and Aunt Amelia and Aunt Nefret and Aunt Lia and baby Abdullah—no, baby, you cannot climb the pyramid, you must lie here on the sand and wait for us, it is very boring, but babies are very boring—and Ramses and"—her voice rose to a triumphant squeal—"and me!"

They were on the summit, of course. This did not bode well.

She called almost everyone by the courtesy titles of Aunt or Uncle, since her precise relationship to us would have been hard to define. It was not hard to explain, but a number of people still believed, despite our denials, that she was Ramses's illegitimate daughter. The resemblance between them was primarily one of coloring—brown skin and curling black hair. Her resemblance to me was stronger; she had the steely-gray eyes and determined chin I had inherited from my father. Sennia had got them, not from Ramses but from my brother's son. My nephew was one of the few truly evil men I had ever encountered. He had abandoned his child to a life of poverty and eventual prostitution, and for years he had been Ramses's bitter enemy. I could only thank heaven that Sennia had forgotten him, and that he was now out of our lives forever.

The unfortunate baby doll, pushed off to one side, gave me a new insight into Sennia's real feelings about Lia and David's son. She behaved impeccably with him, but it was not surprising that she would be jealous of him and the attention he got from the rest of us. (It is quite a normal response, so psychology tells us, and I am a firm believer in psychology when it agrees with my own opinions.) Sennia was the only one who called him by his full name, which was that of his great-grandfather, one of the finest men I had ever known. One day he would be worthy of it, but it was far too formal an appellation for such a fat, jolly little creature. The rest of us employed various pet names, some of which were so silly I hesitate to repeat them. Emerson was one of the worst offenders; he relapsed into babbling idiocy with infants. The infants seemed to like it, though; little Dolly (my name for him) broke into a broad toothless grin whenever Emerson came near him.

I announced my presence with a slight cough, and Sennia came running to me. She threw both arms around my waist and squeezed as hard as she could.

"Goodness gracious," I exclaimed. "I believe you are even stronger than you were yesterday."

"And taller. See?"

I patted the curly black head pressed against my midriff, but felt obliged to point out that she was standing on tiptoe. Sennia grinned. She had very pretty, even, little white teeth. At the moment two of them were missing, which gave her smile a child-ish charm. "You always catch me, Aunt Amelia. Ramses never does."

"He wouldn't. All right, my dear, we must get to work. Where is your reading book?"

She had it and her other books ready, neatly arranged on the desk. She enjoyed her lessons, in part because they gave her the opportunity of being with the people she loved. Eventually she would have to have tutors for music and languages and other advanced subjects, but she was still very young and we took it in turn to teach her what we—and she!— felt she should learn. The curriculum was admittedly somewhat unorthodox. It included not only reading and writing and simple arithmetic, but hieroglyphic Egyptian and archaeology. Sennia had insisted on studying both. If Ramses had been a plumber, she would have demanded to learn about drains.

We were deep in the adventures of little Polly and little Ben and their dog Spot when Basima bustled in. She had been late returning the breakfast tray to the kitchen, she explained, because Sennia had had to be *persuaded* to eat her porridge.

"I do not care for porridge," said Sennia, in Ramses's very tones. "It is boring."

I stifled a laugh. It would not have done to encourage her, but it was amusing to hear her imitate her hero's speech patterns and accent. She was bilingual, speaking Arabic and English with equal facility, and in her haughtier moods she brought back fond (and not so fond) memories of the little boy who had acquired his nickname of Ramses because, to quote his father, he was as swarthy as an Egyptian and as arrogant as a pharaoh.

"Porridge is good for you," I said firmly. "I don't want to hear of you refusing your healthy breakfast again, or talking back to Basima."

"I did not talk back. I would never be rude to Basima. I only pointed out—"

"Enough," I exclaimed, as Basima nodded and beamed fatuously at her charge. She and the other servants, including Gargery, would have let Sennia skin them alive if she had indicated an interest in doing so.

We finished the lesson without further interruption; but when it was over, Sennia had another complaint. "I find little Ben and little Polly very boring, Aunt Amelia. Can't we read a more interesting book?"

"You find too many things boring," I said (though secretly I was just as bored with little Ben and little Polly, to say nothing of the dog). "Sometimes it is necessary to suffer boredom in order to be educated and learn manners."

Sennia, who had heard this before and was not at all impressed with my argument, shifted ground. "It is time for my hieroglyph lesson. Where is Ramses?"

"In hiding" was the correct answer, which I did not give. He wouldn't appear until the storm had passed. The sooner I got it over, the better.

"Come here and sit by me," I said. "We must have a serious conversation."

A quarter of an hour later I left the room, feeling like a villain and a murderer. Sennia lay flat on the rug next to the cat, her face buried in her arms and her body shaking with sobs. Horus alternated between licking her hair and snarling at me. I was in no greater favor with Basima; she had not dared intervene, but the looks she shot me expressed her feelings quite well.

Emerson was waiting for me at the top of the stairs. "How did it go?"

"I am surprised you need ask. Everyone in the house must have heard her initial reaction."

Emerson passed his sleeve across his wet forehead. The house was not especially warm; it was sheer nerves that made him perspire. "But it has been quiet for some minutes," he said anxiously. "You convinced her?"

"I informed her of our decision," I corrected. "You cannot suppose I would allow a child to overrule me."

In late October we sailed from Southampton. Horus shared the cabin of Basima and Sennia.

TWO

The voyage was without incident of a military nature, but it provided one surprise. Gargery did not make his appearance until we were two days out of Southampton. He chose his moment well, waiting until after Emerson had had several cups of coffee and we were taking our morning promenade on deck. No doubt he hoped the presence of several dozen witnesses would force my husband to control himself. In this he was not correct. Emerson came to a dead halt when he saw the familiar form advancing toward him. Gargery drew himself up to his full height of five and a half feet, snapped off a salute, and got out three words—"Reporting for duty"—before Emerson seized him by the collar and began shaking him.

It was the sight of Sennia's scandalized face that stopped Emerson after only a few bad words. "Confound it!" he exclaimed, winding down. "What do you mean by this, you rascal? How dare you disobey me?"

"People are staring, Emerson," I pointed out.

"Don't hurt him!" Sennia cried, throwing her arms round Gargery.

Between Emerson's grip on his collar and Sennia's passionate grasp of his diaphragm, Gargery had not breath enough to speak; I could not help noticing that he looked very pleased with himself, however.

Ramses and Nefret had been following at a discreet distance. Now they joined us.

"Perhaps," said Ramses, "we ought to continue this—er—discussion in private, Father."

Emerson's grip relaxed and Gargery, who had been standing on his toes, staggered and caught himself.

"Haven't got my sea legs quite yet, sir," he remarked. "Soon will. As I was saying, sir, I am reporting for duty."

We had our private discussion, in a corner of the smoking room. It was a fine, bright day, so most of the passengers were on deck enjoying the sunshine. Gargery offered no excuses except the one that was, for him, sufficient. "I couldn't let you go off by yourselves, not after all the terrible trouble you got into last year."

Gargery did not know the details of the "terrible trouble," for the truth of that business was and would be buried deep in the secret files of the War Office, but it had been impossible to hide certain of the consequences from him and the others. I had therefore, with my usual skill, composed a narrative that explained what could not be concealed and avoided what could not be explained. After all, as Gargery admitted, we got ourselves into trouble almost every year with one set of criminals or another. So far as he and our other friends were concerned, the boys' injuries had been incurred in the course of another encounter with our old nemesis, the Master Criminal, and his gang of antiquities thieves.

Pursuing his advantage, Gargery went on with mounting indignation. "What's more, sir and madam, you went and let those two get married out there in Egypt, without us being present or even being told, sir and madam, till it was all over. We took that most unkindly, sir and madam."

Nefret was trying so hard not to laugh, she was incapable of speech, but Ramses managed to interpose a word.

"We got married again in England, Gargery, primarily to please you and Rose. A man doesn't make that sort of sacrifice lightly."

"Well, yes, sir," said Gargery, with the air of one graciously conceding a point. "It was good of you, Mr. Ramses. And very nice it was, I must say, with all the flowers and Miss Nefret pretty as a picture and the master blowing his nose every few minutes and Rose and Miss Lia and Miss Evelyn crying and you the picture of a proud husband and—"

"Yes, quite," said Ramses. He was somewhat flushed, whether with embarrassment or suppressed laughter, I could not tell. "We know all about it, Gargery. We were there."

"Me, too," said Sennia.

In fact, it had been partially on Sennia's account that Ramses had agreed to "make an ass of myself" in full formal dress, in the presence of the press and various curiosity seekers, at no less an establishment than St. Margaret's at Westminster. Sennia had been devastated by the news of his marriage. As she explained indignantly to me, she had counted on marrying him herself, when she was a little older. It required a great deal of tact on Nefret's part to win her over, and part of the price of acceptance was the offer of being a member of an elaborate wedding, attired in her fluffiest frock and bedecked with flowers. (She behaved throughout the ceremony rather as if she were giving the groom away.) Though the whole business was something of a nuisance, it pleased a good many people and satisfied a nagging doubt of my own as to the legitimacy of the original arrangement. Father Bennett of the Anglican Church had been unwilling to act as promptly as I wanted, and the amiable but very elderly Coptic priest who officiated kept forgetting the words.

The handsome flush that had darkened Emerson's cheeks was not caused by embarrassment or laughter. He knew he had lost considerable ground during the exchange and was trying to think how to regain it without offending Sennia.

"You need me, sir and madam," said Gargery. "Especially with Mr. David staying behind and little miss along."

"Oh—er—bah," said Emerson, with a wary look at Sennia. She was watching him like a small protective dragon. He forced a sickly, unconvincing smile. "Hmph."

"So that's settled," said Nefret. "Come, Ramses,

we haven't done our mile round the deck yet. Will you join us, Sennia?"

"I will stay with Gargery." She took his hand.

And stay with him she did, during most of the daylight hours for the remainder of the voyage. It took Emerson several days to get back in her good graces.

"Curse it," he remarked gloomily. "I daren't so much as scowl at the rascal."

"She is fiercely protective of all those she loves, Emerson. She would take your part just as vigorously if someone were unkind to you."

"D'you think so?" Emerson considered this idea.

"I refuse to pick a quarrel with you so that Sennia can defend you. She'll get over it; just be polite to Gargery."

"Damnation," said Emerson.

I have never cared for Alexandria. It has no pharaonic monuments worth mentioning, and the city is a blend of the worst of European and Eastern characteristics, with little of the charm of Cairo's shadowy old streets. This year the harbor was crowded with shipping, including a depressing number of hospital vessels. Alex had been the center of operations for the Gallipoli Campaign; the brave lads from Australia and New Zealand had sailed from there, in high spirits and with promises of a quick return. They had returned only too soon. There were so many wounded, the hospitals could not take them all in; the Red Cross flag flew over many villas and houses in and around the city.

It was a relief to board the train for Cairo, and only the need to hide our feelings from the child kept us from gloomy introspection and gloomier conversation.

However, being back in Egypt was pleasure enough to take our minds off sadder subjects, and when we pulled into the central station in Cairo, we were met by a shouting, cheering crowd—members of the family that had worked for and with us for so many years. Abdullah, our reis and dear friend, was gone now, but his children and grandchildren and nephews and nieces and cousins formed a close-knit clan. As soon as the train came to a stop, eager hands pulled us from the carriage, and we were immediately surrounded. Fatima, Abdullah's daughter-in-law and our Egyptian housekeeper, snatched Sennia out of Basima's arms; Selim, Abdullah's youngest son who had replaced him as reis, began questioning Emerson about the season's work; Daoud, towering a full head above the others, demanded news of his adored Lia and the baby; Ali and Yussuf, Ibrahim and Mahmud embraced us all in turn. They then escorted us in a triumphal procession to the carriages they had waiting.

As soon as we were in our carriage, Emerson began to grumble. "Confound the cursed cabs, they are too slow. Why didn't Selim bring the motorcar?"

I had ordered Selim not to. Emerson would have insisted on driving it, and Emerson's notion of operating a motorcar is to head straight for his destination without slackening speed or changing direction.

This is not a good method with slow-moving carts and camels. There are a good many of both in the streets of Cairo.

Instead of pointing this out, I remarked, with the tact I have developed over many years of marriage, "I expect he wanted to make a spectacle of our arrival. You see how handsomely the carriages are decorated."

"Spectacle is the word," Emerson grunted, throwing himself into a corner and folding his arms.

"Sennia is enjoying it." I looked back at the carriage following ours. Bright-red tassels hung from the horses' harnesses and bells jingled. I could see Sennia jumping around like a cricket, and Gargery trying to hold on to her.

After we had gone a short distance Emerson forgot his pique and began looking for old acquaintances in the crowd. Since he is acquainted with practically every beggar, thief, and merchant in Cairo, he found a good many of them, and his stentorian greetings were answered in kind. "Salaam aleikhum, Father of Curses! Marhaba!"

Our procession made its way through the city, across the bridge, and along the road to Giza toward the house we had taken for the past several seasons. Comfortable in the knowledge that our devoted friends would have everything in order for our arrival, I breathed deeply of the dry, warm air and with greedy eyes took in the sights and sounds that were so dear and familiar. Not even the dust kicked up by the hooves of horses' and donkeys could spoil my pleasure. I was back in Egypt, the home of my heart. What thrilling discoveries awaited me that season! I felt certain the tombs of ancient Giza held undiscovered treasures. And with any luck, we might run across a gang of tomb robbers or even a murderer.

Another group of friends awaited us in the courtyard of the house. Sennia was immediately gathered up by Kadija, Daoud's wife, who had been too shy to come to the railroad station. We had all learned to admire this very large, very dignified woman, who had the dark brown skin of her Nubian mother. She and Nefret were especially close; as soon as Kadija had given Sennia a hearty hug, she passed the child on to the others who were waiting to greet her and turned to Nefret.

"You are blooming like a flower, Nur Misur," she murmured, as they embraced. "Is it happiness or some other cause that puts the light in your eyes?"

I had wondered myself. They had been married for eight months—not that I was counting—and one might have supposed that by this time . . . Naturally I would never have ventured to ask directly, so you may believe I awaited Nefret's response with considerable interest. Unfortunately at that moment Fatima came bustling up to inform me that she had prepared a feast of all our favorite dishes and that the food would be cold if we did not come at once. I asked for a little time to remove the dust of travel, a request which was granted. Our rooms were in perfect order, as I had expected.

"She has put rose petals in the wash water again," Emerson said resignedly.

Though it would have been difficult to fault Fatima's arrangements, there were always a few household matters to be attended to before we could begin work. The house had not the charm of others we had inhabited—I still regretted the loss of our residence in Luxor, which I had had built to my own specifications—but it was comfortable and commodious, with numerous balconies and a flat roof which we used as an open-air sitting room. We were in the habit of taking tea there whenever the weather was fine, enjoying the views of the city and the Giza pyramids and watching the sun go down in a blaze of fiery color.

However, certain members of the family did not find the house commodious enough. Nefret had already spoken to me about her and Ramses taking up residence on our dahabeeyah, which we kept moored at the tourist dock near the house. I could think of no reasonable objection to the scheme; over the years the boat had served as living quarters for various members of the family, and although it had become somewhat cramped for all of us it was roomy enough for two—especially if the two were close. So when Nefret raised the subject again—the first morning after our arrival—I assured her I would do everything I could to facilitate the move.

Emerson was the biggest stumbling block. He always objects to "wasting time" on household chores. When I first met him he was living quite comfortably, by his standards, in an empty tomb chapel, and it took me quite some time (and a lot of argument) to overcome his preference for tents over houses and a splash in the Nile over a nice neat bath chamber. He had us out at Giza the day after we arrived.

The previous season we had begun excavating some of the private tombs at Giza, called mastabas because their shape resembled that of the benches outside Egyptian houses. These splendid tombs belonged to the nobles and princes of the Old Kingdom; laid to rest near their royal master, they hoped to share the eternity of endless bliss that awaited him.

The neatly drawn plans readers will find in volumes of excavation reports, including our own, give a misleading picture. The rows of precise rectangles representing the streets of tombs show them as they were laid out four thousand years ago. When modern explorers first visited the site, it was a wilderness of broken stone and undulating sand. Only the head of the Sphinx showed above the sand; temples and tombs had been buried deep. And, as subsequent excavation proved, the tombs had been robbed and the temples vandalized in ancient times. The same pharaohs who composed pious inscriptions praising their kingly ancestors tore the monuments of those ancestors apart in order to use the stones for their own temples. Some of our archaeological predecessors had added to the confusion, digging more or less at random and carrying off statues and even the painted and carved stones from the walls of the chapels. Many of them hadn't even bothered to keep accurate records of what they found and where they found it. These objects were now scattered across Europe and America in various museum collections. After the founding of the Service des Antiquités, would-be excavators were subjected to stricter rules. No one could dig without a permit, and nothing could be taken out of Egypt without the consent of the director.

At least that was the way it was supposed to work. It had always been impossible to control illegal digging and the smuggling of antiquities, but of late there had been a dramatic increase in these activities. With the Germans gone and French and English archaeologists in the army or preoccupied with war work, many of the sites had been left unguarded. According to Selim, whose family and professional connections extended all over Egypt, there was hardly a site that had not suffered.

It was a relief to find no evidence of disturbance in our work area, but of course the situation was not so bad at Giza, where our loyal men kept watch over our concession and Mr. Reisner's American expedition had its permanent headquarters. The Giza cemeteries were so extensive that the area had been divided between several different expeditions. The Americans had got the lion's share. I do not complain of this, I simply mention the fact. Mr. Reisner was a fine excavator and a good friend.

We had taken over one of the areas that had been assigned to the Austro-German group under Herr Professor Junker. It was a temporary arrangement; God willing, our German friends would return when the war was over. (Friends they were, and friends

I would always consider them, despite the artificial definitions of governments.) I prayed that day would come soon, but I must confess it was a thrill to be working near the mightiest pyramid of Egypt.

Every cultured reader must be familiar with the Great Pyramid, so I will not remind him of its remarkable features. Its builder was known to the Greeks as Cheops; Emerson preferred the more accurate rendering, from the Egyptian, of Khufu. In addition to the pyramid itself, there were a number of subsidiary structures—temples at the base of the pyramid and at the river, connected by a long causeway; three smaller pyramids meant for the burials of queens, and several cemeteries of private tombs, to the south and west. I have nothing against private tombs; some of the rock-cut variety have nice deep burial chambers and long passageways choked with rubble and full of bats. The mastabas unfortunately lack these attractive features. Their burial chambers consist of a perpendicular shaft with a single small room at the bottom. It was particularly frustrating to work at tombs like these when Egypt's greatest pyramid was within a stone's throw of our dig. However, my attempt to interest Emerson in investigating it was met with indignant rebuttal.

"What do you expect to find? The damned place has been explored by dozens of people—thousands, if you include all the cursed tourists. Every foot of every corridor has been seen and mapped, and our contemptible predecessors even blasted their way into the relieving chambers over the King's Chamber."

"I haven't been up there for years, Emerson. I would like to have another look."

"Curse it, Peabody," Emerson shouted. "I cannot allow you to putter around in pyramids, especially in that part of that pyramid. How the devil you made it up the ladders in the first place, with all those petticoats and bustles and—"

"It would be much easier now that I have taken to wearing trousers. It is very selfish of you to attempt to prevent me from doing it this season. I say 'attempt' because, as you know perfectly well—"

"I do know." We were in Emerson's study, collecting his notebooks and the other supplies we would be using that day on the dig. He took me by the shoulders and turned me to face him. "We have put in only one season here, and already you are bored with mastabas. Too open, no deep dark underground passages. I don't even want to think about why you are so fascinated by such things. Supposing you give me your invaluable assistance in excavating a few mastabas. I am not an unreasonable man; four or five will satisfy me. Then . . . then we will see."

"That is very kind of you."

"Are you being sarcastic, Peabody? Hmph. My dear, I am speaking not as your devoted husband but as your professional superior. Am I or am I not the director of this expedition?"

"Yes, of course you are."

"Then give me a kiss."

"That is a very unprofessional request."

"We aren't at the dig yet," said Emerson, folding me in his arms.

Eventually the sound of voices outside the room made him leave off what he was doing. "Well, well, we had better get on," he said. "Is Sennia coming with us again today?"

I had permitted Sennia and Gargery to join us the past two days. She was never happier than when she could play archaeologist, trying to copy an inscription or pretending to act as Ramses's clerk while he called out measurements and descriptions to her, or, when she became tired of sitting, scrambling around the plateau looking for potsherds and bones. Gargery, who insisted on accompanying her wherever she went, thoroughly disapproved of the bones, which he believed to be both morbid and unsanitary, but there was nothing he could do about it since the rest of us considered bones a perfectly legitimate subject of inquiry.

We were soon on our way, since—as Ramses pointed out—they had been waiting for us for quite some time. The beautiful Arabian horses, which had been gifts to Ramses and David from our friend Sheikh Mohammed, had had offspring; there were now six of them, including Nefret's mare Moonlight and the splendid stallion Risha, patriarch of the little herd. We had hired a fat, placid donkey for Sennia and another for Gargery. This arrangement had not been arrived at without arguments from both parties. Sennia demanded to know why Ramses could not take her with him on Risha. Gargery had declared he would prefer to walk.

"Nonsense," said Emerson. "If you cannot keep up, Gargery, you will have to go back to England. You have ridden donkeyback before."

Gargery's countenance lengthened. He *had* ridden donkeyback and he had hated it, but as Emerson remarked—chuckling at his rather clumsy play on words—he hadn't a leg to stand on. He left it to me to convince Sennia, which I did by pointing out that Gargery would have no one to keep him company if she went with Ramses, and that if she intended to take Horus along, he would have to ride in a basket fastened to her saddle. Horus did not like donkeys, or the basket, but he would have allowed himself to be dragged at the end of a rope rather than let Sennia go off without him. His grumbles and growls formed an unpleasant accompaniment to our conversation.

Leaving the horses and the donkeys at Mena House, we proceeded on foot, with Sennia on Emerson's shoulder and Horus stalking along after them. Everyone we met stared and smiled at them: Emerson, tall and stalwart as some hero of legend, the big cat following like a faithful dog, the little girl laughing and chattering and waving at her friends— for by then every gaffir and guide at Giza knew her and adored her. They were always offering her little presents, and we had to keep a close eye on her to keep her from eating the questionable sweetmeats which were presented.

She looked very picturesque in her "working clothes," as she proudly termed them. We had had a pith helmet made to her measure, and after some discussion I had agreed that boys' clothing would be more sensible than frocks. I had allowed her a voice in the selection of these garments (leaving several clerks in the Young Gentlemen's Department at Harrods in a state of shock) and I was not surprised when she favored tweeds and flannels similar to the ones Ramses wore. Except for the long black curls that escaped from under her hat she was a miniature version of her idol, even to the small boots we had had made especially for her.

I had, as is my custom, arranged a little shelter to which we could retire during rest periods. While the others collected their tools, I sat Sennia down on a campstool and gave her the same lecture I delivered every day—for I had discovered, through painful experience, that constant repetition is the only hope of driving an idea into the head of a young person. She was easier to manage than Ramses had been (any child would have been easier than Ramses) because she lacked the streak of Machiavellian logic that had enabled him to squirm out of obeying my orders.

"Remember, you are not to go off on your own, without Gargery or one of us. You are not to eat anything the gaffirs give you. You are not to talk with any of the tourists. Do not get in the way of the basket carriers. Do not stand on or cross the tracks; those heavy cars are difficult to stop once they have started moving."

"Yes, Aunt Amelia," said Sennia.

"Don't you worry, madam," said Gargery. "I will be following in her every footstep."

"Quite right," Emerson remarked. "What are your plans for today, Little Bird?"

"I am going to get more bones for Aunt Nefret."

"Thank you," Nefret said gravely. She had already been presented with several baskets full of miscellaneous animal bones, all of them bleached white and none of them over ten years old.

Sennia nodded graciously. "It is no trouble."

I noticed that Gargery was limping as he followed Sennia's agile little form. Ah well, I thought; he will be back in trim before long, and that sunburn won't be nearly so painful after a few more days. He made her stop and look both ways before they crossed the rails that connected our dig with the distant dump heap.

I lost track of them after that, since Emerson demanded my services. In fact I was not worried about her getting into a dangerous situation. Gargery followed close on her heels, and so did Horus; the beast's vile temper and uncanny resemblance to the hunting cats depicted in the ancient reliefs made even the guards and guides wary of approaching too close. My warning about talking with tourists had quite a different motive. The wretches were insatiably curious about us and our work. Sennia was such a quaint little figure in her boy's clothes that she was bound to attract attention, and she was too innocent to parry impertinent questions.

We had begun work on a new mastaba, next to the ones we had excavated the previous year. (Most archaeologists, I daresay, would have ripped through the lot of them in one winter, but the distractions to which I have alluded had prevented us from putting in a full season, and our tentative plans of returning in the spring had been superseded by familial obligations.) Two days' digging had exposed the top of the walls of the chapel and the openings of several deep shafts that led to the burial chambers of the owner and his family. The roofing stones were gone—collapsed, I presumed, into the chamber below—and the whole upper part was filled with sand and debris. Since Emerson insisted upon sifting every square inch of this fill, emptying the chamber would take a long time.

A long, boring time.

Nefret took a few photographs, but there was nothing much for Ramses to do until and unless we uncovered reliefs and inscriptions. It was he who hailed us from his vantage point above the tomb.

"Here comes Sennia at a dead trot. Looks as if she's found something. Prepare to be enthusiastic, Nefret."

"Probably a camel bone this time," Nefret said. "It's time we stopped for a rest, Aunt—I mean, Mother. You've been crouching over that sifter for hours."

She gave me a hand to help me rise—I am always a little stiff the first few days—it soon passes—and Ramses went to meet Sennia, who had outstripped Gargery by several yards. Swinging her up onto his shoulders, Ramses carried her to the shelter where Nefret and I had retired.

"She's made an exciting discovery," he announced seriously. "But she won't show it to me."

Sennia's clenched fist made a bulge in the front of her jacket. "He said it was for me," she explained. "But of course I will show it to you, all of you."

"What's this?" Emerson demanded.

She took her hand out of her coat, opened her fingers very carefully, and put the other hand under the object to support it. It covered both small palms—a piece of limestone, rounded at the top, approximately six inches long by four across. Several figures in low relief occupied the upper portion; several lines of hieroglyphs ran horizontally under them, ending in a ragged break.

"Very nice," said Emerson, smiling. "Where did you find it, Sennia?"

"There." She gestured. The stone went flying, and Ramses caught it deftly in mid-air.

"One of the gaffirs gave it to her, I expect," he said, examining the lines of hieroglyphs. "Quite an attractive . . . Hmmm."

"What is it?" Emerson asked.

"It appears to be genuine."

We had all assumed the miniature stela was one of the fakes that are turned out by the hundreds to be sold to gullible tourists. The so-called guards often indulge in a spot of private excavation—and who can blame them, considering their pitifully small wages—but fond as they were of the child, none of them was likely to give her something they could sell.

We crowded round. "What does it say?" I asked.

Ramses blew sand out of the incised lines. "'Adoring Amon-Re, Lord of the Silent, who hears their prayers—'"

"How can he hear their prayers if they don't talk?" Sennia asked.

"True prayer comes from the heart, not from the

lips," I explained, seizing the opportunity to instill a bit of religious instruction. "As it says in Scripture, the hypocrites pray on the street corners where they may be seen, but the true believer enters into his closet and speaks in secret to the Father—"

"Quite," said Ramses, who, like myself, had been watching *his* father and had seen the signs of an imminent outburst. "In this case, Little Bird, the silent people are the poor and humble, who dare not address the powerful nobles who rule their lives. So they pray to Amon-Re, who is . . ." He looked again at the inscription. " 'Protector of the poor, father of the orphan, husband of the widow—that I may see him in the course of every day, as is done for a righteous man; said by . . .' The rest is missing. The figures above represent Amon enthroned, with an offering table in front of him and a kneeling figure—that of the offerant, one presumes. A pity his name isn't given."

Emerson snatched the object from him and subjected it to a close scrutiny. "Damned if I don't think you are right," he exclaimed.

"Emerson," I murmured.

"Er," said Emerson. "That is one of the words you are not to repeat, Sennia."

"Damned, you mean?" said Sennia, in her high-pitched chirp. "I know."

"Show me which of the men gave this to you."

"He didn't give it to me, I found it," Sennia said indignantly. "He only told me where to dig."

"Show us," Ramses said. "Please."

"You really like it, then?" Sennia asked, beaming at Ramses. Children are not as dense as we think.

She could tell the difference between the polite thanks she usually received and this concentrated interest. "It is important? Would you like it? I will give it to you, and look for more if you want me to."

"No, Little Bird, you found it and it is yours. I will keep it for you if you like. Now show me where it was."

We all went with them, for this little mystery had captured our imaginations. Holding Emerson's hand, Sennia led our caravan to a rubbish dump southwest of our line of tombs. Some of these mounds were twenty or thirty feet high, formed of the debris removed from various excavations. I remembered this one quite well; it had been the scene of a nasty accident the year before.

"You didn't let her go up there, did you?" I demanded of Gargery, who had not been able to get a word in before.

"No, madam, and I had the deuce of a time preventing her," said Gargery in injured tones. "Madam, the fellow who helped her find the thing was just one of the guards; he never offered to touch her even and he was very polite, madam, at least I think he was, from what I could understand. He was smiling and bowing all the while, madam. You said I was not to be rude to those chaps when they were only—"

"Yes, yes, Gargery, that's all right. No harm was done. It is just rather strange."

"He wanted to give her a little present," Gargery insisted. "And the fun of finding it herself."

"You believe he put it there?"

"He must have done, madam. It was low to the

ground, where she could reach it without climbing, and buried only a few inches deep. Just there, madam."

We had reached the bottom of the mound, and Sennia too was pointing. "There are lots of things sticking out," she explained. "Mostly bits of stone and boring pottery."

The statement was correct. Most excavators do not sift their fill. Emerson studied the side of the mound thoughtfully. "Quite right," he said. "This is more interesting, isn't it?"

"It has writing on it," said Sennia. "So I knew it was important. Is it important?"

"Yes," said Ramses. "And rather unusual. I've seen similar votive stelae, but most of them came from the Theban area. Do you think you could find the kind gentleman who gave—who showed you where to dig?"

We did not find the kind gentleman, though Emerson spent a good half hour trying. The description given by Sennia and Gargery would have fitted most of the guards—turbaned, bearded, wearing a galabeeyah and sandals.

FROM MANUSCRIPT H

It was not until the Friday following their arrival that Nefret was able to move their belongings to the *Amelia*. Fatima had had the dahabeeyah in spotless condition, all ready for them, but somehow it was never quite convenient to make the move. She had refused a number of well-meant offers to make their rooms at the house more comfortable, and, once she had carried her point, more well-meant offers to help her arrange furniture, hang pictures, and shelve books on the dahabeeyah. She wanted to do it herself, to transform the quarters which had belonged to various members of the family in turn into their quarters, their home.

Though it was the day of rest for the workers, Ramses had gone off to Giza with his father that morning. Just like a man—they hated the fuss and confusion of moving. She had scolded him a little, for the fun of it—he knew she was teasing, and she loved seeing his austere features relax into a smile and his eyes reflect her laughter—but she was happy to be alone.

For a while. Straightening, she rubbed her aching back and contemplated the piles of books littering the floor and the tables in the saloon. It was a large room in the bow of the boat, with a curved divan under the windows, and it would be quite charming once she had the cushions re-covered and the new curtains hung and the new rugs on the floor, and the books in their proper places on the shelves.

He ought to have been back by now. He had promised he would leave early, but getting away from Emerson when he had put you to work wasn't easy, at least not for Emerson's son. She had learned how to handle him, but she sometimes wondered if Ramses would ever be able to say no to his father and stick to it. She moved restlessly round the room, glancing out the window and moving a few more books, and then her eyes came to rest on the portrait of her mother-in-law that hung over the bookshelf.

It wasn't the first time that day those painted eyes had held hers. David had done a wonderful job; his affection for his subject and his whimsical sense of humor made the portrait come alive. She stood looking squarely at the observer, parasol in hand, booted feet planted firmly on the sand. Behind her was a mélange of pyramids, camels, minarets, and the Theban cliffs—all of her beloved Egypt—framing her. The direct, steely gaze, and the little half-smile on her lips were Aunt Amelia to the life. Nefret loved the painting. She wondered how long she could stand having it there, staring at her, hour after hour and day after day.

Kneeling on the divan, she looked out the window. The *Amelia* was moored at the public dock not far from the house. The last steamer must be about to leave; the dock swarmed with tourists, all drooping and dusty and bedeviled by the dragomen who were herding them toward the ferry. Her eyes searched the crowd. How could he delay, when he knew she'd be waiting? Once she had wished she could fall in love—head over heels, insanely, madly, passionately. She'd got her wish. Being away from him for more than a few hours left her feeling empty and half alive. She lay down and closed her eyes, picturing him in her mind, recalling the things he had said the night before.

"What's your hurry? I want privacy as much as you do, but another day or two here—"

"Is a day or two too long! Oh, I know I'm being unreasonable and unfair; it's because they're so fond of us that they want us with them. But the only time we can be alone together is at night; if we steal away during the day they know why, and Sennia is apt to come looking for you, the way she did yesterday—I thought I'd have a heart attack when she started knocking on the door and calling your name."

He was laughing soundlessly, his breath stirring her hair. "The moment was certainly not well chosen. Mother would say I had it coming. I can recall at least one occasion when I interrupted them under similar circumstances. It was the only time Father ever threatened to thrash me."

"I don't blame him."

"Neither do I . . . now. My only excuse is that I was too young to comprehend the situation."

"How old were you?"

"Ten." The rhythm of his breathing changed and the arms that held her tightened. "A few days later I saw you for the first time. I was old enough to know one thing—that there would never be anyone else for me. Don't pretend you felt the same. It took me years just to get past the younger-brother role."

They could talk about them now, the misunderstandings and heartaches that had kept them apart so long. Almost all of them. "Was it worth the wait?"

"I'm not sure. Feel free to convince me."

"As soon as you promise you will help me move first thing tomorrow."

"Of course, if it means that much to you."

Another man might have made a jesting reference

to Lysistrata, who had refused her favors to her husband until he agreed to her demands. His ready understanding melted her completely. "It's just that . . . She watches me all the time. I can feel her eyes examining me. Kadija and Fatima do it too. They're wondering if I'm . . ."

That was the one heartache she still couldn't face, the word she couldn't say, the guilt that would not go away. If it hadn't been for her folly and pride, they would have the child they both wanted so much. She had promised she would never talk about it again, but she didn't have to. He knew.

"How often do I have to say it?" he demanded, his voice rough with anger—not at her, but for her. "It wasn't your fault. For the love of God, Nefret, you're a doctor; you know things can go wrong for no apparent reason. There's no hurry, sweetheart. I'm too selfish to share you with anyone else just yet."

She clung to him, too moved to respond, and he added, "Including Mother. Or Father. Or Sennia. Or Fatima and Kadija and Daoud and Selim and the rest. They do hover, don't they? Damn it, you're right. I can't give you my full attention when they're around."

Not since their first night together had they made love with such urgency and tenderness. Nefret went over it in her mind, every word, every gesture. He found her there when he came in, her hands resting lightly on her waist.

Later, while they were having tea on the upper deck, he said, "I assume we aren't dining with the family tonight."

"You assume correctly. Mother and Father are dining at Shepheard's."

"With whom?"

"I don't believe they have an engagement with anyone in particular. It's Mother's annual reconnaissance, to catch up on the gossip and see who's in town. I declined their kind invitation to join them, but I thought we might go out—someplace where we needn't dress and where we're not likely to meet anyone we know. Bassam's, perhaps."

It would have been impossible to find a place in Cairo where the Emerson family was not known, but he understood what she meant. Their Egyptian acquaintances were more courteous—or possibly more intimidated—than the gregarious, gossip-minded members of the Anglo-Egyptian community. The previous year he had been persona non grata with that community because of his outspoken pacifist sentiments. He kept telling himself he didn't care what they thought of him, but it had hurt a little to be cut dead and snubbed and insulted wherever he went.

He shook off the ugly memories and smiled at his wife. "Bassam's it is."

Bassam's was not mentioned in Baedeker. It didn't meet English standards of cleanliness, but then Ramses had always suspected the kitchens of the European-style restaurants wouldn't have passed a close inspection either. The menu, which existed only in Bassam's head and varied according to his whims, was primarily Egyptian. He was chef, headwaiter, proprietor, and, if necessary, bouncer. This situation seldom occurred, since no alcoholic beverages were served and drugs were not allowed, but now and then a drunken Tommy or hashish smoker wandered in by mistake.

He spotted them instantly and came rushing to greet them, the sleeves of his robe tucked up to bare brawny arms, his apron a rainbow medley of spattered food. One could almost guess at the menu by studying Bassam's apron. Obviously that evening's dishes made copious use of tomatoes.

After reproaching them for not having notified him in advance of their coming and asking why the elder Emersons were not with them, he showed them to a table in a prominent position, where they could be seen not only by the other patrons but by passersby. "The lady cat, she is not with you?" he asked, dusting off a chair with his apron.

"She had another engagement," Nefret said.

Bassam nodded. The honorific had been his way of propitiating Seshat, who had sometimes dined with her owners. The Emersons' cats had acquired a certain reputation among Cairenes. Large and well-muscled and strikingly similar in appearance, they did not resemble the spoiled pets of the harems nor the lean, feral scavengers of the streets. Ramses found them somewhat uncanny himself.

They had an excellent meal—with a lot of tomatoes—and relaxed over cups of Turkish coffee and a narghileh. The other patrons pretended not to notice Nefret's enjoyment of the water pipe, just as they had pretended not to notice her, the only woman present. Egyptians had become accustomed to Nefret's turning up in places where she wasn't supposed to be. Like her mother-in-law, who had been doing the same thing for years, she was in a special category, obviously a woman but commanding the same respect as a man.

He couldn't have said what alerted him. It might have been a flicker of surreptitious movement at the door, where the curtain was tied back to admit air into the smoke-filled room. It might have been that odd sixth sense, the feeling that someone was watching him. The hairs on the back of his neck rose, but when he looked directly at the doorway, no one was there.

Nefret passed him the stem of the pipe. "What's wrong?" she asked softly.

"Nothing." Meeting her unblinking blue gaze, he acknowledged her right to a truthful answer. "Nothing I can put my finger on. Are you ready to go?"

The night air, though laden with the ineffable stenches of Cairo, was cool and comparatively clear. Beyond the light from the doorway behind them, the street was a tunnel of darkness. They were only a quarter of a mile from the square where they could expect to find a cab, and he knew every twist and turn of the path, but a quarter of a mile is a long way in the dark when your skin is prickling.

He reached into his pocket. "Take the torch, but don't switch it on yet."

"Right." She smiled back at him. Her eyes were sparkling. Of all the people in the universe she was the last one he would have wanted with him if there was going to be trouble, but what an ally she was—quick and unafraid and unrestrained by silly notions of fair play. He didn't have to tell her not to hang on to his arm. She wasn't the clinging kind.

Neither of them was carrying a weapon. He cursed himself for overconfidence, but who would have supposed they'd encounter trouble so soon? It was there, waiting in the dark; he could feel it like a knife blade pricking his skin.

Nefret felt it too—or was it, she wondered, only her intense awareness of his mood? She let him lead the way; he knew the alleys of Cairo better than she, and if there was danger it could come from behind as well as before them. Her hand light on his shoulder, she stepped softly, every sense alert for a sound or movement.

He heard it before she did. He turned on his heel and pushed her behind him, pinning her against the wall with an arm as hard as a steel bar. Cursing breathlessly, she switched on the torch.

What she saw almost made her drop it. The face was that of a monster or a demon, the only visible features a pair of glittering eyes, inhuman and enormous as those of a magnified insect. The light shivered along the blade of a knife—it had to be a knife, though she could not see the hand that held it. She saw it descend, saw her husband's arm lift to block the blow—but he moved without his usual quickness and he made no other move to defend or attack. The sleeve of his coat darkened. Blood ran down his hand and dripped onto the ground.

Nefret remained motionless and silent, though her vocal cords and every muscle in her body protested. It went against all her instincts to be a passive observer, but she was trying to control her impetuosity, which had led to considerable trouble in the past. Ramses could have easily stopped the attacker before he struck; she'd seen him do it with fighters much more skilled than this one appeared to be.

After a few interminable seconds, the apparition let out a strange moaning cry and vanished. Ramses went after it. Gritting her teeth, Nefret remained where she was, turning the beam of the torch so that it framed the two figures.

Ramses had the man in a firm grip. Only a man, after all; his dark clothing had made him virtually invisible, and the eerie eyes were glasses, reflecting the light of the torch.

"It's all right," her husband said, and although he spoke English she knew he wasn't talking to her. "It's all right. You've done the job. Give me the knife."

The scarf that had masked the lower part of the man's face had slipped, exposing a scanty beard and narrow jaw. He held up his hands. They were empty. He raised them to his face and began to cry.

THREE

In the old days I had been in the habit of giving a little dinner party soon after our arrival in Egypt, to greet friends and catch up on the news. I had not the heart for it that year. Many of our friends were gone, into a better world or into retirement; many of the younger generation had gone to war; and for the first time in many seasons our closest friends, Cyrus and Katherine Vandergelt, were not in Egypt. Cyrus was American and too old for military service in any case (though I would not have cared to be the one who told him so), but Katherine was English by birth and her son Bertie had been one of the first to volunteer. After several minor injuries which had not prevented him from returning to the front, he had been wounded in the leg, arm, chest, and head by an exploding shell and was making a slow but steady recovery, nursed by his mother and sister and supplied by Cyrus with every comfort money could buy. The war was over for him, thank heaven, but at what a cost!

Indeed, a celebration would have been inappropriate. However, I felt it my duty to reestablish relations with various acquaintances who were still in the city. The phrase "idle gossip," which Emerson employed, was just one of his little jokes. It is necessary to know what is going on. I had been out of touch for many months; nowhere was the press controlled as tightly as it was in Egypt, and even letters from friends were reduced to illegibility by zealous censors. I had asked Nefret if she and Ramses would like to join us, but I was not surprised when she politely declined. So we went alone to Cairo, my dear Emerson and I. As I said to him, we were company enough for one another.

Except for the predominance of khaki, the dining salon of Shepheard's was much the same. Fine wines and rich food, snowy damask and sparkling crystal, dark-skinned servants darting to and fro, male civilians in the stark black and white of evening kit, females flaunting jewels and satin. The display struck a particularly offensive note for me that evening. No one admires a stiff upper lip more than I, but these people were not displaying courage under fire. They were in no danger here. Boys were dying in the mud of France while they sipped their wine and enjoyed the servile attentions of the individuals whose country they had occupied.

Having enjoyed this interlude of moral superiority, I decided I might as well take pleasure in the moment, as is my habit. Some of the old familiar faces were there—Janet Helman dressed with her usual elegance and good taste, Mrs. Gorst and her daughter Sylvia, who waved at me with her left hand to make sure I saw the diamond-and-ruby ring on her third finger. Even the plainest girl had no difficulty getting engaged these days, with so many young officers passing through Cairo. A man who expects to be facing death in the near future is not overly fastidious.

I said as much to Emerson, who gave me one of those superior masculine looks that reprimanded me for malicious gossip even as his well-shaped lips parted in a grin. He had never liked Sylvia, who had been one of Ramses's most tireless pursuers until his marriage, and who could have taken a prize for gossip.

I did not really expect to see any of our archaeological acquaintances, so you may conceive of my surprise and pleasure when I beheld a familiar form standing in the doorway of the dining salon.

Howard Carter's face was fuller and his mustache bushier, but otherwise he had not changed much since we had first met him. At that moment he resembled a statue of stupefaction, his eyes wide and his mouth ajar. Not until the headwaiter glided up and addressed him did he give himself a little shake. He questioned the waiter, who nodded and led Howard to our table.

"Why, Howard," I exclaimed. "What are you doing here?"

"Looking for you. I heard this afternoon that you were in town, and hoped I might run into you here, since I knew Shepheard's is one of your favorite spots."

He accepted my invitation to join us, but he kept glancing over his shoulder. "Are you in trouble with the law?" I inquired jestingly.

"I have just had a most unnerving experience,

ma'am. Thought my eyes were playing tricks on me. You don't happen to have a double, do you?"

I requested elucidation of this extraordinary question, and Howard indicated a table near the door. "The lady dining with those two staff officers, the one wearing a green dress. She's the spit and image of you, Mrs. Emerson. I was about to speak to her when I saw you and the Professor and realized I was mistaken."

Curiosity overcame propriety. I stared shamelessly at the lady. Owing to our relative positions, I could see only the back of her head and her shoulders. The latter were covered by a wide lace bertha, and the head by black hair piled high and held by jeweled combs. There was something very familiar about that dark hair.

I said, "Confound it," and Emerson chuckled.

"Well, well," he said. "I believe I can hazard a guess. Miss Minton has turned up again." Anticipating Howard's question, he explained. "We encountered the young lady some years ago when she was writing newspaper stories—it was that nonsensical business about the British Museum mummy. I was struck at the time by the resemblance between her and Mrs. Emerson, but it is pure coincidence; Miss Minton is the granddaughter of the late Duke of Devonshire, and no relation to my wife. She has made something of a name for herself since as a journalist specializing in Middle Eastern affairs."

"Yes, of course," Howard exclaimed. "I remember now. Isn't she the one who was captured by one of those Arab emirs a few years ago? Wrote a book about it. Can't say I've read it."

"You were among the few who did not," I said with a sniff. "It was immensely successful, which is not surprising since it was a perfect example of yellow journalism—sensational and exaggerated."

"Come now, Peabody, that isn't fair," Emerson expostulated. "The reviewers hailed it as a shrewd analysis of relations between the warring desert chieftains."

"That isn't what sold the book. It was her lurid descriptions of the Emir's harem and his women, and his—er—his advances to her."

"Really? Did he—uh—"

"According to Miss Minton," I said, "he was about to overcome his scruples, such as they were, when she was rescued by a handsome, dashing, mysterious hero."

Emerson choked on his wine. After recovering himself, he exclaimed, "Peabody! It wasn't—it couldn't have been—"

"No, Emerson, it couldn't have been," I said. "I don't believe in her mystery man or in her highly colored version of her relations with the Emir. She wasn't captured; she walked into Hayil—rode, rather—in search of a story and I expect Ibn-Rashid evicted her when he tired of her interminable questions. Let us turn to more important subjects. Why aren't you in Luxor, Howard?"

Howard opened his mouth, but before he could reply, Emerson said, "Yes, why aren't you? I hear that the local thieves are at it harder than ever— digging at Drah Abu'l Naga and even stealing statues from Legrain's magazine at Karnak."

"Where did you hear that? Oh—Selim, I suppose. He would know; half the crooks in Gurneh are friends and kin of his. It's not as bad as all that, Professor. Your tomb hasn't been touched, if that is what's worrying you."

More precisely, the tomb was that of Queen Tetisheri, which we had discovered and cleared several years earlier. We had removed the funerary equipment—and a deuced difficult job it had been—but there were painted reliefs of superb quality in one chamber, and thieves had been known to cut out fragments of such reliefs for sale on the illegal antiquities market. They were popular with collectors.

"Have you been in it?" Emerson demanded.

"No one's been in it, sir, since you locked the gates and refused to give up the keys to the Service des Antiquités." Howard grinned appreciatively. He had had a falling-out with the Service, which had resulted in his losing his position as Inspector of Upper Egypt, and he thoroughly approved of Emerson's high-handed behavior.

"Then how do you know it hasn't been molested? Curse it," Emerson added.

I got Emerson off the subject by asking about Howard's recent work in the Valley of the Kings— one of the valleys, that is to say, for there are two of them. The East Valley is the one visited by tourists. The West Valley is seldom visited, for it contains only two royal tombs, both isolated and in bad repair. Howard had spent several weeks exploring one of them.

This proved to be a mistake on my part. Emerson had yearned to work in the Valley himself; after years of frustration watching the inept excavations directed by Mr. Theodore Davis of America, he had seen the concession given to another wealthy dilettante, Lord Carnarvon. In my opinion Emerson was a trifle unjust to this gentleman, who was far more conscientious than Davis had been, and who had the good sense to hire Howard to carry out the ac-- tual digging; but it was still a sore subject. Dismembering his dinner with wild slashes of his knife, Emerson demanded details which he refused to allow Howard to give, interrupting him after almost every sentence.

"You had no business starting on that tomb if you meant to spend only a month at it. Amenhotep the Third was one of Egypt's greatest kings and his tomb could provide vital information about a particularly important period."

"Well, sir, you see—"

"At least there are tourists and a few token guards in the East Valley. Nobody ever goes to the West Valley. Nobody except vandals and thieves; now that you've aroused their interest, they've probably removed everything of value that you overlooked. How far did you get?"

"The entrance corridor and the well—"

"Yes, and what happened to the objects you found? Carnarvon's got them, I suppose."

"Enough of that, Emerson," I said. "This is a social occasion—at least it would be, if you would leave off badgering the poor man. Have a glass of brandy, Howard."

"Thank you, ma'am, I believe I will." Surreptitiously Howard wiped his perspiring brow. "May I smoke?"

"Certainly. Now tell us what you are doing in Cairo."

Howard looked mysterious, or tried to. "I can't talk about it, Mrs. Emerson."

"Ah," I said. "Intelligence. I am sure you are making yourself useful."

"You would be of more use in Luxor guarding the tombs," said Emerson. "Damnation! I am tempted to make a quick trip there myself."

"One must do what one can for the war effort," Howard protested.

The poor man looked so uncomfortable I attempted to change the subject. "Howard, do you happen to know of any unemployed Egyptologist who is looking for a position?"

"Why, are you taking on new staff?"

"No," said Emerson, who had been holding his breath and was thus able to forestall me. "Curse it, Amelia, I thought we had agreed to think the matter over before we took steps."

"I have thought it over, Emerson. You see, Howard, David and Lia are not coming out this year. Without them we will be shorthanded, and we can always use a skilled copyist."

"Ah, yes," Howard said. "Someone told me they would not be with you. They had a child last year, I believe. Is that why Todros has deserted you?"

Gossip, gossip, I thought. Men love it, no matter what they say. I hastened to clear David of the imputation of disloyalty, but I could tell by Howard's cynical smile that he considered a wife and child an inadequate excuse.

"I wish I could offer my own services," he said. "But I am committed to Lord Carnarvon, and I expect to be occupied with—er—other duties. I will put the word out, though I don't know offhand of anyone."

We parted soon thereafter and I managed to get myself and Emerson out of the room without our being seen by Miss Minton. I had a feeling we would hear from her before long, however. She was too good a journalist to let go her hold on a source.

When we passed the dock on our way home we saw there were lights in the saloon of the *Amelia*. Emerson brought the motorcar to a jolting stop. "They are still awake. What do you say we drop in and—"

"No, my dear."

"Ramses will want to know what Carter said about—"

"Emerson, this is their first evening alone. I expect Ramses will have other things on his mind."

However, when we got to the house we found them waiting for us in the drawing room. "Ah," said Emerson, shooting me a triumphant look. "I felt certain you would want to hear the news. What about a final whiskey and soda, eh? We ran into Carter—"

"Do be quiet, Emerson," I exclaimed. My intuition is seldom at fault, and I had known at once that they had news of graver import than ours. "Something has happened. What?"

"Nothing to worry about," Ramses said. "I tried to persuade Nefret it could wait until morning, but she insisted we come."

"A spot of whiskey is definitely in order," Nefret said grimly.

"That bad, is it?" I inquired, taking the glass Emerson handed me—for he had proceeded to act on his own suggestion. Ramses reached for his, and I remarked, "You are favoring your right arm. Another shirt ruined?"

Ramses let out a sputter of laughter, and Nefret's tight lips relaxed. "Trust you, Mother, to put the matter in proportion," she said. "Not only a shirt, but his best linen coat. No, Ramses, you are not allowed to speak; you'll try to make light of it, and I won't have that. I will tell them."

Ramses listened in silence, his eyes moving from her expressive face to the equally expressive movements of her slim hands. He did not interrupt, it was Emerson who exclaimed, "Hell and damnation, Ramses! Why didn't you defend yourself? You deliberately let him—"

Ramses shrugged. "It was only poor Asad trying to be heroic. He scuttled off as soon as he'd made his point."

"Was that a pun?" I inquired.

"Inadvertent," said Ramses.

"Stop that," Emerson bellowed. "Both of you. All right, Nefret, go on. The assassin burst into tears, and Ramses consoled him? I suppose you then took him somewhere for coffee and a chat? Good Gad!"

"Not exactly," Nefret said. "The fellow broke

down completely. He was weeping into his hands, and Ramses was patting him on the shoulder—leaving bloody prints all over his robe, I should add. He'll probably keep it as a sacred relic."

"Wait just a minute," Emerson said, rubbing his chin. "I confess I am having some difficulty taking all this in. Asad. Wardani's lieutenant? You had a sneaking sympathy for the fellow, I believe?"

"Yes." Ramses leaned forward, cradling his glass in his hands. "He was the best of Wardani's lot—a scholar, not a man of action, and the bravest of them all because he went on with the job despite his fear. He'd developed a certain . . . attachment to me. Only, of course, he didn't know it was me. Can you imagine what a shock it must have been for him to learn he had been deceived by an impostor, that all his devotion and loyalty and—and admiration had been lavished on a man who had deceived him and betrayed the cause in which he believed? He had to do something to prove his manhood. Now he's done it, and that will be the end of it. He's quite a gentle soul, really."

I said, "How did he find out it was you?"

"Ha!" Emerson cried. "Just what I was about to ask. The official story was that Wardani was arrested at the same time as his lieutenants and exiled to India—where, in fact, he had been all along. The others were sent to prison or to one of the oases, so that there would be no chance of their communicating with Wardani. That's another thing. This fellow Asad was supposed to be locked up. How did he escape?"

There are five major oases in the Western Desert: Siwa, the northernmost; Bahriya, Farafra, Kharga, and Dakhla. Except for Farafra, they are each large enough and fertile enough to support a population of several thousand, but I would not have cared to endure a long exile in any of them. Sanitation was virtually nonexistent and diseases of various kinds were endemic. They served as quite effective prisons, since they were separated from the Nile by miles of barren waterless country, and were accessible only by camel caravan. All of them except . . .

"Oh, good Gad," I exclaimed. "Don't tell me they sent him to Kharga!"

"Right as always, Mother," said my son. "The fellow bought him a nice new suit and a ticket and put him on the train."

"It isn't funny," Nefret said, but the corners of her mouth curved up in sympathy with his amusement. It was nice to see him smile as often as he did these days, even if, as in the present case, the situation was really too serious for laughter.

"But it's so wonderfully humdrum," Ramses explained. "Escape from the oasis—doesn't it conjure up an image of a wild dash for freedom on camelback, under the desert stars, with the enemy in hot pursuit, and all that rot? The train from Kharga only takes nine hours to the junction, and from there he could catch the express to Cairo."

"Damned fools," muttered Emerson.

"That is a trifle harsh, Emerson," I said. "Even if he had had the initiative and the means to escape on his own, what harm could he do, alone and leaderless? Someone supplied him with both means and incentive—and, I expect, encouragement. We hold Kharga, don't we?"

"Only a token force," said Emerson. "The Senussi undoubtedly have emissaries—or spies, if you prefer the word—at Kharga and the other oases. Everyone knows an attack on the Egyptian-Libyan border is imminent. The Turks have been training and arming the Senussi for years, and the tribesmen of the Western Desert support them. We haven't the manpower to defend the oases. We are spread thin enough as it is."

"Weren't you able to get any more information out of Mr. Asad?" I inquired, attempting against all odds to stick to the point.

"Not really," Nefret admitted. "He said his benefactor was a man he'd never seen before; he was dressed like a Bedouin and his Arabic, though fluent, was not that of an Egyptian."

"Not that of a Cairene," Ramses corrected. "Local dialects vary a great deal."

"So do the dialects of Syria and Turkey," Emerson muttered. "And Senussi. Ah, well, we mustn't leap to conclusions. Was that all?"

Nefret nodded. "He was so upset it was almost impossible to get anything sensible out of him. He kept saying he was sorry, he was going away, he would never bother us again, but there were others, and we must be on our guard. So Ramses let him go."

"Damnation," said Emerson. "Why the devil did you do that?"

"What was the alternative?" Ramses demanded, with unusual heat. "Turn him over to the police or

the military? I did that before. I couldn't bring myself to do it again, not to him. He knows how to
find me and I told him I would help him if I can."

"Very sensible," I said, anticipating another indignant comment from my impetuous husband, who
prefers less subtle methods of extracting information from reluctant witnesses. "He is now indebted
to you, and if he is a man of honor, as you believe, he
will wish to repay that debt. You think he will seek
you out again?"

"I hope so."

"That's all very well," Emerson grumbled. "But
what about the others? You might at least have
asked him who they were."

"I don't believe he knew himself," Ramses said.
"The movement's not dead, but it has been driven
underground and I can't believe anyone is going to
bother about me." He put his glass on the table and
rose to his feet. "However it's agreed, isn't it, that
none of us is to mention this incident to the family
in England?"

"Hmmm." Emerson stroked his chin. "You are
in the right, my boy. If David got wind of it—"

"He'd be on the next boat." Ramses's grave young
countenance softened into a smile. "He thinks I
haven't enough sense to take care of myself. I can't
imagine what gave him that idea. The fact is, David
would be in even greater danger from Wardani's
people. I was never a member of the organization.
David was. Asad's motives were personal and—er—
emotional, but he and the others would regard David
as a traitor."

After they had taken their departure I waited for

Emerson to comment. He said nothing for a while; deep in thought, he took up his pipe and went about the messy business of filling it. Having scattered bits of tobacco all over his knees and the floor, he struck a match and started puffing.

"Well?" I demanded. "What are we going to do about this?"

"You are of the opinion we should do something?"

"I suppose we could sit back and wait for one of those wild-eyed fanatics to assassinate Ramses."

"I'm inclined to agree with his assessment of Asad, you know. However," said Emerson, anticipating my indignant protest, "I don't like the sound of this. Ramses's role was known to Sahin Bey of Turkish intelligence and to Sidi Ahmed, the Sheikh of the Senussi. I had a little chat with General Maxwell the other day—"

"Why did you do that? I thought we had agreed we would have nothing to do with the military. Confound it, Emerson, if you suspected something like this was going to happen you ought to have told me."

"I didn't suspect anything like this, and one of the reasons why I went to the trouble of seeing Maxwell was to reemphasize the position we took with Salisbury and that bastard Smith. I was pleasantly surprised to learn that Maxwell agreed with me that Ramses should stay out of the intelligence game, though his reasons were probably not the same as mine."

"No. Military persons do not care about the safety of the men they send into battle. Mark my words, Emerson: if he thought of a way in which Ramses could be useful he would try to recruit him again. What do the Senussi have to do with this, anyhow?"

Emerson enjoys lecturing, so I let him, though much of what he told me was already known to me. The Senussi tariqa, or "way," was a religious movement, a return to the purity of Islam, founded by a descendant of the Prophet and deriving its name from that of his family. Sidi Mohammed ben Ali ben Es Senussi (he had a number of other names, which I have forgotten) had been a man of high principles and moral worth, who preached tolerance and forswore violence.

It was foreign invasion that turned a spiritual movement into a political and military force. The French, infiltrating from the south and the west, and the Italians, attacking Cyrenaica on the north, awakened a flame of resistance in the inhabitants of the region. By 1914, the descendants of the great spiritual leader had joined forces with the Sultan. Turkish officers and Arabic-speaking Germans were supporting the Senussi in their effort to dislodge Italy from her foothold on the coast, and informed persons believed it was only a matter of time before Sidi Ahmed would be persuaded to mount an armed attack on Egypt's western border. Though Britain was ill-equipped to counter such an attack, after the heavy losses at Gallipoli, the real danger was that even a temporary success by the Senussi might cause their sympathizers in the Western Desert and the Nile Valley to rise.

"Not again!" I groaned.

"No, my dear. Ramses managed to control a small group of would-be revolutionaries in Cairo, but not even Kitchener would be fool enough to suppose he could single-handedly counter the influence of the Sheikh el-Senussi. I don't know precisely what sort of harebrained scheme they had in mind, but I suppose it involved sending Ramses to spy on the Senussi in one of his bizarre disguises. There's no need to worry about it, because it won't happen."

"That is very interesting, Emerson, but it doesn't explain who sent that fellow Asad after Ramses."

"No, it doesn't," Emerson admitted. "In fact the whole business is somewhat odd. Sidi Ahmed knew of Ramses's masquerade and it may well have been one of his people who got Asad away from Kharga, but I can't see him going out of his way to seek a petty revenge. Ramses acquitted himself well in the affair, and the Senussi admire a courageous enemy. The same is true of Sahin Bey, who is the real professional and who obviously respected a fellow professional, even if he was on the opposite side. You overheard some of the complimentary things he said about Ramses—"

"'He is a brave man and deserves a quick death.' I cannot say I find that attitude particularly reassuring, Emerson."

"That's how these fellows think," said Emerson, shrugging his broad shoulders. "It's all part of the Game. He'd cut the boy's throat in a second if they crossed swords again, but I don't believe he would try to get back at him for a past defeat."

"That's very consoling."

"Believe me, Peabody, I am not taking this lightly. I have an idea."

"Would you care to discuss it with me?"

"Dear me, you are in a sarcastic mood this evening. What I propose is that we send Ramses and Nefret off to Luxor for a time. The danger, if it exists, is here in Cairo."

"He won't go, not if he thinks we are trying to get him out of harm's way."

"He will if we can convince him he is needed in Luxor. According to all the reports I've heard, the Gurneh tomb robbers are running wild, with no supervision of the sites. If Ramses can't round up a few of the more pertinacious lads he can put the fear of God into them—and make certain *my* tomb is not molested."

"I see through you, Emerson!" I exclaimed. "You aren't concerned about Ramses; you are worried about your confounded tomb."

"I am concerned about both," said Emerson, giving me a reproachful look. "They don't call Ramses Brother of Demons as an idle compliment; his very presence will make the lads think twice about breaking the law."

"Well, it is not such a bad notion," I admitted. "It will get Ramses—and Nefret, who is equally at risk, since she won't let him out of her sight from now on—away from Cairo, and stop your ranting and raving about tomb robbing. They can sail on the *Amelia*. It will be like a honeymoon for them; the poor things never had one, you know, not really."

"Honeymoon? With Reis Hassan and a full crew, not to mention Sennia and Basima?"

"I have no intention of allowing Sennia to go with them."

"Good luck," said Emerson. "I am glad you approve. I will propose the scheme tomorrow."

Though we used the *Amelia* primarily as living quarters, she had been completely overhauled the previous spring and I did not suppose it would take long to get her ready to sail. The question of what to do about Sennia was more complex. I was determined she should not accompany Ramses and Nefret; if she went along, Gargery would go too, and so would Horus, and Basima, and in the close confines of the dahabeeyah the poor dears would have no more privacy than animals in a zoo. I wanted them to have that time alone, in the romantic ambience of which I had such fond memories. Removed from the distractions of daily life and from the attentions of their loving family, they would stand side by side at the rail watching the ripples of moonlight on the dark waters, and . . . and do whatever persons passionately attached to one another do under such conditions.

Anyhow, it was time Sennia got some formal schooling. She soon would be, or had just become, six years of age. We did not know the precise date of her birth, so we had selected an arbitrary date in September on which to celebrate that anniversary. The festivities had been extravagant and well-received; more to the point, Sennia herself had announced that now she was six she was practically grown up and should be treated accordingly. This seemed an appropriate time to remind her that persons of six were old enough to attend school.

I trust I will not be accused of insularity when I say that the only proper institution was the English School. Most of the others, especially the American Mission schools, had a strong religious orientation, and I knew Emerson would never stand for that— nor was I keen on having my grandniece turned into a Methodist. Methodists are worthy individuals, but we have never had one in the family. The English School was coeducational, which was another point in its favor. I do not believe in wasting time, so I went round to the school the day after my discussion with Emerson, to inform the Headmaster that our ward would be attending.

He knew our family—everyone in Cairo does— and he knew about Sennia. Every gossip in Cairo did—or thought they did. When I informed him that her father was my late nephew and her mother an Egyptian woman—additional details being, in my opinion, irrelevant—his high forehead creased into rows of parallel wrinkles, and he said, without much hope, "Perhaps the—er—child would be better off at Saint Mary's."

Saint Mary's English School was for "natives."

"Had I believed that to be the case I would not be here," I retorted. "Kindly give me a list of the clothing and supplies she will need. I will bring her here on Monday next. Thank you."

Emerson was genuinely worried about the Luxor tombs—his in particular—so it was not difficult for him to put on a convincing show of concern. We were eating our luncheon in the courtyard of the small tomb we had begun to excavate when he raised the subject for the fifth time in two days.

"I'm tempted to take a quick trip to Luxor myself," he declared.

"It couldn't be quick," Ramses said, watching his father bite savagely into a sandwich. "You would have to spend some time there if you were to have any lasting effect."

"Quite, quite," Emerson agreed.

"And it is unlikely that you would succeed in having anyone arrested. You remember what happened to Carter, after the tomb of Amenhotep II was robbed; not only did the guards state they had recognized two of the Abd er Rassul brothers, but Carter photographed the footprints of one of the thieves and found they matched those of Mohammed. Yet the court refused to convict."

"I don't intend to waste time trying to get anybody arrested," said Emerson.

Nefret chuckled. "You intend to beat them up, I suppose."

Her fair skin glowed with the golden hue it acquired after a few days in Egypt, and her laughter was as carefree as that of a child; but I sensed she was concealing something from me. She had spent the morning at the hospital for women she had founded several years earlier, and her eyes kept returning to the bandage on Ramses's forearm. Its primary function was to keep sand and dirt from infecting the wound, which was not deep. I had inspected it myself.

"Physical force would not be necessary," Emerson

declared. "Moral persuasion is what I had in mind." He sighed. "I really cannot spare the time, though. A pity. I wonder if—"

I interrupted before he could go on. Emerson has not the patience for subtle hints, and that was what we needed now.

"How were things at the hospital, Nefret?" I asked. "I trust Dr. Sophia is well. She must be very busy with all the wounded in addition to her usual patients."

The color rose into Nefret's cheeks. "There aren't any wounded."

"But every hospital in Alex and in Cairo is full," I said. "And the military is sending them on to England. Why—"

"Why do you suppose?" Nefret's voice rose. "Because the bloody military won't let a woman surgeon or a woman physician treat their men, that's why! Sophia went round to headquarters in person as soon as the casualties from Gallipoli began pouring in. They thanked her and sent her away."

"Damned fools," Emerson grunted.

"It is worse than folly, it is criminal negligence," Nefret said angrily. "By the time the wounded are taken onto the hospital ships, many of their injuries are gangrenous, and the surgeons have to amputate. They don't suture the wounds, they just apply wet dressings and pray. An even greater number of the men are suffering from dysentery, jaundice, typhoid, and God knows what other diseases. We could save some of them if we were given the opportunity."

"How do you know this?" Emerson asked.

Nefret shrugged. "Not all the army doctors are blind fools. Sophia spoke to one of them, who had come round—without official permission—to ask for supplies. He was rather bitter."

At the end of the day Ramses and Nefret came back to the house with us for tea. We were a little late—as we often were, since Emerson would have gone on working till sundown if I had not insisted he stop—so we found Sennia waiting for us on our rooftop salon, vibrating with indignation and, as she explained, faint with hunger.

"How was school?" I inquired, for this had been her first day.

"I did not like it," said Sennia, through a mouthful of cake. "It was very—"

"Do not say 'boring,'" I warned.

"But it was, Aunt Amelia."

She was sitting on the settee between Ramses and Nefret. Nefret put her arm round the child. "Did you make any friends?"

"No. The other children are—"

"Boring?" Nefret laughed, but her lovely face was a little sad. "A new school is always hard at first, Sennia."

"Was it hard for you?"

"Oh, my, yes." Nefret and I exchanged reminiscent smiles. "Just ask Aunt Amelia. I didn't know the things the other girls knew, languages and music and deportment, and they were horrid to me."

"It *was* very hard for you, my dear," I said. I still regretted having put Nefret into a situation whose difficulties I ought to have anticipated. She had been thirteen when she came to us, straight from the remote oasis in the Western Desert where she had been born and raised. Intelligent and anxious to please, she had adjusted to civilized customs so quickly that I had believed her ready for school. I had forgotten that young children of both sexes are inherently vicious.

Sennia would not have an easy time either. Socially and educationally she was better off than Nefret had been, since she had been with us long enough to learn our ways, but while Nefret had been a fair blossom of English loveliness, some of the little beasts would make fun of Sennia's dark skin and call her names. I wondered whether Saint Mary's might have been easier ... Well, we would have to see. Sennia was a fighter, and should the occasion arise I would pay a few calls on the parents of the offenders—or send Emerson to call on them. If she really hated it we would have to reconsider the case.

I said cheerfully, "In some ways it was more difficult for Nefret than it will be for you, Sennia. Children of six are not expected to know French and German or play a musical instrument. That is why they are sent to school, to learn those things."

"I can play two tunes on the piano," Sennia said hopefully.

"Thanks to your aunt Nefret."

"Yes!" She threw her arms around Nefret. "Will I be able to play as well as you one day, if I practice?"

"You will play much better," Nefret assured her.

Horus had joined us, stamping up the stairs with a tread as heavy as a man's. Sennia began feeding him bits of biscuit and cheese, and I looked through the post, which I had brought up with me.

"Anything of interest?" Emerson inquired.

"No."

FROM LETTER COLLECTION M

My dear Mrs. Emerson,

I was delighted to learn that you and your family are back in Cairo. Will you—one or all of you—do me the honor of lunching with me on Thursday next? If I should be so fortunate as to receive an acceptance, I will reserve a table at Shepheard's for half past one, unless you would prefer another place.

With sincere regards,
Margaret Minton

My dear Mrs. Emerson,

I am so sorry that Thursday is not possible for you. Would Friday, which I understand is the day of rest for your men, be more convenient? If it is not, please suggest a date.

Sincerely,
Margaret Minton

My dear Mrs. Emerson,

You can continue to refuse my invitations, but in the small world of Cairo society you can't avoid me

*altogether. I have a particular reason for wanting
to see, not only you, but your husband and your
son. It isn't what you think. Won't you meet pri-
vately with me so I can explain?*

> *Yours,*
> *Margaret*

Margaret, indeed, I thought, after perusing this last
epistle. Our letters had been whizzing back and forth
with the speed of bullets; I answered hers the instant
they arrived and she did the same with mine. Obviously she had not changed since the days when she
first incurred my ire, initially by pursuing us merci-
lessly in the hope of a story, and finally by falling in
love with my husband. She had actually disguised
herself as a housemaid in order to gain a position in
our home, and it was during this period that she had
succumbed, as many women did, to Emerson's numerous attractions. Servants are always hearing and
seeing things, since one does not pay attention to
them. At least one didn't used to. I did now.

Was she still in love with him? She was a very
determined woman, and few men can match Emerson. I was not in the least concerned about his being
attracted to her. Not until the knowledge was forced
upon him did the innocent man realize the depth of
her affection, and it had embarrassed him horribly.
All the more reason, I thought, to spare him additional embarrassment. I wrote a brief, forceful response in the negative and told Ali the doorman to

have it sent by messenger to the Semiramis, where Miss Minton was staying.

She turned up at Giza the following day.

There were not many tourists in Egypt that winter. Citizens of the countries of the Central Powers were of course personae non gratae, the French and English were most of them deeply involved in the deadly business of war, and many Americans had been deterred from travel abroad because of the submarine threat. Desperate for work and baksheesh, the guides swarmed like flies over the visitors who did come. It was a piercing, poignant chorus of pleas that attracted my attention; I looked up from the rubble I was examining to see a crowd of the rascals scampering toward me. Not until they were close at hand did I recognize the form they surrounded. I leaped to my feet, hoping to head her off before she could get to Emerson, who was down below in the tomb. Seeing me, the guides retreated to a safe distance and Miss Minton proceeded to accost me.

"Good morning, Mrs. Emerson." She held out her hand.

Instead of taking it I inspected her from head to foot and back again, noting that her well-cut skirt was a trifle fuller than was fashionable and that her buttoned boots had practical, low heels. Her figure was still trim and her black hair was untouched by gray; but the marks of the passing years were visible at the corners of her eyes and around her mouth.

A silent stare is often the best way of disconcerting an unwanted guest. It had no effect on Margaret Minton. Her smile broadened. "You ought to have known you wouldn't be rid of me so easily."

"What do you want?"

"I told you. A private conversation."

"You won't get it here," I pointed out. "I will have tea with you on Friday next."

"Will you? Or is that just a way of putting me off?" She removed her hat, a stylish Panama with a rolled brim and red ribbon, and pushed a loosened black lock back into place. "So long as I am here, I would like to have a look at your excavation. I've become very interested in Egyptology, you know."

I considered various means of removing her by force. None seemed practicable. "I fear that is impossible," I said frostily. "My husband does not allow sightseers to interrupt his work. Go look at the pyramids."

She had chosen her time well. I had been about to stop work and summon the others to luncheon. As we stood with eyes locked, like two dogs trying to stare one another down, Nefret emerged from the tomb chamber. "Aren't you ready for lunch, Mother?" she called. "Come and join us."

She had taken Miss Minton for a tourist. Emerson, who was the next to appear, did not fall into that error. He had, as was his invariable and uncouth habit, removed his shirt as soon as the temperature began to rise; seeing Miss Minton he started, swore, and dashed back into the tomb.

"Dear me," said Miss Minton, laughing. "Was that a hint that he doesn't want to see me?"

"We are very busy," I began.

"What a magnificent-looking man he is."

"As I was saying—"

Emerson forestalled my feeble attempt to dismiss

the lady, reemerging with his shirt on. Tucking it in as he walked, he came toward us.

"Miss Minton, isn't it?"

"I'm so flattered you remember me, Professor." She gave him her hand. Emerson let it go as soon as he decently could, but the blunt manners he exhibits toward other men are softened by his hopeless sentimentality about women. He finds it very difficult to be rude to them.

"Are you joining us for luncheon?" he asked.

"No, no, I wouldn't dream of intruding," said Miss Minton. She glanced at me. "But if it wouldn't be too much trouble . . . A glass of water, perhaps, before I go on my way? The air is so dry here."

It was a request one could hardly refuse. Forcing a smile, I led the way to the shelter.

We had taken Sennia with us that day, as it was a school holiday. She and Gargery were investigating the picnic basket Fatima had prepared while Nefret looked on and Ramses discussed with Sennia the relative merits of tomato versus cheese sandwiches.

"What a charming domestic group!" Miss Minton exclaimed, her keen dark eyes taking in every detail, from Sennia's dusty black curls to Nefret's working costume of trousers and boots and sweat-stained shirt. "Please, let us not be formal; I am certain I can identify everyone except—"

"Miss Minton," I said, with malice aforethought. "You remember our butler, Gargery."

I failed to embarrass her. The corners of her rather wide mouth turned up. "I remember him very well. He gave me a memorable tongue-lashing one afternoon when he found me loitering near the library, a room outside the sphere of my regular duties. How are you, Gargery?"

"Quite well, miss—madam—er—miss. Thank you."

"And this must be the young Mrs. Emerson," said Miss Minton, offering her hand to Nefret. "I have heard so much about you."

"I have heard a great deal about you too, Miss Minton."

"You don't know me," said Sennia. "My name is Sennia. Are you a friend of ours?"

Miss Minton gave her a sickeningly sweet smile. I could see she had had very little to do with children. "Why, yes, my dear. I have known your—er—family for a long time."

Miss Minton then turned a stare like a searchlight on Ramses, who had risen to his feet. He was decently covered, at least, but the casual clothing he wore on the dig set off his frame to best advantage.

"You know my son, of course," I said.

"I remember him very well, but I would not have recognized him. What a difference a few years can make!"

"More than a few years, I think," said Ramses. "Are you in Egypt on a journalistic assignment, Miss Minton, or for pleasure?"

"A little of both."

I filled a glass with water and pushed it into Miss Minton's hand. "So it is the truth you are after?" I inquired ironically.

"As always, Mrs. Emerson." She sipped daintily at the liquid. "Thank you. Most refreshing. What I would really like, of course, is to make my way to the fighting lines."

"There's not much going on in the Sinai just now," Ramses said.

"I was thinking of the western front." Her lips twisted ironically. "The western front of Egypt, that is. The Senussi have crossed the border and we haven't enough men to drive them back. I'd like to see some action."

"No, you would not," Emerson said. "Anyhow, you haven't a prayer of getting to Mersa Matruh. If you tried it on your own you'd be turned back before you left the Delta, and the War Office would never allow a woman into a fighting zone."

"They aren't allowing any journalists into that area," Miss Minton said, her eyes flashing. "There are only four correspondents who have a War Office license; needless to say, I am not one of them. Ah, well. They will be evacuating the rest of the poor devils from Gallipoli before long; I am hoping to interview some of them. It is an open secret that the campaign was fatally mismanaged from the start. The inadequacy of medical care is a scandal the War Office is attempting to conceal."

I glanced warningly at Nefret. There was no need; though her intent expression indicated her interest in and agreement with Miss Minton's statement, she remained silent. The dear girl had learned discretion from bitter experience, and she had heard a great deal from me about the untrustworthiness of journalists.

"You appear to have unofficial sources of information about matters that are not common knowledge," I said, hoping to provoke Miss Minton into an indiscretion.

I ought to have known better. She shrugged, and took another sip of water. "All journalists rely on such sources, and there is always someone open to bribery. Well, I must be going. It has been a great pleasure to see you all again and to meet your lovely wife, Ramses . . . if I may use the name by which I used to call you."

"It was Master Ramses," said my son coolly. "While you were employed as our housemaid."

She gave him an appreciative, unembarrassed smile. "Touché—Mr. Emerson. You still favor plain speaking, I see. Good. So do I."

To my surprise, for I had expected her to prolong her leave-taking, she started to walk away.

The surface was uneven. There were pebbles and bits of broken stone littering the ground. However, I suspected it was not a coincidence that she tripped and lost her balance just as she was passing Ramses.

He put out a hand to catch and steady her, and was visibly taken aback to find himself in a close embrace. Clinging to him, her arms around his neck and her body pressed against his, she looked up at him with a smile. "Thank you. How quick you were! You saved me from a nasty fall."

"Bruised knees and scraped hands, rather," said Ramses, recovering himself. It is very difficult to disconcert Ramses for long. "Are you able to walk, or shall I call one of the dragomen to help you to your carriage?"

"No, that won't be necessary." She detached herself with brisk efficiency. "I hope you didn't hurt your arm again when you caught me. What happened to it?"

"Accidents frequently occur on a dig," Ramses said.

"Ah." Miss Minton straightened her shirtwaist and tucked it in. "Well, then, good-bye. I will see you tomorrow, Mrs. Emerson. Five o'clock at the Semiramis?"

"What was that all about?" said Emerson, as the trim little figure strutted away—there is really no other word for the way the woman walked when she was pleased with herself. I remembered that walk very well.

I wondered too. Her stumble had been no accident, and her embrace had been deliberately calculated. It had not been a romantic advance. She was far too clever and sophisticated to resort to a trick like that one to get a man's attention, especially with that man's wife only two feet away. If it had accomplished nothing else, it had aroused my curiosity and convinced me that I had better accept her "invitation."

FOUR

When I entered the Semiramis shortly after five I was met by the concierge, who informed me that Miss Minton had requested that I take tea with her in her room. Aha, I thought, I was right. She has something to tell me, or demand of me— some matter that requires privacy. This was not an ordinary social encounter. Not that I had ever supposed it was.

I took the lift to the fourth floor, where the safragi escorted me to her door. It was a pleasant little suite, consisting of parlor and bedchamber; the parlor also served as her office, for there were books scattered about and piles of papers neatly arranged on a table under the window. After she had greeted me and offered me a chair, Miss Minton sat down behind the tea tray.

"How do you take your tea, Mrs. Emerson? If I had remained in your household long enough to reach the exalted station of parlormaid I would know the answer, but—"

"Milk, please. I marvel at your audacity, Miss

Minton. You ought to recall your shameless masquerade with embarrassment and regret, not make a joke of it."

"Ramses did. At least I assume he was joking. Come now, Mrs. Emerson, it was a long time ago; haven't you forgiven me for that harmless prank?"

"I am not concerned about the past, but the present. You haven't changed your spots, Miss Minton. You would not have been so persistent if you only wanted to renew old acquaintances. What are you after now?"

"Straight to the point, eh?" She put her cup on the table and leaned forward. "Believe it or not, renewing old acquaintances was one of my motives. I was particularly curious to see Ramses."

"You did more than look."

"Mmmm." The sound was like a cat's purr. "I knew he must be a grown man by now, but who would have supposed that infuriating, unprepossessing little boy would change so much? He's even handsomer than his father, and those shoulders . . ." She rolled her eyes and pursed her lips in an unseemly manner.

"You are certainly in a position to know," I replied coldly. "What was the reason for that performance?"

"I have every intention of telling you. However, I beg you will allow me to tell it in my own way, without questioning or interrupting me. You have heard many strange stories in your time, I expect, but this is one of the strangest. Perhaps I should begin by asking if you will do me the honor of accepting a copy of my latest book."

She handed it to me. "I haven't inscribed it. You may keep it, give it away, or burn it, whatever you like; but first read the pages I have marked."

"Now?"

"Yes, please. It won't take long."

A strip of paper indicated where I was to begin. I opened the book and glanced at the page. "It won't be necessary for me to read it. I remember this scene very well."

The lines in her cheeks deepened, forming an attractive frame for her firm mouth. "One of the most thrilling scenes I have ever written," she said complacently.

"You used the word 'silken' twenty-six times."

Miss Minton threw her head back and laughed. "And 'voluptuous' twenty-eight times. Very well, if my style offends you so much I won't ask you to suffer it again. You recall, I am sure, that after requesting an interview with the Emir, I was escorted to a room in the palace where I remained for eight days, seeing no one except the slave girls who brought me food. I was treated with the utmost courtesy, but my repeated demands to see the Emir were ignored and I was prevented from leaving my room by guards outside the door—"

"Until, on the eighth night, three burly eunuchs—wearing silken garments—came and escorted you to the audience chamber where the Emir—swathed in silken robes—awaited you. You attempted to ask him about the political situation in central Arabia; he responded with fulsome compliments, his bold black eyes scanning your form. You persisted. He offered to show you his secret correspondence with the spies he had set on his rivals and on the Turkish governor. Fearing the worst but knowing you had no other choice, you accompanied him to a small chamber—"

"Voluptuously appointed with soft divans and silken cushions," said Miss Minton, grinning broadly. "It was where he kept his private papers, though."

"And there," I continued, "the Emir cast off his silken robes; clad only in trousers and sleeveless vest—"

"—of silk brocade—"

"—he seized you in his arms. Struggling in his grasp, knowing it would be futile to call for help, you were on the verge of swooning when suddenly he released you and spun round, his hand on the hilt—"

"—jewel-encrusted *golden* hilt—"

"—of his sword. You sank trembling upon the silken cushions of the divan and what to your wondering eyes should appear but the form of a man, who had entered the room through a curtained doorway. Was he a rescuer or another foe? you wondered (pressing your hand to your heaving bosom, if I remember correctly). He wore the coarse cotton garments (I must say, that was a pleasant change) of a peasant, and in his hand he carried a naked blade. In deadly silence he rushed at the Emir, who drew his sword. The blades clashed. A grim smile playing about his well-shaped lips, the newcomer . . ."

Miss Minton fell back against the cushions, whooping with laughter. She wiped her eyes on her napkin and remarked, "I knew it was bad, but I didn't realize it was as bad as that. Spare me the rest, Mrs. Emerson."

"The end was never in doubt," I continued remorselessly. "Your defender's mighty thews (really, Miss Minton!) and tigerish agility soon overcame the Emir, who sank wounded and unconscious to the floor. Lifting your fainting form as easily as if you had been a child, the stranger carried you to the window and . . . well, to make an unnecessarily prolonged story short, he lowered you down to the ground with a rope—a silken rope, wasn't it?—led you through the dark deserted streets to where your men were camped, awaiting your return, and clasped you to him in a long passionate embrace before lifting you onto your camel and vanishing into the night."

"Oh, dear," murmured Miss Minton. "Very well, Mrs. Emerson, you have had your fun. I hope you enjoyed that."

"Why do you write such rubbish? You are capable of better; some of the passages in that same book are cogently argued and well expressed."

"Why? Because it sells, of course. You know my financial situation; my father left me nothing but the empty title of 'Honorable,' and I am dependent on what I earn." Another smile deepened the lines framing her mouth. "You must have been struck by my rubbishy prose, or you wouldn't remember the very phrases I used."

"You made it up out of whole cloth, didn't you?"

"The story is true up to the point where the Emir took me to his private room. Would you like to know what really happened after that?"

Dignity warred with curiosity and lost. "Well . . ."

Miss Minton rose and went to the table. Selecting

a small sheaf of papers from one of the piles, she came back and handed it to me. "Here is the true version. I composed it soon after the event."

FROM MANUSCRIPT COLLECTION M
(MISCELLANEOUS)

The Emir was only a boy, seventeen or eighteen at the most. A black mustache and goatee gave him a warlike look, but his cheeks were as smooth as those of a girl. He reeked of attar of roses and clanked with jewelry. I wondered he could raise his hands; there were rings on every finger and both thumbs. Enameled brooches set with emeralds and rubies pinned his garment; through his sash had been thrust a dagger that had to be purely ornamental—the hilt was so heavily encrusted with gemstones it would have been impossible to get a good grip on it—and on the front of his turban was an ornament many a woman would have sacrificed her virtue to possess—a spray of diamonds eight inches long and four inches across, with a white egret feather sticking up from it.

We were alone in that vast-columned audience chamber, but I knew there were guards at the doors. The invitation, though courteously couched, had been a command. I couldn't be any worse off than I was, and after all, what choice had I? When he gestured again for me to follow him, I did so. He managed to keep a step or two ahead of me, as male dignity required, but he had to trot, and he kept shooting resentful glances at me over his shoulder. I stifled a laugh. Which only went to prove that I had a lot to learn about boy emirs.

The room we entered was a surprise. There was a divan, there were cushions, and a low brass table with vessels of silver containing dates and sweetmeats; but there was also a modern, workmanlike desk covered with papers.

"The most important papers are there," the Emir said, indicating a curtained doorway. "But first let us sit and talk like friends. You appear warm. Take off your coat."

"I am quite comfortable, thank you." Involuntarily I drew the garment closer around me.

"You will be more comfortable without that heavy garment." He rolled his eyes and moved slowly toward me. "It does not become you. Why do you dress like a man, Sitt, when you are very much a woman?"

"The papers—"

"Later."

I had stood my ground and not backed away as he approached. I was suffering from that inconquerable and imbecile sense of superiority which is born and bred in our class, and fool that I was, I could not help thinking of him still as a boy. I was honestly rather surprised when he caught hold of me. He was stronger than his foppish attire had led me to believe; I had conveniently ignored the fact that the Rashids were fighters, and that this "boy" had probably killed his first man before he was fourteen. Instead of struggling, which would have been wasted effort, I looked him straight in the eye and said haughtily, "I am not one of your women. Let me go and we will talk like friends and equals."

"You are not my equal. No woman is. Come, embrace me. I promise you will enjoy it."

His lips crawled across my cheek. So much for moral superiority; I had always suspected it wasn't effective except in fiction. To my surprise and disgust, I heard myself scream. I won't put that in the book; I hate to admit it even to myself. Not only was it contemptible, it was futile. Who would come to my rescue here?

I am going to write this down just as it happened, but I wouldn't believe it if I had not been there. The Emir pushed me away, with such force that I staggered back, tripped on the edge of a rug, and fell ungracefully onto the divan with my heels temporarily higher than my head. By the time I got my breath back they were engaged in hand-to-hand combat, the Emir and another man who had appeared from nowhere. The boy was no coward; closing with his opponent, he got both hands around his throat. Instead of trying to break his hold, the other man delivered a series of hard blows with his knee, his elbow, and the edge of his hand. The first two were well below the belt, or in this case, sash; the last caught the Emir on the back of the neck as he doubled up, clutching his stomach. He crashed to the floor and lay still.

The newcomer took a step toward me and then stopped as if he had run into a glass wall. He was a tall man, broad-shouldered and well-built, the skirts of his cotton galabeeyah tucked up to display muscular calves. The black beard and the folds of his kaffiyeh concealed all his features except for a prominent hawklike nose.

"Who the devil are you?" he demanded.

I gaped at him, too astonished to answer. His complexion, his costume, and what I could see of his features were those of an Arab, but he had spoken educated English, without the slightest trace of an Eastern accent.

Two quick strides brought him to my side. He took me by the chin and tilted my face toward the light. "The resemblance is not so exact after all," he remarked. "You must be the damned fool English journalist they're gossiping about in the bazaars."

The reassurance of the language, the speech of a man of my own nation and class, restored my courage. I tried to pull away from him, but he only tightened his grip. My chin felt as if it were being squeezed in a vise. "Who the devil are *you*?" I asked. "Were you sent here to rescue me?"

"You came here of your own free will, didn't you? What makes you suppose you need rescuing?"

"He tried to make love to me!"

"He did?" The unknown released his grasp and grinned. "That's Ibn-Rashid for you. Can't resist a joke."

"A joke? How dare you? He was about to—to . . ."

"Oh, I doubt it. He knows better. Since his uncle was assassinated—they're heavy on assassination here—his mother and his maternal uncles are the real power behind the throne, and he wouldn't dare go against their wishes. Raping and/or murdering a British subject would get them in serious trouble, and they are not ready to risk that. Too busy playing one side off against the other." Picking up a heavy brass vase, he bent over the Emir, who was beginning to stir, and struck him smartly on the head. "You've really complicated matters," he said in tones of mild vexation. "You had better come along with me. Rashid is going to be a trifle annoyed about this, and he might take it out on you. At least you're sensibly dressed. That fetching ensemble was another thing that misled me; she favors trousers too."

"She? Who? What are you going to do?"

"First I'm going to tie him up." He removed the Emir's beautifully embroidered sash and bound his hands behind him. "If you hadn't distracted me I'd have done the job and been gone without his knowing I was here."

"Why should I go with you? I don't know who you are. I could be going from the frying pan into the fire."

"You could be. If I were in your place I'd risk it, though. The frying pan has begun to sizzle." He finished binding and gagging the Emir with bits of his clothing and rose to his feet. "You can come willingly or draped inconveniently over my shoulder. I'll have to knock you unconscious first, you understand. It will hurt. Well?"

"I—"

"Oh, for God's sake, stop dithering." He caught hold of my wrist and raised his other arm. His fist was clenched. He *was* going to hit me!

"Don't, don't! I'll come."

"I should damn well think so." A muffled groan from the Emir drew his attention away from me. Ibn-Rashid was conscious. His eyes were the only part of his body he could move, but they were eloquent. I no longer doubted that a possible fire was preferable to a certain grilling.

My rescuer—if that is what he was—threw his shoulders back and planted his hands on his hips. His pose, the tilt of his head, a dozen small changes I could see but not define, turned him into the ruffian he had first appeared to be. "Forgive my rude treatment, lord," he said in fluent Arabic. "But you see how it is. You are a rich man and I am a poor man. Does not the Prophet teach that helping the poor is pleasing to God?"

Bending over the Emir, he deftly removed the brooches and chains and unfastened the glittering turban ornament. "I will take the woman too," he said, tucking the objects into his pouch. "She would not bring much from the brothel owners, but perhaps the Inglizi will pay."

Ibn-Rashid's eyes were popping and his forehead was beaded with sweat. I hoped he had begun to realize he might be in a spot of trouble if someone came looking for me, and he had to admit his impetuous behavior had caused him to lose me. The other man made him a mocking salute, hands together under his chin, head bowed, and then walked toward me, with a slow, insolent stride. I backed away. I would like to claim my movements were calculated and that I understood what he intended, but honesty compels me to admit my retreat was purely involuntary. His back to the Emir, he bared white teeth in what I hoped was a smile, and swung his fist.

It barely grazed my jaw. In case I hadn't got the idea, he administered a brisk kick on the ankle, and as my knees buckled he scooped me up and tossed me over his shoulder. I had the sense to close my eyes and let my body go limp, though it was a damnably uncomfortable position. He carried me through the curtained doorway and set me on my feet. The room was unlighted except by moonlight, but I could see cupboards lining the walls. The door of one of them was open; papers had spilled out onto the floor. I picked one of them up.

"What do you think you're doing?" His voice was almost inaudible. "Put that down and come here."

"It's his private correspondence." I tried to keep my voice as soft as his. "What a story I could write if I had some of these letters!"

"And what a pretty sight you would be hanging upside down from the gate of the palace with crows picking at your eyes." He struck the paper from my hand, added it to the others that had fallen on the floor, and put them back in the cupboard.

"Uncle Ismail and Mama won't bother pursuing a worthless female they were about to send on her way anyhow, but if you had those letters they wouldn't rest until they got them—and you—back." He went to the window and then turned, holding something I couldn't identify in the darkness. "I don't suppose you can climb down a rope? Young women today have so few useful skills. I'll lower you. As soon as you're on the ground, untie it and get out of the way."

He fastened the end of the rope round my waist and hoisted me unceremoniously into the embrasure. The window gave onto a walled garden, shadowy with trees and flowering shrubs; the sweet scent of some night-blooming flower reached my nostrils. The ground looked a long way down.

I took a deep breath and turned round, so that I was lying across the sill, with my feet dangling and my hands gripping the window frame.

"You took the jewelry to make him believe you are a common thief," I whispered.

"My dear girl!" His voice was light with laughter. "I took the jewelry because I *am* a thief, though not a common one. The turban pin alone is worth several thousand pounds. Stop talking and let go. I've got you."

The only thing that gave me nerve enough to loosen my grip was the knowledge that if I hesitated he'd shove me out. The rope tightened; it felt as if it were cutting me in two. He lowered me in a series of quick, breath-stopping jerks. My feet hit the ground so hard my knees buckled. He was already halfway down before I had loosened the slipknot and stepped aside.

"How did you get up there?" I asked breathlessly.

"Climbed the wall. I took a rope along since it is sometimes advisable to beat a hasty retreat. Good Lord, you talk almost as much as she does. Follow me and keep quiet."

He led the way through shadowy aisles of

shrubbery to the far wall. It was of mortared stone and over ten feet high. Moonlight glittered off a fractured surface.

"That's broken glass," said my companion informatively. "I cleared a space, but it's only about two feet wide, so be careful where you put your hands. You'll have to stand on my shoulders. How are you at acrobatics?"

"I'll soon find out, won't I?"

His lips parted in a smile. "Quite. Here we go."

I managed it by leaning against the wall to keep my balance while he lifted me and pushed from below. Nimble I was not, but I got there. Squatting, I looked down and saw two astonished faces looking up.

"Allahu akhbar!" said one. "It's a woman. Where does he find them?"

The other man said, more practically, "Turn, Sitt, and lower yourself by your hands. I will catch you."

My palms as well as my knees were bleeding by the time I got myself down. We must have been outside the confines of the palace now; a narrow lane led off to right and left. The high walls on either side cut off the starlight; I couldn't see anything except the pale robes of the two men and some shadowy shapes that appeared to be horses. A few moments later my rescuer dropped down beside me.

"Stand still," he ordered. "Don't move."

Taking the other two aside, he spoke to them softly and urgently. I couldn't make out the words, but I was pretty sure he wasn't speaking Arabic; the rhythms of the language are quite distinct from those of English. One of the other men laughed; their leader, for so he must be, responded with a curt reprimand. Then he came back to me, leading a horse. He pulled his robe off and handed it to me. "Put this on."

I got the thing over my head and tried to find the sleeves. He swung himself into the saddle and reached down. "That's good enough. Leave your head and face covered."

It sounds so romantic when one reads about it. Held in the curve of his arm, my face pressed to the hard muscles of his chest, riding off into the night through a city filled with enemies! I couldn't see, I couldn't draw a deep breath without inhaling folds of coarse cotton, something was jabbing into my left hip, and . . . and I wished it could go on forever. Finally he pulled the fabric away from my face. "We're almost there. Your men should be packed and ready to go. We took the long way round, just as a precaution, but Ed—one of my people—went directly to their camp and warned them. I am telling you this much so you won't delay me with a lot of damned fool questions that I don't intend to answer."

"Who—"

"Especially that question." After a brief silence he went on, in quite a different tone of voice. "You don't owe me anything. They'd have let you leave eventually, with your virtue and your skin intact. The boy has a rather crude sense of humor, that's all. I expect you will be unable to resist the temptation to describe tonight's little adventure for your newspaper, in the most lurid terms you can invent;

but if you would care to do me a service you won't mention my—er—linguistic abilities."

"You mean I mustn't say you were English."

"You're jumping to conclusions. I might have been a Rooshian, or French or Turk or Prooshian—"

"Who quotes Gilbert and Sullivan?"

"Why not? Look here, I gave myself away once, out of sheer astonishment—and no, I won't explain that either—but—"

"I promise. I won't say a word. Will I—will I ever see you again?"

"I devoutly hope not." The horse had stopped. He lowered me to the ground and dismounted.

I'd been so intent on listening to his voice, trying to get a closer look at his face, I hadn't been aware of my surroundings. We were on the edge of the city, at the place where my men had set up camp. They crowded round me, apologizing and exclaiming with relief.

"Enough," said my companion in Arabic. "Take the Sitt and begone. Here is money to bribe the guards."

He tossed the leather bag to Ali, who weighed it in his hand and smiled. "It is enough to bribe the vizier himself. We are almost ready, Effendi. There is only the Sitt's bathtub to be loaded onto the pack camel."

He trotted off, leaving me facing my rescuer.

"Bathtub?" he said under his breath. "No wonder the sun never sets on the British Empire."

"At least I'm not traveling with crystal stemware and fine china and damask tablecloths, like Miss Gertrude Bell."

"Oh, so it's Miss Bell you're trying to outdo, is it? I'm afraid she would consider you had let the side down." He was wearing only a loose shirt and a pair of knee-length drawers. The moonlight gave them a pale luster but left his face in shadow, except for the tip of that arrogant nose. He started to turn away. "Good night."

"Wait. Er—don't you want your robe back?"

"Keep it. And borrow a kaffiyeh or scarf from one of your men."

"Yes, I understand."

"What are you waiting for? Oh. This?"

He drew me into his arms and kissed me.

It was a long, lingering kiss, and I think he enjoyed it more than he had expected; but it was he who broke away, detaching my clinging hands and pushing me unceremoniously toward my kneeling camel. Ali was there to help me mount; when I looked round, he was gone.

I turned the last page over. She was waiting for me to speak, her hands tightly clasped and her lips parted.

I cleared my throat. "It is even more preposterous than the other version."

"But it's true, every word. You know it's true. You were the woman he meant. I was too confused to think straight at the time, but when I went over it in my mind—over it and over it—I realized it could only have been you. Who—"

I interrupted. Rude of me, but I wasn't ready for

that question yet. "Why didn't you publish this version?"

"I had promised I would not betray him."

"Dear me, how noble."

She jumped up. "Don't patronize me, Mrs. Emerson! That summer, the summer before the war, the commitments of the tribal chieftains were of vital importance. Could we count on them to remain neutral, or were they secretly dealing with the Turks? That's why he was there, to find out, and he endangered his mission and himself by helping me. That knowledge has haunted me ever since. I must find out what happened to him. If he came to harm because of me—"

"I see. You had better sit down, Miss Minton, and finish your tea. Pacing in that agitated fashion will only tire you."

She flung herself down onto the sofa. "I don't want any more confounded tea. Are you going to answer me or not?"

"After you have satisfied my curiosity on one final point. What made you suspect that Ramses might have been your rescuer? I presume that was why you embraced him?"

Her tight lips relaxed. "I quite enjoyed it, even with his wife looking daggers at me. Your son, Mrs. Emerson, has a certain reputation in certain circles. It was the sort of thing he might have done, and there was something about my rescuer—his voice, his gestures—oh, I can't explain it, but it was oddly familiar, somehow. Ramses is very like his father, but as soon as I was—er—close to him, I knew he wasn't the man. Now it's your turn. I've been honest with you; please tell me the truth. He knew you, and knew you well; it is impossible that you should not know him."

I had postponed answering her in order to give myself time to think what to say. How much could I—should I—disclose? Part of the story must be told; a flat denial of facts that she knew to be true would only sharpen her curiosity, and I feared my face had given me away not once but several times as I read that bizarre narrative. I was only too familiar with Miss Minton's persistence. And in this case, I felt certain, she was driven by a stronger motive than journalistic curiosity.

I said slowly, "I knew him."

"Knew . . . Do you mean . . . ?"

I suspected she had developed a sentimental attachment to her unknown hero; it had echoed in every word of her story; but when I saw the color drain from her face I realized the attachment was deeper than I had supposed. Sympathy for the pain of a fellow woman loosened my tongue.

"I am sorry. It had nothing to do with you; he died saving my life, and that of—of others."

"I knew he was not a thief," she whispered.

"Oh, but he was. One of the best. For years he controlled the illegal antiquities game in Egypt—tomb robbing, forgery, illicit digging. He had built up a criminal network that covered all of Egypt and parts of the Middle East. I never knew his name; his men referred to him as 'the Master.' He also used the sobriquet of Sethos. Nor did I ever see his face when it was not disguised. The general description matches his, however, and the statements you reported were completely in character. He had a strange sense of humor."

"He was in love with you, wasn't he?"

"That is irrelevant and immaterial and none of your business, Miss Minton."

"That was why he kissed me. Because I look like you."

"I assure you, Miss Minton, that Sethos undoubtedly kissed quite a number of women who did not resemble me in the slightest." She bit her lip and bowed her head. It was the only sign of weakness she had exhibited; admiration for her self-control made me speak with a candor I had not intended. "It doesn't do to romanticize a man, you know. None of them is perfect. Sethos had some admirable characteristics, but he broke every commandment except the seventh, and that was only because he was not in a position to do so."

I left her sitting bolt upright with her hands folded in her lap and her face composed; but I knew that as soon as the door closed behind me, she would weep. I could hardly blame her for romanticizing that strange encounter. It *had* been romantic—blatantly, deliberately, and outrageously. Sethos was . . . had been . . . a consummate actor; he had slipped into the role of dashing hero as easily as he would have drawn on a pair of gloves.

It had been odd, though, her sense of recognition. Not until the previous winter had we discovered that the Master Criminal, the man who had harassed and tormented us for so many years, was Emerson's half-brother. That part of the truth Miss Minton would never know; there was no reason why she should. There was a very good reason why I had not enlightened her about another matter. I had sworn never to disclose it, for it might compromise others, including Ramses. It was for her own good, really. Let her remember her rescuer as the thief and criminal he had been, before he turned his unique talents from crime to counterespionage, and died in the service of his country.

FIVE

The interview had taken longer than I had expected. Darkness had fallen when I left the hotel. It was a lovely evening and I did not hurry the cabdriver; accustomed as I am to the bustling traffic and interesting odors and cacophonous street sounds of Cairo, I quite enjoyed the drive. It gave me time to think over what had transpired. All things considered, I believed I had handled the matter quite well.

When the cab stopped in front of the house, Ali the doorman rushed at me waving his arms and thanking God in a loud voice. Ali is an excitable fellow who enjoys theatrics, but he tends to take his cues from certain other persons, so I was not surprised when Emerson burst through the open door and added his voice to Ali's. Emerson was not thanking God.

"What kept you so long? How dare you be so late? What happened?"

"Pay the driver, Emerson," I said, as soon as I could make myself heard. I had been about to do so myself, but knew this little task would distract him.

"What? Oh." He was not wearing a coat. After fumbling in his trouser pockets he found a fistful of coins, handed them to the driver, put his arm round my waist, and propelled me into the house.

"You gave him far too much," I said. "Why are you carrying on like this? I told you where I was going."

"Hmph." Emerson stopped outside the door of the parlor. He was still holding me very tightly. "Perhaps I had a premonition."

"You? You don't believe in premonitions and forebodings. You always sneer at mine."

The parlor door opened, and Emerson released me as if I were red-hot.

"Ah," I said, seeing Nefret and Ramses side by side in the doorway. "Good evening, my dears. Are you dining? You didn't tell me."

"I told Fatima," said Nefret. "She always prepares food enough for a dozen. When you didn't turn up I asked her to put dinner back."

"Mahmud won't like it," I said. Our cook is somewhat temperamental.

"I had a few words with him," said my daughter-in-law firmly. "There's time for your whiskey and soda, Aunt Amelia. Come and sit down and tell us what that woman wanted."

I realized that Ramses must have discussed with her our earlier encounters with Miss Minton, and that they had concluded—correctly—that the lady had an ulterior motive for wanting to see me. I had intended to tell them the whole story anyhow. After a number of unfortunate incidents, resulting from the misguided attempts of certain persons to shield other persons from knowledge they (the certain persons) considered dangerous, we had made a pact, the four of us, to conceal nothing. At least Nefret and I had. Emerson and Ramses had agreed in principle, but both of them suffered from the innate conviction of male persons that they are the natural protectors of helpless females, and although both of them knew that Nefret and I were far from helpless, I did not trust either of them to stick to his promise.

So I took off my hat and took a chair and a glass of whiskey, and launched into my narrative. I was able to render it with all the panache of the original because I had brought the original away with me, slipping the pages into my handbag while Miss Minton's vision was blurred by tears. (It was not a nice thing to do, but as I had once remarked, all is fair in love, war, and journalism. In this case all three considerations applied.) I fully intended to return it, with my apologies—or perhaps without them—after I had taken a copy.

Nefret was the first to speak. "So that was it. I was afraid she'd heard some rumor about what Ramses did last winter. It would make a sensational story."

That idea hadn't occurred to me. Perhaps it would only have occurred to a woman so passionately devoted to her husband that she was blind to anything that did not directly affect him.

"She's not such a fool," Ramses said. "Publishing anything at all about that episode would violate the Official Secrets Act and get her in serious trouble."

Emerson had not said a word.

"Well, Emerson?" I inquired.

"Well," said Emerson. "We had better go in to dinner before Mahmud burns the soup."

In a normal household the discussion would have ended there, or been postponed until we four were alone. In this respect (as in certain other ways), ours is not a normal household. Emerson had always discussed anything he felt like discussing in front of the servants, sometimes asking them for their opinions or appealing to them for support (usually against me). It was this ill-bred habit of Emerson's that had encouraged Gargery to offer his opinions even when Emerson did not ask for them.

We took our places at the table and I waited for Emerson to introduce the subject, which I felt sure he would sooner or later. I was tempted to introduce it myself, in the hope that it would get Gargery's attention off his butling duties. He had, as was only natural, assumed he would take on the same duties in our Egyptian household. The only trouble was that Fatima considered it her duty and her right to serve our dinner. She seldom contributed to the conversation, but she liked to know what was going on.

So did Gargery. It would have been amusing to watch the two maneuvering for advantage if it hadn't been so inconvenient. Neither would yield to the other, so dishes were slapped onto the table and snatched up with such efficiency that I had not eaten a full meal since we arrived. I had been meaning to have a little talk with the two of them, but had not yet found the time.

So, when Gargery reached for my soup bowl, I said, "I haven't finished, Gargery. Emerson, what have you to say?"

"Miss Minton's narrative," said Emerson, fending Gargery off with his elbow, "is of purely academic interest. I see no reason to discuss it."

"Do you believe her?" Nefret asked.

"Yes," said Ramses. He glanced at Fatima, who was neatly blocking Gargery's attempt to get at his soup. She insisted on his finishing every bite of every dish, because she considered he was too thin. He hastily swallowed the last spoonful and went on, "It was Sethos, unquestionably. The reference to one of his lieutenants, incomplete but faithfully recorded by Miss Minton, leaves no room for doubt. I understand now why she was so determined to see us and speak with you, Mother. She was obviously fascinated by him. What did you tell her?"

"It required some careful thought," I said. "The resemblance between me and Miss Minton, and the references to certain of my characteristics, made it impossible for me to deny that I was the woman to whom he had referred. I felt obliged to disabuse her of her assumption that his purpose in being there was anything other than the one he had admitted."

Gargery's brow furrowed. "I beg your pardon, madam, but I can't quite work my way through that sentence."

"No one expects you to, Gargery," I replied.

Gargery took offense at my dismissal of his implicit request and retaliated by removing my fish plate before I had taken more than two bites.

"What else did you tell her?" Nefret asked.

"I gave her a brief summary of his career as a thief, and I informed her that he had passed away. I hope that will put an end to her romantic notions, but I don't count on it. A woman of a certain age . . . I wonder why she has never married."

"Gargery," said Emerson. "If you try to take my plate again before I have finished, I will pin your hand to the table with my fish fork."

"Yes, sir," said Gargery. He folded his arms and looked sternly at Emerson. "I think, sir, that you should tell us what this is all about. If that Master Criminal person has come back to life and is after you and the madam, we must take steps to protect you. What has he got to do with Miss Minton? I remember her; she gave us quite a lot of trouble over the British Museum case."

Emerson turned rather red in the face.

"You may as well tell them, Emerson," I said. "If you don't, Gargery's imagination will run riot and he will do something silly."

Emerson looked from Gargery to Fatima. Both of them were nodding vigorously. Despite their competitiveness in regard to serving the food, they were allies in all matters that might affect our safety and well-being, and if Fatima believed the situation was serious she would inform Selim and Daoud and Kadija, and then the whole lot of them would be trailing after us. Recognizing the logic of my remark, Emerson said, "It seems Miss Minton ran into Sethos summer before last, when she was in Arabia. She was unaware of what happened this past winter."

"Ah," said Gargery. "So he is dead, then. You wouldn't lie to me, would you, sir?"

"No," said Emerson.

I hoped we had seen the last of Miss Minton, but I did not count on it, especially since I had taken the liberty of borrowing her manuscript. In the hope of forestalling further communications I copied the pages out before I went to bed that night and sent them back to her by messenger the following morning, with a little note explaining politely but firmly that I had told her all I could and saw no reason for further contact. Somewhat to my surprise, there was no response. Perhaps she had regretted her decision to confide in me. It had certainly been a most revealing document.

With Miss Minton on the trail, I was all the more determined to get the children away from Cairo. There was no reason why they could not leave immediately; the *Amelia* was ready, and after remaining blandly indifferent to his father's increasingly blunt hints, Ramses had finally announced that he was willing to go. He had given up hope of hearing from Asad, who could easily have communicated with him had he chosen to do so. We concluded that he had left the city for parts unknown.

It was Nefret, however, who had been the deciding factor. We had had a little chat one day, while we were cutting flowers for the saloon. The roses were particularly pretty that year.

"Did Father agree?" she asked.

"Emerson proposed the scheme himself," I assured her. "Not that I believe there is any cause for concern. Emerson really is worried about the Luxor tombs. You wouldn't mind leaving the hospital for a while?"

For a few moments she was silent, her attention apparently fixed on the perfectly formed crimson rose she held. Then she said, "You know that when I went back to Switzerland to complete my medical training it was a form of penance."

"My dear girl, we agreed not to refer again to those unhappy times."

She went on as if I had not spoken. "The hospital was in desperate need of a woman surgeon. It still is. Aunt Amelia—Mother—" She put the secateurs down and turned to face me. "Is it wrong to care so much about someone that nothing and no one else matters to you?"

"I don't know whether it is right or wrong, my dear; but I understand."

"I thought I loved him before we were married, but it was nothing to the way I feel now. You know how much the hospital means to me. I would abandon it forever, without a backward look, if it would help to keep him safe."

"Now, my dear, there is no need for such a theatrical gesture," I remarked, for I felt it advisable to lower the emotional temperature. "Ramses would not want you to give up your professional career on his account; in fact, he would be extremely vexed if you considered such a thing. So we are agreed? You can persuade him?"

"Oh, yes." Her pensive features relaxed into a little smile. "I can persuade him."

I had not doubted she could. To say that her slightest wish was his command would not have been strictly true—and a good thing, too, for a man who will give in to a woman's every whim is not worth having—and the other way round, of course—but one had only to see them together to know that the attachment was as strong on his part as it was on hers.

The only remaining difficulty was Sennia. However, she returned from school that afternoon looking quite pleased with herself, and started telling us about her friends Mark and Elizabeth.

"There, you see?" I said. "I told you that you would soon make friends if you were polite and well-behaved."

Sennia had been trying to learn how to raise her eyebrows as Ramses did. His were very thick and dark and expressive, rising and lowering and tilting at various angles according to his state of mind. Thus far Sennia's best attempt had been to open her eyes very wide and wrinkle her forehead, with no visible alteration in the position of her brows. She did this now.

"Far be it from me to contradict you, Aunt Amelia," she said, in a fair imitation of Ramses's best drawl. "But being polite was a waste of time. They didn't like me till I cursed them."

I dropped the scone I had been buttering. Horus extended a paw, pulled the scone to him, and ate it.

"Cursed them?" I said weakly.

"In ancient Egyptian. I know a lot of bad words in Arabic and English but the Professor told me I mustn't use any of them." She reached for a cream bun and bit into it.

"Emerson! You didn't teach her—"

"Certainly I did. Children are natural bullies, my dear, and the only way to deal with bullies is to overpower them, physically or morally. Since it did not seem right to teach Sennia how to knock someone down—"

"Ramses taught me that," Sennia volunteered. She licked cream off her fingers. "But I only did it once, and not until after he pushed me."

I turned my indignant stare toward my son, who avoided my eyes and began to mumble. "It was just a little harmless trick of tripping someone up—self-defense, really—it's only effective if the person has got too close for comfort . . ."

Nefret began to laugh. "Never mind, darling. Mother may not approve your methods but they seem to have been effective. So, Sennia, you are now enjoying school?"

"Oh, yes. The lessons are not too boring and everyone wants to be on my side when we choose up for games."

So that was all right. Sennia kindly consented to continue her education and I informed the parties concerned that they would sail next day. It was as well that I did, for the evening post brought a letter from Howard, who had returned to Luxor for a brief visit, containing news that brought Emerson's fury to the boiling point.

The latest theft had been extraordinarily bold and daring; the miscreants had actually carried off part of a monumental black granite statue of

Ramses II from his mortuary temple on the west bank. The statue had been in fragments, but the head had been very well preserved. The head had been the first element to disappear. Its absence had been noted, not by any of the guards, but by a tourist—one of those tirelessly compulsive persons who reads his Baedeker line by line. He had reported it to the authorities, who had promised to investigate. By the time they got round to visiting the Ramesseum, two other large chunks of the statue were gone.

"How the hell did he do it?" Emerson demanded, waving Howard's letter like a battle flag. "The cursed head must have weighed hundreds of pounds. Then he had the damned effrontery to return the following night, after the original theft had been reported—"

"He?" I repeated.

Emerson broke into a fit of coughing.

"Whoever he was," said Ramses. "Father, would you like a glass of water?"

"I would like to—er—hmph. No, thank you, my boy. I suppose," said Emerson, "one of the Abd er Rassuls might have done the job."

The men of Gurneh were among the most accomplished tomb robbers in Egypt. One could not help suspecting there was a hereditary factor; their ancestors had been locating and looting tombs since pharaonic times. The Abd er Rassul brothers had had an almost uncanny aptitude for finding hidden burials; the cache of royal mummies had been only one of their discoveries.

"That's not really their line of work, though,"

Nefret said thoughtfully. "The fragments of that statue have been lying about for years. One can't really blame the authorities—such as they are—for failing to guard them. One would need a block and tackle to lift the pieces, wouldn't one?"

"Not necessarily," I said. "You have seen our men raise objects even heavier by sheer brute strength and skill. Well, it will be a nice little mystery for you and Ramses to solve, my dear."

Nice and safe, I thought to myself. The Gurneh thieves were a wily lot, but none of them was given to violence.

We stood on the dock waving good-bye as the men poled the *Amelia* away from the bank. The great sail caught the wind and swelled. The strength of the northerly winds and the skill of Reis Hassan would carry her upstream, against the current. The steam engine we had installed, at hideous expense and against my wishes, reduced the travel time to little more than a week, but they were in no hurry, and if they followed my advice they would only use the confounded noisy odorous machine when the wind failed.

Emerson's arm stole round my waist. "Curse it, Peabody," he said, in a voice gruff with emotion.

"Yes, my dear. It has been too long. Shall we plan a voyage of our own, later in the season?"

"Why not? We should be able to get the other business settled before too long."

"What other business?"

Emerson drew my arm through his and we started back toward the house. "Why, the little matter of the weeping assassin. Not a bad title for a thriller," he added musingly.

I turned my head and looked up at him. The morning breeze ruffled his hair and the morning light cast his strong features in sharp outline.

"Come now, don't pretend you hadn't thought of it," he said. "You always claim you anticipate my intentions and deductions."

"I had, of course. I was waiting until Ramses was out of the way before I raised the question with you. He won't like our interfering, you know."

"If things work out as I hope, he won't know about it. He's too softhearted by half," said Ramses's father. "Not that I mean any harm to the poor devil. I only want to question him and help him, if he is in need of help."

"I would like to help him back into prison," I said. "You are as softhearted as Ramses. How either of you can be so tolerant about a murderous attack—"

"I don't think you quite understand the—er—motivation, Peabody."

"Explain it to me, then."

Emerson drew me behind the shelter of a wall, out of the wind, and took out his pipe. He made quite a long business of filling and lighting it. After puffing meditatively, he said, "No, my dear, I would rather not. There are some subjects a gentleman does not discuss with a lady, and you are still delightfully naive about—er—"

"Oh, good Gad!" I cried. "Do you mean that wretched boy is—has—was—"

"Not so naive as that, I see," Emerson remarked as if to himself. "I believe so, yes. That assumption goes a long way to explaining Asad's emotional behavior."

"But—but—"

"My dear girl, don't look so stricken. It is perfectly natural—for some individuals—and perfectly harmless—for most of them. Ramses couldn't help it, if a young man—er—took a fancy to him, any more than he can prevent females from doing the same. He handled the matter very well, I thought. I only hope Asad hasn't cut his throat in a fit of remorse."

"Would he do such a thing?"

"He might. That is one of the reasons why I am anxious to locate him. And before you condemn him for that rather pathetic attack," Emerson added, "bear in mind that in matters of the heart the female can be deadlier than the male."

I certainly could not deny that. I was turning over in my mind various examples, from my personal experience, as we proceeded on our way. Emerson took my hand and hurried me along. He was, as always, anxious to get to the dig.

"Not so fast, if you please," I said. "We haven't decided how we are to go about locating this elusive youth. If he had wanted our help he would have sought it by this time."

"It will be difficult," Emerson admitted. "But there are certain steps we might take . . ."

We took the first that same night.

Mr. Bassam was delighted to see us. Some form

of green vegetable figured prominently in the menu for that evening, and a strong smell of onions filled the room.

"Whatever you have," said Emerson, cutting short Bassam's traditional offers of varied food substances, none of which was on hand.

We had our usual table, next to the open door of the restaurant. I was not aware of watching that doorway until Emerson kicked me on the ankle and suggested, in what he thinks is a whisper, that I stop being so obvious. After an excellent meal Emerson invited Bassam to join us for coffee and a pipe. The last was a habit I had never acquired, and I wondered, as the men passed the mouthpiece back and forth, how on earth Emerson could ingest so many dubious substances without the slightest alimentary inconvenience.

Bassam gave him the opening he wanted by asking after Nefret and Ramses. "They have gone to Luxor, I hear."

Emerson glanced at me. If Mr. Bassam knew, so did everyone else in Cairo. The speed with which gossip spreads in that city is astonishing. "Yes," he said. "They told us what a fine dinner they had here. Did you happen to see their friend?"

"They were alone," Bassam said, looking puzzled. "Not even the lady cat was with them."

"They ran into him just after they left," Emerson explained. "Ramses asked me to look him up, and give him a message, but he seems to have moved. I thought he might be one of your regular customers."

"Ah. What is his name?"

Emerson had no choice but to give the only name we knew, though it was unlikely the fellow was still using it. Bassam shook his head. The description Emerson proceeded to give struck no chord either.

"Eyeglasses, young, a thin beard," Bassam mused, stroking his own bushy appendage fondly. "It could be any one of several who come from time to time. Shall I watch out for him and tell him the Father of Curses wishes to speak with him?"

"Tell him the Father of Curses has news for him. Good news, that he will be glad to hear."

"Well done, Emerson," I said, after we had taken leave of our host and left the establishment.

"I doubt anything will come of it. If Asad learned anything from his temporary leader, he has probably altered his appearance."

Nothing came of it that night, though we strolled with snail-like slowness through the dark alleys. We could only hope that the word would spread. It probably would; Emerson's activities were always of consuming interest to the citizens of Cairo. He dropped a few more words the following night, in various coffee shops around the University.

"People tend to return to familiar surroundings," he explained. "He was a student at Al-Azhar and knows the area."

Nothing came of that visit either, though we sat late in the garden every night and informed Ali that if anyone approached the house in a surreptitious manner he was not to raise the alarm but come quietly to inform us. I suggested, therefore, that we try a more direct approach by informing the police of Asad's reappearance and asking what they knew about him.

Emerson was against the idea. "I would rather not have anything more to do with British official-dom, Peabody. Thus far they have left us alone. Why invite their interest?"

"What shall we do, then?"

"Wait," said Emerson. "Someone is bound to at-tack you sooner or later, it happens every year. In the meantime, if you can bring yourself to put up with mundane mastabas, we will get on with our work."

I forgave him his ill humor, for the work was not progressing as quickly as he had hoped. We had already been shorthanded; with Ramses and Nefret both gone, our workforce had been cut in half. The tomb on which we had just begun was a double mastaba, of a man and wife, its perimeter cluttered up with a hodgepodge of later tombs; it had no fewer than six burial shafts and a chapel with the remains of painted reliefs. One morning I was try-ing to help Selim with the photography—he wasn't much better at it than I—while the unsifted rubble piled up and Emerson cursed Daoud for not hold-ing the measuring stick level, when a soft voice ad-dressed me.

"Mrs. Emerson? Er—good morning? Uh—I hope I am not interrupting you?"

I assure the Reader that the interrogation marks are necessary to indicate the indecisive tones. The speaker, who had approached while my eye was fixed to the viewfinder of the camera, was a youngish man of medium height who looked vaguely familiar. I had to take a second look before I recognized him. In my surprise I heard myself also talking in questions.

"William? William Amherst? Can it be you?"

"Yes, ma'am," said William. (At least he had enough confidence in his own identity to make it a statement instead of a question.)

For a number of years William had worked for Cyrus, supervising the latter's excavations in the Valley of the Kings. I had known him well, but my disbelief was understandable. He had been a fine, upstanding young chap, with a ready smile. The man who faced me now stood with shoulders hunched and head bent. His clothing was shabby, his boots had been patched, and the once neatly trimmed mustache drooped raggedly over his mouth.

"Well!" I said with somewhat forced heartiness. "How good it is to see you, William, and how kind of you to drop by. We were about to stop for a bite of luncheon. Will you join us?"

It was as if I had wound the spring of an automaton. The drooping figure burst into speech. "I wouldn't have come at this time, Mrs. Emerson, but I know the Professor does not like to be interrupted when he is working, and I would not have ventured to call on you at home—"

"Why on earth not? Emerson will be delighted to see you too. He is down in a burial shaft. I will call him."

"No, ma'am, please! Not until I have told you . . .

I would rather ask you than the Professor, ma'am. You can explain it to him—if you will be so very good—"

"Explain what? Get a grip on yourself, William." He looked so guilty, I couldn't help asking, "Have you committed a crime, or got yourself in trouble with the Service des Antiquités?"

"Oh, no, Mrs. Emerson! Nothing of the sort. The truth is . . . well, Howard Carter told me you were looking for . . . And then I heard that Ramses and Miss Nefret had . . . So I thought perhaps . . ."

I felt as if I were trying to translate a language of which I knew only a few words. Fortunately I am experienced at conundrums. "Are you applying for a position on our staff?"

"Uh—yes."

"Why?"

"Er—"

"Our minimum requirements demand that any individual we employ be able to express himself in ordinary English," I said impatiently. "What I am endeavoring to ascertain is why you want a position. The last I heard of you—for I take an interest in my friends, William—was that you had enlisted."

"I tried to." He bowed his head. "They wouldn't take me. I have a—a medical condition . . ."

Delicacy forbade further questioning on that point. I felt sure I now understood how the unfortunate young man had come to his present state. I could have wrung the truth out of him, sentence by sentence, but it seemed simpler to state my conclusions.

"You felt disgraced and ashamed," I said. "That

is very silly, William, but such a reaction is typical of the male sex. So you decided to drown your shame in drink, abandon a promising career, and wallow in self-pity? Quite characteristic. What reason have I to believe you have reformed?"

"None," William said humbly. "But if you will give me a chance, I swear I will prove myself."

At that unpropitious moment Emerson's head appeared. He was standing on a ladder, with the rest of his body in the shaft, but the suggestion of decapitation was somewhat uncanny. "Who's that?" he shouted. "Why aren't you working? Isn't it time for luncheon?"

"It is," I shouted back. "Come up, Emerson, and greet an old friend."

Before he joined us there was only time for me to say softly, "I am inclined to believe you, William, and I will do my best to persuade Emerson. Only straighten up and face him like a man!"

Emerson required very little persuasion. He was so frustrated he probably would have hired an ax murderer if that individual had been able to translate Egyptian. Encouraged by a series of surreptitious pokes from me, William managed to speak coherently and look Emerson in the eye. He explained he had a room in a so-called hotel in Giza village. I knew the place, and would not have kenneled a dog there, but I decided I would wait awhile before offering the hospitality of our home to an individual whose habits might not be acceptable.

His initial efforts were promising. He turned up smack on time the following morning, washed and shaved and sober, and worked tirelessly and well. I had him to tea; I had him to dinner; he began to put on flesh and gain confidence. Even Sennia approved of him. "He is rather boring," was her verdict. "But nice." After a few more days I proposed that he move into one of the guest chambers.

To my surprise he refused, courteously but decidedly. "You have already done so much for me, Mrs. Emerson. I cannot accept additional favors until I have earned them." He was sufficiently at ease with me by then to add, with one of his shy smiles, "It isn't because I spend the evenings drinking, you know."

I had already been certain of that; I am well acquainted with the signs of overindulgence. I did not press him, for an individual is entitled to his privacy.

Do not suppose, Reader, that the pressure of professional labor had made me lose sight of another objective. The children had been gone for almost a week when I decided Emerson's laissez-faire approach was not going to work. No one had attacked us. It was extremely vexing, so I worked out a few little schemes of my own. I arranged matters so that I could take care of at least two of them on the same day. Efficiency is my strong point, if I may say so; and besides, I did not suppose I could get away from Emerson a second time after he had found out what I had done.

I slipped away one afternoon when he was fully occupied with a burial shaft. I knew he would be there for a while, since several interesting bits of mummy had turned up. Naturally I left a message for him at the house, but I expected I would have an hour or two to myself before he tracked me down.

The Turf Club was a bastion of British bigotry in the heart of Cairo. (The description is that of Emerson.) Egyptians were not admitted to membership. Neither were noncommissioned officers. We were not members either, but I did not anticipate I would be prevented from entering.

Such proved to be the case. The doorman was a large, very gloomy-looking fellow, who had once occupied the same position at Shepheard's. He took one step forward. I waved my parasol at him in a friendly manner. He backed hastily away, and flung the door open.

I had never been in the Club, since Emerson and I refused to patronize establishments of that sort, but I had heard that many of the officers and high officials were in the habit of meeting there for drinks and gossip before they went on to various evening appointments. The large hall appeared to be where these activities took place; it was not yet crowded, for the hour was still early, but I saw a number of familiar faces. They saw me as well. Some looked away, as from a visual obscenity, while others stared and muttered amongst themselves. I realized I was the only female present. Apparently the sacred precincts were out of bounds to women as well as other lower breeds.

I found a spot from which I could get a good view of the proceedings and made myself comfortable. I believe my appearance could not have been faulted; I was wearing a smart calling suit of saffron silk and my second-best hat. The parasol might have been regarded as a slightly discordant note, for it was larger and plainer than the frivolous parasols carried by fashionable ladies. I have had occasion in the past to remark on the all-round usefulness of a good stout parasol; it proved its usefulness once again, for, failing to capture the attention of a waiter, I hooked one of them by the arm and ordered a whiskey and soda.

The buzz of conversation, which had halted upon my entrance, resumed, though on a lower note. Sipping my whiskey, I looked around. There was no one to whom I cared to speak. Evidently no one cared to speak to *me*. I had been there a good half hour before the gentleman to whom I had addressed a little note finally appeared. He appeared a trifle ill at ease, and as he stood in the doorway I thought how much he reminded me of another Edward, the lieutenant of the Master Criminal, who had been with us on several occasions. Like Sir Edward Washington, Lord Edward Cecil was tall and fair-haired, with the faintly supercilious expression that marks the product of our public schools. He did not see me at first; then someone caught his sleeve and whispered in his ear, and he turned with a forced smile, and came to me.

"Good evening, Mrs. Emerson. I am sorry to have kept you waiting."

"Do not apologize. I made certain you did not receive my message until a short time ago, and since I expect my husband will turn up before long, please do me the favor of answering my question promptly and without equivocation. Is the War Office still trying to force my son into cooperating with them?"

His faint smile vanished. "For heaven's sake, Mrs. Emerson, don't talk so loudly! I don't know what you mean."

"I find that very hard to believe, Lord Edward," I said severely. "The man whom I met at your brother's house under an assumed name is in Cairo. Don't bother asking how I know; I have my sources. He is a newcomer, and therefore of interest to the Anglo-Egyptian community, and the description I extracted from Mrs. Pettigrew fits him exactly. I presume he is the new head of the group of disorganized individuals who make up our intelligence department. I asked you to bring him here this evening. Where is he?"

Never had I seen the imperturbable Lord Edward so uncomfortable. Shifting his weight from one foot to the other and glancing uneasily about, he cleared his throat but did not speak. I felt certain he was trying to invent a lie that would put an end to my interrogation, though he could not possibly have supposed that he would succeed. He was spared that difficulty when he saw the man who had just entered.

"Ah," I said. "The mysterious Mr. Smith. Perhaps you will be good enough to introduce us, Lord Edward. Otherwise I will be forced to hail him, in a clear and carrying voice, by the name he gave me."

"You would, wouldn't you?" Lord Edward muttered. He gestured, hastily and without his usual grace. The mysterious Mr. Smith had seen us. His mouth tightened into invisibility, but knowing he was fairly caught, he made the best of it. "Sorry to have kept you waiting, Cecil," he said smoothly, and bowed to me, as to a stranger.

Lord Edward presented him: the Honorable Algernon Bracegirdle-Boisdragon. "How do you do," I said. "You are new to Cairo, I believe. I hope you find it pleasant." I did not give him time to reply, for I could see he was about to make his excuses. Lowering my voice, I went on, "Do try to look a little more affable; you must have known you would encounter me sooner or later. I do not enjoy your company any more than you like mine, so let us get to the point. Why didn't your office inform us that one of Wardani's lieutenants had escaped?"

"I was unaware—"

"Come now, don't lie to me. If you didn't know, you are even more inefficient than I had expected. Are any of the others on the loose?"

He was not an easy man to keep off guard. His eyes narrowed into slits. "How did you know about Asad? If you did, why didn't you notify the police or the military?"

"Well done," I said approvingly. "It is a pleasure to fence with an adversary of your skill, but you cannot put me on the defensive. I asked you first."

"You had better tell her," Lord Edward warned. "The Professor is on his way, and you don't want *him* asking the questions."

Bracegirdle-Boisdragon's face hardened. "The fact is, we are no longer concerned about that lot of ineffectual revolutionaries. They cannot do any harm now."

"Do you mean you let the rest of them get away too?" It was my tone of voice, rather than the words themselves, that brought a flush of anger to his face. He looked much more human and, as I had hoped, rising temper produced a prompt answer.

"No, madam, we did not! We have kept them under closer surveillance since Asad escaped. I am sorry if our failure to notify you caused you trouble . . ."

I recognized this as a disingenuous attempt to extract information from me; after considering the pros and cons, I decided to provide it.

"One might call it that. Fortunately Ramses was not seriously injured."

If I had not known the fellow to be a professional dissembler, I would have taken his surprise at face value. "Injured? By Asad? When did this happen?"

"It was not serious. Now, Mr.—oh, good Gad, never mind— don't let us waste time; I have one more question and I want a direct, honest answer. I expect Emerson momentarily. Have you or any of your associates approached Ramses again about the matter we discussed at Lord Salisbury's?"

He hesitated—weighing the pros and cons, as I had done—but not for long. "I understand why such a suspicion might have entered your mind, Mrs. Emerson. Let me assure you that Asad's attack on your son must have been motivated by resentment of his earlier activities. To the best of my knowledge there is no present cause—"

Lord Edward was guilty of the discourtesy of interrupting. "I say! Isn't that . . ."

It was. There is no mistaking the noises with

which Emerson brings the motorcar to a stop, particularly when he is in a hurry or in a rage. On this occasion he was both, as he promptly demonstrated. The door crashed back against the wall, and there he stood, like Hercules or some other hero of antique legend, fists clenched and eyes blazing. He must have found my message as soon as he returned from the dig, for he was still wearing his dusty, sweat-stained garments, and of course he had lost his hat. The other men were in uniform or lounge suits, but Emerson was superbly indifferent to the inappropriateness of his attire and at that moment so was I. He outshone every man in the room.

Emerson headed straight for me, brushing aside people who were not quick enough to get out of his way. By the time he reached me I was alone. Lord Edward had not even excused himself, and Mr. Smith had simply melted away. I did not suppose Emerson would swear at me in public, but just to be on the safe side, I spoke first. "Good evening, my dear. Will you join me in a whiskey and soda?"

"Not in this hellhole," said Emerson. He did not bother to lower his voice. "Come along, Peabody. Er—if you are ready, that is."

Once we were outside, Emerson expressed his opinion of people who did not have the common courtesy to consult their husbands before dashing off on some harebrained expedition.

"Well, my dear," I said, "your little scheme of waiting for someone to attack us has not borne fruit. It is no wonder, really, when you consider we haven't gone anywhere except to the dig and back. We need to get out and about, away from—"

"But why the bloody Turf Club? You know how I feel about the place, and if you are hoping to instigate a violent attack, I can think of more likely areas."

"It is where many of the officers and most of the officials spend their spare time. I took it for granted that Mr. Asad's escape must have been known to some of them, and such proved to be the case. You will never guess who I ran into."

"Yes, I will. I saw the bastard before he scuttled off, like a beetle behind the baseboard. Did you know he would be here?"

"Yes. I learned of his presence in Cairo when I took tea at Shepheard's with Mrs. Pettigrew, Mrs. Gorst, and Madame Villiers. As I have often told you, Emerson, the sources of information you rudely refer to as gossip—"

"Leave off, Peabody. I am already in a state of extreme exasperation."

"Very well, my dear. I asked Lord Edward to bring him to the club. His real name is Bracegirdle-Boisdragon, with an Honorable, no less. No wonder he chose a monosyllabic pseudonym! Upon interrogation he admitted he had known of Asad's escape, professed disinterest in the comings and goings of the ex-rebels, on the grounds that they had been rendered harmless, and asked how I knew of it."

"Did you tell him?"

"Yes. It occurred to me, you see, that it might have been the War Office that set Asad on Ramses's trail, in the hope of frightening him back into the service."

Emerson dropped the pipe he had been about to

fill. "Frightening?" he repeated, in a rumble like thunder.

"The word was ill-chosen," I admitted. "Ramses is not to be intimidated so easily. However, those who do not know him well—"

"Peabody!" The roar was muffled. Emerson was fumbling under the seat for his pipe. He came up red-faced and sputtering. "That theory is absolutely insane."

"So are many of the people in the intelligence service."

"Hmmm," said Emerson.

"I don't insist on that interpretation, I merely present it as a possibility. Supposing we dine at Bassam's and ask if he has heard from Asad. Afterward we might stroll the streets of the old city arm in arm and hand in hand—"

"Back-to-back is more like it," Emerson grumbled. But his eyebrows had resumed their normal position and a smile tugged at his lips. "You are incorrigible, Peabody, and you are not really dressed for a melee, supposing we should be fortunate enough to inspire one. Is that a new frock? It becomes you."

"It is not new, and you have seen me wear it several times, but I appreciate the compliment. Fear not, my dear, I am armed and ready."

Though the restaurant was crowded, Mr. Bassam had kept a table for us. I had sent ahead to tell him we were coming, and I was rather touched when I saw how much effort he had made. The cloth on the table was very clean (and a little damp still) and a vase of flowers adorned it. The roses were beginning to wilt. He had not put any water in the vase. After all, they would last until we were finished dining, and it was the immediate impression that mattered.

The genial fellow greeted us with a cry of triumph. "I have found him!"

"Splendid!" I said, taking the chair he held for me.

Emerson was less enthusiastic. "How do you know it was the right man?"

"One of them must be the man. There were three who wore glasses and I told your words to each."

"Doesn't mean a cursed thing," said Emerson, after Bassam had gone off to the kitchen. "If one of them was Asad, which is doubtful, he did not take the hint."

"Perhaps he will approach or attack us when we leave," I said.

Emerson grinned. "Always the optimist, my dear."

We lingered over our dinner. The hour was fairly late when we left. My hopes were high, but they were soon dashed; though we walked slowly along some of the darkest lanes I have ever seen, even in Cairo, the shadowy forms of other pedestrians passed us without speaking.

We had left the motorcar at the Club and taken a horse-drawn cab. This sensible suggestion was mine; as I pointed out to Emerson, once he was behind the wheel of the vehicle it would have been virtually impossible for anyone to stop him. When we reached the Place de Bab el-Louk, where we had told the driver to wait, we found the fellow had gone to sleep, slumped forward with his head bowed. Emerson announced our arrival in a loud voice and helped me into the cab, which was, to my disappointment, otherwise unoccupied. Ah, well, I thought, settling myself, there is still a chance we will be waylaid before we reach the Club.

It did not happen quite as I had expected. All at once the driver pulled the horse up with a sharp jerk on the reins and began striking the poor creature with his whip. Cursing volubly, Emerson sprang to his feet and reached for the driver. It was well known that we never allowed that sort of thing, so the fellow was prepared; he met Emerson's lunge with a blow that made him fall back onto the seat. By that time I found myself busily occupied with another individual, who had opened the door of the cab and was attempting to pull me out of it. He was quite surprised, I believe, when instead of resisting I descended instantly from the vehicle and stepped heavily onto his bare feet. Our positions were now reversed; he was trying to get away and I was determined he should not escape me. My parasol was in my hand; with a quick twist I freed the nice little sword concealed in the handle and thrust. He let out a thin scream, but I must not have hurt him very much because he hit out at me, and although I blocked the blow quite efficiently, it was hard enough to throw me back against the open door of the carriage.

It all happened very quickly. I must have uttered an expletive, though I do not remember doing so; Emerson hastened to me and took hold of my arm.

"Go after him!" I gasped, for the man I had attacked was no longer to be seen.

"Be damned to that," said Emerson. "Curse it, don't you realize you are wounded?"

"Nonsense," I said, wondering why my voice sounded so far away. "It was only . . ."

The next thing I knew I was half sitting, half reclining on the seat of the carriage, with Emerson bending over me. I heard something rip. It was the sleeve of my coat. The glow of light surrounding us came, as I discovered, from Emerson's torch, which he had propped on the seat. With the gentleness and efficiency that mark his movements, he bound strips of cloth around my upper arm, muttering all the while. "Not so bad as I feared. My darling girl, what a bloody idiot you are! Hang on, my love, I'll have you back at the Club in a few minutes and we will find a physician—"

"There is no need for that," I replied. "Where is my parasol? Find my parasol, Emerson, I think I may have dropped it."

Swearing vehemently with relief and exasperation, Emerson located the object and tossed it into the cab before he mounted the box. The poor horse was in an extreme state of agitation, but Emerson's firm hands and calm voice soon had it under control. As he drove he kept turning to look back at me, uttering exclamations of concern and complaint.

"How many times have I told you not to attack an armed man with that confounded parasol? Are you conscious, sweetheart? You have no more sense of self-preservation than Ramses, and considering that you are only half his size, your impetuosity verges on feeblemindedness. I ought to have you locked up. Speak to me, my darling. Have you fainted?"

"Certainly not. It is only a scratch. Curse it, I believe I have lost my second-best hat."

SIX

"What an inept, amateurish attack," Emerson remarked sourly.

"And after all the trouble we went to," I agreed.

Meeting one another's eyes, we simultaneously burst out laughing. It had been a ridiculous performance, especially the ending, when we tiptoed through the darkened house like a pair of burglars in order to avoid waking Fatima or Gargery. I doubted we could conceal the truth from them indefinitely, though. Emerson's thick hair had absorbed the worst of the blow and the bump was not very conspicuous, but my nice ensemble was ruined and even if I managed to hide it, Fatima would notice it was missing and demand to know what I had done with it. I allowed Emerson to help me out of my bloodstained garments and tend to my little wound. Wrapped in a comfortable but becoming rose silk dressing gown, with a glass of whiskey in my hand, and my husband sitting close by me on the settee, I felt fully restored and ready to discuss the events that had transpired.

"The most interesting aspect of the evening,"

Emerson went on, "is that we seem to have attracted a new group of enemies. I don't believe Asad had a hand in the business."

"Their intent may have been to keep him from approaching us."

"That doesn't make sense, Peabody. One of them took the place of our driver, which could be easily accomplished. The other must have been nearby, waiting and watching; if Asad had tried to get to us, the second man had only to knock him on the head or drag him away. By all accounts he's a timid, undersized chap. We, on the other hand, are known to be formidable fighters. Why tackle us—and with only two men? By Gad, it's a confounded insult!"

"Perhaps the attack was not meant to succeed. The fellow who attempted to pull me out of the carriage did not draw a weapon until after I had him pinned against the wall with six inches of steel in his body."

Emerson let out another guffaw and threw his arm round my shoulders. "Don't exaggerate, Peabody. If you had put six inches of steel into him he wouldn't have been able to scamper away so handily. I am profoundly sorry I ever gave you that damned sword-parasol."

"You are confusing the issue, my dear."

"Hmmm, yes." Emerson put his glass on the table and took out his pipe. "You have a theory, do you, as to who is behind this latest encounter?"

"An idea only. What Cyrus would call a hunch."

"Ah. Would you care to tell me what it is?"

"No, I would not."

Emerson removed his arm and drew a little away. "I have a hunch too."

"I expected you would."

"I am not going to tell you either."

"I expected you would not."

Emerson scooped me up and put me on his knee. Holding me close, he remarked, "I could go on sparring with you all night, my darling, but you need to rest. You lost a half cup or so of blood tonight. Before I tuck you in, tell me what you want to do about this. Are we going to tell the children?"

"Oh, Emerson, I don't know . . ." I had not realized how weary I was until I lay against his broad breast and felt his strong arms enclosing me. "We agreed not to keep things from one another, but if Ramses and Nefret discover that we have been attacked they will come dashing back to Cairo in order to protect us."

"I suppose they might," Emerson said, in tones of mild surprise. "No need, of course, but . . . Well. Hmmm. What about Gargery and Fatima and the others?"

"I would like to keep it from them if we can, and I believe we have a good chance of doing so if I can get rid of that suit. I will bundle it up and take it to the dig tomorrow and bury it."

"Won't Fatima notice it is missing?"

"By the time she does, I will have thought of something."

"I'm sure you will. Good Gad, life would be much simpler if we didn't have to deceive our friends as well as our enemies." He rose and carried me into the next room.

Naturally I felt perfectly well next morning and was ready to return to work. Some persons might have found it strange that we would go on with our excavations as if nothing had happened, but for the moment we were at an impasse. There was no way of tracing the men who had attacked us; they had only to lose themselves in the crowded byways of Cairo. We had left the cab at the Turf Club, in charge of the doorman, on the assumption that its owner (assuming he was still alive) would look for it there, since it was there we had hired him. Such proved to be the case, as we learned later that day from the driver himself, who came looking for us to remind us that he had not been paid. He added, somewhat plaintively, that we owed him something extra for the inconvenience. I could not but agree. Being struck over the head, bundled up in a sack, and thrust into a dark corner behind a rubbish heap is unquestionably inconvenient. Unfortunately the driver had nothing useful to contribute. He had not even seen the man who took his place, for he had been asleep when he was knocked unconscious. It had taken him some time to free himself.

The actual work of excavation was proceeding well enough. William Amherst had proved to be a great help, and I took a certain modest pride in having being instrumental in his reformation. However, his abilities were limited. He was a fair copyist—though not in Ramses's league—and a trained excavator, but he was no use at all when it came to bones, and we were getting a lot of them. The day after our little adventure we cleared the third of the burial shafts and found another set of bones, enclosed in a rather attractive wooden coffin. The bones themselves were not attractive. Bits of them protruded at ungainly angles from the mass of rotten mummy wrappings, and the skull had been separated from the body. It had been placed at the foot of the coffin, between two large cylinder jars. Its fleshless grin was the first thing we saw when the lid was raised.

"Dear me," I remarked. "How odd. Was the injury pre- or post-mortem, do you think?"

"I don't know," Emerson growled. "And I won't, until Nefret can examine the cursed thing. There's another skeleton behind the coffin. No sign of mummy wrappings . . ."

It took the rest of the morning to get the coffin out and up the narrow shaft. I feared that the bones had got shaken up in the process, but I did not look, since we were about to stop for luncheon. After the men had taken the coffin off to the house we opened the picnic basket and William said, "I will get on with clearing the burial chamber this afternoon, sir, if you like."

"Photographs first," Emerson grunted. "That second skeleton is all jumbled about."

"We might leave it in situ," I suggested. "Until Nefret gets back. And perhaps it might be advisable to wait for her before we investigate the other burial shafts."

Emerson's eyes narrowed. "And wait for Ramses before we clear the chapel? Curse it, Peabody, I can read your mind like an open book. What alternative were you about to propose? If it is one of the queens' pyramids—"

"You promised me I could have one of them."

Emerson removed his pith helmet, flung it onto the ground, wiped his sweating forehead with his sleeve, and took a deep breath—preparatory, I presumed, to a long, loud lecture. His broad breast swelled.

"Buttons, Emerson," I reminded him. "Some of them are about to pop off, and I do get tired of sewing them on."

"What? Oh." Emerson looked down. "Peabody, you have a positive genius for getting me off the track."

"I beg your pardon, my dear. Do go on."

"Hmph. I was about to say that there is nothing in those damned pyramids, that they are in a dangerous state of collapse, and that they are not mine to dispose of. We are here on sufferance as it is."

"That is just an excuse. They are part of Herr Junker's concession, and you have never hesitated to break the terms of a concession when you felt like it. Who is going to prevent you?"

"Prevent *you*, you meant. He stands before you, Peabody."

"It was only a suggestion," I said, for I had learned that the best way of handling Emerson when he gets his back up is to wait awhile and come at him from another direction at another time. "We will, of course, finish with the mastaba." And then I made the fatal mistake of adding, "We've been hauling the fill all the way out to the edge of the escarpment. Perhaps we could find a dump site closer at hand. The one to the southwest, for instance. Junker and Reisner have both used it."

Emerson said, "Hmmmm," and stroked his chin.

I did not see him again until late afternoon. William had finished clearing the burial chamber, and wanted to know what he should do next. He had become fairly comfortable with me, but he would not have dared pick up a potsherd without Emerson's permission.

Not until after I had scanned the farther terrain and shouted his name several times did I behold the familiar form striding toward me. He was bareheaded, as usual, and covered with dust from the top of his black hair to his boots. The pockets of his shirt and trousers bulged. His hands looked like those of a laborer, the nails torn and the fingers scraped raw.

"For pity's sake, Emerson, what have you been up to now?" I demanded.

"Digging," said Emerson. "That is the occupation of an archaeologist, my dear. I found—"

"Where are your gloves?"

"Cursed if I know. Stop fussing, Peabody. I decided to investigate the dump you were talking about. Do you know that none of our predecessors bothered sifting the fill? That heap of rubble is full of objects they overlooked. I found several interesting things."

He began unloading his pockets. At first glance the fragmentary scraps of stone looked like rubbish, but Emerson's eye cannot be faulted. A closer look assured me that one bit was a miniature foot that must have been part of a statuette.

"Very nice," I said. "But hardly worth the effort."

"That statement," said Emerson, giving me a stern look, "violates every principle of archaeology I have endeavored to teach you. No scrap is too small, no effort too great."

"The stela fragment Sennia found was planted, Emerson."

Emerson flinched. He hates it when I appear to read his thoughts. "That was Gargery's theory. What does he know about excavation? I rather enjoyed it, you know. It has been a long time since I got my hands dirty."

"Nonsense, you are always getting them dirty—and scraped and bruised and cut. You might at least have worn your gloves."

"What gloves?"

A hideous foreboding filled me. "Emerson, you are not planning to move and re-excavate that dump, are you? It is twenty feet high and covers hundreds of square feet!"

"Someone will have to do it someday, Peabody. Can't leave a thing like that standing. There may be tombs under it."

"There are plenty of tombs right here. And pyramids."

Emerson was beginning to react unfavorably to that word. After he had finished expressing himself, he announced we would go back to clearing the chapel before we opened another burial shaft, and I congratulated myself on finding something with which to distract him from his wretched dump heap. Little did I know that we were about to come on something that would distract him even more effectively.

We found it an hour later. To be strictly accurate, the discoverer was Ismail, one of Daoud's young sons, whom he was training as a basket man. Working under the critical eye of his father, Ismail was removing the fill from the interior of a small chamber that had been added to the larger adjoining mastaba at a much later date by a man who could not afford a separate tomb of his own. Like most of the later additions, it was in wretched condition, and if there had been any reliefs on the upper parts of the walls, they were completely gone. Many excavators demanded no particular skill from the men who performed this heavy task, but our men were taught to watch for anything that might be an artifact or a piece of one. Sometimes, if one of them came across a particularly interesting item, he would call out.

Ismail did not call out; he screamed at the top of his lungs. His cry was echoed by a bellow from Daoud that brought Emerson running and jolted me out of the dreamy state which generally affects me after several hours of sifting rubbish. When I arrived on the scene, Emerson was down into the pit brushing sand away from something and William had joined me, and Daoud was shaking the afflicted Ismail.

"What way is that for a man to behave? You will not hear the Sitt Hakim scream when she finds a dead body."

"No," Emerson said. "She is accustomed to them. Don't scold the boy, Daoud. Let's have some light down here."

"What is it?" William asked. "Another skeleton?"

He turned on his torch and aimed it at the corner where Emerson was kneeling.

I was able to catch the torch before he dropped it. I had been conscious of the smell for several minutes. It was no skeleton Ismail had found, nor an ancient mummy. Some of them can be rather nasty looking, but a fresh corpse in which the process of decay is well advanced is even nastier. The unfortunate youth had uncovered, not a hand or foot, which would have been bad enough, but a face. The eye sockets and open mouth were filled with sand.

I heard the unmistakable sounds of someone being violently sick, and deduced, since he was no longer beside me, that the sufferer was William. I was not feeling very well either, but I kept the torch steady. Emerson rose to his feet and held up an object for my inspection. It was the twisted wire frame of a pair of eyeglasses.

FROM LETTER COLLECTION T

Dearest Mother and Father,

I write from your "open-air drawing room" on the upper deck of the Amelia. *It is late afternoon, almost teatime, and the awning has been rolled back; there is a lovely breeze and the cliffs on the east bank are turning gold. We will stop tonight at el-Til and spend a few days at Amarna checking on the condition of the tombs and "making our presence known," as you suggested. We will of course invoke the dread names of the Father of Curses and the Sitt Hakim, and I don't doubt that will be all the authority we need.*

I meant to begin this letter earlier and give you a kind of running journal of the voyage, to be posted when we reach Luxor. Laziness is my only excuse—if that is an acceptable excuse! It is astonishing how quickly the time passes on the river, and how easy it is for even energetic persons to relapse into a pleasant languor. Mother and Father, I cannot tell you how grateful I am to you for suggesting and arranging this—especially for arranging it as you did. Believe me, I know how complicated it was, especially with regard to Sennia. I love the dear little thing, but she would have been all over the boat, hanging from the rail and trying to climb the mast and coaxing the crew to tell her stories, with Gargery puffing and panting in her wake.

Ramses is looking better than he has for a long time. He is even putting on a bit of weight, if you can believe it! Fatima must have taught Maaman some of her favorite recipes, and instructed him to feed us every few hours.

Two days later. I've lost track of the date. Isn't that shameful? The days blend into one another. This time I really will write a proper report. I suggested to Ramses that he ought to do it, and he said he would, and then he went off to the saloon, and the next time I saw him he was reading some ponderous tome in German and admitted he hadn't set pen to paper. So here it is.

You will be relieved to hear that the situation at

Amarna is not as grave as you feared. According to Ramses, who seems to remember every confounded scene on every wall of every tomb—how does he do it??—the locals have not damaged them or the Boundary Stelae. He did have a few critical remarks to make about Mr. Davies's copies of certain scenes, notably in the tombs of Ay and Parennefer. I think it was Parennefer. Never mind; it will be in his notebook. I had to drag him out of the tomb in question.

As for the city site, it is so extensive one can only make general observations. The area the Germans were excavating in 1913–14 has been partially recovered by blowing sand. Ramses says you will know the precise location, which is more than I do, even after having it shown me. It's all so flat and featureless. We walked the plain from end to end— it's over five miles!—and to think I was worrying about gaining too much weight!—without seeing any signs of recent digging. Really, the area is so large I can't imagine how a would-be thief would know where to start.

We made a sentimental pilgrimage to the Royal Wadi one day. It is an incredible place, isn't it— quiet as death and empty as a lunar landscape.

We had, of course, called on the Sheikh el-Beled as soon as we arrived. The Sheikh remembered you very well—especially you, Mother. As we drank coffee together, Ramses explained in his most flowery Arabic that you had a great interest in the site and would be very sorry if anything were damaged or stolen. The poor chap turned as pale as a gentleman of his coloring can turn. Did you really tell him you wanted someone's head in a basket? You never told us that.

Later.

Oh, dear, I did it again. Ramses called me to come and look at the sunset, and one thing led to another. It was a spectacular sunset. The river looked as if it were on fire.

It is several days later, to be honest. I should be ashamed of having accomplished so little—I meant to read several medical journals and the new publication of the Egypt Exploration Fund, and practice drawing hieroglyphs so I can help Ramses copy texts—he never criticizes mine, but when I'm not looking he does them over! He thinks I don't know, but I do.

It hasn't been wasted time, unless being happy is a waste of time. We've been cut off from everything—no newspapers, no letters, no telephone calls. Ramses is getting a little restless, though; I know the signs. He can't stand inactivity too long. We reach Luxor tomorrow, so our idyll will soon end. I will get this letter off to you as soon as we arrive and let you know in due course about the situation in Luxor.

Dear Mother and Father,

Nefret insists I add a few words. I can't think why; she writes much more entertainingly than I, and she has told you everything you need to know, for the present at least. I certainly did not mean to speak disparagingly of Mr. Davies. There were

*only a few minor points, which is not surprising
when one considers the vast extent of his work and
the speed with which it was published.*

*As Nefret mentioned, the tombs at Amarna are
undamaged. I did notice a number of new graffiti,
all from the hand of a single tourist who may be a
member of some odd cult—he didn't leave his name,
only a peculiar symbol. They are on the rock face
outside. At least the fellow had the decency not to
scratch his wretched monogram across the reliefs,
which is more than can be said for some.*

*Your affectionate son,
Ramses*

FROM MANUSCRIPT H

Ramses was well aware of his parents' real reason
for sending him away from Cairo. His father's hints
had the subtlety of a cavalry charge: in case you
didn't get the idea the first time, he turned round
and rode over you again. He understood their
concern—he'd given them the devil of a time last
season—but sometimes he wished they would back
off and let him manage his own affairs.

It was good to be back in Luxor, though. The
morning after their arrival he finished dressing
before Nefret and went up on deck. They had a
new steward, a fresh-faced boy who was having a
little trouble getting used to his new duties. He
kept dropping things, especially when Nefret was
present. She reassured him so sweetly, Ramses had

begun to wonder whether young Nasir did it on purpose.

While he waited for Nasir to pull himself together and bring the coffee, he leaned on the rail looking out across the cultivation toward the western mountains, flushed with the reflection of sunrise. They were moored at the dock Cyrus Vandergelt had built for his *Valley of the Kings*, and Ramses could make out all the familiar landmarks: the narrow road that led to the Valley of the Kings; the rocky slopes of Drah Abu'l Naga; and dim in the distance the ruined temple of Hatshepsut, where he and David had copied some of the reliefs. He missed David, but not as much as he would once have done; marriage was turning out to be a much more time-consuming business than he had expected and more confusing. He had loved her so long, and had finally won her; yet his need of her grew stronger every day, and with it the fear of losing her. It was on her account that he had agreed to leave Cairo. She'd have stuck with him wherever he went, and fought with him if the need had arisen— and she had the right—he couldn't deny that, no one had a better right—but it had been hard enough for him to accept her as an equal companion and ally when she had been only (only!) the woman he loved. Now she was also his wife, caring for him as he had never dared hope she would, and he wanted to lock her up and keep her safe. She wouldn't stand for that, nor should she . . . but the thought of harm coming to her made him break out in a cold sweat of terror. I wonder how the hell Father does it, he thought.

He felt her presence and turned.

"Damn," she said, laughing. "I was trying to creep up on you."

"I always know when you're near." He took her hands and drew her to the rail. They stood side by side in companionable silence until a crash of crockery announced the arrival of Nasir.

"He does it on purpose," Ramses said, after the boy had carefully swept up every splinter of china and Nefret had dismissed him. "Sweeping up the broken bits gives him an excuse to linger. You must start scolding him, or we won't have a cup left."

"We can always buy more."

Ramses laughed and shook his head.

"What were you staring at so intently?" she asked.

"Everything. I've missed it. I didn't realize how much."

Her eyes followed the same sweep his had made, from one end of the plain to the other. The rosy light on the cliffs had faded into pale gold. "I think Mother and Father miss it too," she said. "She has her pyramids, but this was home for a long time. There are so many memories . . ."

"My God, yes. Murder and torture and every year another dead body, as Abdullah ed to say."

"Some of them quite horrible," Nefret agreed. "Poor mummified Mrs. Bellingham——"

"And the two who were mutilated by the mechanical crocodile, and Dutton Scudder, and Bellingham himself. I must have left someone out, that can't be all."

He was trying, with fair success, to emulate her

detached tone, but she saw his long, sensitive lips tighten and cursed herself for not changing the subject. She had learned during her medical training that sardonic humor was one way of protecting oneself against the grisly sights of the dissecting room, and the pain of losing patients, but Ramses still had a hard time pretending to be indifferent. It was one of the reasons why she loved him so much.

"So where are we going today?" she asked, buttering a piece of leathery toast.

"Gurneh. I sent word to Yusuf last night."

"Yes, of course."

He looked up from his plate. The dark eyes that were so often half hidden by drooping lids and long lashes met hers directly. "Don't be patient with me, Nefret. Slap me down when I go all brooding and theatrical."

"Eat your eggs," Nefret said tenderly.

"They're stone cold." He pushed his plate away. "I hear voices. It must be the fellow who's brought the horses. He's early. Take your time, I'll go down and—"

"No, I've finished."

They descended the stairs to the lower deck, where they found Ashraf, the crewman on guard duty, confronting the newcomer. It wasn't Yusuf or one of his sons. It was a girl, wearing a blue tob, whose wide sleeves had been turned up over her head to get them out of the way. The long face veil was not as common in this area as it was in Cairo, but no respectable woman would go about with her head bare; the kerchief she wore instead of a tarhah was tied at the nape of her neck, covering her hair except for two long curling locks on either side of her face. At the moment the lower part of her face was concealed by a fold of the tob. Turning her back on Ashraf, she let the cloth fall and addressed them in a piercing shout, and in carefully enunciated English. "Welcome—good morning—please, I must talk to you, now, before Jamil comes; I ran very fast so I would be here before him and now this person will not let me pass!"

Nefret poked her husband in the ribs, reminding him of something he knew only too well: that a fixed stare at a Muslim female was worse than rude. She couldn't blame him for staring, though. The girl must be one of Abdullah's far-flung and extensive family. They were a handsome lot, but she was something special: big melting brown eyes, rounded cheeks, and a full, pink mouth. She was a tiny creature, barely five feet tall and at the moment every inch was rigid with indignation.

"Yes, of course," Ramses said. Ashraf was trying to look as if he weren't there. He hadn't done any harm or meant any, but he had no business making advances, even harmless advances, to female visitors. "Come into the saloon. Would you like coffee?"

"Yes, thank you. If it is not too much trouble." She gave Ashraf a triumphant look and swept past him.

"No trouble at all," Nefret murmured. "At least I hope not."

If Ramses heard, he pretended he hadn't. Like his father, he was genuinely and endearingly bewildered by the effect he had on susceptible women (which included most women, Nefret thought).

By the time Nasir had stumbled through the coffee-serving process they had established the girl's identity. She was Jumana, the daughter of Selim's uncle Yusuf, the head of the Luxor branch of the family. It was no wonder they had not recognized her immediately; five years ago she had been one of a cheerful pack of children, indistinguishable from the rest. Jamil was her brother.

"He is lazy," she said, pursing up her pretty mouth. "He should have been here with the horses before this. But it is good for me that he is so slow. I ran all the way."

"All the way from Gurneh?" Nefret asked.

"No, from the house of the Father of Curses. He told my father to stay there to look after it. Do you want it back now?"

"No," Nefret said. They had discussed the matter with the senior Emersons before they left Cairo. "We will only be in Luxor for a few weeks, and we would prefer to stay on board the dahabeeyah."

"That is good, but someone should have told my mother. She has been cleaning everything and making me work too."

Ramses was smiling. He spoke to her as he would have to Sennia. "You don't like to do housework?"

"No. I want to work on the excavations, like the men." She leaned forward, slim brown hands clasped, eyes wide and serious. "I have been to the school of Mrs. Vandergelt. I can read and write and speak English; I speak it well, you see. I can learn anything, I am much better than Jamil. He is too lazy to study. But it is Jamil my father says will be your reis while you are here. Why not me?"

"The work is very hard," Ramses said.

Nefret knew this approach was not going to be effective. Ramses wasn't taking the girl seriously, but she was not deceived by the pretty face and childish figure. Jumana had got more than an education at Katherine Vandergelt's school. If she had been English she would have been out with the Pankhursts, chaining herself to railings and demanding the vote.

"How old are you?" she asked.

"Sixteen. But I am very strong. I can climb the cliffs as well as Jamil, and carry heavy baskets."

Ramses leaned back and looked helplessly at Nefret. Unlike some men, he had sense enough to know when he was out of his depth.

"What you want is impossible," Nefret said. "In the first place, your father would never agree to that arrangement. In the second place, you are too young for such a responsible position. The men wouldn't take orders from you and you have not had the proper training."

The big brown eyes filled with tears. "I thought you would help me. You do all the things I want to do. And they said you were kind."

"It took me many years to learn to do those things. When I was your age . . ." She saw the corners of Ramses's mouth twitch, and stopped herself. Good Lord, I sound like one of those sententious old ladies I always despised, she thought. "I will tell you what we will do," she went on. "We will speak with your father and if he agrees you can spend some time with us while we are here. We will see how you get on, and then, perhaps, it might be possible for you to have the training you want. I make no promises, you understand."

The girl jumped up and flung herself at Ramses's feet. Grasping his hands, she began pressing kisses on them. "The blessings of God be on you, Brother of Demons! You will do it? You will speak to my father?"

"Yes, yes, of course." Flushed with embarrassment, he tried to free his hands. "Uh—please don't do that. You had better run along now, before Jamil gets here."

She gave him a radiant smile—spared a noticeably dimmer one for Nefret—and darted out.

"You're perspiring," Nefret said critically. "Where is your handkerchief?"

He hadn't misplaced it yet; the day was still young. After wiping his forehead, he demanded, "What did she do that for? I didn't say anything! You were the one who promised we'd give her a try."

"Because you're a man. She thinks I need your lordly permission to carry out my promise, and," Nefret added with a grin, "she knows men are susceptible to big brown eyes and fawning flattery."

"I'm not. If I have to put up with that sort of thing every time she comes round—"

"Well, you may, though now that she's got her way she won't be quite so attentive. She's a calculating little baggage. It's a good thing I was here. What would *you* have promised her to stop her crying?"

"I hate to think. Did you really mean what you

said? Yusuf isn't going to like it. He's probably selected a husband for her. Most Egyptian girls of
sixteen are already married."

"Of course I meant it, and I don't care whether
Yusuf likes it or not. We'll see how she works out.
You of all people are not going to tell me she doesn't
deserve a chance because she is female?"

"I of all people am not." Taking her hand, he
raised her to her feet. "There's Jamil at last. She's
right, he is slow."

Jamil looked like his younger sister—big brown
eyes, well-shaped features, brilliant smile—except
for his mustache, which was large and luxuriant.
He was of medium height and obviously conscious
of his lack of inches; when he shook hands with
Ramses he rose onto his toes and straightened his
shoulders. He made no mention of Jumana, so
Ramses concluded the girl must have made good
her escape before he got there.

"The horses have been washed," Jamil announced, stroking his mustache fondly.

Ramses nodded. His mother had begun that
custom on her very first visit to Egypt, starting
with the hired donkeys and moving on, over the
years, to other animals. One of his fondest memories was of watching his mother calmly scrubbing a
camel with a long-handled brush while the camel
bellowed and kicked, and four of their men tried to
control its thrashing legs. He could only dimly
imagine the incredulity with which her initial efforts must have been received, but it had now become an accepted tradition, and Abdullah's kin took
pride in the care they gave their animals. These ap-

peared to be in good condition and sturdily if not elegantly built.

Nefret was getting acquainted with her mare, whispering into its pricked ear and stroking its neck. She was wonderful with animals and impossibly tenderhearted; every year she collected a me nagerie of injured or abandoned creatures. Ramses hoped she wouldn't want to adopt a few stray cats, dogs, and goats while they were in Luxor. He gave her a hand up, and mounted his horse, a massively built black with white blazes on forehead and chest.

They set off along the road that led through the cultivated fields toward the cliffs of the high plateau. The air was already warm. What with their unexpected visitor and Jamil's nonchalance about time, they had been late in getting off, but it was necessary to pay a courtesy call on Jamil's father before they went on with the day's business.

The house his parents had built was near the hill and the village of Sheikh el-Gurneh. They had all lived there, in comparative harmony, for almost seven years; but Ramses had no particular desire to live there again. If we come back to Luxor for a long period of time, he thought, I'll build another house—one that will be ours from the start. His mother's energetic personality imprinted itself on every place she had ruled as mistress. At least he didn't have to face that penetrating stare of hers whenever he walked into the saloon. Nefret must have felt the same; without discussing it or asking his opinion, she had replaced the portrait with another of David's paintings, the copy he had made of the offering scene from Tetisheri's tomb.

Word of their coming had preceded them by several weeks, and someone—probably everyone—had worked like the very devil to get the house in order. It had been freshly painted and reroofed. The flowers in the boxes on the veranda had a suspiciously youthful look, but they would show up nicely in the photographs he meant to take for his mother.

The whole family, men and women and children, poured out of the house to greet them. Then the women retired, leaving them on the veranda with Yusuf and the other men.

The years had changed Yusuf, and not for the better. He had got quite stout. A roll of fat framed his bearded chin, and when he smiled his cheeks swallowed up his eyes. After the usual compliments had been exchanged, they settled down on the veranda with coffee, cigarettes, and several platters of food, and Yusuf asked how he could be of service.

"Where will you be digging? I can find all the men you want, good men who have worked for the Father of Curses before."

Ramses explained that they had not come to excavate and felt sorry when he saw Yusuf's fat, affable face fall. Times were hard for the men of Gurneh.

"But the Father of Curses said you would be digging in the Valley of the Monkeys," Yusuf protested.

"Oh, did he?"

Ramses didn't verbalize the expletives he would like to have added. The Valley of the Monkeys was what the Egyptians called the West Valley, because of the wall paintings in one of the tombs. It was part of Lord Carnarvon's concession, and nobody else had the right to excavate there. Emerson had mentioned in an offhand manner that they might just have a look at the tomb of Amenhotep III—as a favor to Howard Carter. Carter would probably not regard it as a favor. Emerson was up to his old tricks, trying to maneuver people into doing what he wanted them to do, by fair means or foul.

"We may go out there one day to have a look round," Ramses said. "First of all I want to inspect Tetisheri's tomb. It is my father's chief concern."

"Yes, yes." Yusuf's chin wobbled as he nodded. "You wish to go there now? Jamil will come. He is at your service while you are in Luxor, for anything you need. You will take him wherever you go. If you need more men, he will hire them for you."

Nefret was looking at the open door of the house. Ramses glanced in that direction, and saw a small brown hand. The fingers were wriggling furiously.

"Right," Nefret said, half to herself and half to the almost invisible eavesdropper. "Yusuf, I understand your daughter Jumana has been attending school. We would like her to work for us while we are here."

"Yes, you will need a maidservant," Yusuf said complacently. "She is a good girl, clever with her hands. I will send her to the dahabeeyah—"

"No!" Nefret moderated her voice. "I don't want a maid, Yusuf. I have heard she is clever in other ways, that she can read and write. We can use her as a—a secretary."

"Secretary? You mean to write letters for you? On the dahabeeyah?"

"Not on the dahabeeyah," Nefret said decidedly. The last thing she wanted was a bright, inquisitive young girl sharing their quarters. "We want her to come with us when we inspect the tombs."

"You want to take her with us?" Jamil demanded, scowling. "She will only be in the way. She is a nuisance, always following me and wanting to do what I do."

The little brown hand clenched into a fist. Yusuf glanced uneasily at his son, who was sitting at his feet. Jamil had spoken out of turn, anticipating his father's response, but it was obvious that he could do no wrong in Yusuf's eyes.

"I don't know," Yusuf muttered. "I have never heard of such a thing. A woman's place is in the house."

"Not always," Ramses said, with an amused look at his wife. "Think about it, Yusuf. We would be grateful for her help. And we would pay well for a skilled scribe."

"Ah. Hmmm." Yusuf tugged at his beard. "So. I will think. Bokra (tomorrow) perhaps."

Yusuf insisted on accompanying them to Tetisheri's tomb. Ramses tried to dissuade him; unlike his cousin Abdullah, who had been fit and capable into his seventies, Yusuf couldn't even get out of a chair without puffing and wheezing. He waved Ramses's objections aside.

"The Father of Curses would be angry if I let you go into the hills without protection. Jamil, bring me my gun."

The boy jumped up and ran out. When he returned, Nefret's eyes widened and Ramses stared in consternation. The weapon was an antique Martini, at least forty years old. It had been kept oiled and polished, but it was a single-shot, wildly inaccurate at long range, with a kick like a mule's. The only way you could be sure of damaging someone with it was to hit him over the head, and Jamil was fondling it in a way that made it more than likely he would shoot himself in the leg.

"Yusuf, none of the men of Luxor would threaten us," Ramses said. "You don't need that."

"No, no one in Luxor," Yusuf agreed, snatching the weapon from Jamil. "They all fear the Father of Curses and the Brother of Demons. But the Senussi have taken Kharga and Siwa and the Bedouin are in arms."

"When did this happen?"

"Some days ago," Yusuf said, with the vagueness about time typical of a man who does not own a clock or a calendar. "There is fighting in the north, near the coast, and it is said the Inglizi are falling back. The desert tribes from Cairo to Nubia are waiting to see who will win. If the Inglizi lose, they will attack."

Ramses wondered how accurate Yusuf's report was. He wasn't surprised to hear that some, if not all, of the oases were no longer in British hands, but the chance of a band of bloodthirsty Bedouin attacking Luxor was preposterous. However, Ramses abandoned hope of persuading the old fellow to give up his cherished weapon.

It took two of his sons to hoist Yusuf onto his

horse, which was almost as fat as Yusuf, with a belly like a barrel and a decided disinclination to go faster than a walk. It seemed to take them hours to cross the desert stretch between Gurneh and the hills of the high plateau. As they plodded along side by side Yusuf explained that he had everything ready for them.

"Every day there was a letter! From the Father of Curses, from Selim, from the Sitt Hakim, telling us what to do. Never have I had so many letters in a few days!"

"It is a good thing you had Jumana to read them to you," Nefret said without so much as the hint of a smile.

Jumana's father grunted.

The tomb was in an inconvenient location, halfway down a narrow cleft that split the cliff from top to bottom, and originally it could only be reached from above, by means of a rope. Emerson had widened the lower opening and had had steps built for their convenience while they were working on the tomb; he had torn them down when they finished, in order to make access less convenient for thieves (and the members of the Service des Antiquités). In place of the former stairs there was now a rope ladder, with odd-shaped pieces of wood fastened to the supporting ropes at irregular intervals.

"It is safe," Yusuf insisted, as Ramses eyed the structure dubiously. "I have been up and down it many times. And it was Jamil, Brother of Demons, who took it to the tomb, descending a rope from the top of the cliff, with great danger to himself."

"It was not difficult," Jamil said. "Dangerous, yes, but not difficult for me."

Modesty was not an attribute admired by Egyptians. Jamil's boasting was not unusual; and, Ramses had to admit, it was probably justified. The boy was slim and well-built for his size, and the young men of the west bank were accustomed to scrambling up and down rock faces and along precipitous paths that would have daunted most Europeans.

However, he refused Jamil's offer to ascend first—"to help you and Nur Misur." Even with Yusuf's weight anchoring the structure from below, it swayed alarmingly, but it seemed sturdy enough. When he reached the ledge outside the tomb entrance he called down to Nefret to follow. Jamil stood staring up at her as she climbed. That will teach him not to underestimate women, Ramses thought; she was unafraid and as nimble as a boy. The cleft was narrow and the sun was not high enough to shed light into it; when she joined him on the ledge they stood in a gray shadow, enclosed by stone, with only a slit of sky visible high above.

"I'd forgotten what a gloomy place this is," Nefret murmured.

Ramses put his arm round her and drew her away from the edge. "Let's have some light."

The heavy iron gates added a Gothic touch; oil had been pumped into the locks with such excessive zeal that it had dripped, leaving dark streaks and a puddle or two. Nefret held the torch while Ramses got out the keys his father had given him. The locks yielded at last and he pushed one of the gates back. It groaned appropriately and Nefret chuckled.

"All we need now are a few bats and a perambulating mummy."

"I doubt if there are any bats. We sealed the place up as tightly as we could."

There were no bats and no mummy, only stale air that caught at the throat. When they reached the antechamber with its beautifully painted reliefs, Ramses was pleased to see that the preservatives they had used, with all due caution, had not darkened or flaked. The rock-cut steps leading down to the burial chamber were uneven. She let him take her hand. He continued to hold it when they stood in the room they had emptied of its incredible litter—broken boxes, fallen jewelry, the queen's dismembered chariot. The only thing remaining was the huge stone sarcophagus.

Nefret moved the torch slowly round the walls. The closed-in chambers were very warm. Her face glowed with perspiration and curling locks of hair had escaped from under her hat to frame her temples. Ramses said, "I've never kissed you in the burial chamber of a tomb, have I?"

"Not yet." She turned into his arms.

A short time later the torch went out. He didn't know whether she had switched it off or dropped it, and by then he didn't care. The darkness of that enclosed space, deep in the cliff, was like a black blanket, muffling all sensations except the exquisitely refined and concentrated sense of touch.

Then she tightened her grasp and something hit him on the back of the head.

"You didn't drop the torch," he murmured.

"Darling, I'm so sorry. I didn't mean to smack you with it."

"Quite all right. I suppose we'd better get on with the job, though. I was thinking," he went on, as the light reappeared, "that it might make a nice little hobby to kiss you in every tomb in Luxor."

"What a lovely idea. One down, how many hundreds to go?"

"We'll keep track as we proceed. Everything seems to be in order here. We might come back another day and take a few photographs for Father."

They made their way back to the entrance. Ramses closed and locked the gates. He took out his own torch and moved the beam slowly and methodically over the locks and the hinges. "I don't see any signs of tampering, do you? Remarkable I rather expected some of the local lads would have a go at breaking in."

"They know we removed everything that was portable. And didn't Father put a curse on the place?"

"One of his best. He invoked every god in the pantheon from Anubis to . . . Well, I'll be damned. Somebody's been here. Look at that."

Cut deep into the rock above the doors was the same odd device they had seen near several of the Amarna tombs—a circle divided by a sinuous waving line.

"He didn't get in," Nefret said practically.

"But how did he get here in the first place? One wouldn't want to climb up from below, the rock is too unstable. From above the only practicable method is sliding down a rope, and I wouldn't want to tackle that without help."

"You wouldn't, but some of these he-man explorer types behave very stupidly. We can ask around. If he hired any of the locals, they'll tell you." Drops of perspiration slid down her face. He knew her throat must be as dry as his, and that she was anxious to get into the open air, but the oddity of the little cryptogram held him.

"What does it remind you of?" he asked.

Nefret blinked wet lashes and wiped her eyes with her handkerchief. "Something. I can't think . . . Oh, I know! It's like the yin and the yang symbol—the opposing forces, masculine and feminine, dark and light, that make up the world. Perhaps our busy tourist is Chinese."

"Someone is making his presence known, certainly. All right, love, down you go. Be careful."

"You too." Her foot already on the topmost rung, she smiled up at him. "You can let go my wrist now."

Ramses waited until she had reached the bottom before he started his descent. Further examination of the odd little symbol had told him nothing he did not already know or suspect. He hadn't mentioned it to Nefret because he didn't want to put ideas into her head. If she came to the same conclusion independently, it would be confirmation of his . . . One couldn't even call it a theory, not yet. There were not enough data. He knew what he was looking for, but he still didn't know how to go about it.

SEVEN

As we stood staring down at the gruesome thing and Ismail sniveled in the corner, with his back to the scene, Emerson said, "That takes care of the question of whether or not to consult Russell. The police will have to be told of this."

I was not at all averse to a little chat with Mr. Thomas Russell, the Assistant Commissioner of Police. I did not hold him wholly accountable for getting my son half killed (a number of other people shared the blame for that, including Ramses himself), but I had not had a chance to express my recriminations as forcibly as I would have liked.

"It is the usual procedure after one has discovered a corpse," I remarked.

"Hmmm, yes. Shall we telephone or send someone?"

"The latter, I think. We must stay here with the body."

"It isn't necessary for both of us to stay. You go back to the house and—"

"You go."

"Oh, bah," said Emerson. "Very well. Selim!"

Selim was within earshot—by that time most of the men had gathered round, drawn by Ismail's howls of woe—but Emerson shouts as a matter of habit. Selim was as unwilling as we to leave the scene, so he delegated one of the other men as messenger, and Emerson scribbled a note on a page from his excavation journal. "Russell: Have found corpse at Giza. R. Emerson."

"Is that all you intend to say?" I inquired.

"What else is there to say? Anything more would be pure conjecture. Russell thinks he is a detective, let him come and detect."

The messenger reluctantly tore himself away and the other men stood by, watching avidly as Emerson squatted by the body. I knew what he intended to do, and I was content to leave it to him. Mummies I have become accustomed to, though I never have liked them very much, and I have encountered quite a number of fresh corpses, but this one did not appear to be as fresh as it might have been.

Rather than confess this weakness to Emerson, I found a more practical objection. "If you mean to finish excavating that corpse, Emerson, you ought to follow your own professional standards. You will need more light, to begin with."

Emerson had to agree. The body lay in the shadow of the wall and a single torch gave limited light. While he was locating his own torch and showing Selim where to point it, I found one of the brushes we used for clearing delicate objects. He was gracious enough to accept this as well. It was not really necessary for him to mention fly larvae.

"But that is rather odd, isn't it?" I asked, as detective fever overcame my temporary attack of squeamishness. "Surely a body buried in sand would be protected from insects, and it would suffer desiccation rather than decay."

Emerson did not look up. He had brushed the sand away from the face and was working his way down. "Flies, of which there are a great number in Egypt, gather on a motionless body almost instantly. I would guess that the body was left unburied, long enough for a busy insect population to infest it."

"You need not go into detail, Emerson."

"Rigor mortis, as I hardly need tell you, has come and gone," Emerson continued. "Hmmm. The effects of desiccation on top of decomposition are quite fascinating. It's a pity Nefret isn't here, she would appreciate this. Are you sure you wouldn't like a closer look, Peabody?"

"It is most considerate of you, my dear, but I think not."

"Too much even for you, eh?" Emerson chuckled. "There are no signs of animal attack, which suggests that the murderer did not leave him lying in the open."

"So you agree it was murder."

"He didn't walk out here on his own, dig a hole, lie down, and cover himself with sand," Emerson said acerbically. "Now why the devil would a killer keep the body of his victim lying round the house instead of burying it in the desert or throwing it into the river?"

"Because he wanted us to find it. He couldn't

carry it here in broad daylight, and the moon has been at the full. Last night was overcast."

"The past several nights, in fact. He's been here for a while." Emerson went on digging carefully around the remains. "I wonder what they did with . . . Ah. Here it is—a sizable piece of canvas. I knew they must have bundled him up in something of the sort in order to facilitate transport and keep bits of him from falling off along the way. Considerate of them to remove it before they buried him, so that the lucky discoverer would get the full effect." He stood up.

The body lay completely exposed. It was dressed in the ragged and horribly stained remains of a cotton galabeeyah. I will not describe the condition of the face and hands.

"Let's get him out of here," Emerson said coolly. "Tell Ibrahim to rig some sort of litter."

"I don't think Mr. Russell would approve of that, Emerson. Disturbing the crime scene—"

"The devil with Russell. His CID people are blundering idiots. I won't have them tramping around in my tomb. However," Emerson conceded, fingering the cleft in his chin, "we will take a few photographs. Selim!"

"I am here, Father of Curses," said Selim reproachfully.

"I don't want you here, I want you to get the camera."

Watching Emerson's methodical procedures, and adding a few little suggestions of my own, I agreed that we were quite within our rights to proceed with the investigation. At a location like this one, the techniques of excavation applied, and of course we had both had considerable experience with murder in all its forms.

Selim took a number of exposures, from various angles, of the corpse and various parts of it. In the light of our pocket torches the makeshift grave and its occupant resembled a scene from a horror story. The shifting shadows gave an illusion of movement. Emerson, who is not at all sensitive to such things, went briskly ahead. I sat on a stretch of wall eating a sandwich left over from lunch, for we had missed tea. I rather regretted doing so when Emerson and Selim lifted the piece of wood that had been inserted under the body. The head rolled to one side, and the jaw dropped, opening the mouth in a silent scream.

"All right, are you, Peabody?" Emerson inquired.

"A fragment of cucumber caught in my throat," I replied, coughing. "Is it possible to tell how he died?"

"No doubt of that," Emerson said, wiping his hands on his trousers. (I made a mental note to have them laundered immediately.) "His throat was cut. The poor devil may never have seen his killer; a man under attack from the front generally throws up his arms to protect his face, and his hands and forearms are unmarked. No skin or dried blood under his nails . . ."

"It was quick and relatively merciful, then," I murmured. "Thank heaven for that."

"Bah," said Emerson. This is his usual reaction to a mention of God or heaven. Bending over, he examined the ground. "There are no signs of blood or other fluids under the corpse—another indication, if one were needed, that he was killed elsewhere. I would guess he's been dead at least two or three days. Hard to tell, without knowing where he's been during that time."

"So he was killed before last night. The attack on us was not designed to keep him from speaking to us."

"Not unless our attackers and his killer were not connected. That seems unlikely, on the face of it."

"You had better hurry, Emerson. Russell will be here before long and it is getting too dark to see what you are doing."

By the time Russell arrived, the velvety dusk of Egypt had fallen. Stars twinkled in the sky over Cairo. The moon had risen; it was several days past the full but still bright. Russell was accompanied by three of his men. Our people had left, except for Selim and Daoud. I had dismissed William, since he kept throwing up.

"What kept you?" Emerson demanded. "I want to get this thing off my hands and go home to dinner."

Russell took off his hat. "Good evening, Mrs. Emerson—Professor. My apologies for the delay. I was out of the office."

"Playing cricket or some other damn fool game at the Sporting Club, I suppose," said Emerson. "Well, take him away. We've got him nicely bundled up for you."

Russell turned his torch onto the recumbent form and examined it. "He's Egyptian."

"Brilliant!" Emerson exclaimed.

"Don't be rude," I said.

"Conversations with you, Professor, are excellent exercises in self-control," Russell said. "I swore I would never again allow you to provoke me, but don't push me too far. I see you've moved the body. What else have you done that is improper if not actually illegal?"

Brushing this bit of irony aside, Emerson proceeded to explain how and where we had come upon the remains. Russell did not interrupt, but I could hear him breathing stentoriously.

"You took photographs? Well, that's something. Any clues as to the man's identity or the identity of his killer?"

"I sifted the debris under the body and for several feet around," Emerson said. "The murderer did not leave his name and address. I can identify the victim for you, however. His name—his nom de guerre—was Asad."

After a time I said, "Really, Mr. Russell, you need more practice in self-control. Such language!"

Russell was bent over the body, inspecting the awful face more closely. "It could be," he muttered.

"We found his eyeglasses," Emerson said.

Russell snatched the twisted frames from his hand. "Anything else you forgot to mention? How, for example, you recognized a man you'd seen only once and whose present appearance is certainly not—er—lifelike?"

"As to that," said Emerson, hands on hips, shoulders thrown back, brows thunderous, "how is it that you neglected to warn us that Asad had escaped?"

"Stop shouting, both of you!" I exclaimed, for the

constables, awaiting their chief's orders, were listening with openmouthed interest. "Take the body away," I continued, addressing those individuals. "At once. Mr. Russell will follow you shortly."

They did as I directed, of course. As soon as the cortege was out of earshot, I addressed Russell. "There are several points that need to be cleared up. We will discuss them here and now. I apologize for not inviting you to return to the house with us, but I prefer to have as little to do with you as is possible. Nothing personal, you understand."

I described Ramses's encounter with Asad and our futile efforts to locate him. Russell and Emerson kept trying to interrupt my orderly exposition, but I was in no mood for displays of masculine illogic. I was hungry and it was past dinnertime. Mahmud would certainly have burned the soup.

"So you see," I concluded, "that Asad must have had information that was dangerous to some unknown party—presumably the same party who told him of Ramses's masquerade. The identification is certain to my mind. If you doubt it, you must have on file a description of his physical attributes which will settle the matter. You will of course keep us informed of the progress of your investigation. And," I added, for I was unable to resist a little touch of sarcasm, "if you hear that any other spies or terrorists have escaped, it would be kind of you to inform us before one of them succeeds in assassinating Ramses. Good night, Mr. Russell. Come, Emerson."

"Just a moment, Mrs. Emerson. Please."

"Be quick, Mr. Russell. It is probably too late for the soup, but I have hopes of the roast beef."

"I . . ." He shook his head vigorously, like a dog after a dip in a pond. "I forget what . . . Oh, yes. Is it true that Ramses has left Cairo?"

"He is in Luxor and will remain there for several weeks. I am glad you reminded me, Mr. Russell," I went on. "I meant to tell you that this business must be kept quiet. There must be nothing in the newspapers."

"I can't control the press, Mrs. Emerson!"

"Yes, you can. You people do it all the time. I do not want to be badgered by journalists and I do not want Ramses to hear of Asad's death. He might feel obliged to do something about it."

"I see." He tugged at his ear. "I'll do my best. The fellow was Egyptian, so perhaps the press won't take much of an interest."

Emerson growled deep in his throat but did not deny this outrageous remark—outrageous because it was true. I was turning away when Russell spoke again.

"After they were arrested, the members of Wardani's organization were handed over to the military. I was not informed of this man's escape."

"Really? How strange."

"I trust you are not questioning my word, Mrs. Emerson."

"No," said Emerson, before I could reply. "It's typical of the bastards not to trust anyone outside their own little circle. Who the devil was it, I wonder, who was responsible for keeping the information under wraps?"

"I don't know," Russell said shortly. "I wish I did. If you had seen fit to report what were unquestionably police matters, I would have been able to ask questions. You and the rest of your family have the most terrifying nonchalance about people trying to kill you!"

"We didn't want the police getting in our way," I explained.

"I expected you would say that. May I suggest that cooperation might be to our mutual advantage? I will pass on any information I get if you will do the same. We are on the same side, you know."

"Against the bloody War Office," said Emerson, with a chuckle.

"At least we have the same aim," Russell said, tactfully avoiding a direct answer. "The safety of your son. I think well of him, you know."

The roast beef was rather dry, but we were too hungry to be critical. We did not discuss the case during dinner, despite some rather pointed questions from Fatima, who was serving, and some coughing and shuffling from Gargery, who was listening at the door. They knew we had discovered a body—the word had spread with the rapidity of a brushfire, as it always does—but insofar as they were aware, the dead man had been a stranger. I was determined to keep it that way.

By morning Gargery was in a state of extreme exasperation. He was delighted that we had a corpse on our hands; he had been secretly hoping for some such thing ever since we arrived. Not that he was an unkind or uncaring individual, but as he had once remarked, "If there's got to be a murder, madam, it might as well be us that gets the use of it." He had got his wish, and here we were selfishly trying to keep him from getting the use of it. Fortunately the morning post included the long-awaited letter from Nefret, which served as a temporary distraction.

It also roused Emerson from his normal state of early-morning stupor. Gargery's attempts to read the letter over his shoulder were not well-received, however.

"She says they are well and happy," I informed my surly butler. "The rest of it concerns archaeological matters, which would not be of interest to you."

"I do not know why you should suppose that, madam," said Gargery stiffly. "We all of us take a deep interest in that there tomb you were so busy with for so long."

"Tetisheri? Well, there is nothing in the letter about that. They had just arrived in Luxor."

"Was there anything for Miss Sennia, madam?"

"They sent their love, of course. Emerson, what on earth is the matter?"

"She will expect more than that, madam. She will expect—"

"Hell and damnation!" Emerson bellowed.

"—a personal letter," Gargery finished.

"I am sorry, but they—"

"I had a feeling—a hideous foreboding—"

"Emerson!" I shouted.

"You needn't scream, Peabody!"

"Miss Sennia will—"

"Gargery!"

"There is nothing wrong with my hearing, madam."

They were both glaring at me, but at least I had got them to be quiet. I decided to deal with Gargery first. "There is no letter for Miss Sennia, so she will have to accept it."

Emerson examined his cup. "More coffee, Gargery."

"Are you sure you want more, sir?"

"Yes, I'm sure. What an idiotic question."

Gargery added a dribble of coffee to Emerson's cup. "Far be it from me to hurry you and madam, sir, but I must leave shortly to take Miss Sennia to school."

"Yes, quite," Emerson said absently. He was re-reading Nefret's letter. The import of Gargery's comment finally penetrated. He looked up with a scowl. "Since when has it been necessary for you to stand over me while I finish my breakfast? Go."

Gargery's jaw set. After a chat with me, he and Fatima had agreed on a compromise. They would take it in turn to serve breakfast and dinner, alternating each week. (Implicit in the agreement was the right of both to listen at the door.) He was a man of his word and would stick to it, but he was unwilling to give up a single minute of his allotted time. After he had stamped out, taking the coffeepot with him, I turned to my husband.

"Now, my dear Emerson, what is the trouble?" I inquired sympathetically. "Tell me about your premonitions."

Emerson's eyes narrowed into sapphirine slits.

"I never have premonitions, and I don't believe in yours—never have, never will."

"You just this minute said—"

"Did I? No, I didn't. And if I did, I didn't mean it." Emerson snatched up the pile of unopened letters and began looking through them. "Nothing from Russell," he remarked.

"We can hardly expect word so soon. Let's not discuss it here. Have you finished breakfast?"

"I want another cup of coffee." Emerson's wandering eye moved across the table and failed to find the object it sought. "Where the devil is the coffeepot?"

"Gargery took it away," I replied. "Pure spite, I presume. I fear you were right when you— Ah, Fatima. Thank you. The Professor was just asking for more coffee."

She offered more of everything, which we refused. Still she lingered. "Was there a letter from Nur Misur?"

"Yes. She posted it as soon as they arrived in Luxor. They are well and happy. You can read it if you like, and tell the others."

Her face glowed with pleasure. "Thank you, Sitt Hakim. Is there any more news?"

"Here's a letter from Katherine Vandergelt," said Emerson, tossing it to me. "Do you want to wait while we read it, Fatima?"

Sarcasm was wasted on the good woman. "Yes, Father of Curses, please."

"Well, this is good news!" I exclaimed. "Bertie has got pneumonia—"

"Really, Amelia!" Emerson exclaimed. "Your habit of looking on the bright side has gone too far. What is good about pneumonia? It is preferable to gangrene or lockjaw, I suppose, but—"

"If you will please allow me to finish my sentence, Emerson? In fact," I admitted, "it was something of a misstatement. He has had pneumonia and is much better, but the doctor believes a warm dry climate will hasten his recovery. Katherine and Cyrus are bringing him to Egypt. They will be here next week."

"Ah," said Emerson. It was certainly modified rapture, but I had not expected him to admit how much he missed the Vandergelts. His pleased expression was admission enough.

Fatima was more effusive. "It is very good, Sitt. Will they stay with us?"

"I hope we can persuade them to remain with us for a time, but Katherine expressed her intention of taking Bertie on to Luxor. The climate there is much more salubrious, as you know. She has asked us to make sure *The Valley of the Kings* is got ready for them."

"I will begin the cleaning," said Fatima.

"We may as well be on our way," said Emerson. "There is no privacy in this house. Peabody, I warn you: If there is a confounded journalist lurking outside, I will throw him in the river."

"The newspapers cannot have got wind of this so soon. Anyhow, they won't be interested in the death of an anonymous Egyptian."

How I could have overlooked the obvious, I cannot imagine. How often in the past had we found ourselves and our activities featured in sensational newspaper stories? Should the Reader be unfamiliar with that past, I will answer what would otherwise be a rhetorical question.

Very often.

Egyptological exploration fascinates the general public. That is understandable. I would not have objected to a reasoned, accurate description of our excavations, but—purely by chance—we had been involved in several cases of mysterious death with seemingly supernatural overtones, and it was those criminal cases that attracted the lurid imaginations of the press. Kevin O'Connell of the *Daily Yell* had been the first and the worst offender; it was he who invented "the Curse of the Pharaoh," and that word—curse, that is, not pharaoh—was to haunt us for years. But Kevin had become a friend and had toned down his rhetoric accordingly, and it had been awhile since our criminal cases had involved any but normal murderers, thieves, and forgers.

What I had overlooked was the fact that Miss Minton was in Cairo, looking for an excuse to seek us out and willing to revert to the most despicable variety of yellow journalism in order to gain her end. When we reached Giza she was already there, notebook and pencil in her hands, confronting Selim. Her back was to us; Selim's back was flat against the wall of the mastaba. He had retreated as far as he could and could retreat no farther, for she had him neatly cornered. She had always been good at that.

Emerson let out a roar and broke into a run. Miss Minton turned, cool and smiling. Selim could have got away then, but I give him credit; he stood his ground, though he looked as if he were glued to the wall, and his lips were moving—probably in prayer.

"Don't be angry with him," Miss Minton said. "He hasn't told me anything I didn't know."

"Curse it," Emerson began.

"Now, Emerson, be calm," I said. "I ought to have anticipated this. I suppose, Miss Minton, that you have informants in the police department?"

"In all government departments," she corrected. "It is customary. Now, Professor, perhaps you will tell me in your own words how you happened to discover the body."

Emerson's eyes bulged. "I will be everlastingly damned if I do!"

"Emerson, can't you see that she is trying to get you worked up so that in the heat of anger you will say something indiscreet? It is an old trick of the profession."

Miss Minton's insufferable smile faded. Her prominent chin jutted out. "You are mistaken, Mrs. Emerson. I had to follow up the story, it was too delicious to resist, and God knows I haven't been able to get anything of interest out of the military."

Emerson's countenance resumed its normal shade. He has a frightful temper, but he can control it if he must. He saw what she was getting at, and so, of course, did I.

"Very well," he said. "Selim, you may go."

Selim was glad to do so. I indicated one of the packing cases we used as seats. "Sit down, Miss

Minton. Let us not beat around the bush. What do you want from us?"

"A story, Mrs. Emerson. What can be the harm in that? Half Cairo knows of the body by now, its discovery cannot be kept secret. If you won't give me an interview, perhaps I might talk with your son and daughter-in-law."

"Unfortunately my son and daughter-in-law are not in Cairo."

"So it is true that they have gone to Luxor. Why?"

"What the devil business is it of yours?" Emerson demanded.

"Don't make a mystery of it, Emerson," I said sharply. "They are taking a little holiday and making a brief tour of inspection of the Luxor monuments, particularly the tomb of Tetisheri."

"There has been an increase in theft, I believe."

"It is only to be expected under present circumstances. The more remote the site, the greater the difficulty of proper supervision."

"But the situation is serious enough for you to send Ramses there. That leaves you badly short-handed, doesn't it?"

"No," said Emerson. "Er—somewhat. It is a question of—"

"Of priorities," I interrupted, seeing that he was about to make a mess of things. "We have answered your questions candidly and openly, Miss Minton." I rose from my packing case to indicate the interview was at an end. "I trust you will not make a sensational story of the extraneous corpse. It has nothing to do with us, and we don't want a lot of ghoulish sightseers coming round to bother us."

"You have no idea why the murderer buried it in your tomb?"

"None whatever."

She did not even say good-bye. Emerson waited until she had passed out of sight before he spoke. "Well done, Peabody. You are a damned fine liar when you put your mind to it."

"Thank you, my dear. As you know, I never prevaricate unless it is absolutely necessary. I fear, however, that you missed the point of that exchange. I shall write immediately to Nefret and tell her she must prevent Ramses from seeing the newspapers. I only hope my letter reaches Luxor before Miss Minton."

"Good Gad, Peabody, aren't you jumping to unwarranted conclusions? What makes you suppose she is going to Luxor?"

"Didn't you understand those questions about tomb robberies? She believes I lied to her, which of course I would have done had I felt it to be expedient. The silly, romantic creature is hoping Sethos is still alive."

FROM MANUSCRIPT H

The inspection of Tetisheri's tomb had been paramount. That accomplished, Ramses couldn't make up his mind what to do next—or rather, he knew what he ought to do, but he didn't know how to go about it. Assuming, he told himself sourly, that his imagination hadn't got completely out of hand.

For the next two days they wandered with seeming aimlessness and great enjoyment around the west bank—carrying out a preliminary survey, as Ramses thought of it—revisiting the scenes of our misspent youth, as Nefret put it, rather more accurately. A visit to Abdullah's tomb was one of their first acts; they stood in silence by the simple monument for some time before Nefret said quietly, "It would be nice to believe that he knows we're here."

"Do you believe it?"

Her hand slipped into his. "Mother does. I told you she dreams of him. He said Lia's baby would be a boy and that they would name it after him. Now, don't tilt your eyebrows at me, I know the odds as well as you do! It's strange, though, that she always sees him in the same place—the cliff behind Deir el Bahri, on the way to the Valley. He loved that view and so did she—watching the sun rise over the eastern cliffs, seeing the light spread across the river and the fields."

And that is why she dreams of it, Ramses thought. He found it rather moving, though, and because he was embarrassed to admit it, he said practically, "I wish I could dream about him; I'd ask for advice on where to look for our hypothetical tomb robbers."

"My dear boy, they aren't hypothetical. Just because we haven't found them yet—"

"It's not likely that we will. This whole trip is a waste of time. Do you suppose I don't know why everyone conspired to get me to Luxor?"

"Do you mind?"

"Mind being alone with you, sans friends, family, and Sennia? I expect I can endure it a little longer." She twined her fingers more tightly through his, and he went on, "If we were looking for one mastermind, like Sethos or Riccetti, we might have a chance of solving the case, but this is the same old business that's always gone on here. There are probably a dozen people involved, all local men and all extremely good at their trade. Catching one or two of them wouldn't put a stop to the thefts."

He waited for her to contradict him, hoping she would—and hoping she wouldn't—but she accepted his statement without appearing to question it. "A more sensitive woman might consider she'd been insulted by that remark about wasting time," she remarked, dimpling. "It's true you've only kissed me in eleven tombs—"

"So far." He put his arm round her and kissed the dimples and her smiling mouth. It might have seemed incongruous, even profane, in the silence of that deserted cemetery, but if he had been given to fancies, which of course he was not, he might have imagined he heard a deep, satisfied chuckle in a well-remembered voice.

So they climbed the cliff behind Deir el Bahri at dawn and stood in silence watching the sunrise, and wandered around the village of Gurneh, where ancient tombs stood side by side with modern houses, and he kissed her in ten more burial chambers. Getting into several of them were exercises in endurance, since they were partly filled with rubble and popular with bats. On only one facade did he find the strange cryptogram. The tomb, which had belonged to the vizier Ramose, was of great historical importance and outstanding beauty. Ramose had served under Amenhotep III and his heretic son, and one wall of the tomb showed the latter king in two startlingly different ways: on the left, King Amenhotep IV, depicted in conventional Egyptian style, with the goddess Maat; on the right, the same man after he had changed his name to Akhenaton and abandoned the classic canons of Egyptian art and the gods of his fathers in favor of the one god, Aton.

If Nefret had observed the cryptogram she made no comment. Ramses was not surprised to see it there. The reliefs of the vizier and his family were among the most exquisite in Egypt. They were particular favorites of his mother.

Among their other obligations was to be royally entertained by various members of the family. When they returned to the *Amelia* one evening after an interminable dinner given in their honor by Yusuf, Nefret flung herself down on the divan in the saloon and groaned.

"I can't go on eating like this! And did you see the way Jumana was glowering at us? We promised we'd let her come with us, and we haven't."

"I will be damned if I am going to feel guilty about not encumbering myself with that child." Ramses stretched out next to her, wondering if he would ever want to eat again. "But perhaps it's time we got to work."

"We've been working," Nefret protested. "Think of all those bat-infested tombs we've explored."

"In a rather haphazard fashion. We haven't been on the east bank at all."

Nefret pulled her feet up and knelt beside him. "Why should we? The tombs are all on the west bank."

"Well, we ought to have a talk with Legrain. His storage magazines were robbed. And we could try terrorizing the antiquities dealers."

"Not for another day or two. We still have a lot of tombs to visit." She slid her fingers into his hair and began stroking his temples. "Does your head ache?"

"No, but feel free to go on doing that. By the way, I keep forgetting to ask—has there been anything of interest in the post?"

"Not much."

"Nothing from Mother?"

"Oh, yes. But it was just family news. Turn over and I'll rub your back."

"It's not my back that needs to be rubbed," Ramses muttered, rolling over. Nefret burst out laughing. He turned his head to look at her in surprise, and then laughed too. "That wasn't what I meant."

"No? Well, we'll see." She pulled his shirt up and slid her hands slowly along his ribs, pressing lightly.

"What did Mother have to say?" he asked.

"Close your eyes and relax."

"I'm practically comatose already. At least I was until you started doing that . . . Did she say something rude about me, is that why you don't want to tell me?"

"Goodness, but you have a one-track mind. I was just trying to remember. Let me see . . . Sennia is enjoying school; Mother has settled the controversy between Gargery and Fatima—they're taking turns—and she is annoyed because the Professor won't let her investigate the queens' pyramids. She had just received the letter I posted the day we arrived, but they are anxious to know what we found here. We really ought to write them."

"May I see it?"

"See what? Mother's letter? If you can find it. You've got papers and books spread over every surface, as usual. Oh, I almost forgot—the Vandergelts are coming out. Bertie has had pneumonia and the doctors have recommended a winter in Egypt. They should be arriving any day now. There was a letter from Lia, too. Mother forwarded it. The baby had a cold, nothing serious, but she told me about every sniffle and sneeze! David's leg is better; the doctors think he will regain full use of it eventually."

She paused to take a deep breath.

"That's good. So long as he doesn't think he's well enough to come out. Have you written Lia lately?"

"I owe her a letter," Nefret admitted. "You should write Father; he'll be impatient to know what progress we've made in our investigations."

She stretched the word out, pronouncing each syllable with portentous emphasis. Ramses laughed.

"Not even Father could expect results within two

days. He will want to know that Tetisheri is safe, though. I'll write him tonight, unless you would rather."

"I'll end up having to do it," Nefret grumbled. "I always do."

"Poor girl. What a miserable life you lead."

"Do you really want to write letters tonight?"

He turned onto his side and pulled her into his arms.

EIGHT

The war had drastically curtailed excavation, but Legrain was still at Karnak and Ramses decided to visit him first, since he had already suffered a loss of statues from his storage magazines. One of the men took them across the river in their small boat, and landed them near the temple. From a distance it was still an impressive sight, though much of it was in ruins and the oldest structures had vanished, quarried by later kings for their own monuments. Vandalism had taken its toll, and so had time and natural disasters. Ramses well remembered the year several of the mammoth columns of the Hypostyle Hall had collapsed, with a crash that could be heard all over Luxor.

They found the Frenchman in the Hypostyle Hall directing a crew who were moving a stone drum from one of the fallen columns. After he had shaken Ramses's hand and kissed Nefret's, they walked back between the masses of tumbled sandstone blocks that had once been twin pylons, into the sunlight of the forecourt. Ramses congratulated him on all he had accomplished since they were last there.

"It will be a lifetime's work," Legrain said. His gesture took in the fallen pylons, the uneven bramble-strewn surface of the court, the ruined columns that flanked it on the north and south. "And this is only one small part of the whole. So where will you be working? I had thought you were at Giza."

Ramses explained their ostensible mission, and Legrain shrugged.

"I fear it is a hopeless cause. To guard everything, it is impossible, and the thieves have grown bold. You heard of the theft from my magazines?"

"Yes. Have the police found any clues?"

"Ah, the police!" Legrain's cynical smile showed his opinion of the local gendarmerie—an opinion Ramses shared. "No, there were no clues—although if Madame Emerson had been here she would have found some, n'est-ce pas? Whoever the thieves were, they knew their antiquities. They took four of the best—a charming little alabaster statue of Thutmose III, virtually intact, and three larger statues from the late Eighteenth Dynasty."

"No sign of them on the antiquities market?" Ramses asked.

Legrain shrugged again, and fondled his impressive mustache. "I notified the authorities in Cairo, of course, but I do not expect results. What is difficult to understand is how the villains moved such heavy objects. Mais, c'est la vie!" He chuckled and smiled at Nefret. "I think I will hope not to find anything more for a while. My work, it is primarily that of restoring and rebuilding. The discovery of the statue cache was an accident, as you know."

"Not much help," Nefret said, as they walked toward the river. "Are we going back to the west bank now?"

"I thought we might have lunch at one of the hotels."

"It's still early. I'm not hungry yet."

"Whatever you say."

"It seems logical to talk to the other Egyptologists who are working in Luxor, doesn't it? There aren't that many of them, and they are all working on the west bank except for M. Legrain, and they might be able to give us a lead."

"All right."

"You're so damned agreeable I could kick you," Nefret muttered. She was stamping along beside him, her head bowed, her face hidden under the broad brim of her hat. "And don't say you're sorry!"

"All right."

Nefret stopped dead in her tracks. He turned to her in surprise. Her face was flushed, and her eyes fell before his puzzled gaze. "What's wrong, darling?" he asked.

"Nothing." She bit her lip. "I'm being beastly. But—but if you'd only yell at me when I behave like this, or shake me, or—"

"Beat you? Anything to oblige. I hope you won't object if I put it off until we're alone, I do dislike providing entertainment for tourists."

There were several parties heading toward the

temple, and a few people had stopped to stare at them—probably, Ramses thought, because they took him for a jumped-up Egyptian in Western clothing being too familiar with an English girl. Nefret glared at a rather large woman in a very large-brimmed hat and quantities of veiling, and made a vulgar gesture. The woman turned red and went on her way, muttering indignantly. Having relieved her feelings by this bit of rudeness, Nefret began to chuckle.

"You're impossibly even-tempered," she murmured. "Kiss me?"

"In front of all these people? Not on your life. Anyhow, you don't deserve to be kissed. Where did you learn that gesture? Not from me!"

"From Father," Nefret said calmly. She slipped her arm through his and they walked on. "So where shall we go first?"

"The Valley, I suppose. MacKay is one of the few people who's still working, and he ought to be there today."

Ernest MacKay, who had replaced Weigall as head of the Theban Tombs Conservation Project, was an Englishman in his mid-thirties. They found him in the tomb of Thutmose III, where he was inspecting the paintings. He greeted them courteously but with a conspicuous absence of warmth.

"I'd heard you were in Luxor."

"The word does spread, doesn't it?" Nefret gave him a dazzling smile.

"Yes." The smile had no effect this time; Mac-

Kay's face remained glum. "To the best of my knowledge, Tetisheri hasn't been touched. I'd have notified Professor Emerson at once had I had reason to suppose that."

"Yes, quite," Ramses said, thinking he understood the change in MacKay's manner. He'd been friendly enough the last time they encountered him. "No one could possibly expect you to watch over all the tombs on the west bank, and carry out your other duties. It must be horribly frustrating."

"There are no longer any inspectors between Cairo and Assuan," MacKay said. "I felt obliged to do what I can. I don't think I can stick it much longer, though. One feels a bit of a slacker, doesn't one, when one's friends are on the fighting lines."

It wasn't a question, so Ramses did not answer. MacKay's replies to his tactful inquiries about theft and vandalism were curt and unhelpful. He might be resentful of anything that smacked of criticism, but that comment about slackers had suggested another reason for his hostile attitude.

Nefret had said very little. When they left the Valley, Ramses could tell she was seething.

"You can't blame him, you know," he said.

"I can if I like! What business has he sitting in judgment over you? I wish you couldn't read my mind as easily as you do a—a line of hieroglyphs."

"Your face is a good deal more expressive." At the moment it bore a scowl that almost matched Emerson's for pure temper. He took her hand in his.

"Nefret, all he knows about me is the story we were at such pains to cultivate last year. We can hardly complain if it succeeded in convincing people I was—well, what I pretended to be."

"Coward, slacker, pacifist." She spat the words out. "It's not fair!"

"If refusing to engage in the indiscriminate slaughter of people who've never done me any harm is being a pacifist, that's what I am." Her fingers curled into a fist, and he said quickly, "Darling, it's not important. Forget it. I think we can eliminate the East Valley from our inquiries. MacKay said there'd been no signs of illicit digging or intrusion."

"That's what he would say," Nefret muttered.

She wasn't easy to distract once she had got her mind fixed on a grievance. He tried again. "Shall we go to the Asasif tomorrow? Winlock is in the States, but Lansing is holding the fort for the Metropolitan Museum people."

"Whatever you like."

"I'll send word to Yusuf. And we might have your little protégée along."

Even that concession failed to win a smile from her. The Valley was almost deserted. The more energetic tourists had followed the path over the gebel to Deir el Bahri, where they would lunch at Cook's Rest House, and the others had returned to the donkeys and carriages that would take them to the river and their hotels. They passed the entrance to the tomb of the sons of Ramses II—the last excavation they had carried out in the Valley, before Emerson's explosive temper had caused Maspero to ban them from the area.

"It's a pity we never got a chance to finish in Number Five," Ramses said.

"We'd still be at it," Nefret said. She stopped and turned to look up at him. "Ramses . . ."

"Yes?"

"I didn't lose my temper with him." She sounded like a little girl who is afraid she has behaved badly. "I wanted to, but I didn't. It's just that I love you so much."

"You were wonderful."

"Yes, I was, wasn't I?" She put her hands on his shoulders and leaned toward him. Her lips were parted and her eyes were blue as cornflowers.

A pair of belated tourists hurried past; they were complaining in shrill voices about the heat and the dust.

"Come on," Ramses said, taking her hand.

·"Where are we going?"

"Back to the *Amelia*. I promised you a beating, remember?"

And that took care of the remainder of the day.

J amil was early next morning and pouting like Sennia in one of her moods. The reason for his ill humor was with him. She was riding astride, her skirts hitched up to show nicely turned ankles and small feet. The only incongruous note was her headgear. By some means or other she had got her hands on a pith helmet. It was an old one, which had been made for a larger head, and it came clear down to her eyebrows, but it had been carefully cleaned and painstakingly patched with bits of cloth.

"Good morning!" she shouted. "How are you? It is a beautiful day. We should have a pleasant time. I have brought my notebook and a pencil."

She was showing off her English and showing up her brother, who gave her a sour look. Nefret grinned. Jamil had only a few words of the language, and she doubted he could read and write. If he had had those skills, he and/or his father would have mentioned them. It wasn't for want of opportunity; most of the members of the family were keen on education—for boys—and Selim and David were always on the lookout for promising youngsters.

Promising *boys*. It would be a comeuppance for them if this girlchild turned out to have the qualities that would make an archaeologist. Men were all blind, even the best of them; Ramses's benevolent expression suggested he was about to pat the girl on the head and give her a sweet. Nefret had a feeling Jumana was going to show him up too, and she was prepared to cooperate to the fullest.

The three of them rode side by side, with Jamil trailing after them with the basket of food and water bottles. Jumana chattered, giving them her opinions of her father, her brother, various cousins, the school and its faculty, and she would have gone on to the wider environs of Luxor if Nefret had not stopped her. "The first thing you must learn," she said, "is to be quiet except when you ask a question. This is your chance to learn from a man who knows more about Egyptology than any teacher you could have."

Ramses, who had been listening indulgently to the girl's chatter, gave Nefret a sidelong grin. Nefret gave him a frown. He could be authoritative, even brusque, with his professional associates and the men who worked for him, but like his father he was too damned polite to women.

The morning air was cool and crisp. They followed the road through the fields into the desert beyond. The group from the Metropolitan Museum of New York was working in an area between the cultivation and the great temple of Hatshepsut at Deir el Bahri, where the cliffs of the high desert enclosed the plain in a series of bays. In the largest and most spectacular of them the female pharaoh Hatshepsut had constructed her mortuary temple, next to the earlier Eleventh Dynasty temple. The ruined monuments of other kings stretched along the edge of the cultivation. Few of them had been properly excavated. Then there were the tombs. They were everywhere, dug into the hills of Gurneh and Drah Abu'l Naga and Deir el Medina. In the broken terrain behind the cliffs lay the Kings' Valleys, east and west, and the Valley of the Queens, and dozens of smaller wadis, any one of which might contain undiscovered tombs. It was an embarras de richesses, a long lifetime's treasure hunt, with no map and few clues. The Asasif itself was a rich site, from an archaeological point of view. Ramses envied the Met people their concession, but even his father admitted they were doing an excellent job.

Ambrose Lansing, a slender dark man with a neat little mustache, was directing a crew of workmen in an area near the foot of the Asasif. When one of his men drew his attention to them he jumped up and came to greet them.

"We heard you were in town. It's good to see you." He looked curiously at Jamil and Jumana, who had remained at a discreet distance, and grinned. "I see Yusuf has foisted his best-beloved son off onto you. Who's the girl?"

Nefret explained. "I take it you don't think highly of Jamil?" she asked.

"He's worked for practically every Egyptologist in Luxor at one time or another," Lansing replied. "To use the word 'work' loosely . . . Hey, George, come here and meet the Emersons."

The man he addressed had been waiting for his summons; he was obviously a subordinate, and, as Lansing explained, a new member of the staff. He was several inches taller than his superior, with features that suggested words like "craggy" and "rugged," but as he approached at a shambling trot Ramses realized he was even younger than Lansing. Barton gaped admiringly at Nefret and tried to find words in which to express how honored he was to meet Ramses, whose book on Egyptian grammar . . .

"Good of you to say so," Ramses said, feeling approximately a hundred years old. "Are you enjoying Egypt?"

"Yes, sir!" Barton brushed sweat-soaked sandy hair out of his eyes. "I've been all over the west bank and Karnak and Luxor temples—when I'm allowed time off, that is."

"Everyone knows what a slave driver I am," Lansing said amiably. "Come and have a look around. I think you'll find this interesting . . ."

Not until Nefret started showing signs of impatience did Ramses realize they had been there for

over an hour and he had not yet raised the question
of thefts. As she had predicted, Lansing was unable
to offer any useful information.

"We've found very little that would interest
thieves. MacKay's the one you ought to talk to; the
poor guy's supposed to be looking after all the
Theban tombs, more or less single-handed."

"We spoke with him yesterday," Ramses said.

"Or Alain Kuentz."

"German?" Ramses asked in surprise.

"Swiss," Lansing corrected. "You don't know
him? He started working at Deir el Medina a
couple of years ago. It was after you folks left, so
maybe you never met him. Reason I mentioned
him is that he actually caught one of the Gurnawis
in the act of digging out a tomb up behind the
Ptolemaic temple."

"Who was it?"

Lansing shrugged. "You'll have to ask Kuentz.
He knew there was no point calling in the police,
so he gave the fellow a good hiding and kicked him
down the hill."

"That's the method the Professor favors," Nefret
said. "We'll have a little chat with Alain. I didn't
know he was back in Luxor. It was good to see you,
Mr. Lansing, and to meet you, Mr. Barton. We
didn't mean to take up so much of your time."

Lansing was young, still in his early twenties,
and unmarried. He accompanied them to where
they had left the horses and insisted on helping
Nefret to mount.

"You going to be here long?" he asked hopefully.
"It would be swell to have you all back in Luxor."

"There's not much chance of that this year," Ramses said. "But one never knows. We'll stay for a few weeks anyhow."

"Come by any time." He stood by Nefret, his hand on the saddle, looking up at her.

"And you must come to us one evening," Nefret said. "Both of you. We will decide on a time and let you know."

"Any time," Lansing repeated.

"Another victim," Ramses said, as they rode off, trailed by Jumana and Jamil. "Or two."

"Now don't start behaving like Father. Not every man I meet falls in love with me."

"Kuentz did, though. Didn't he?"

He tried to speak lightly, but the attempt was not a success. Nefret glanced at him in surprise. "Darling, it was years ago! You were off on one of your solitary excursions, trying to avoid me, and he was . . . well, he was very attentive and rather attractive and . . . I told you about him."

"I'd forgotten until Lansing mentioned his name."

"I told you about all of them," Nefret said. "Which is more than you've done. You know everything about my past affairs, if they can be called that, but you've never talked about yours, and I'd be willing to bet they were a lot more interesting than mine! There was that girl in Chicago, and Christabel Pankhurst, to mention only two, and I've always wondered what went on between you and Enid Fraser, and—"

"Men don't discuss such things," Ramses said self-consciously.

"It wouldn't be gentlemanly, would it?"

"Are you trying to start a quarrel?"

"I'm ready whenever you are!"

She was absolutely right; he was in no position to criticize her past behavior, or even ask about it. He said so, adding, "We'll talk about it another time."

"Ha," said Nefret. "Where are we going now?"

"Deir el Medina. It's the first specific piece of information we've had. If one of the shifty beggars was digging there, Kuentz will be able to tell us where."

When they reached the site of the workmen's village, there was no sign of life. The mud-brick walls of the simple houses stood in regular alignment. Only a small part of the site had been cleared. Perhaps Kuentz was investigating the tombs that lay in the slopes of a shallow bay near the ruins. Some of the entrances gaped open, black against the pale sandstone of the cliff.

On the chance that the excavator was stretched out somewhere in the shade, taking a nap, Ramses called out. Initially there was no response. They were about to turn back when a voice hailed them, and a man came scrambling down the slope. He was wearing a galabeeyah and turban, and as he trotted toward them Ramses thought he looked familiar.

"You are looking for the Mudir? He is not here. He left me to stand guard."

Over what? Ramses wondered. The workmen's huts had yielded no treasures, only a few objects the former occupants had left, and the tombs were those of the workers themselves—relatively humble sepulchres, most of them robbed in antiquity.

There had been one spectacular exception, that of the tomb of a royal architect, which an Italian expedition had discovered in 1906 with its grave goods intact, but another such find was highly unlikely.

"Have thieves been at work here?" he asked. He remembered the man now; he had once worked for them at Drah Abu'l Naga. Like so many of the locals, who could not afford medical or dental care, he had aged rapidly, his face wrinkled, his beard graying.

"No. But if they come, I will be ready for them!" He flexed stringy arms and bared decaying teeth in a threatening grimace.

He had ignored Jumana, but when she began scribbling in her omnipresent notebook, he gave her an uneasy glance. "What is she writing?" he demanded.

"I don't know," Ramses said truthfully. "Tell the Mudir we were here and will come again."

"Do I ask questions now?" Jumana demanded. "I have much to say."

"I'm sure you do," Ramses said. "Nefret, are you ready for a rest?"

Her hand shielding her eyes, she was scanning the slopes of the hills. "Perhaps it was one of the workmen's tombs the thief was clearing."

"Lansing said it was behind the temple, but he may have been mistaken. Shall we have a look?"

Jamil, who was carrying the water bottles, shifted the bag to his left shoulder. "It is a hard climb, and there is nothing to see," he announced. "The tombs are empty."

"You've been in them, have you?" Ramses's tone was not accusatory. Jamil grinned and stroked his beloved mustache.

"I and many others, Brother of Demons."

"''Tis true 'tis pity, and pity 'tis, 'tis true,'" Ramses said. He didn't bother to translate; Shakespeare would be wasted on Jamil. He went on, addressing Nefret, "Weigall finally got round to installing gates over the most interesting of the tombs, but not before the reliefs had been damaged."

The climb was not precipitous, but it was steep and long, involving a scramble up the loose stones at the base of the cliff, and by the time they reached the crumbled remains of a small mud-brick pyramid Ramses had had second thoughts. "This is wasted effort. I haven't seen any signs of recent disturbance, and we may not be in the right place."

"Let's rest a bit before we go back." Nefret dropped gracefully into a sitting position, legs crossed, and beckoned to Jamil. "It's not a very thrilling site. All those poor little battered pyramids! Not even Mother would get excited about them. Where are the tombs of the Saite princesses?"

"The what? Oh, those." Ramses handed Jumana one of the water bottles. "They weren't the ladies' original tombs."

"Where were they buried, then?"

"Medinet Habu. You can still see their chapels, or parts of them. The tombs themselves are empty. Two of the sarcophagi were dragged all the way over here and up the hill, by people who wanted to use them for their own burials."

Seeing that Jumana was watching his mouth as if

pearls of wisdom were about to fall from it, he sighed and prepared to do his pedagogical duty. "The princesses were the high priestesses of Amon at Thebes during the last dynasties. They had the titles of God's Wife of Amon and Adorers of the God—"

"Adoratrixes," said Nefret, through a mouthful of bread.

"Far be it from me to deny a lady her feminine ending," said Ramses, "but I find that title frightfully clumsy. Anyhow, the ladies were daughters or sisters of the pharaoh, sworn to celibacy—er— sworn to remain unmarried, for they were the brides of the god. Each of them adopted a successor, who was also a royal princess."

"So they were very powerful and very veeery rich," murmured Jumana. "If they were not in their tombs at Medinet Habu or in their sarcophagi, where are they?"

"A good question," Ramses admitted. "Three thousand years ago most of the royal tombs had been robbed and the mummies violated. The priests gathered up what was left and hid it in the royal cache at Deir el Bahri and in the tomb of Amenhotep the Second. But that happened five hundred years before the last of the God's Wives died and was buried at Medinet Habu."

"So perhaps," said Jumana, her eyes shining, "their tombs were also robbed, later, and their bodies were moved to a secret hiding place like the one at Deir el Bahri."

She was a sharp little thing, and the gleam in her dark eyes aroused what his mother would have called strong forebodings. He hoped he hadn't stimulated a hereditary interest in tomb hunting. Nefret was thinking the same thing; he heard her chuckle. He was glad she found it amusing. He had a horrible vision of Jumana scrambling over the hundreds of square acres of broken cliff on the west bank, looking for the "lost tomb of the princesses"— falling, breaking her leg, or fracturing her skull . . .

"That is what we call pure speculation," he said sternly. "It means we do not know. Scholars do not waste time looking for something that may not be there."

"Where?" Jumana asked, not at all disconcerted by his minatory tone.

"Anywhere! Didn't you understand what I said?"

"He means you are not to go into the mountains alone," said Nefret, corking the bottle.

"But we do it all the time! Don't we, Jamil?"

She stretched out her leg and nudged Jamil with her foot. He glowered at her. "No. Not since we were children. You are not a child, you are a woman. Women do not climb the cliffs, they stay at home. Our father should have found you a husband before this. He will not allow—"

"That's enough, Jamil," Nefret said. Jumana's eyes were bright with tears. She was a fine little actress, but Nefret thought her distress this time was genuine. She and her brother must have been good friends when they were young, before the conventional separation of the sexes and Jamil's masculine ego destroyed their closeness.

They spent the rest of the day at the Ramesseum, climbing over fallen walls and columns and chatting with the local men who lay in wait for tourists.

"Ramses the Great" was one of the few pharaohs known to most visitors, and the ruined colossus of that monarch was famous because of its association with Shelley's sonnet.

> "I met a traveller from an antique land
> Who said: 'Two vast and trunkless legs of
>   stone
> Stand in the desert. Near them, on the sand,
> Half-sunk, a shattered visage lies . . .'"

Since the poet's time, the legs had been shattered too. As they passed the tourists gathered round the pieces, they heard a plummy voice declaiming the only phrase the average person seemed able to remember—Shelley's ironic commentary on the futility of human vanity: "'Look on my works, ye mighty, and despair.'"

The entire court was littered with statue fragments, bits of column and other debris; but the black granite head, which had been part of a smaller but even finer colossus of the king, was conspicuous by its absence. They hadn't expected to find any evidence of how the thieves had managed to remove it—tracks of feet, carts, or animals had been well trampled by now—and Ramses's attempts to question the "guards" were unsuccessful. Some melted quietly away when they saw what he was looking at; the ones he managed to corner expressed complete ignorance of the affair. They had all been somewhere else at the time.

"Some of them must have been bribed to be elsewhere," Ramses said.

"No doubt," Nefret agreed. "But they know we can't prove anything."

She led the way into the Hypostyle Hall. "At least the reliefs appear to be untouched," she said.

"Yes, I don't see any fresh gaps. Old Ramses was a combative has—fellow, wasn't he?" The scene they saw showed the Egyptian forces attacking a city in Palestine. Mounted in his chariot, the pharaoh drove over the bodies of the slain, while his sons thrust and struck at a row of kneeling enemies. "Even Thutmose III didn't revel in fallen bodies so enthusiastically."

"You're aching to copy them, aren't you?" Nefret asked.

"I'd leave that to David. Ramses lost the damn—" Out of the corner of his eye he saw Jumana scribbling busily, and revised his comment. "He lost the battle, you know. All this is pure propaganda. Reminds one of the War Office, doesn't it?"

"All war offices," Nefret murmured. "Down through the centuries."

The back part of the temple was in ruinous condition. Nudged by Nefret, Ramses delivered another lecture. "The chapels dedicated to the king and various gods were the most remote and sacred parts of the temple, where only priests could go. In the morning the attendants would open the doors of the shrines, anoint the statues and dress them in fresh robes, and make offerings."

"They put clothes on the statues?" Jumana asked incredulously.

"Fine linen and royal linen, and ornaments of gold and precious stones. The offering vessels were also of the finest materials—or so we assume." He added, "The actual food was eaten by the priests, after the god had finished with it."

Jamil was leaning against a fallen pillar, arms folded and eyes half closed. His ostentatious boredom inspired Ramses to continue. "The most important shrines were at Karnak and Luxor Temples, but the gods, especially Amon-Re, were represented in various other temples. He traveled around quite a lot, too; his statue was carried from Karnak to Luxor every year, and he also visited his sanctuary at Deir el Bahri. It must have been quite a thing to see: the barges on which he was carried shining with gold, the crowds of devoted worshipers lining the route."

Jamil covered his mouth with his hand, presumably to hide a yawn.

"Where shall we go tomorrow?" Jumana asked, as they retraced their steps.

She was taking it for granted that she would make one of the party. He hadn't the heart to deny her, especially with Nefret watching him.

"The West Valley, I think."

"Mr. Carter won't like that," Nefret said.

"I am not planning to steal his damned tomb, just see if there are any signs of recent activity."

"Don't swear," Nefret said, in a fair imitation of his mother's voice. She laughed, and added, "You sounded alarmingly like the Professor."

"Good Lord, did I? Unlike Father, who would like nothing better than an excuse to interfere with someone else's excavation, I meant precisely what I said. We'll head out that way tomorrow."

When they reached the *Amelia* they turned the horses over to Jamil, and Ramses said, "What about a change of scene and cuisine tonight? Maaman's cooking is first-rate, but it's becoming a bit repetitive. We could have dinner at the Winter Palace or the Luxor and perhaps buy a newspaper. We've been out of touch for weeks."

"Not tonight. Do you mind? I'm a little tired and we really ought to write a few letters."

FROM LETTER COLLECTION T

Dear Mother and Father,

I'm afraid we haven't much to report thus far, except the most important thing—Tetisheri is safe! Not even a bat got past those iron doors, though some idiot tourist—the same one who left his odd little cryptogram all over Amarna—risked his neck climbing up—or down—into the cleft. It was an eerie experience, to stand in the dark, empty burial chamber and remember all the excitement of that wonderful season. There's no place quite like Luxor, is there? We've spoken with M. Legrain and Mr. Lansing and a few others, but haven't learned anything of interest. However, I have acquired a protégée. I never had one before! She is Yusuf's daughter, a bright and beautiful little person who aspires to be an Egyptologist. Yusuf agreed to let her go with us when we visit the various sites. He thinks it's only a temporary arrangement, and I see no reason to inform him of my intentions until I see how she works out; but prepare yourself for piteous complaints from Luxor if and when I remove her from under the paternal roof.

Her brother Jamil is our official escort. He's beautiful too, but not at all bright, and as vain as a peacock. There's no way of ridding ourselves of him without offending Yusuf, though. That's about all the news, except that we are suffering from permanent indigestion! You know the family. It's getting late, so I must stop. Here's Ramses.

Dear Mother and Father,

Nefret has covered the main points. Nothing else to report as yet, but we will keep you informed. Sorry to hear about Bertie. I'm sure Mother will soon set him right.

> *Your affectionate son, Ramses*

Dear Mother and Father,

It's two o'clock in the morning. Ramses is sleeping— soundly, I hope—and I am crouched over the table in the saloon scribbling as fast as I can by candle- light and glancing guiltily over my shoulder at every sound. I am glad you warned me about find- ing that poor man's body, but please don't tell me anything else you don't want him to know; he kept asking to see your letter and I had to lie like a trooper to keep it from him. It makes me miserable to lie to him, and when I'm miserable I act like a shrew because I feel guilty, and he's so sweet and un-

derstanding and that makes me feel even guiltier!
I'll slip this note into the envelope with my other
letter before I post it.

Fondest love,
Nefret

Jamil was hollow-eyed and half asleep next morning. He sat on his horse like a bag of rags. Jumana greeted them in her usual high-pitched shout. "Good morning! How are you? It is a fine morning! Did you enjoy a happy night?"

"Yes, thank you," Nefret replied, avoiding her husband's meaningful look.

"That is good. I have read all the notes I wrote down yesterday and I have sharpened my pencil. Jamil would not tell me where we are going today, but I asked my father and he said—"

"What did I tell you about keeping quiet unless you are asking questions?" Nefret prompted.

"It is true," said Jumana. "I am as stupid as Jamil. I will ask the right question. What are you looking for in the Valley of the Monkeys?"

"What do you know about the place?" Ramses asked.

"I thought I was to ask the questions. Oh—it is a test?" Her face fell, and so did the pith helmet, down to the bridge of her nose. She pushed it back. "I have never been there. I have been in the other valley many times; I worked as a basket carrier for Vandergelt Effendi when I was little. At the school of Mrs. Vandergelt the teachers took us to see the tombs. I have seen Seti and Thutmose and Amenhotep—"

Nudged by a stern look from Nefret, Ramses cut in. "It is the tomb of another Amenhotep we are visiting today. His is one of the few in the West Valley, which you call the Valley of the Monkeys. Mr. Carter worked in the tomb this past spring for a short time. We want to see if anyone else has been digging without permission." He would have left it at that, but the concentrated regard of two pairs of eyes, one blue, one black, demanded more. Reluctantly, for he disliked lecturing, he went on, trying to use words simple enough for her to understand. "Amenhotep the Third was the builder of the temple of Luxor and the two colossi on the road to Deir el Medina. He ruled at a time when Egypt was at the pinnacle—the high point—of its power and wealth. His chief queen, Tiy, was a commoner—that means she was not of royal birth—but she had great influence. Kings of other countries wrote to her asking her for gifts and favors. Their son was Akhenaton, who abandoned the worship of the old gods in favor of one . . ." Jumana was nodding vigorously. "Oh. You know about him from school? Good."

They had followed the road that led from the public ferry landing past the temple of Seti I and the slopes of Drah Abu'l Naga, into the wadi that formed the approach to the two valleys. Several hundred yards before the entrance to the East Valley a track led off to the right. They were the only ones to turn into it. Few people came this way; the ground was uneven and littered with fallen stones. The rough trail twisted and turned between rugged cliffs and rocky outcroppings. They went on in single file, holding the horses to a walk. No one spoke, not even Jumana. It was so still they might have been the only living creatures for miles.

The weird wavering call fell into the silence like a scream. Nefret's hands clenched on the reins. The others had stopped too. She laughed self-consciously. "A jackal."

"At this time of day?" Ramses's head lifted. The sound was not repeated, but he must have heard something, for he turned in the saddle and spoke to her. "Stay with them."

He dug his heels into the black's sides and urged him into a trot, bending low over his neck and guiding him with hands and voice. Nefret swore under her breath. He'd been too quick for her. Jackals prowled and hunted by night. The cry must have been a signal. It had certainly not been a shout of welcome.

Jumana and Jamil were also familiar with the habits of jackals. Both of them looked hopefully at her. Jamil was not interested in archaeology, but he would probably love a fight. Nefret felt an unexpected stab of sympathy for her mother-in-law. Was this what she had had to deal with all those years—young people who didn't have sense enough to be afraid?

Someone had to stay with them. Of course it would have to be me, Nefret thought. She acknowledged the logic behind Ramses's decision; he was a better rider, and better equipped by size and strength to handle a thief if he caught one. If there was only one . . . Ramses was already out of sight, behind a spur of rock, when she reached her decision.

"Stay close behind me," she ordered, and started forward.

After a short distance the wadi opened up into a wider gorge, walled by cliffs like the ruined ramparts of a giant's fortress. The sun was high enough to paint the rock walls with a bewildering mixture of light and shadow, where deep clefts and ragged apertures broke the surface. There was no sign of life, and no sign of her husband. Nefret went on. She was afraid to let the mare go faster than a walk, the surface was bad and the uneven contours of the rock face offered concealment for any number of men.

The tomb they'd come to see was about halfway between the entrance and the far end of the valley. They were almost upon it before she saw Ramses's horse. The saddle was empty.

She heard the rattle of loose rock and he came into sight, halfway down the cliff next to the tomb entrance, and she realized that the sharp line of shadow above him was a fissure or chimney. He was a skilled climber, but she always hated watching him; even an expert could miscalculate, and the cliff face below him was practically sheer. Bits of rock broke away from under his feet as he lowered himself from one hold to the next. She dismounted and handed the reins to Jamil. "Stay here," she said again.

By the time she got to him he was on the ground.

"Damn it!" he said furiously. "I was too slow. He got away. So did the others, I suppose. I could only follow one of them."

His narrowed eyes scanned the surroundings. There was no one else in sight and no sound of movement. The futility of pursuit was obvious; there were hundreds of hiding places in the cliffs and probably a dozen ways out of the Valley for those who knew the paths.

His hands were scraped and bleeding. He'd lost or removed his hat; perspiration trickled down his face from under his hair. "Come and have a drink," Nefret said, torn between brushing the damp curls off his forehead and shaking him. "Why the devil couldn't you have waited for me before you went off like that? Following someone when he is climbing above you is asking for a kick in the head."

"I never got that close to the bastard," Ramses said sourly. "I take it none of them passed you on their way out?"

"No."

In emulation of her mother-in-law she had taken to carrying first-aid supplies and a few other useful "accoutrements." He let her bathe his hands and apply alcohol to the open cuts while he talked.

"They heard the signal and were out of the tomb and running in all directions by the time I got here. It was quite an orderly retreat, almost as if they had rehearsed it beforehand. I never imagined they'd have the bloody gall to operate in broad daylight."

"Why not?" Nefret said. "Nobody ever comes

here. They did have enough common sense to post a lookout."

"Yes." He took a long drink and passed the water bottle to Jamil, who was squatting on the ground watching him. "Jamil, did you tell anyone where we were going today?"

Jamil choked. Water spilled down his chin. He wiped it with his sleeve and looked guilty. Sensing that he was trying to think of an acceptable lie, Nefret said, "There is no reason why you should not have spoken of it, Jamil. We did not forbid you to do so."

"Ah." The boy's handsome, sulky face brightened. "I told my father, yes, of course. You did not forbid—"

"It was talked about at the house when two of my uncles and five of my cousins were there," Jumana broke in. "No doubt they talked of it in the coffee shop later, and Jamil too. He is always at the coffee shop. If you wonder who could have known of your plans, the answer is: the whole of Luxor. But none of them would face the Brother of Demons."

She was so much quicker than Jamil. For the first time Ramses spoke to her as he would have spoken to an equal. "I thought the same. Does that mean these men were strangers?"

"That, or they had found something so important they were willing to take the risk. It was not such a great risk, perhaps. They did get away."

"So they did," Ramses agreed ruefully. "Shall we see what they were doing?"

It was a bit of a scramble up the slope of loose talus to the wide cleft in the rock. Sunken and deeply shadowed, the tomb entrance had been closed by an iron door. It stood open. Piles of fresh debris, presumably from Carter's recent excavations, surrounded it.

"Foundation deposits," Ramses said, indicating several pits. "Carter must have cleared them out. Jumana, why don't you stay—"

"I am your scribe," Jumana said, brandishing her notepad and pencil.

"Yes, of course. Take my hand, then. It's rather rough going."

Nefret motioned Jamil to follow them. This was a far cry from the popular tombs of the East Valley, with their electric lights and accessible chambers. The long entrance passage sloped steeply and was broken by several flights of steps. The tomb had lain open for years before the Department of Antiquities installed the iron door, long enough for a considerable amount of windblown sand and water-driven rubble to accumulate. Rock fragments and bits of plaster from the walls added to the debris. Emerson would not have approved of Carter's methods; he had left a lot of stuff underfoot. The daylight faded as they descended, their torches the only illumination. The well at the end of the passage had been bridged with planks. They crossed it and stopped, at Ramses's low-voiced order. His voice echoed in a rather unpleasant manner, and the beams of the torches were lost in the enclosing darkness. The air was hot and dry.

"Carter cleared the well," Ramses said. "He couldn't have done much more, he was only here for a few weeks." He moved the light slowly around the room, which had two pillars and the opening of a flight of stone-cut steps that led down. The floor was inches deep with debris, an unholy mixture of broken stone, bits of wood, and unidentifiable fragments of other kinds. Except . . .

Before she could get a better look, Ramses turned the light up. The ceiling was moving.

Jamil let out a howl, and Nefret said irritably, "It's only bats. Keep quiet, they are attracted by voices."

Jumana hadn't uttered a sound but she had edged closer to Ramses. Maybe she knew bats would approach a taller target first. Ramses handed her his torch. "Go back up and wait for us outside," he said.

"I am not afraid of bats," Jumana said.

"Nor I," Jamil said. "I stepped on a sharp stone, that was why I cried out. It was not fear."

"Do as I say," Ramses snapped. "We won't be long."

The two retreated, bickering in low voices.

Nefret moved closer to her husband. Carefully though she stepped, things crunched under her feet. "You should have let her stay. Jamil was the one who was making all the noise."

"I wanted them both out of here."

"Why?"

"Several reasons. First and most important . . ." One arm went round her waist. The other hand took firm hold of the torch, and she was laughing as she raised her face for his kiss.

"That makes twenty-two," he said, after awhile.

"Did you think I was going to hit you on the head again?"

"I can hardly blame you for losing your wits when

I kiss you," he said magnanimously, and kissed her again.

"There's another reason," he went on. "The thieves were able to get out in a hurry, so they couldn't have been far inside. I think they were in this room when we interrupted them."

He pointed the torch toward the left-hand wall. Someone had certainly been doing something. She would have assumed it was Howard Carter; the cleared space was neatly defined, leading from the door to the base of the wall and along it for several feet.

The hiding place was a rough hole which had been hastily enlarged from a fault in the stone. She could only guess at what it might once have contained; the only things remaining were a scattering of beads and a narrow strip of gold— a spacer or part of the fastening of a bracelet. Swearing softly and comprehensively, Ramses scooped up the objects, handed them to Nefret, and swept his fingers through the dust. He found one small item the thieves had overlooked: a ring, the golden hoop surmounted by a bezel of turquoise or blue glass with several tiny figures in gold relief.

"They must have had most of it out before they heard the signal," he muttered. "Then they grabbed and ran. Damn!"

"Damn," Nefret agreed. "How did they know where to look?"

"Good question. It was probably an ancient thief's cache; some enterprising workman or priest scooped up a handful of jewelry—or maybe a small box, there are splinters of wood here—possibly when the tomb was being inspected, or was re-opened for another burial, and tucked it away, meaning to come back for it later, when nobody was around. Carter would have found it if he had gone a bit farther. He'll be sick when he hears about this."

He rose to his feet. Nefret said, "You didn't answer my question. How did they know where to look for the jewels?"

"I don't know the answer. But he has an uncanny talent for finding such things."

The backlight from the torch cast odd shadows across his face.

"He's dead," Nefret said, after a moment.

"Is he?"

They had been talking too loudly. An irritable, dry rustling began. They left the chamber and started back up the sloping passage to the entrance.

"Don't mention what we found to Jamil or Jumana," Ramses said.

Nefret nodded agreement. She knew as well as he did the effect the word "gold" had on the men of Gurneh, and how gossip would exaggerate the find. Upon their emergence they were greeted with flattering enthusiasm by their companions.

"Is it time to eat?" Jamil inquired hopefully.

"We may as well," Nefret said. "Ramses?"

He was inspecting the rock surface around the entrance. She saw it almost as soon as he did: a rough circle cut into the rock, divided by a flattened curve.

There were times when the man Nefret adored with all her heart and soul made her so angry she wanted to hit him. According to her mother-in-law, this was a normal, even positive, feeling. "Not that I would ever condone striking a man," she had added. "It would not be playing the game. A firm expression of annoyance generally inspires a loud response and a brief discussion, which serves to clear the air." It seemed to work for her in-laws, but Ramses didn't have his father's explosive temper.

She had assumed they would go straight back to the boat so they could discuss the astonishing idea he had planted in her mind. It inspired other ideas, other conjectures, other theories; but instead of letting her talk about them, her husband proceeded to spend the rest of the day methodically exploring the valley and dictating notes to Jumana, who trotted after him like an energetic puppy. They went into the other royal tomb, where Ramses muttered over its neglected state and pointed out the wall painting of little baboons which had given the valley its name. By the time he announced they would return, her head was so full of unspoken comments it felt as if it would burst.

They parted from Jumana at the point where the path to Gurneh diverged from the main road to the ferry landing. Jamil, who would take the horses back to the house, trailed along after them.

"She held up well," Ramses said in a low voice. "It's a pity I can't dismiss Jamil, he's more of a nuisance than a help, but I'm afraid Yusuf would be offended."

"Yes, I suppose. Ramses, what makes you think Sethos is—"

"We'll talk about it later."

"But—"

"Later."

It was at this point, Nefret thought, that her mother-in-law would have expressed her annoyance—firmly—and insisted on continuing the discussion, and then she and Emerson would have shouted happily at one another and the air would have been cleared. There was no hope of any such thing with Ramses. She bowed her head and said nothing more.

She had finished bathing and changing when he joined her in their room.

"I had to wait for Jamil," he explained unnecessarily. "Do you mind if I clean up a bit before we talk? I'll be as quick as I can."

He finished unbuttoning his shirt and tossed it in the general direction of a chair, then sat down to unlace his boots. When he bent over she saw the faint scars that ran across his shoulders and down his back. Thanks to the use of a "magical" ointment supplied by Kadija, the wounds had healed well and were not visible except in certain lights, but Nefret knew they were there. It was morbid and self-indulgent to blame herself for those injuries; her inadvertent blunders would not have affected the outcome of that awful business. She kept telling herself that. One day she might be able to believe it.

"I'll have tea ready," she said, and fled, before he could see the tears in her eyes.

She took it out on poor young Nasir, spurring

him into a flurry of activity that actually got the tea-things on the table before Ramses came up-stairs.

"Cucumber sandwiches again?" he inquired, settling into a chair.

"It seems to be an unalterable law. Your mother started it and I can't get Maaman to stop. He won't even do cheese."

"It doesn't matter."

She poured the tea. When she handed him his cup she saw he was watching her, his eyes bright and steady, his lips slightly curved.

"You do it on purpose, don't you?" she demanded.

"You're adorable when you're in a temper." He began to laugh, raising one hand in a mock posture of defense. "I thought that would stir you up. No, honestly, I don't do it on purpose. I thought we ought to conduct the discussion of what is unquestionably a complex and controversial subject—"

"When we are comfortable and not likely to be interrupted," Nefret broke in. "All right, I've had all afternoon to think about it, so you can let me talk first. You think Sethos is back, don't you? Ramses, he can't be. I saw the wound. It must have penetrated his lung."

"People have survived such wounds, haven't they?"

"People have survived worse," Nefret admitted. "Miracles, they're called, but they do happen. So let's grant that he had a good surgeon, and a miracle. I'll also grant that it would make excellent sense to let *everyone* believe he had died. You wouldn't dare make an exception for fear word would get back to his counterparts in the intelligence services of Turkey and Germany. They must have known of his existence, if not his real identity, and he'd have been high on their list of people to be eliminated. They'd write him off if they thought he was dead."

"I agree." He watched her, his eyebrows tilted and a smile curving his lips. "Anything else you want to say?"

"Yes. That peculiar mark you pointed out to me—the one like a yin-and-yang symbol. He'd find that appropriate, wouldn't he—the light and the dark sides of his nature, his criminal past and his most recent role as an agent of British intelligence. And the wavering line looks like a flattened *S*! The sign is meant to warn thieves away from places that are under his protection, and they include sites in which we—especially Mother—take a personal interest. That occurred to you earlier, didn't it? Why didn't you tell me?"

"I hoped you'd arrive at the same conclusion without my prompting. It was such a far-fetched idea."

"Not so far-fetched now," Nefret said thoughtfully. "I have to admit it fits together rather neatly. Is he back in the antiquities business?"

He answered with another question. "Did he ever leave it? He may have been in touch with his old confederates all along. Random digging wouldn't have located that jewel cache so easily. Someone must have known where it was—the same thief, perhaps, who found and marketed those carved plaques that Carter bought for Lord Carnarvon a few years ago. They showed Amenhotep the Third and his queen, and may well have come from the tomb."

"And when they appeared on the market, Sethos got wind of it and passed the word to leave the tomb alone? I have to admit, your idea is looking more and more plausible. That was a well-planned operation in the West Valley—a lookout posted, an orderly retreat—more his style than that of the locals."

"It's possible," Ramses said cautiously.

"What are we going to do about it?"

"Flush him out."

"I expected you'd say that. Should we tell Mother and Father what we suspect?"

"Father already suspects, I think. Discretion is not his strong point; he's let a few things slip. He wouldn't say anything to Mother, and you know what a confounded romantic she is; she's convinced that Sethos died nobly serving his country, and saving her life." Nefret was silent. After a moment Ramses added, "And mine, and yours. Do you suppose I've forgotten what I owe him?"

"Then couldn't we just pretend we don't know?"

"You're a bit of a romantic yourself." He smiled at her and her heart quickened. "I have several reasons for wanting a private chat with him."

"How do you propose to go about it? Start a rumor that we've found some unique antiquity and left it sitting here in the saloon, unguarded and unprotected?"

The sun had set and the afterglow lingered on the western cliffs. Ramses pushed his cup away and lit a cigarette. "He won't touch anything we've got or come anywhere near us. But there's one thing that might bring him out into the open. What did you do with that portrait of Mother?"

They took the painting to Luxor next day. By the time they reached the river, half the population of the west bank had had a look at it. Several times they had to stop while a curious crowd gathered round to admire and comment. "By the life of the Prophet, it is the Sitt Hakim herself! Her very look, her smile, her parasol!"

They used the English word. The parasol was so famous it rated a special designation. Some of the older, more superstitious residents of Gurneh thought it had magical powers. It had certainly come into contact with enough heads and shins.

"Where are you taking her?" one of the men asked respectfully.

Nefret explained. The picture was so fine they had decided to have another, more elegant frame made for it. Abdul Hadi in Luxor was known for his wood carving; he had promised he would finish the job by the following evening.

"Who is going to believe that?" Nefret asked, after they had detached themselves from the art critics. "Abdul Hadi is the slowest craftsman in Egypt."

"Well, I'm damned if I am going to spend more than one night in the back room of Hadi's shop."

Because Ramses did not underestimate his quarry's intelligence, they went back to the *Amelia* and remained on board until after dark. When they left the boat it was through the window of their room. The crewman had the dinghy in position; he helped Nefret down into it—Ramses could hear her cursing her cumbersome robe and veil—and as soon as Ramses had joined them he pushed off.

"I do miss Luxor," Nefret said, moving closer to him. "It's so quiet and the stars are as bright as candles. Aren't you going to put your arm round me? I'm feeling very friendly."

"With Isam watching us?"

"I don't care who sees."

"All right."

It had not been a sufficiently enthusiastic response, and he could tell she was annoyed, but even if he had been in the habit of public displays of affection, he couldn't get his mind off what was about to—what might—happen. They could be dead wrong about everything. In a way, he hoped they were.

Abdul Hadi had left a back window open for them. He had been effusive in his promises of assistance and of silence, but Ramses didn't count on the latter promise holding for more than a day, which was one of the reasons why he had made a point of mentioning that the portrait would only be in the shop for twenty-four hours. Luxor men were formidable gossips. If nothing happened that night, they would have to abandon the scheme and try another.

Nefret wasn't too pleased when he stationed her behind the curtain that led into the front room of the shop and took up a position nearer the window, behind a wooden chest. (Or was it a coffin? It looked like one.) She wanted to be near him, ready to pitch in if there was a struggle. His excuse, that having her close would distract him, was only partly true. He had politely requested that she refrain from switching on her torch until *he* told her to. She hadn't been pleased about that either.

Flat on the floor behind the chest—he preferred not to think of it as a coffin—he settled himself for a long wait, putting his watch near his hand and shielding it so the radium-painted numerals would not be visible from the window. He didn't expect any activity before midnight, but he had been there less than an hour when a soft sound from outside drew his attention and a shadow darkened the window. He ought to have known. The fellow never did what one expected.

The shadow remained motionless for over a minute, which is quite a long time when one is counting seconds. Will he risk a light? Ramses wondered. I would. It is not a good idea to enter a dark room through a narrow window without making certain that someone isn't inside ready to grab you by the throat.

When it came, the light was a pencil-thin circle, just bright enough to show the outlines of objects. Ramses didn't dare turn his head; he felt certain Nefret had been watching through a gap in the curtain and hoped she had seen the shadow or the light in time to close it. The light flickered back and forth and went out, and the shadow moved.

He didn't make much noise, but he couldn't avoid the brush of cloth against plaster, or the creak of the old wood of the windowsill. Ramses moved at the same time, rising slowly to his feet. He waited until the dark form was half in and half out of the room before he abandoned silence for speed. Vaulting over the chest, he got a firm grip on the first body part that came to hand—it turned out to be a leg—and pulled. He didn't want to hurt the fellow, he just wanted to make sure he couldn't get away. The second part of the plan worked. Instead of trying to free himself, the other man let go his hold on the window frame and collapsed heavily onto Ramses.

Approximately a second and a half later it occurred to Ramses that he might have been guilty of a slight error in judgment. He was flat on his back, pinned by a body as hard as leather and steel, with a hand squeezing his right wrist. The bones felt as if they were about to crack.

The fellow was thirty years his senior. Sheer embarrassment made Ramses forget his kindly intentions. He raised his head sharply and felt his opponent's nose bend with a nasty squashing sound. The grip on his wrist loosened. He pulled his hand free, grabbed a handful of hair and a fistful of sleeve, twisted his legs around the other pair of legs, and flipped the man over.

A sudden glare of light half blinded him. "Goddamn it, Nefret, I told you—"

"Shut up," said his bride. "That's enough. From both of you."

Ramses looked down at the man whose limp body he straddled. He was not unconscious, just completely and infuriatingly relaxed. The face was unfamiliar and, at the moment, somewhat monstrous. His beard had been pulled loose, and the putty that had enlarged his nose had been mashed into a grotesque lump, like that of a boxer who has lost too many fights. The substance had probably saved him from a broken nose, but blood trickled from his nostrils. Ramses got awkwardly to his feet.

"That was a filthy trick," his uncle said admiringly.

NINE

The arrival of Nefret's second letter—or letters—brought to my attention a difficulty I had, of course, already considered. After food and several cups of coffee had revived Emerson somewhat, I handed him what I must call the official or overt epistle. His reaction was not what I had expected. A particularly vehement expletive burst from his lips.

Men! I thought to myself. I did not say it, since I have been happily married for many years and intend to remain so. Temperately I inquired, "What was it in that letter that could possibly upset you? Tetisheri's tomb is safe, the children are well and obviously very happy—if one reads between the lines, which I can easily—"

Sounds of altercation in the hall, including a scream from Gargery, interrupted my speech. Sennia must have forgotten to shut Horus in her room. The cursed cat was bound and determined to go with her to school, and since that would have been inadvisable (the Reader will note that I have avoided the temptation to employ the word "cata-strophic"), we had to lock him up until after she had left the house with Gargery. He and the cat had never got on, but mutual dislike had blossomed into open enmity since Gargery had appointed himself Sennia's escort. He ought to have known better than to catch hold of the beast.

The sounds of combat died, and I heard Sennia scolding Horus in her high-pitched voice as she carried him off. I also heard Gargery cursing. I took no notice. Emerson took no notice either; it was a fairly frequent occurrence and he had become accustomed to it. He had also regained control of himself.

"The letter? Oh, the letter. Nothing. It is a—er—fine letter. I could wish that Ramses had been more communicative; neither of them gave any details about their investigations."

"Ramses is not much of a letter writer. I don't believe he is hiding anything, if that is what you suspect."

Emerson said nothing. "Do you suspect him of hiding something?" I demanded.

"No, why the devil should I? What's that?" he added, as I handed him the enclosure—the covert epistle, as one might term it. He glanced through it, and his face lengthened.

"What precisely did you tell her?" he asked.

"Everything. Nefret and I agreed not to hide things from one another. She is quite right, you know. We cannot keep these little disturbances from him indefinitely. He is going to be very annoyed with us, and it isn't fair to Nefret to put her in the position of conspiring with us against him."

"Us? It was your idea to keep these—little disturbances, good Gad!—secret. Have you changed your mind?"

"Would you like more coffee, Emerson?"

"I have been trying to get the coffeepot away from you for several minutes, Peabody."

"I beg your pardon, my dear." I filled his cup.

"Well? Answer my question, if you please."

"I dreamed about Abdullah last night."

This might have struck some as a non sequitur, but Emerson understood, or thought he did. His dour expression became even darker. He is such a thoroughgoing skeptic that he continues to deny the validity of premonitions, dreams, and other "superstitions," as he terms them. I had not told him of my strange sleeping visions of our dear departed reis until the previous year, and although the effort almost choked him he refrained from pouring the ice water of his disbelief on them because he believed the dreams comforted me—as they did. I would always miss Abdullah, who had been very dear to me; to see him again, fit and handsome and strong, in the setting he loved as much as I, was like meeting a living friend. Many of the things he had told me in those dreams had come to pass; he had warned me of danger and consoled me when I was in distress, and I now had a strong if illogical faith in the import of such visions.

Since Emerson could not quite bring himself to ask for details, I proceeded to inform him. "He did not advise me on what course to pursue. I would have asked him if I had had the opportunity, but this was different from the other dreams. The setting was the same—the cliffs behind Deir el Bahri, at sunrise—but this time when I reached the summit he wasn't there waiting for me. I saw him walking away from me, along the path toward the Valley, and called out to him. He stopped and turned, but instead of coming back he raised his arm and gestured me to follow. Then he went on . . . And I woke up."

"Ah," said Emerson. "Hmph. Er—he was looking well, I hope?"

"Oh, yes. Well and happy. He smiled as he waved me on. What do you suppose it meant?"

I had pushed my amiable spouse too far. "The interpretation of dreams is your specialty, Amelia, not mine. What are we going to do about Ramses?"

"Nothing at present. I have a pre—I have a feeling that the business will settle itself."

"How?" Emerson demanded.

"Either he will learn of Asad's death from someone else, or Nefret will break down and tell him. The dear girl learned discretion in a hard school, but in this case we are pushing her too far, and, I suspect, putting something of a strain on their relationship. Their natures are so unalike—her quick temper and openness, and his reticence—"

"You said they were obviously very happy," Emerson protested. "What are you reading between the lines now?"

"It is obvious that they love one another dearly, but that does not prevent them from having differences. I anticipated that they would."

"What sort of differences?" Emerson asked anxiously.

"For one thing, I expect both of them will be

ridiculously overprotective of one another—you know, the way you used to be with me. And Ramses isn't as easy to deal with as you, my dear; he keeps his feelings to himself, and broods instead of bellowing. She will have to give a little, and so will he. It takes awhile to smooth out the wrinkles in a marriage. As you ought to know."

"Hmph," said Emerson. "Well, curse it, I would hate to think we are making it more difficult for them. You were the one who—"

"Recriminations also put a strain on a marriage, so I will not stress the fact that you were in full agreement with me." I went on quickly, before Emerson could recriminate. "Nefret's primary loyalty, after all, is to her husband. As the Scripture says, a married person should cleave only unto—"

"Don't quote the bloo—blooming Bible, Amelia, you know how I hate that."

"Certainly, my dear. Shall we be off, then? We will have to stop work early. You haven't forgotten that the Vandergelts are arriving this afternoon?"

"Today? Oh. I suppose you will want us to meet them at the train station, though I don't see the sense in it, when they will be coming on to us."

"It is a courtesy, my dear. If I had followed my own inclinations, I would have gone to Alexandria to meet them."

Katherine had said she did not want us to go to the trouble of meeting the boat, so I bowed to her wishes; but unbeknownst to Emerson, I had sent Daoud to Alexandria the night before. With the city in such chaos and an invalid in the party, I felt sure his strength and sympathy—for he had the kindest heart in the world—would be welcome. Emerson was bound to complain when he discovered Daoud's absence, so after we had mounted our horses and set out toward Giza, I decided to distract him by tactfully reintroducing a subject I had raised before.

It really was the most logical next step. We had worked our way down the row of large mastabas parallel to the south face of the Great Pyramid, except for the one we were presently excavating. A pedant might have claimed we had not the right to proceed farther in any direction, since it was this part of his concession Herr Junker had asked us to take over. He had not set any limits, however, and how were we to consult his wishes when he was officially an enemy, cut off from us by the cruel laws of war? As for permission from the Antiquities Department, I did not see how they could possibly object to our extending our work, so long as we did not intrude on the areas given to Mr. Reisner. He had the lion's share of the cemetery as it was.

My conscience being entirely at ease on this point, I saw no reason why I should not investigate the southernmost of the three queens' pyramids, which was adjacent to our row of mastabas. It was the most complete of the three, having in addition a small chapel attached to one side. This structure had been a temple of Isis during the late dynasties, several thousand years after the pyramid was constructed.

"However," I remarked to Emerson, "I feel certain that the remains of the queen's original mortuary temple lie under the later one, since all pyramids had such temples, and that is the location—"

"Peabody," said my husband. "Do you suppose I require to have the architecture of the pyramid complex explained to me?"

It was a fine, clear day, with only a little wind, and although the hour was still early, there were a good many people on the road, some on foot, some employing various means of transportation. We passed an object that looked like a pile of perambulating green vegetation: a donkey, all but his four patiently plodding legs hidden by the load. A motorcar filled with tourists, their veils flapping, passed us. Emerson waited until the cloud of dust raised by its passage had subsided before he continued his complaint. "You are attempting to distract me from the greater provocation by supplying a lesser. I will not be provoked, Peabody."

"But you love temples, Emerson."

"The word is inappropriate in that context!" Emerson shouted. "I do not 'love' inanimate objects. I love you and—"

"That is very kind, Emerson, but you need not broadcast your feelings to the entire world."

"Hmph," said Emerson. His teeth shone white in the handsome brown of his countenance. It might have been a smile . . . "I see what you are up to, Peabody. There may be some interesting problems of stratification if there are, as one may reasonably expect, the remains of different temples of different periods on that spot—"

"And no one is better than you at unraveling such complications."

"Flattery has no effect on me, my dear," said Emerson, looking pleased. "You want me to excavate the temple so that you can poke around inside the confounded pyramid."

"Of course."

"Well, I suppose we might have a look. At the temple ruins," Emerson added hastily. "Not the interior. At least not today."

"Bokra?" The Arabic word for tomorrow is frequently heard in Egypt. It is always tomorrow, not today, that an order can be carried out.

Emerson acknowledged my little witticism with a grimace and an excuse. "The Vandergelts will be here."

"Life is getting a bit complicated," I agreed. "I am vexed we have heard nothing from Mr. Russell or the enigmatic Mr. Smith."

"That isn't his name. His name is—"

"I know what his name is, Emerson. I prefer Smith. It is shorter and not so silly."

Emerson opened his mouth, closed it, shook his head, and remarked, "Have it your own way, Peabody. You always do. Your point is well taken, however. If the information we want from the police is not forthcoming, we will have to extract it by guile or force. But not today. And probably not bokra."

When the little party descended from the train in Cairo, I was glad I had had the foresight to send Daoud to meet them. If the others had not been with him I would never have recognized Bertie. I do not suppose I had encountered him more than half a dozen times over the years, but I had liked what I saw of him. Though he was more interested in sport than in scholarship, he was a cheerful, considerate young chap, utterly devoted to his mother and obviously fond of his stepfather. Of medium height and sturdy frame, he had always been the picture of health, his cheeks ruddy and his hazel eyes clear. Now . . . it was an old man who leaned against Daoud's supporting arm. Gray streaked his brown hair, his wandering eyes were dull, his cheeks sunken. I heard a muffled oath from Emerson and forced my lips into a smile as I hastened to embrace Katherine and Cyrus.

It did not take me long to decide what should be done, and I proceeded to do it. Leaving Daoud to arrange for the luggage, we got into the motorcar, Katherine and I in the tonneau with Bertie. After I had surrounded him with cushions and covered his knees with a robe, I directed Emerson to proceed. For once I did not have to tell him to drive carefully. He had been as shocked as I at the lad's wasted appearance.

"You will stay with us for a few days," I said to Katherine. "Fatima has your rooms ready and everyone is anxious to be of use. Now, my dear, don't argue, I have it all worked out. Ramses and Nefret are in Luxor just now, so there is plenty of room."

At that, Bertie sat up a little straighter and spoke with the first indication of interest I had seen him display. "Ramses isn't here? I had looked forward to talking with him."

"You will be able to do that very soon," I assured him. "The most important thing now is for you to rest and get your strength back."

He nodded and closed his eyes. His face looked like a death's head, gray skin stretched tightly over the bones.

I took Katherine's hand and gave it a little squeeze. That was all I could do then. She could not talk freely in his presence.

As soon as we reached the house I sent Katherine and Cyrus to their room and put Bertie to bed, ignoring his feeble protests. By the time I finished with him there was some color in his face—primarily embarrassment and wounded masculine pride. I considered this a hopeful sign; he had enough energy, at least, to resent me! I made him drink a quantity of water and pointed out the little bouquet, an indiscriminate mixture of marigolds and weeds, that Sennia had arranged in a glass on his table. That brought a faint smile, and before I left the room I had the satisfaction of seeing his eyes close.

Katherine and Cyrus were in the drawing room with Emerson. "How is he?" Katherine asked at once.

"Sleeping." I took a chair and accepted a glass of whiskey from Emerson. "The wounds appear to have healed nicely and although his breathing is still short, I believe it is a matter of weakness and lack of exercise rather than permanent injury to his lungs. However, if you feel we ought to have a doctor look at him . . ."

"He wouldn't accept that," Katherine said wearily. "He is bitterly resentful of the entire medical profession. I cannot imagine how you managed to examine him."

"Ah, well, I have had a good deal of practice overcoming the objections of injured and recalcitrant male individuals," I said, glancing at Emerson. "Which reminds me . . . why is he so anxious to talk with Ramses? They got on well enough, but were never close friends."

"Can't you guess?" Cyrus demanded. His long countenance had been lined and weather-beaten ever since I had known him, for seasons under the hot Egyptian sun has that effect on fair-skinned people. Some of the lines were deeper now. Bertie was the only son he would ever have, and he had always been proud of the boy, his only regret being that Bertie did not share his passion for Egyptology. "He heard a lot from Anna last year about Ramses's objections to the war," Cyrus continued. "He has a new sympathy for that point of view."

"Yes, of course. Well, we will build up his strength and improve his spirits."

"If anybody can do that, it's you," Cyrus said, smiling at me.

"Quite right," said Emerson. "She never lets up until you do what she wants."

Katherine laughed. It was almost her old laugh, and her drawn face had brightened. "I feel happier and more optimistic already. It is his mental state that worries me most, Amelia. He won't talk to me about his experiences at the front, and he hasn't said much even to Cyrus. He is bitter and angry, and he has no interest in anything. In living, even, I think."

Her voice broke. His handsome face concerned, Emerson immediately poured her a whiskey and soda. Knowing that sympathy would cause her to break down completely, I said briskly, "We will find an interest for him. I have several ideas. On the whole, I believe it would be advisable for you to go on to Luxor as soon as possible. *The Valley of the Kings* is, of course, ready for you, but in my opinion the long, lazy voyage would be inadvisable. He needs to be stirred up mentally. He indicated some wish to talk with Ramses. That would be good for him, I think. Nefret is a qualified physician and can watch over his physical health. Yes. That is unquestionably the wisest course. A day or two of rest, then the train to Luxor. We will telegraph ahead, you to your majordomo at the Castle, and I to Ramses, informing them of your plans."

I leaned back and raised my glass in salute. "So that is settled. Drink your whiskey, Katherine. I know you seldom touch spirits, but it will do you good. Cheers!"

With unusual tact, Emerson waited until we had retired to dress for dinner before he expressed his opinion. "'Pon my word, Amelia, that was extraordinarily high-handed, even for you."

"They agreed, didn't they?" I removed my frock and hung it up. "Katherine appeared to be in a much more cheerful frame of mind."

"Both of them would walk off the edge of a cliff if you proposed it," Emerson muttered. "Do you want to bathe first, or shall I?"

"I haven't time for a bath." I poured water into the washbasin and began my ablutions. "I will just freshen up a bit and then see if Bertie is fit enough to dress and come down for dinner. It would be good for him, in my—"

The breath went out of me as Emerson wrapped his arms round my waist and squeezed. "Your opinion! By Gad, Peabody, if you ever failed to give your opinion on any subject whatever, I would have you put in hospital."

After a few brief exchanges of affection—for, as I reminded him, we must not keep our guests waiting—we resumed the activities Emerson's impetuous embrace had interrupted, and I responded to his remark.

"My reasons for suggesting they go on to Luxor are unarguable, Emerson, but there is an additional reason I could not mention to them. We cannot proceed with our investigation of Asad's death while they are with us. Cyrus would insist on taking a hand, and that might be dangerous."

"He is already suspicious. He took me aside before we came up and asked how often we had been attacked since we arrived."

"He was just making a little joke, Emerson. He cannot know about the body in the mastaba, and if we get them away within the next few days, there is little chance of his finding out. I warned Daoud and Fatima and Selim not to speak of it, and told

Gargery I would send him back to England on the first boat if he said a word."

"You seem to have thought of everything."

"I believe I have. The only remaining problem is to find a new interest for Bertie."

"You haven't solved that little difficulty yet? Good Gad, Peabody, what is wrong with you?"

I turned. Emerson had removed boots, stockings, and shirt. Meeting his speculative eye, I said, "I have an idea or two. Do hurry, Emerson."

"We ought to leave the bath chamber free for our guests," said Emerson, grinning. "Will you share the washbasin, my dear?"

After I had dressed I hurried to Bertie's room, leaving Emerson looking for a clean shirt in every drawer but the one in which they were always kept. The door was ajar; as I approached I heard a small clear voice.

"So the brave princess filled a saucer with beer and waited, while the prince slept; and soon the snake crept out from under the bed and started to bite the prince, but when it saw the beer it drank it and was drunk, and then the brave princess took her knife and cut its head off."

"That *was* brave of her," said Bertie.

I opened the door and went in. Sennia had dragged an armchair close to the bed and was sitting on the very edge of the seat so as not to crush her ruffles. She was wearing her best frock, of embroidered white dimity with a pink satin sash and matching pink hairbow. Horus was stretched out across the foot of the bed, forcing Bertie to pull his knees up, but he appeared fairly benevolent—for Horus. "I am telling him a story," Sennia explained.

I tried to look severe—for I had not given Sennia permission to join us that evening, or to visit the invalid—but when I saw the smile on Bertie's face I decided to let the little minx off the scolding she deserved. She knew she had won; giving me a smug grin, she added, "I washed his face too."

Her son's laughter was the first sound Katherine heard when she came along the hall. As she told me later, she had not heard him laugh for weeks. Sennia was in her element: a sick person to be fussed over and an attentive audience. At her invitation Katherine sat down to listen to the rest of the story. Before long, Emerson and Cyrus had joined us, and Fatima had taken it upon herself to bring the decanters and glasses and plates of sandwiches, and glasses of lemon water for Bertie and Sennia, and everyone was talking at once. Bertie declared he had never heard such an interesting story.

"It was 'The Doomed Prince,'" Sennia explained to Emerson and Cyrus, who had come in at the end. "The one Aunt Amelia translated. She translated lots of other stories. I will tell them too, if you want."

"Another time," I said firmly.

"One story a day, like Scheherazade," Bertie suggested.

She liked that idea, but was quick to point out that Scheherazade had left off in the middle of her stories—"so the Sultan wouldn't chop her head off next morning"—so perhaps she should start another one.

"Bertie is not going to chop your head off," I said. "And it is time you went up to the nursery for supper. Say good night—and take Horus with you."

She gave Bertie a kiss, which he returned. There was no need to carry Horus away; he jumped down off the bed and followed her, snarling at Cyrus as he passed him.

We chatted for a while longer, while Fatima bustled about clearing away the plates and glasses, and then left Bertie to rest.

"He has had quite enough excitement for one evening," I explained, as Katherine and I went arm in arm along the corridor. "Sennia is getting to be as Machiavellian as Ramses used to be. She knew that if she asked permission to visit Bertie I would say no, so she simply neglected to ask."

"She did him so much good, though," Katherine said. "Perhaps she could be that new interest he needs just now."

"I think not. We will administer small doses of Sennia for a few days, but she will wear him out if we let her. An individual must be in excellent physical condition to deal with a small energetic child."

"So you still recommend our going on to Luxor immediately?" Cyrus inquired.

"My opinion on that matter is unchanged."

Emerson gave me a quizzical look but remained silent. He knew, as did I, that it was imperative to get our friends away from Cairo. They would be safe in Luxor. Everything was quiet there.

The man *was* his uncle. Sethos, the Master Criminal, the War Office's most valued secret agent, his mother's ardent admirer, his father's deadliest enemy—and illegitimate half-brother. They had learned that astonishing bit of information only the previous winter, and Ramses still hadn't fully adjusted to the idea. Even more unbelievable was the fact that the man he had last seen on a stretcher bleeding from a bullet hole through the lung was still alive. He had attacked a man who was not only old enough to be his father, but who had suffered a near-fatal injury less than a year ago—and he'd had to use several of his "filthier" tricks to come out ahead. He caught Nefret's cold blue stare, and wondered whether an apology was in order, and if so, to which of them it ought to be addressed.

"You promised you wouldn't hurt him," she said accusingly.

The bloody wad of cloth Sethos was holding to his nose was her handkerchief. He lowered it and sniffed experimentally. The bleeding had stopped.

"I hurt him first," he pointed out, with visible satisfaction. "My apologies, Ramses. One reacts instinctively, as you know. May I sit up now, Nefret? I hope you don't mind the familiarity. It's all in the family, after all."

She had inspected him from head to toe to make sure a bloody nose was his only injury. He'd enjoyed it too, flinching theatrically when she touched one spot or the other and then bravely denying it hurt. Ramses rubbed his aching wrist and winced. There was no reaction from Nefret. He decided he would be damned if he would apologize.

"So what are we to call you?" he demanded. "'Uncle Sethos' doesn't sit trippingly on the tongue."

"Never mind the Uncle," the other man said with a grimace. "It's rather late to acknowledge a relationship of that sort. Sethos will do. I haven't used my real name for so long, I wouldn't respond to it."

He had declined Nefret's invitation to return with them to the dahabeeyah. Now he sat up, crossed his legs, and, with a courtly gesture, offered them a seat on the coffin. It *was* a coffin. Yet the smell of wood shavings and varnish gave the room a homely feel, and Nefret had placed the torch so they could see one another.

Ramses stared. He had seen Sethos on several occasions in various disguises—an elderly American lady, a priest, an effete young aristocrat, and, most recently, a Scottish engineer with red hair— but this was the first time he had been able to study the man's actual features. He was wearing native dress, but his head and feet were bare. At the moment his hair was black, which didn't signify much, but at least Ramses knew it was his own, thick and slightly waving. His eyes—what the hell color were they? An ambiguous shade between gray and brown, with a hint of green, according to Ramses's mother, who had been in closer contact with Sethos than anyone else in the family. Ramses couldn't tell, the light wasn't strong enough. He had peeled off the loosened beard and attached mustache. Chin, jaw, and mouth were undistorted, and since this was to have been a quick raid under cover of darkness, he hadn't bothered to stain his square white teeth. The nose was au naturel too, now that Nefret had removed the squashed lump of putty. The contours of that nose were strangely familiar.

Sethos was well aware of his intent scrutiny. With an amused smile, he said, "Do you have a cigarette? The trouble with these garments is that they are limited as to pockets."

Wordlessly Ramses offered the tin and a packet of matches.

"Be careful with those matches," Nefret said. "You don't want to start a fire."

Sethos blew a perfect smoke ring. "Is she always this high-handed?"

"No worse than Mother," Ramses said.

Sethos turned to look at the portrait. "Clever of you to use that to lure me out of hiding. Nothing else would have done it. I've taken considerable pains to avoid you. Please don't tell me you went to all this trouble to get me to return Queen Tiy's jewelry. I won't, and that's flat."

"I didn't suppose you would," Ramses said. "You're back in business, then?"

"I never left it. My recent activities on behalf of a government that rewards its servants rather poorly did not interfere with the practice of my principal profession."

"Such as the time you relieved Ibn-Rashid of his diamonds?"

"How do you know about that?"

He sounded surprised and a little angry. Pleased to have cracked that bland facade, Ramses was tempted to keep him in suspense, but time was passing and they had a good many things to discuss.

"Margaret Minton is in Cairo. She told Mother what really happened in Hayil. She's not told anyone else."

"Ah." Sethos took his time about selecting and lighting another cigarette. "Why?"

"Why did she tell Mother? One can only suppose—"

"That she realized Mother was the woman you had mistaken her for, and she wanted to find out what had happened to you," Nefret said impatiently. "Don't be disingenuous. You deliberately set out to make her fall romantically in love with you."

"Of course. I wasn't sure I had succeeded, though. Women are so unpredictable. Well, well. What's she after now?"

"Not you," Nefret snapped. "Mother told her you were dead."

"I hope that's all she told her." His faint smile had vanished. "It wouldn't do me any good if a journalist found out about my noble sacrifices on behalf of dear old England."

"She told Minton you were a thief and a swindler," Nefret said bluntly.

"Ah."

Seeing his downcast eyes and tight lips, Ramses was conscious of an unexpected feeling of sympathy. He knew what it was like to have people misjudge you and despise you because of it. Sethos *was* a thief and a swindler, but Ramses didn't doubt that his business in Hayil had been on behalf of the

War Office. He'd have left the Emir's jewels untouched if he hadn't been interrupted while he was examining that devious young man's private correspondence, and if he had been as cold-blooded and pragmatic as he pretended to be he would have ignored Margaret's call for help.

"One more person for me to avoid," said his uncle, so coolly that Ramses wondered if he had imagined that fleeting expression of regret. "I appreciate your telling me. Was that why you arranged this meeting?"

"Not entirely," Ramses said. "There's been a leak. Wardani's people know I took his place last winter. At least one of them is free. We had a brief encounter in an alley in Cairo not long ago."

"Who?"

"Asad. He was one of Wardani's lieutenants."

"I know who he was. That explains it."

"Explains what?" Ramses demanded.

"Why you are in Luxor. Mama and Papa and your loving wife thought you'd be safer here."

"Damn it," Ramses began, caught himself, and started again. "I had another reason for wanting to see you. I never got the chance to thank you—"

"Let's not descend into sentimentality, please. I didn't do it for you."

"You tricked the others into leaving before they finished me off," Ramses said, sticking doggedly to the point. "You didn't take that risk for Mother; you didn't even know she was there."

"Ah, but your death would have distressed the dear woman. I got my thanks," he added, with a smile that certainly would have driven Emerson to violence. "When she kissed me. It was quite a touching scene, I believe."

"She thought you were dying. We all thought so."

"As you see, I was not obliging enough to finish the process. How did you know I was still alive and in Luxor?"

"I wasn't certain," Ramses admitted. "But those artistic symbols you carved outside various tombs were new, and the incident in the West Valley had your trademark. It was well planned."

"Good of you to say so. If that's all—"

"No, it isn't all. How many people are aware of the fact that you are still alive?"

The other man's face didn't change. There was a brief pause before he replied. "Aside from Kitchener and General Maxwell—and you? What about your father?"

"He suspects, I think. Mother doesn't."

"Are you going to tell them?"

"That depends," Ramses said, savoring a brief—and, as he was soon to discover, illusory—feeling of power. "Would you prefer that I didn't tell them?"

"Yes, I would. But if you are thinking of using that threat to blackmail me into doing something I don't want to do, dismiss the idea. I don't care that much. It's just that my life would be a good deal simpler without Amelia trailing me all over Luxor trying to catch me and reform me. Can you imagine the trouble she'd get herself into?"

Ramses could. Damn the man. Sethos had seen the trap and stepped neatly over it.

"Get back to the point," he said harshly.

"Point? Oh, you mean is there anyone out for my blood at the moment?" He spoke slowly, thinking aloud. "When they carted me away that night, the only people who knew I was working for the department thought I was dying. The doctor and the nurses were told that I'd been an innocent bystander in an encounter between the police and a group of revolutionaries. Your repellent cousin is dead. The only other people who were there that night were Sahin Bey and Sidi Ahmed; they accepted me as one of theirs, and were long gone before the dramatic denouement. I can't see how anyone could have made the connection. There's even a neat little RIP after my name in the files of the department."

"I thought you should be warned," Ramses said.

"Your concern touches me deeply." Sethos's eyes narrowed, fine lines fanning out from their corners. "Did you think I was the one who betrayed you to Wardani's people?"

The suspicion had never occurred to Ramses—until that moment. His silence provoked Sethos into heated speech. "For God's sake, the two men who knew your real identity and the role you'd been playing were the head of the Turkish secret service and the chief of the Senussi! There are literally dozens of people, not counting the bloody Germans, who now have that information. Why suspect me?"

"The idea had never entered my mind," Ramses said.

"Ah." The quick flash of anger had passed. Sethos lit another cigarette and pondered for a few moments before he went on. "You haven't been fool enough to take on another assignment, I hope?"

Ramses shook his head.

"Stick to that. Your cover was blown sky-high, my lad, and they'll be on the lookout for you. If you will take my advice, you'll lie low and concentrate on excavation."

"I've every intention of doing so. What about you?"

"The same." His uncle gave him a wolfish smile. "I came to the conclusion that espionage has very little to recommend it. The pay is poor and few people live to collect the pension, such as it is. Anyhow, the present situation in Egypt is irresistible. There's no one to stop me from doing whatever I like."

"No?"

His uncle sighed. "You mean to try, I suppose. The young are so idealistic. All right, then, you force me to revise my plans. There are plenty of other sites in Egypt. Enjoy your holiday."

He rose to his feet and returned Ramses's cigarettes to him. "Good night. I can't tell you how much I've enjoyed this evening."

"Oh, no, you don't," Ramses said. "Not until you've answered a few more questions."

"I've told you everything you need to know. Look after him, Nefret. He's not very good at looking after himself, and Amelia would be upset if he came to harm. Which reminds me—you haven't heard anything more about the body she found at Giza, have you?"

"Body?" Ramses stiffened. "What body?"

"You didn't know? It was in the newspapers. The story didn't mention his name, but it just now occurred to me that it might be . . ." He peered inquiringly at them. "Oh, dear, I hope I haven't spoken out of turn. Perhaps it was just one of those jolly little fortuitous corpses Amelia keeps encountering. Good night again."

He slid neatly out the window, feet first. Ramses turned very slowly and looked at his wife. She met his gaze squarely, but her face was flushed.

"You said you had misplaced Mother's letter," he said. "All the charming chatter—and charming attentions—were designed to keep me from insisting upon reading it."

The flush deepened. "She was afraid you'd see the story in the newspaper."

"And you made certain I didn't see a newspaper."

"I didn't want you to—"

"I don't have to ask who it was, do I?" He took her by the shoulders. "You wouldn't have gone to such lengths to keep the truth from me if the body had been that of a stranger. The newspapers might not know his identity, but Mother must; she always does! It was Asad, wasn't it? Murder or suicide?"

"Murder."

She had told him the truth because she knew the alternative would have been even worse. It didn't lessen his sense of guilt. He should have anticipated the danger and taken steps to prevent it.

"They, whoever they were, put the body where she and Father would find it," he said. "Why? No, don't tell me, the answer is obvious."

"It isn't at all obvious. Strewing corpses in their path is one sure way to provoke Father and Mother."

"Not Father, not Mother. Me. He was my friend. So you all took it upon yourselves to keep me in the dark? You expected I'd dash off to Cairo and go after his killer, and perhaps hurt my poor little self?"

"Don't you dare talk that way to me!" She slipped out of his grasp and faced him, breathing hard. "We did it for your own good!"

What with one thing and another, the past hour had tried Ramses to the limit. That infuriating, condescending comment finished the job. He reached for her. If she had protested, or apologized, or even looked at him reproachfully, he'd have let her go at once, but she was as angry as he was; she squirmed and twisted and swore, and in pure self-defense he caught her in a grip he had used once before, pinning her flailing arms to her sides and holding her close. From that point on, self-defense wasn't a consideration. He put his hand on her cheek and forced her head back against his shoulder.

It might have been the softness of her skin under his hand, or the slight sound she made, hardly more than a squeak of breath. He couldn't believe what he had just done. Horrified and repentant, he relaxed his hold and started to speak.

"If you apologize I'll kill you," Nefret whispered. Her arms went around his neck.

When they left the shop a little later there was only one thing on both their minds, and the few words they exchanged that night had nothing to do with Sethos or corpses. Ramses's last coherent thought, before exhaustion overcame him, was that she had been right when she told him he didn't understand women. Obviously he had a lot to learn even about his own wife.

Nefret was in one of her sunniest moods next morning. He woke to hear her clear voice singing little snatches of her favorite melodies—the more saccharine bits from romantic operettas—as she moved around the room. "'When you're away dear, How dreary the lonesome hours . . . Never again let us part, dear, I die without you, mine own! Hold me against your—'"

The high note wobbled. "Wrong key," Ramses said with a laugh. "You're a mezzo, not a coloratura."

"And you are very lazy." She leaned over him and sang it again, straight into his face. "'Hold me against your heart!' But not now. Mohammed is heating your bathwater."

When he came up she was already at the table, and Nasir was nowhere in sight. "I told him we didn't need him," she explained. "We've a lot to talk about."

"Yes." He waited until she had filled his cup and put the pot down. Then he took her hand in his. "Nefret, I—"

"I told you not to apologize."

"No. I mean, yes, you did. But—"

"I've been wanting you to do that for months." The dimple in her cheek deepened. "You're adorable when you're in a temper."

"I suppose I deserved that," Ramses said ruefully. "But I don't understand why—"

"You've been treating me as if I were someone you didn't know very well and were afraid of offending," Nefret said indignantly. "Do you realize that was the first real, loud, honest-to-goodness argument we've had since we were married?"

"An argument's one thing, and if that's what you want I'll do my best to cooperate from now on. But handling you like that—"

"Well, I wouldn't want you to crrrush me in your arms and overpower me every day of the week! But now and then it makes for an interesting change."

"Oh." Still mildly confused but infinitely relieved, he said hopefully, "I suppose if it weren't spontaneous it wouldn't be the same? I mean, you couldn't drop me a hint when you—"

"Absolutely not." A little gurgle of amusement escaped her lips. "You might give me my hand back; I need it to pour. Drink your coffee and I'll tell you the whole story."

It was a lurid story; certain of the details must have come directly from his mother's letter, they had the ring of her prose. The police had found nothing that would lead them to the killer, but the identification of the body was certain.

"The name wasn't in the newspaper story," Nefret added. "You can thank Mr. Russell for that."

"I'm surprised the newspapers picked it up. An anonymous Egyptian—"

"Discovered in an ancient tomb by a lady who has a certain notoriety," Nefret finished. "Russell couldn't keep that information from the press, most of the gaffirs at Giza were on the scene at the time. And there is a journalist presently in Cairo who once specialized in the extraordinary adventures of the Emerson family."

"Damnation, that's right. Miss Minton."

"Mother and Father make wonderful copy," Nefret said with a smile. "With press censorship so strict, there's not much in the way of real news. One can hardly blame the woman for exploiting this."

"I suppose not. Were there any references to curses?"

"Several." Nefret hesitated, but only briefly. "There was something else in her letter I didn't tell you about. Miss Minton may be on her way here."

"I am dense, amn't I? That's why you didn't want to dine at the hotel, you were afraid we'd run into her. Is there any other little detail you've neglected to mention? Assault, attempted abduction?"

"Well . . ."

"Good God!" He jumped to his feet. "Who? When? Why the hell didn't you—"

"I'm sorry," Nefret whimpered. "She swore me to secrecy."

Ramses got a grip on himself. "You don't whimper convincingly, Nefret. You're enjoying this, aren't you?"

"No." The corners of her mouth drooped. "I've hated keeping things from you. I almost told you the other day, when you were being so sweet and reasonable and I was snapping at you because I felt guilty. Sit down and I'll tell you about it. She wasn't much hurt."

"Mother? Of course, it would be Mother."

As she went on with the story, curiosity replaced his outrage. He contented himself with a few mild damns before remarking, "So if Father is right, Asad was already dead when the attack on him and Mother took place. It doesn't make sense. Are you sure that's everything?"

"Well . . ."

"I can't stand much more of this," Ramses remarked conversationally.

"It's nothing serious, honestly. At least I hope not. Our Mr. Smith is in Cairo, ostensibly attached to the Department of Public Works. That's not his real name, of course; it's something hyphenated and unpronounceable. Mother tracked him down through her usual sources—tea at Shepheard's and rude gossip."

"She's been a busy little creature, hasn't she?" He ran distracted fingers through his hair. "I might have known she and Father were just waiting to be rid of me before they went on the offensive. What did she do to Smith, threaten to thrash him with her parasol if he didn't leave me alone?"

"Well . . ."

Ramses glared at her.

"I'm sorry," Nefret gurgled. "I suppose it isn't funny, but if you could see your face . . . That's more or less what she did, I guess. Ramses, she went to the Turf Club—by herself—and ordered Lord Edward to bring his friend to meet her there. Heaven only knows what she threatened, but it was enough to bring Smith promptly to heel. He admitted he had known of Asad's escape, but hadn't bothered to inform us because—how did he put it?—'we aren't worried about that ineffectual bunch of revolutionaries.' Something like that." Another irrepressible gurgle of laughter escaped her. "Can't you see her sitting in the lounge, surrounded by all those scandalized men, wearing her second-best hat and genteelly sipping her whiskey?"

It *was* funny, if one didn't happen to be related to the lady in the second-best hat. "She's unbelievable," Ramses muttered. "Even I don't believe in her, and I've known her for over twenty years. Well, I'm not surprised 'Smith' is in Cairo. We knew he was with the Department and that his new assignment had something to do with Egypt. There is no reason to suppose he has any evil designs on me. I wish to God Mother would stop treating me like a child!"

"Darling, you have every right to be angry," Nefret said soberly. "I'll never do it again, I promise."

"Perhaps it's as well you did." He pushed his plate away and lit a cigarette. "In the heat of the moment I might have done something ineffectual and idiotic like catching the first train to Cairo. Then we'd have missed that charming family reunion."

Nefret got up and looked over the side. "There's Jamil with the horses. Where are we going today? Gurneh?"

"You know better than that."

She turned, leaning against the rail. The morning breeze lifted the loose hair on her forehead. Her face was grave. "I know what you've got in mind, anyhow, but I don't agree. Mother claims she can recognize him, whatever disguise he may assume, but I certainly couldn't. He could be anywhere; he could be anyone!"

"Well then, what the hell do you suggest we do? Let him loot every tomb in Luxor? Dash wildly up and down the west bank, trying to guard all of them at once?"

"He said he was leaving Luxor."

"You didn't believe him, did you? For God's sake, Nefret!"

Instead of shouting back, she gave him a provoking grin. "My, my, that's twice in twenty-four hours. When you're angry, you are absolutely—"

"Adorable. Right. I wasn't angry with you."

"You were angry with him. You still are. Why?"

"He manipulated both of us as if we were puppets," Ramses said between his teeth. "He had you feeling sorry for him, and me feeling guilty, and he directed every word of that conversation, do you realize that? He told us what he wanted us to know and we told him what he wanted to know! He waited until the end to drop his little bombshell so he could make a quick exit before we had the chance to ask any more questions. He's hiding something, and I'll be damned if I'm going to let him get away with it."

"He really got under your skin, didn't he?"

"Ever since I can remember he's been the enemy, the one man who defeated even Father, time after time. Coming to grips with him became my greatest ambition. And now—" He realized he was gripping the rail so tightly his fingers ached. "Now he's a bloody hero, and my uncle! How can I set the police on his trail? If I tell Father we've encountered him, Father will want to go after him himself, and Mother will find out, she always does, and he was absolutely right about that, damn him, she'd poke her nose into every trouble spot in Luxor!"

Nefret slipped her arm through his and leaned her head against his shoulder. "So we're back to the old habit of keeping things from one another," she said soberly.

"You're a fine one to talk."

"I said I was sorry!"

"I'm just being adorable."

Nefret chuckled. "Well done. If you keep practicing you'll soon be able to shout me down when I'm horrid to you. No, but seriously, darling, why not tell the parents? If anyone can influence Sethos, it's Mother."

"That's what I'm afraid of." He turned his head and found her mouth in a convenient location, so he took advantage of it. "You may be right, but let's see if we can find him before we decide. And if I get my hands on him again I'll tie him down until he's answered all my questions! How did he know about Queen Tiy's jewelry? What else is he after? Who is working for him? We've got to stop him somehow, and if we can do it before Mother gets involved, we'll save ourselves a lot of grief."

Nefret didn't argue. She knew that look—mouth set, eyes hooded—but she wondered whether Ramses understood his own motives for pursuing a search that was almost certainly doomed to failure. Really, men could be so obtuse at times. After having come up with the brilliant idea of using his mother's portrait to attract Sethos, he was now rejecting the logical next step—that of using his mother in person. His feelings about his uncle were ambivalent, a bewildering mixture of admiration, resentment, and unwilling fascination. She felt the same, but in her case the resentment was almost entirely secondhand. For Ramses, and his father, it must still rankle—the many times Sethos had slipped through their fingers, his unrepentant devotion to his brother's wife.

And when you came to think about it, using one's mother as bait to catch a thief wasn't very nice.

Preceding her husband down the stairs to the lower deck, she told herself that though it might be a waste of time to search for a man so elusive and so determined to avoid them, at least it wouldn't be dangerous. Neither of them had anything to fear from Sethos.

TEN

FROM MANUSCRIPT H (CONTINUED)

They had neglected to inform Jamil there might be a change in their plans for that day. Jumana was with him, and she looked so crestfallen when Ramses explained that they wouldn't need her that Nefret said impulsively, "Why can't she come with us?"

"She can't come to the dealers with us," Ramses said. "It will be difficult enough bullying them into giving away useful information without a wide-eyed female child present."

Nefret had to admit he was right. She and her mother-in-law had a unique status, but Jumana would be treated like any other Egyptian female. She was also a member of a family with connections all over Gurneh and Luxor, some of them legal, some not. Abdullah's uncle had accrued a sizable fortune by methods no one was rude enough to inquire into. The dealers wouldn't speak freely in front of her. But the wide, imploring eyes were difficult to resist.

"Jamil can take us across the river, and she can stay with him."

Jamil gave Nefret an outraged look. He probably had plans of his own, involving a long leisurely gossip with friends in the glamorous coffee shops of Luxor. She really couldn't blame him for not wanting his sister trailing along.

"Then she might visit the school. You can talk with your teachers, Jumana, and tell them what you are doing."

"I will do that, yes, I will! They will be very proud of me!"

I must teach that child not to shout, Nefret thought.

Once they reached the other side of the river, Jamil tied the boat and sat down to chat with the other boatmen. As she and Ramses walked toward Luxor Temple, Nefret saw that Jumana had also stopped to talk with several girls of about her own age. It was no wonder news spread so fast. Gossip was one of the chief amusements in a semiliterate society where other means of entertainment were lacking. This was brought home to her a few minutes later, when a voice hailed them and they saw one of the clerks from the telegraph office trotting toward them.

"It came just now," he explained, handing Ramses the telegram. "I was about to send a man to bring it to you when I heard you were in Luxor."

Ramses handed over the expected baksheesh and ripped open the envelope. He let out a breath of relief and handed the paper to Nefret. "The Vandergelts will be arriving in Luxor on Sunday."

"You expected bad news?"

"One always does, doesn't one?"

"Telegrams are so damned uninformative," Nefret murmured, rereading the brief message. "If this isn't just like Mother! She doesn't say why they are coming by train instead of sailing, but wastes four words on 'Find Bertie new interest.' What on earth do you suppose that means?"

"The phrase 'shell-shocked' comes to mind."

"Yes, of course." Nefret's smile faded. "Poor boy."

"It's not really such good news," Ramses went on. "With Sethos on the loose they could be jumping from the frying pan into the fire."

"Shall we try to put them off?"

"I don't suppose there's any danger to them, really . . ." He stroked his chin, in unconscious imitation of his father, and his frown of concentration smoothed out into a smile. "However, I think I'll wire Mother. Let's go to the telegraph office."

"You're going to tell her about Sethos?"

"No."

He wrote out the telegram and then showed it to her.

"All is discovered. Kindly refrain from conspiring with my wife against me."

Nefret laughed, but shook her head. "Now you're the one putting me in an impossible situation."

"I am not. Your first loyalty is to me. It's in the Bible, as Mother would say."

The first shop they visited was near the Luxor Temple, conveniently located to catch the tourist trade. The proprietor greeted them with a show of surprise that didn't fool either of them, sent one of his sons out for coffee, and began complaining. The thrice-cursed war had ruined his business. How could an honest man make a living when so few tourists came?

"That is why *we* came to you," Ramses said. "Your honesty is well known, and since there are no tourists, you must have many fine antiquities for sale. What have you got to show us?"

After considerable hemming and hawing, Omar finally brought out a small bronze figure of a seated cat wearing a gold earring, and a fragment of carved relief. The latter showed the head and shoulders of a man wearing a short, tightly curled wig.

"Late Twenty-fifth or early Twenty-sixth Dynasty," Ramses murmured, turning it in his hands.

"Very good," Nefret said. "I wish I had your eye."

"Eye be damned. This comes from the chapel of Amenirdis at Medinet Habu. It was in situ last time I saw it. How much damage—"

Nefret cleared her throat warningly, and he controlled his anger, as his father would not have done. There was nothing to be gained by berating dealers like Omar; they wouldn't stop cooperating with the local thieves, but they would stop showing him the objects.

"Who was responsible for the robbery of Legrain Effendi's storage magazines?" he asked abruptly.

He knew better than to expect a truthful answer but he hoped his sudden question would induce a reaction, however fleeting and faint, that might give him a clue. It did. The other man's face became as hard and blank as a plaster mask, glazed with sudden sweat. He shook his head dumbly.

"No one else will hear of it if you tell us," Ramses persisted. "Do you doubt my word?"

"No." The dealer's eyes rolled from side to side. "But—but I know nothing, Brother of Demons. I have nothing for you. I must—I must close now. It is time for prayer."

It lacked a good quarter of an hour until noon, but Ramses did not argue. Omar barely waited till they were outside before he slammed and bolted the door. The second shop was closed. So was the third. "We may as well give it up for today," Ramses said. "Omar's son warned the others. There is definitely something out of the ordinary going on. The dealers are accustomed to having me come round trying to winkle information out of them, they rather enjoy the game. They wouldn't be so wary unless they had been warned not to talk with us."

"Threatened, perhaps," Nefret said. "He wasn't just wary, he was frightened."

"Yes. Our estimable kinsman is good at terrorizing people. In his heyday there wasn't a dealer in Egypt who would dare cross him." He added feelingly, "Damn him."

"Yes, darling." She took his arm. "It's still early, but we might have lunch—sit on the terrace of the Winter Palace and watch the passing throngs. Sethos may be playing the part of a waiter."

He was not amused. Walking slowly, with his head bent and his hands in his pockets, he said absently, "Whatever you like."

"Or we could go by Abdul Hadi's shop and pick up the portrait. You don't really want a new frame for it, do you?"

"For what? Oh, the portrait. No, I . . ." He came to a dead halt. "Hell and damnation!"

"What's wrong?"

"We left it there." Ramses slammed his fist into his other palm. "How bloody stupid can I get? Come on!"

She had to trot to keep up with him. The midday call to prayer floated down from the mosque of el Guibri, and when Ramses burst into the shop, Abdul Hadi was about to lower his rheumaticky knees onto his prayer mat. For a moment Nefret feared her husband was too overwrought to remember his manners, but she need not have worried.

"I beg your pardon. I came for my mother's picture. It can wait."

The amiable old gentleman looked bewildered. "But—did you not take it? Last night? It was not on the easel this morning. I thought—"

"Never mind," Nefret said quickly. "Malesh. Thank you. Good-bye."

She pulled Ramses out of the shop and closed the door. He turned to look at her. His features were as impassive as granite; but his effort to keep his voice low was not entirely successful. "What are you laughing about?"

"But it is funny," Nefret gurgled. "Instead of fleeing into the night, like a proper crook, he waited coolly outside that window until we . . . until . . . Oh, dear."

"Finished the performance," her husband said

wildly. "He must have found it quite amusing. I seem to remember telling you . . . And then didn't I . . . ?"

"The Savoy's closer than the Winter Palace." She took his arm. "I prescribe a stiff whiskey or a glass of wine."

"I do not need a drink." He stalked along beside her, scowling blackly. "What I need is revenge. Not only for last night, but for a long history of affronts."

"You can't—"

"I don't want to torture him, sweetheart. I want to humiliate him and get the better of him. For once!"

Remembering some of the things they had said—and done—in the belief they were unobserved, Nefret felt a certain sympathy, but she tried to be fair. "He wasn't deliberately playing Peeping Tom. He was only waiting to see whether we'd leave the portrait."

"And now he's got it. How are we going to explain that to Mother?"

They selected a table in the garden of the Savoy and ordered. Bougainvillea spread ruffled arms along the wall behind them, and a sparrow alighted on the table and cocked a bright eye at Nefret. She fed it crumbs from her hand until it suddenly took flight, and she looked up to see Margaret Minton standing beside her.

"May I join you?" she asked.

"How did you find us?" Nefret asked, watching Ramses's face go blank. He rose and held a chair for the journalist.

"The usual methods," Minton said blandly. "Bribery and baksheesh. I paid some of the loafers on the dock to come and tell me if you turned up on the east bank. I've been trailing you all morning—to no avail, I might add. Why were you visiting antiquities dealers? It's common knowledge that the Professor won't buy from them."

"Father won't, but I occasionally do," Ramses said. Nefret saw him brace himself, like a duelist en garde. "One must sometimes sacrifice principle to expediency or lose an important piece to a private collector."

"You weren't surprised to see me. Did Mrs. Emerson tell you I was coming to Luxor?"

"Had you informed her of your plans?"

With a faint smile she acknowledged her second failure to get past his guard, and attacked from a third direction. "Surely she told you about the body she found in the mastaba."

Nefret decided to intervene. She had read the letter and the clipping from the *Gazette*. Ramses had not. Besides, she was tired of fencing.

"Is that why you're here?" she demanded. "If it is, you are on the wrong track. All we know is what Mother told us in her last letter, and that was little enough."

The waiter came with the food they had ordered. Miss Minton waved away the menu he offered her and asked for tea. While he hovered, arranging the dishes to his satisfaction, she glanced round the garden.

"Who is that man?" she asked suddenly. "He's been staring at me ever since I sat down."

He was still staring—a burly man with a heavy, neatly trimmed beard and a bush of curly brown hair—but not at her. Catching Nefret's eye, he stood up and came toward them, smiling and holding out his hand.

"Hello, Nefret. It's wonderful to see you again. I've not met your husband, but of course I've heard of him. May I offer my felicitations to you both?"

Ramses rose and took the extended hand. A soft brown fuzz covered the back; it felt like a cat's fur, but his grip was almost painfully hard. Ramses met it with equal strength, thinking how childishly they were behaving, flexing their muscles to impress a woman.

"Sorry I missed you the other day," the other man went on. Nefret pronounced the formal words of introduction, and Kuentz kissed her hand. Introducing Miss Minton could not be avoided; she was firmly settled in her chair and had no intention of leaving.

"She is a well-known journalist," Ramses added.

"Ah. Then I must be careful what I say!" His booming laugh made heads turn.

"Not unless you've done something you're ashamed of," Miss Minton replied.

"Me? No! Never! To blow up the German House, that was not a shameful thing."

The sentence contained three words that would have aroused any journalist's curiosity. Miss Minton's fingers twitched. "Blow up? German? What's this about?"

"She is wanting to write it all down," Kuentz said with a grin. "See how she crooks her fingers as if they were holding a pen. So you had not heard of our humble effort on behalf of the Allies?"

"We had heard of it," Ramses said. "But no one seemed to know who was responsible."

The journalist turned her hungry gaze on him, and since he saw no reason to conceal the facts, he went on to explain. It might get Miss Minton off on another track.

"The German government built the place a few years ago to serve as headquarters for their archaeologists. Without wishing to denigrate your effort, Kuentz, I can't see that blowing it up did the Allied cause much good."

"It was very ugly," Kuentz said airily. "Too large, too red, too German."

"Hardly sufficient cause for destroying someone else's property," Ramses said.

"It was not the only reason." Kuentz glanced around, like a stage conspirator, and lowered his voice. "Carter and I found out that the place had become a center for the illicit antiquities trade—among other undesirable activities. I say no more, eh?"

"But I'd like to hear more," Miss Minton said eagerly. "Was Mr. Carter involved, then? Who else?"

"I did not say that," Kuentz declared. Ramses had the impression he was quite enjoying himself. "I and I alone was responsible. And now I must return to my labors, I have been too long away."

"Then perhaps you would dine with me this evening. I am staying at the Winter Palace."

"So you will write it all down and then my name will be in your newspaper?"

"I won't print anything without your permission."

Nefret's face twisted into a look of exaggerated incredulity. Kuentz laughed. "So what do I care? A poor hungry archaeologist does not refuse a free meal, especially with a beautiful lady. Thank you, I will come. At eight, yes? And you, my friends the young Emersons, will visit me again at Deir el Medina, where I will show you many things of interest."

He bowed and walked away. Ramses pushed his chair back. "I forgot to ask him about something. Excuse me."

"Was it true?" Miss Minton demanded. "What he said about the German House being a center for dealing in illegal antiquities?"

"It's the first I've heard of it," Nefret said truthfully. Ramses was still talking with Kuentz. Knowing that if they were discussing archaeology he might go on at length, oblivious of the time, Nefret raised her hand to summon the waiter.

"But there has been an increase in such activities this year, hasn't there?"

"I didn't know you were interested in the subject, Miss Minton."

"Didn't you?" There was a note in her voice that made Nefret look up from the coins she was counting out on the table. "Don't tell me you did not read the manuscript Mrs. Emerson took—oh, quite by mistake! I'll wager you talked it over at length, all of you, dissecting my emotions and speculating about my feelings. Perhaps it gave you a good laugh."

Nefret felt her face heating up. At the time, she had not questioned her mother-in-law's bland appropriation (she would never have called it theft) of the document. Yet it was really like stealing someone's private diary and showing it to others. The author had spared herself very little, because she had never meant anyone else to read it; no doubt she had explored every other possible source of information before she consulted a woman whom she knew disliked and mistrusted her.

"No one laughed," she said. It was a rather feeble stab at reassurance and tacit apology, but the other woman nodded in acknowledgment. She was blushing too—and I don't wonder, Nefret thought. I know how I would feel if I had spread my heart out on a sheet of paper and someone else had read it.

"I wouldn't blame you for laughing," Miss Minton murmured. "I wrote it for myself, you know—soon afterward—while the details were still fresh in my mind. I never meant anyone else to see it."

"What made you decide to show it to Mother?"

"Desperation," the other woman said simply. "I don't suppose you can understand, you with your happy marriage to a man who is everything you could ever want, and that close-knit, magnificently eccentric family. I had no lover, no family, no friends. The competition in my business was keen; I didn't feel I had time for such distractions. I was ripe for the plucking, and he . . ." Her wide mouth expanded into a sudden grin. "My dear, he was superb. There wasn't a single false note! Oh, I knew he was putting on a performance, but I didn't care. Something told me that if I didn't find out who he was and what he was really like, I would spend the rest of my life measuring other men against that impossibly romantic image, and having them fail—and hoping against hope that I would meet him again. That's not a very practical program for a woman of my age."

The grin and the glint of self-deprecating humor that brightened her eyes struck a responsive note in Nefret. She wasn't moved to confess all, however.

"I am sorry," she said.

"Did you ever meet him?"

"Sethos?" She hesitated for a moment, trying to anticipate where a truthful answer might lead her, and then decided it could do no harm. "Yes. He unquestionably had a knack for making himself . . . interesting."

"You felt it too?"

Nefret smiled. "Not really. But I was already head over heels about someone else."

"You love him very much, don't you? And he feels the same for you. You are both lucky, Mrs.—" She broke off with a little sound of amused vexation. "It is almost impossible for me to think of anyone else by that name! I don't suppose you would consider calling me Margaret? You may or may not believe me, but I didn't come here to trap you into an indiscretion. I would like us to be friends. And," she added, with another of those wide, rueful smiles, "if either of us is at a disadvantage, it isn't you. You know too many things to my discredit."

Nefret didn't know whether that offer of friendship was genuine, but she knew it would be foolish to reject it.

"Thank you," she said. "Margaret. I had better go and collect my husband. He seems to have gone off with Mr. Kuentz."

He was alone, in fact, just inside the door of the hotel. When he saw her approach he came out, trying not to look as if he had been hiding, and took her arm.

"I thought my absence would give you an excuse to get away," he explained. "What were you going on about so long?"

Nefret repeated the conversation.

"I've nothing against the woman," Ramses said thoughtfully. "I rather admired her. But those questions about illegal antiquities, and her interest in Kuentz's story make me wonder about her real motive for coming here—particularly in view of our recent encounter."

Nefret shook her head decidedly. "She still wants to believe he is alive, but she can't know anything. Unless . . ."

"Unless what?"

"Unless *he* told her."

"The last thing he wants is an infatuated female—and a journalist at that—on his trail," Ramses said.

"Then it's just a forlorn hope," Nefret said softly.

"Stop a minute," Ramses said. "I've had an idea and I don't want to discuss it in front of the kiddies."

The pylons of the Luxor Temple glowed in the afternoon sunlight. Ramses turned to look at them.

He'd never finished copying the reliefs in the Hypostyle Hall. There was so much to do, so many irreplaceable records that were deteriorating daily . . .

Nefret joggled his elbow. "Well? Don't get lost in archaeological speculation, not now."

"Well. Let's suppose that after the initial shock, Minton was canny enough to realize that Mother might have been lying in her teeth."

"Which she was."

"Except for one vital piece of information. My omniscient mama wasn't lying about that, but she was, as we have just learned, dead wrong. Let us also suppose that as a journalist and a member of a 'superior' social class, Minton has access to certain sources of information. And don't ask me what, because I haven't the faintest idea. All I'm saying is that she might have learned something from someone that strengthened that forlorn hope."

"Someone in the War Office, you mean? It's awfully vague," Nefret said dubiously. "So what do you suggest we do?"

"Cultivate the confounded woman. You can do it," he added hastily. "Exchange girlish confidences, and all that."

"Why don't *you* cultivate her? You do look a bit like him, and she clearly enjoyed that fond embrace at Giza."

"Damn it, Nefret, you know that wasn't my idea. Oh. You're joking?"

"Yes." She slipped her arm through his and leaned against him.

"I will defend my honor to the best of my ability," Ramses said. "So we cultivate her. It's worth a try. Searching for Sethos all over Luxor is a waste of time and energy. We need to come up with another scheme to make him come to us."

"He'll be on his guard now—if he hasn't already left."

"I'll believe he's gone when I hear that someone has made off with a pyramid or the temple of Dendera," Ramses muttered. "No, he's still here. The only other thing I can think to do is try to locate his confederates. This is where we miss Selim and Abdullah. They had and have connections with most of the jolly little tomb robbers of Gurneh. I'll see what a few carefully chosen curses will do."

"So we're going to Gurneh?"

"Not today. Do you remember Lansing telling us about the tomb robber Kuentz caught in the act? Kuentz gave me the location. I thought we might have a look at it." He ran long fingers through his hair and added morosely, "Who knows, the fellow may have been considerate enough to leave a footprint or a scrap of paper with Sethos's cryptogram on it."

"We'll have to collect Jumana first."

"Damnation, that's right. I forgot about her."

However, she was waiting when they reached the dock. Jamil was nowhere to be seen. When Ramses asked for him, his sister shrugged slim shoulders. "In the coffee shop, where do you think? I told him to come but he would not. Shall I go now and tell him again?"

"I'll fetch him," Ramses said. The length of his stride and his formidable scowl told Nefret that the unfortunate Jamil was in for a lecture. It wasn't really fair, since they had not told him when they would return, but they would not have had to go searching for Selim or Daoud or any of their other men. Nefret turned to the girl, who was sitting on the edge of the dock. "Did you have something to eat?" she asked.

"Yes. They gave me food at the school."

The brief answer and the downcast eyes were so unlike her that Nefret asked, "Is something wrong?"

"They would not let me have a book!" She raised an indignant face. "I wanted to read about the God's Wives. I would have taken care of it."

Nefret sat down and put her arm round Jumana's shoulders. "I have books you can borrow."

"Do you? Will you? I will wrap them in cloth and take veeery good care of them!"

The child's face was radiant. She was no child, though; in Egyptian terms she was a grown woman and ripe for marriage, and with a face like hers she probably had dozens of suitors panting after her. It would be a crime to let enthusiasm and intelligence like that be lost to a traditional marriage, though. The girl deserved a chance—and I haven't done much to help her, Nefret thought guiltily. Lending books was the least she could do. That pitiful stub of a pencil and tattered notebook—why hadn't she thought of supplying something better?

When Ramses came back, Jamil was trotting at his heels, mumbling excuses and looking more resentful than chastened. He took them across to the dahabeeyah, and Nefret made them all wait while she put together a parcel for Jumana: the first volume of Emerson's classic *History of Ancient Egypt*, pencils and pens and a bottle of ink, a pristine book of blank paper. With that treasure clasped to her bosom, Jumana did not object to being dismissed for the day. They mounted the horses that had been left in Ashraf's care, and headed toward the western cliffs. Jumana left them at the point where the track divided. Her face shone.

"First time I've seen her struck dumb," Ramses said. "That was a nice thought, dear."

"I didn't do it to be nice."

"So you say. My God, she's a beautiful little creature. If she ever looks at a man like that—"

"If she ever looks at *you* like that—"

"She probably thinks I'm as old as Methuselah," Ramses said wryly.

"You aren't as old as the man Yusuf will select for her. No young man could pay the bride price he will ask. I won't let that happen, Ramses."

He didn't ask what she meant to do to prevent it. She'd manage it somehow. Her jaw was set. He took her hand. "She'll get her chance, I promise."

"I thought Mr. Lansing said the tomb was behind the Ptolemaic temple," Nefret said, when they reached the Asasif.

"He was mistaken. Kuentz said it's closer to Deir el Bahri. The easiest approach is by way of Hatshepsut's causeway."

It was after three o'clock. The sun was in their eyes when they headed west, and heat rose from the baked bare ground. There were few people about; the tourists had retreated to their hotels, the guards were napping in the shade, and like all sensible excavators (except Emerson), Lansing had stopped for the day. The site was not completely deserted, however; as they passed, a man stood up and ran toward them, his arms waving wildly.

"It's Mr. Barton," Nefret said, bringing the mare to a halt. "I wonder what he wants."

"Another look at you, I expect."

"Don't be absurd. He reminds one of Don Quixote, doesn't he, or perhaps one of the windmills . . . Good afternoon, Mr. Barton."

Barton rocked to a stop. "Good afternoon. Are you looking for me—us—Lansing?"

His eyes were fixed on Nefret, like those of a dog who is hoping for a pat on the head, so Ramses left it to her to answer him. "We didn't think you'd be here so late," she said tactfully. "We were planning to have a look at the place where Alain caught the would-be tomb robber."

"Alain? Oh. Kuentz. Yes, that's right. You know where it is?"

"I think so," Ramses said. "If you'll excuse us—"

"Mind if I tag along? I can keep up, I walk really fast."

Nefret was too softhearted to resist. She gave him the hoped-for pat. "If you like. We'll have to go on foot most of the way anyhow."

They left Jamil and the horses beside the second terrace of the temple and went on, following a narrow path that climbed steadily upward, skirting heaps of loose debris. There were many such paths, used by the surefooted and often barefooted people of Gurneh or by goats; some had been in use since ancient times. When they stopped to catch their breaths they were high enough to see clear across the cultivation to the river. The line between the green and the barren desert was as sharp as if it had been drawn with a knifepoint. Nefret could feel perspiration puddling between her breasts and running down her back. There were dark patches on Ramses's shirt too, and Barton was breathing hard. He had followed so close behind her that once or twice she had had to skip to avoid tripping over his extremely large feet. If he had hoped to leap to her assistance he had been disappointed.

"That's where they found the cache of royal mummies," Ramses said, pointing toward the base of the cliff.

"Where?" Barton asked eagerly. "I read about it but I haven't seen it yet. Can we get in?"

"No, *we* can't," Ramses said forcibly. "Not without ropes and certainly not today." Barton looked so disappointed, he relented. "I'll show you where it is, but don't entertain any notions about exploring the place on your own. The shaft is over forty feet deep and the last time I was down there the ceilings of the corridors had begun to collapse."

"You've been there?"

Damn, Ramses thought, I should have known he'd take that as a challenge instead of a warning. "It was some years ago. I wouldn't risk it again without assistance."

Another climb brought them to the base of the cliff. There wasn't much to see, only a gaping irregular black hole. Ramses took hold of Nefret's arm and waved Barton back.

"Careful. The Service des Antiquités ought to have covered the opening, it's too much of a temptation to impetuous idiots. There's nothing down there, you know."

That wasn't strictly true. Emil Brugsch had removed the coffins and miscellaneous funerary equipment over thirty years earlier, but it had been a rushed job and Emerson had always been of the opinion that the tomb ought to be properly excavated. Ramses wasn't about to mention that to Barton, who had edged closer and was peering down into the hole. Ramses understood his fascination; it was one of the great stories of Egyptology: the bodies of Egypt's royalty, violated and robbed and stacked up like cordwood, to lie hidden for almost three thousand years, discovered by a family of modern tomb robbers who surreptitiously marketed stolen objects until they were caught by the Antiquities Department.

"We'd better go on," he said.

The going wasn't easy; the path rose and fell, twisted and turned, over the piles of loose debris that bordered the Theban cliffs, the result of centuries of weathering by wind and rain. Barton kept catching Nefret's arm, throwing her off balance and then steadying her. He didn't seem to realize that was what he was doing, and she was kind enough not to complain.

The opening of the royal cache was not far behind them when Ramses stopped. "That looks like it."

There was a long vertical shadow at the spot he indicated. It was only one of many. Splintered and cracked, the rock face rose high above them.

"How can you tell?" Nefret asked, shaking off Barton's hand.

"It's the right distance." Ramses looked around. "He said there is a boulder to the south of the cleft that resembles a sheep's head."

"They all do," Nefret muttered.

"I'll go up and have a look," Ramses said. "Stand back a bit."

The climb wasn't particularly difficult. He had been up and down cliffs like these a hundred times. The surface was so uneven it offered plenty of hand- and footholds; one only had to test each one before putting one's weight on it. Moving slowly but surely, he was almost at the crevice when Nefret screamed.

A louder, deeper sound followed, drowning out her voice, but he had already reacted, flinging himself to one side, his feet and hands groping for holds. The boulder passed within inches of his right hand, accompanied by a shower of smaller stones, and struck the ground with a force that sent splintered fragments fountaining upward. They rained down on the two bodies huddled against the cliff.

Ramses couldn't remember how he got down. The rents in the front of his shirt suggested he had slid most of the way. Of the three of them, Nefret had come off best, thanks to Barton's prompt action. When Ramses reached them, the young man was still holding her, his long arms wrapped tightly around her body and his head bowed over hers. Ramses removed him with rather more force than was necessary and bent over his wife. She pushed her hair out of her eyes and let out a cry of relief.

"Thank God. The last thing I saw was that rock coming straight at you. Help me up."

"Are you sure you—"

"Yes, I'm fine. Thanks to Mr. Barton."

Ramses let go her hands and turned apologetically to Barton.

"I'm frightfully sorry."

Sprawled on the ground with his arms and legs at odd angles like a four-legged spider, Barton grinned feebly. "No, I'm sorry. I didn't see . . . I should have . . . I was almost too slow. Did I hurt her? I didn't mean . . ."

"Yes, all right," Ramses said, interpreting the incoherent comments. Barton had been gaping at Nefret and hadn't noticed anything amiss until she cried out.

Nefret was on her feet, a little pale but steady. "There was someone up there." She pointed. "I saw his head and shoulders, and then . . . oh, my God! Look out!"

The figure seemed to float rather than fall, full sleeves and flowing garments billowing gracefully, like the wings of a giant bird, but it hit the ground with a solid and sickening thud. Ramses was not conscious of having moved until a pained grunt from Nefret brought him to the realization that he had pushed her down and was lying on top of her.

"Get up," she gasped, shoving at him. "Is he dead?"

The body had landed practically at Barton's feet. It was facedown, and as far as Ramses was concerned it could stay that way. The fellow had to be dead, there was blood spattered all over the ground and on Barton's boots. He knew his wife wouldn't be satisfied until she'd made sure, though. She turned the body over.

The face was unrecognizable, a ruin of broken bone and raw flesh. Barton spun round, covering his mouth with his hand, and Ramses patted him absently on the back while he watched Nefret go through the ritual and, in his opinion, unnecessary motions. She looked up at him and shook her head. Her hair was coming down, long strands of gold curling over her shoulders. She's so beautiful, he thought. Aloud he said gruffly, "Find something to cover his face or Barton will throw up."

"No. Listen, I am really sorry . . ." The young man wiped his mouth on his sleeve and said pathetically, "I never saw a dead person before. Not a fresh one."

"This one is bad," Ramses admitted. "Never mind covering him, Nefret, take Barton away from here."

"Yes, of course." She slipped her arm through the young man's. "Don't be embarrassed, Mr. Barton. I'm a doctor, you know, and we're used to this sort of thing."

"So I've heard." Barton managed to summon a feeble smile. "Uh—do you think . . . Do you think you could call me George?"

Ramses waited until "George" and his wife were out of sight before he bent over the body. He had to clean his hands with sand after he had finished.

When he joined Nefret and Barton she was kneeling beside the young man, inspecting him for injuries. Her hair fell over her shoulders, framing a face becomingly flushed with heat and excitement. Her lips were slightly parted and the tip of her tongue protruded, the way it did when she was concentrating.

"There is a bump," Nefret announced, probing a spot on the left side of Barton's head. "How many fingers am I holding up?"

Barton's glazed stare was suggestive of concussion but Ramses felt sure it wasn't the bump on the head that had addled his brains. He finally got the word out. "Uh—three."

"Good. Why don't you come back to the boat with us and let me give you a proper examination. Those cuts ought to be disinfected."

The house the Metropolitan people had built was closer, but by then Barton would have agreed to accompany Nefret into the fires of hell. He made only a feeble protest. "It's too much trouble . . ."

"It's the least we can do," Ramses said. "You saved my wife from serious injury. Can you make it back to Deir el Bahri?"

"Sure."

"Good. I'll meet you there."

Nefret bit off a particularly ripe swearword as he turned toward the cliff face. Barton's eyes widened. "Are you going up there? What for? It was an accident, wasn't it? I mean, the fellow must have been drunk or . . . no, Moslems don't drink, do they? Sick, maybe or . . . He was leaning against that rock, and it fell, and then he . . . It must have been an accident!"

Ramses did not reply. The climb was easier this

time, and before long he had reached the place from which he was sure the missile had come—the path leading along the side of the cliff from Deir el Medina to the Valley of the Kings. It had been used by the men who lived in the village and worked in the royal tombs almost four thousand years ago. There was no one in sight in either direction when he climbed onto the level. He looked down. Nefret and Barton were still there; he'd known she wouldn't leave the spot until she was sure he was safe. She raised her arm in salute, and he waved back, gesturing them to proceed on their way.

The surface of the path was disturbed by the passage of feet, shod and unshod, animal and human. There were no distinctive prints. At one spot a fresh break showed pale and clean, where a section of rock had been levered away. It wouldn't have required much time or effort to do the job, nor would there have been any reason to suspect foul play unless one was looking for evidence of it. Bits of the time-weathered rock were always crumbling and falling. But the man had used a lever of some sort. The marks were there. And there were other marks, scuffed and rubbed, but not entirely obliterated.

Ramses met only one person as he wended his way toward Deir el Bahri—a jovial villain from Gurneh, who greeted him without surprise, gave him a knowing grin, and asked if he was looking for lost tombs.

He went the long way round, scrambling down the steep but safe path behind the north side of the temple. Nefret and Barton were waiting, with Jamil and the horses, when he reached the level of the second terrace.

"Find anything?" the American asked.

"No."

"Listen, I didn't mean to pry. It's just that I've heard so many stories about you folks . . . It was an accident?"

"No doubt." Ramses turned to Jamil. Nefret must have told him what had happened; he looked more alert than Ramses had ever seen him. "Someone will have to go to Luxor, Jamil. The—er—accident must be reported to the police."

"They will do nothing," Jamil said indifferently.

He was probably right. Ramses thought guiltily of the dead man, abandoned and prey to predators, but the idea of retrieving the battered remains was too much even for him.

"Nevertheless, they must be told," he said. "And at once."

At Nefret's suggestion, he sent one of the gaffirs, motivating him with a generous tip. Jamil would stop off in every coffee shop in Luxor before he went to the taftish, if he bothered to go there at all.

They had drinks in the saloon while Nefret worked on Barton. He had turned bright pink, like a schoolboy, when she insisted he remove his shirt. His injuries were superficial—cuts and abrasions and bruises, almost all of them on his back. Nursing his own whiskey, Ramses made courteous conversation and thought inhospitable thoughts.

But it was hard to remain aloof with a man who was drinking your beer and making admiring comments about your work. By the time Barton left, they were using one another's first names. Barton was in no hurry to go. Nefret had to remind him twice that Lansing might be wondering what had happened to him before he put his glass down and rose to his feet, and then he started thanking her again. Ramses took his arm and led him out.

"Shall I tell Ambrose what happened?" Barton asked.

"Why not?"

"Uh . . . No reason, I guess. Well. Thank you again."

When Ramses returned to the saloon, Nasir was setting the table for dinner. He was less clumsy than he had been, but he had found a new excuse to linger by folding the napkins into intricate shapes. His ambition exceeded his skill; tonight's effort was probably meant to be a flying bird, though it more resembled a decapitated duck. Ramses dismissed him with a few brusque words and went to stand by Nefret, who was curled up on the divan.

"You hurt his feelings," she said reproachfully.

"Stop him doing that, then. It takes forever to untie the knots."

"All right, darling, I'll try. George is a nice boy, isn't he? It's a pity he had to have such an unpleasant experience."

"He'd better get used to it if he stays in Egypt."

"Oh, really, Ramses! One doesn't have bodies dropped at one's feet every day. We might ask him and Mr. Lansing and Monsieur Legrain for dinner one evening—with Miss Minton."

"If you want to waste time on social encounters,

that is up to you. I was under the impression that you meant to persuade the woman to confide in you. She's not likely to talk freely when others are around."

"Goodness, but you're in a grouchy mood this evening. All right, we'll make it a threesome. You can excuse yourself after dinner and I'll get to work on her."

"When?"

"The sooner the better. The Vandergelts are arriving on Sunday, and we'll be busy with them for a few days."

"Tomorrow, then?"

"If she's free. Why are you looming over me like that?"

"I thought you liked being loomed over."

"Only when something interesting is likely to develop. Shall I put dinner back?"

"No, I'm hungry."

Her smile faded, but she waited until after Nasir had served the first course before she went on the attack.

"What is it? Something you found when you searched the body?"

"There was nothing you didn't see for yourself. No means of identification, nothing distinctive about his clothing."

"It might have been an accident."

"If you believe in unholy coincidences, it's conceivable that a chunk of rock crumbled away just when I happened to be climbing, but he couldn't have fallen unless he was standing on top of the ridge that bounds the path on the cliff side. It's not a straight drop."

"You think he was pushed," Nefret said slowly.

"It's not a straight drop," Ramses repeated impatiently. "He was lifted and pitched over. You saw how he fell—backward, faceup. He landed on his head, but the damage shouldn't have been that extensive. He was hit in the face before he was thrown over. There were drops of blood on the rock."

"So there were two people up there. One who tried to kill you, the other who tried—"

"You don't know what either of them intended," Ramses said. "Nor do I."

"Damn it, Ramses, stop interrupting me!" She broke off, biting her lip, as Nasir trotted in with the next course, but the argument didn't end there. Ramses knew he wasn't behaving well, but she'd come so close to injury that afternoon, and it had been that gawky young American who had shielded her, and Luxor wasn't safe after all—and he hadn't the faintest clue as to the motive or the man behind the attack.

"I tell you, it couldn't have been—" He glanced at Nasir, who was so unnerved by their loud voices that he was juggling plates in his anxiety to get out of the room. "It couldn't have been one of that lot."

"Who else could it have been? You haven't . . . You didn't . . ."

"No! How many times must I tell you before you believe me?"

"Then who was the second man?"

"What second man?"

"You said—"

"I was theorizing. We don't know there were two people up there."

"Could it have been—" She broke off and directed an inimical glance at their unfortunate steward. Completely undone by a sign of disfavor from his goddess, Nasir burst into tears and fled.

"Christ!" Ramses slammed his knife down. "My fond uncle, you mean. Nursemaid or guardian angel? You think we need one, don't you? Obviously I can't take care of myself—or you—"

"You're impossible! I'm going to write the parents and tell them what happened."

Her hair always came loose when she was angry. The lamplight ran golden fingers along the curling locks. Her cheeks were flushed and her eyes shone with tears of fury.

"Do as you like," Ramses said shortly. "I'm going to bed. It's been rather a long day."

He was tired and he'd acquired several new bruises during his precipitate descent of the cliff, but he was still awake, open-eyed in the dark, when Nefret slipped in and closed the door. She stood still for a few moments, waiting for him to speak; when he remained mute and motionless, she moved quietly to the other side of the room and began to undress. She took her time about it, hanging her clothes neatly over a chair before she slipped into a nightgown. His night vision had always been excellent and he had a hard time keeping his breath even. She tiptoed toward the bed. He was about to reach out for her when she threw herself down beside him. The bedsprings squealed.

"I know you aren't asleep! How dare you behave this way?"

He caught her in his arms. "I'm sorry."

"And don't apologize!"

"Aren't you being a little inconsistent?"

"I was afraid." She hid her face against his shoulder. "That's why I was so horrid."

"I wasn't at my best either."

"Oh, I don't know. It was a jolly good argument!"

He couldn't joke about it. "I didn't lie to you, Nefret. I'd never take on another job without telling you."

"Consulting me."

"That's what I meant to say. I can't make sense of what happened today, but I'm certain it had nothing to do with—"

"I don't want to talk about it." Her lips moved from his throat to his chin. "You shaved!"

"Well—uh—I thought . . ."

"Oh, darling, you really are adorable!" She was laughing as his mouth found hers.

Sometime later, he said drowsily, "I'm beginning to understand why Mother and Father argue so often. Making up afterward is awfully pleasant."

"Mmmm." It was hardly more than a breath against his shoulder. He thought she was asleep until a very quiet, very firm voice said, "Now tell me about Enid Fraser."

FROM LETTER COLLECTION T

Dearest Mother and Father,

You'll have received Ramses's telegram by now. I won't apologize; I told you I couldn't keep things from him. In order to set a good example, I will now tell you several things you need to know—with, I should add, the agreement of my husband. First, Miss Minton is here—Margaret, I should say—she asked me to use her first name. I don't trust her one inch, but I can't make out what she's after, unless . . . But that would be insane, wouldn't it? She seemed very interested in tomb robberies and antiquities theft. We met her at luncheon today, and Alain Kuentz joined us—he's back at Deir el Medina—and she pounced on him with all her claws extended when he casually mentioned that it was he who blew up the German House—because, he claimed, it was a center for the illicit antiquities trade—and other things! See what you can find out about that. Howard Carter is back in Cairo, I understand; Alain denied that Howard was involved, but in a way that implied the reverse!

The other point of interest is that someone dropped a rock on us today. We were near Deir el Bahri, looking for a tomb Alain said had been robbed, and Ramses was halfway up the cliff when it happened. The rock missed him, but not by much, and shortly thereafter a body followed the rock. It landed practically on top of poor young Mr. Barton, who was with us. The man's face had been smashed, possibly before he fell.

I'm giving you the bare facts. I don't know what they mean—at least I hope I don't—but I beg you will not come rushing to our rescue. Ramses would hate that, and so would I. WE have refrained from rushing to YOUR rescue, you know. I thought Ramses was going to explode when I started telling

*him about your recent activities. Do try and stay
out of trouble, will you?*

*On a brighter note, we look forward to seeing
the Vandergelts. I'll do my best for Bertie.*

> *Much love to all,*
> *Nefret*

FROM MANUSCRIPT H

Margaret Minton did not respond to Nefret's note
inviting her for dinner. They were lingering over a
rather late breakfast when their messenger returned with the information that the Sitt had left
the hotel early that morning and that the concierge
had no idea when she would return. Gossiping, as
was customary, he had asked several questions and
learned a few more facts: she had taken a picnic
basket and hired one of the dragomen, so it seemed
likely . . .

"That she had planned a long excursion," Ramses
interrupted impatiently. "Which of the dragomen?"

"Sayid." Their informant chuckled. "He won out
over the others who wanted to go with her by saying he was a trusted friend of yours, Brother of
Demons, who had helped you to capture many
thieves and murderers."

"Sayid." Ramses ran agitated fingers through his
hair. "Good God, the fellow has to be a hundred
years old, and he's still the biggest coward in Luxor.
If she gets in trouble he'll be about as much use as
Jumana."

"Less. Why should she get herself in trouble, though?"

"Because she's a busybody and a journalist and a woman of dangerous self-confidence. And she dined with Kuentz last night."

"I think you are needlessly concerned. Anyhow, there's nothing we can do about it."

The messenger, who was squatting on the floor listening interestedly, volunteered, "They were coming to the west bank."

Ramses handed over the expected baksheesh and the man left. Jamil and Jumana had arrived by then; as they descended the stairs, Ramses said, "Did you write the parents?"

"Yes." She glanced at him from under her lashes. "I sent the letter off this morning."

"What did you tell them?"

"The bare facts."

"You didn't mention *him*, did you?"

"No. But I still disagree."

Their first step that morning was at the Vandergelts' house, to make sure all was in readiness for the travelers. The steward—or majordomo, as he preferred to be called—was a Belgian who had been in Cyrus's service most of his life. Though the Vandergelts had not been in residence often of late, Albert prided himself on keeping the place immaculate and ready for occupancy at a moment's notice. Nefret assured him they would meet the Vandergelts at the station and bring them home.

"All right, that's done," she said, as they headed down the track away from the house. "I suppose now you want to look up Alain."

"How did you know?"

"I know practically everything about you," his wife murmured. "And I intend to find out the rest of it before I'm done. There's Christabel Pankhurst and Dollie Bellingham and Layla and the girl in Chicago and Sylvia Gorst—"

"I never had anything to do with Sylvia—can't stand the woman—never could."

"Well, I thought she was probably lying," Nefret said calmly. "We'll talk about it later."

Not if I can help it, Ramses thought. He was fairly sure he couldn't, though.

Kuentz was at work, supervising a small crew excavating one of the workmen's houses. He came running toward them and took Nefret's hands, cradling them in his furry paws. "I heard. Horrible! Dreadful! My poor girl!"

Nefret managed to free her hands. "I've almost certainly seen more corpses than you have, Alain. Your concern is needless."

"But I feel responsible. Did you find the worthless tomb, then?"

"No," Ramses said. The man even had hair on the palms of his hands.

"Perhaps my directions were not clear enough. Believe me, though, the place is not worth your trouble."

"We didn't come about that," Nefret said. "We were curious about what you told Miss Minton last night."

"It was a curious conversation," Kuentz said with a grin. "Come and join me in my humble quarters and I'll have Mahmud make tea."

They were humble enough, only a small tent pitched against a slope, with a camp stove and a few other minimal comforts.

"Is this where you stay?" Nefret asked, accepting the single stool.

"Part of the time. I rent a room at Hussein Ali's hotel—if you can call it that. I keep my clothes and notes there, and it is possible to have a bath, if one doesn't mind curious onlookers and an occasional dead fish in the water. The tub's in the courtyard." Her look of disgust made him shout with laughter. "It's not so bad. Not the way you people live, but it has a certain charm."

"I'm sure it does," said Ramses, who had lived under even less comfortable circumstances when he was engaged in certain of his undercover jobs. "We tried to reach Miss Minton this morning but were told she had gone off for the day. D'you have any idea where?"

His brusque tone sobered Kuentz. "She didn't say anything to me. No reason why she should. Hold on, though . . . She was very curious about the German House. In fact, all she'd talk about was the illegal antiquities game. Said she was thinking of doing a series of feature stories about some of the more notorious players—the Rassuls, that Italian fellow your parents rounded up a few years back— what was his name?—and Sethos, of course."

It was always startling to hear that name, but it wasn't really surprising; the Emersons had tried for years to enlist the aid of the police and the Service des Antiquités in tracking down "the Master Criminal." Those who had doubted his very existence to begin with had changed their minds after certain of Sethos's activities became public. He had once written a letter to a London newspaper explaining, with the greatest politeness, that he was sorry to have offended Mrs. Emerson by robbing a well-known politician while she was picketing his house.

"I told her what I knew," Kuentz went on. "She'd bought me a very good dinner and a quantity of excellent wine. She kept prodding me for more details, so I finally pointed out that you and your family knew more about the subject than I."

"Not that much," Ramses said. "Our encounters with Sethos and Riccetti are public knowledge."

"Riccetti! That was the name. I wasn't here at the time, but I heard about it. And about Sethos. Some of the stories rather strain one's credulity. Is it true that he was after the Dahshur treasure, and would have got to it before de Morgan if you hadn't stopped him?"

"The story has undoubtedly been exaggerated," Ramses said.

Kuentz let out a whoop of laughter. "Not as much as Margaret will exaggerate it. Whatever happened to the fellow anyhow? Could he be the one behind the latest outbreak of thefts?"

"He's dead," Ramses said. He rose to his feet. "We mustn't keep you any longer."

They had to remove Jumana from the edge of the dig, where she sat scribbling in her notebook, to the barely contained indignation of the workers.

The ruins of the former German expedition house were behind the Ramesseum. The local people had rummaged through them, removing anything that was salvageable; all that was left was a pile of blackened ashes.

"I hadn't realized they had done such a thorough job of it," Nefret said.

"Complete destruction," Ramses agreed. "One can't help wondering why. Carter and Kuentz, if it was they, acted without authority—illegally, in fact."

"I expect Margaret will make a dramatic tale of it."

"Yes. There's no sense hanging about here. Let's go on."

Minton had been on the west bank. Several of the people Ramses questioned had seen her with Sayid, and helpfully pointed them in various directions, none of which led to anything. Finally Nefret said, "This is a waste of time. If you're all that determined to locate her, she'll be at the hotel this evening. Shall I tell Maaman we are dining out?"

However, when they reached the Winter Palace, they discovered that the Sitt had not returned. Ramses tugged fretfully at his tie. He hated wearing evening dress almost as much as his father did.

"Where could she have gone?"

"Led on a wild-goose chase by Sayid, perhaps," Nefret said. She didn't share his concern; she knew the amiable willingness of Luxor guides to supply anything the client asked for. In a fair imitation of Sayid's whine, she went on, "You look for tomb robber, Sitt? Yes, I know many tomb robber! I take you to see them, you give me baksheesh!"

Ramses's tight lips relaxed into an unwilling

smile. "So you think she's sitting in Sayid's house drinking vile tea, while he parades half the population of Gurneh past her?"

"Each of them with a more lurid story," Nefret agreed. "Stop fussing, darling, and let's have dinner. If she's not back by the time we finish . . . well, we'll worry about that later."

The elegant dining salon was only half full, though it was Saturday. Most of the guests were Americans, with a scattering of other nationalities, including a few British officials. Luxor was a popular weekend excursion for the archaeologically inclined and for those who were bored with the routine of Cairo life. The service at the Winter Palace was so good as to be mildly annoying; waiters, wine steward, and innumerable flunkies hemmed them round.

Ramses handed the ornate gilded wine list back to the maître d'. "There are no German wines on the list, but I feel certain you have them. A Riesling will suit, 1911 or '12."

"You're being deliberately provocative, aren't you?" Nefret demanded.

"Yes. I despise the politicizing of harmless ideas and people and objects."

Nefret snatched up her evening bag in time to save it from a sprinkle of water. One of the underwaiters had been too quick or too clumsy filling her water glass. He received a low-voiced reprimand from his superior and cringed away.

"Malesh," Nefret said impatiently. "Leave the fellow alone, he did no harm."

An hour later they were finishing their dinner and there had been no sign of Margaret. Nefret picked up her bag. "I'm going to freshen up," she announced. "I'll stop by the desk first and ask about Margaret."

She hadn't been worried—not really—but she was relieved to hear that Miss Minton had returned and gone directly to her room, after collecting her messages.

"She looked very tired," the concierge volunteered. "And—er—warm. Do you want that I should ring her room?"

"No, that's all right. Thank you." The tactful euphemisms conveyed a picture of a woman staggering with exhaustion, sweat-stained, and grubby. Sayid must have led her a merry dance. Grinning, Nefret went on her way.

Square in the middle of the marble-floored passage that led to the Ladies' Parlor was a kneeling figure—a woman, black-robed and veiled. She wrung out a cloth into the pail beside her and went back to scrubbing the floor. One of the "ladies" ahead of Nefret, bejeweled and befurred, drew her satin skirts aside.

"One would suppose the management would not allow these filthy females in the place until after the guests have retired."

The scrubwoman crouched lower and rubbed even harder. She might not have understood the words, but the tone of contempt was unmistakable. Nefret said, "One of your elegant friends probably threw up. You are quite right, though; the management should have left it. Wouldn't that have been nice for you?"

Voice and stare sent the two "ladies" scuttling off. Nefret reached into her evening bag and took out a few coins.

"Thank you, but I really cannot accept baksheesh," said a voice from around the level of her knees. The "scrubwoman" stood up and took her hand. "Let's get out of this, there will be more of them."

Three other women entered the corridor. The scrubwoman dropped Nefret's hand and scuttled past them, head bowed. Nefret staggered after her . . . him. By the time she joined him, in a pillared niche nearby, he had removed the robe and veil and might have been an ordinary guest of the hotel, clad in well-cut evening clothes, wearing a look of bland superiority and displaying a set of large protruding teeth. It was his hands that gave him away; she'd observed them earlier, fumbling with the pitcher of water.

"You were the waiter! Hell and damnation!"

"Not the waiter, only his clumsy assistant. I've been working here for almost a week. I had expected you would come round before this. Do sit down, won't you?"

Nefret sank onto the velvet-cushioned bench. "You left your bucket."

"And there it will remain. Let's hope someone falls over it. I was forced to that role because it's so damned difficult to get you alone."

"You couldn't have known we would come tonight."

"You sent Margaret a message this morning; I

thought it likely that when she didn't respond you would come looking for her."

"How did you know?" Nefret gasped.

"Oh, I've been on duty for hours. We oppressed members of the working class put in long days, but we are lazy beggars, who are unable to resist stopping to gossip. I saw her go off with Sayid and later I recognized your crewman, who obligingly told me to whom he had delivered the note. I had, of course, made my preparations in advance. It's quite easy to change roles, when you've had as much practice as I." He waggled his teeth at her. Amusement won out over outrage; she started to laugh. Sethos put his hand over her mouth.

"No uncontrolled hilarity, if you please; it might attract attention. Listen carefully, Nefret. I want you and Ramses out of Luxor. Get him back to Cairo. You're the only one who can do it."

"Why?"

"God, you're as bad as Amelia. All I can—all I will—tell you is that he's in danger here."

"From whom? Not you!"

"Thank you for your skepticism. No, not me. Let me think how to put this. I discovered, when I tried to rebuild my old organization, that someone had got in ahead of me."

"Someone like Riccetti?"

"It's a lucrative business," Sethos said, somewhat evasively. "There are always enterprising souls ready to take advantage of a vacancy. How many bodies have to fall on you before you get the point?"

Nefret said slowly, "You heard about what happened yesterday."

"Everyone's heard about it. If you two go on prying you'll be hurt."

Nefret put her hand on his sleeve. "What about you? Won't you please reconsider what you're doing? It's a dangerous game, and the other players are dangerous men. Surely you've enough put by to retire permanently."

She spoke quickly and earnestly, trying to hold his eyes with hers, using the little tricks every woman knows to convince him of her sincerity and her interest. She thought his face softened for a moment, but then he laughed and said lightly, "Into the bosom of the family? I can't really see Radcliffe being pleased at the prospect. Besides, he'd want me to give up my ill-gotten gains."

"So would Mother."

"They couldn't make me do it, though," Sethos said, with a toothy smile. "Prettily done, Nefret. You're a charming creature, but don't waste your charm on me. I've a little present for you."

He took it from his inside breast pocket—a bag of colorful cotton, clumsily stitched together, with a drawstring of thin cord. Even before she took it and felt the weight, she knew what it was.

"I've heard he won't carry a gun," Sethos said. "I hope you don't share his sentiments."

"I share them. But I'll do anything that will keep him safe."

"Just like a woman. Your principles always yield to expediency. Do you know how to use it?"

"Yes."

"Good. I'm in dead earnest, Nefret. Get him away from here. And try to take that damned woman with you."

"Margaret? Why?"

"That, at least, should be obvious," said her uncle by marriage in exasperation. "She's as obstinate and inquisitive as Amelia. She's no fool, either. If she goes on the way she has begun . . . Tell her some fantastic yarn that will induce her to follow you to Cairo. Offer her a scoop—a corpse—a curse—something. Now you'd better get back to him before he comes looking for you. Doesn't he ever let you off the lead?"

He was five feet away, moving with a deceptive quickness that reminded Nefret of his brother, before she could react. She jumped up, took two steps, and stopped. She'd have to run to catch him up. A pretty sight that would be—Mrs. Emerson the Younger pelting through the lobby of the Winter Palace in pursuit of a strange man. A second later he was out of sight.

He'd done it again. From now on I'll be on guard against provocative comments like that, she told herself firmly. He used them like slaps on the face, jarring the listener into temporary immobility. Off the lead—as if she were a faithful hound!

She managed to stuff the crude cotton bundle into her evening bag, but she knew Ramses would notice the bulge. He noticed everything.

He noticed. Not the evening bag at first, but her air of suppressed excitement. "You've been a long time," he said, searching her face. "Has something happened?"

"Yes. I don't want coffee, let's go. I'll tell you as soon as we're alone."

They had hired a felucca instead of having one of their men row them across; Nefret loved sailing the dark waters under the starlit sky. As soon as they took their places and the boat was under way, she launched into her story.

He didn't interrupt until she repeated what he had said about Margaret Minton. "So he calls her Margaret, does he? Try to remember his exact words, Nefret. It may be important."

She went over it again. She left the gun until last. His only comment was, "I saw there was something. Don't show it to me now."

Accustomed as she was to his self-control, the cool tones worried her a little. "Are you angry because I didn't tell you while we were at the Winter Palace?" she asked meekly.

He put his arm round her shoulders. "No, there was no sense in staying there. It would have been futile to try and find him."

But the arm under the fine broadcloth of his coat was hard as granite.

They had coffee in the saloon. They were to meet the train next morning, but it was still early and Ramses wouldn't rest until he had picked over that conversation word by word and syllable by syllable.

"You told him we cared about his safety? It must have been a very affecting performance."

"I do care," Nefret protested. "How could I not, after what he's done for us? He has a lot of admirable qualities, and a lot of the family charm. He reminds me more and more of Father, and of you."

Ramses had removed coat, waistcoat, and tie as soon as he was on board. Pacing up and down the saloon, he pushed a lock of hair out of his eyes and said caustically, "Mother tried for years to redeem him, as she put it. Do you suppose you can succeed where she failed?"

"He's older now and he's been through a lot," Nefret said temperately. "And I think he was sincere when he said he was concerned about you."

"Far be it from me," said her husband, "to cast cold water on that touching assumption, but there is another, less sentimental interpretation of his seeming concern."

"I know."

"He's after something," Ramses muttered. "Something big. Something that requires time and privacy. He's not worried about the locals; he's always used a judicious blend of intimidation and rewards to win their support, and they'd have nothing to gain by turning him in. Hell, there's nobody to whom they could turn him in! The local police are useless or corrupt, and the Service des Antiquités hasn't the manpower, and the British authorities are too busy with the war to care about a few artifacts. The only person they might approach is—"

"You."

"Yes. Not as myself, but as Father's representative. There's an outside chance that one of the lads might be moved by old loyalties or by fear of the Father of Curses. I'll give him this much credit," Ramses added grudgingly. "I don't believe he would do me an injury, and he certainly wouldn't harm you. But he's not going to let us stop him either.

What he did tonight was typically ingenious—appealing to you on my account, with veiled hints of danger."

"They weren't so veiled. He said there was another player in the game."

Ramses dismissed this with a brusque gesture. "We've seen no sign of anyone else."

"Right. People drop rocks and dead bodies on you all the time."

"Maybe he only meant to frighten us off."

"Sethos? He wouldn't take the risk of hurting either of us."

His lips tightened in exasperation. "You've gone soft on him, like Mother and Margaret. Giving you the gun was a particularly clever touch. Did he ask you not to tell me about it?"

"No," Nefret said.

"Let's have a look at it."

He threw himself down on the divan next to her and drew the weapon out of its clumsy container. "Pretty little thing," he said, with a curl of his lip. "It's the newest model of Mother's beloved Ladysmith. Fully loaded . . ." He swung the cylinder out. "Except for the seventh shot, the one in the chamber under the hammer. Since there's no safety catch, that would prevent a nasty accident in case the gun was dropped."

"I know."

"Mother let you play with hers, did she?"

"Would you rather I didn't carry it?"

"You're asking for my approval? Nefret, you know why I don't carry a gun. This isn't the first time I've asked myself whether I have the right to take that position, but I can't . . ." He bent his head so that she couldn't see his face, and when he went on his voice was tired and defeated, like that of an old man. "You were worried about my accepting another assignment. You needn't have been. I won't. I can't. I've lost my nerve, Nefret. The very thought of violence makes me sick. How does it feel to have a coward for a husband?"

Nefret almost laughed, as one does at a statement so outrageously false it is tantamount to a joke. He wasn't joking, though. He really meant it! She wanted to put her arms around him, but the situation was too serious for caresses and soothing denials. It's me, she thought. This is what I've done to him—he's afraid for me, not for himself, and he can't see the difference, and he won't believe me if I tell him.

"That is one of the most ridiculous statements you've ever made," she said. She knew it wasn't enough.

"Good of you to say so." He smiled at her, but his eyes were hooded and opaque. "Well, that's the end of tonight's little drama. Keep the gun. One can't refuse a gift from a fond uncle, can one?"

ELEVEN

The "train de luxe," first class only (except for a second-class car reserved for the servants of the travelers) departed on Monday, Wednesday, and Saturday. It was not deluxe enough for Cyrus, who would have borrowed the Sultan's carriage and had it hitched to the train had he been able. Failing that, he reserved an entire car for his party, which included Daoud. There was no one better than Daoud to look after an invalid, and Bertie had taken quite a liking to him. They carried with them every comfort Cairo could provide, from hampers of food to linen sheets for the berths. A flurry of telegrams had assured us that everything was in readiness for the travelers upon their arrival, and that they would be met at the station. When the train pulled away on Saturday evening, only an hour late, Emerson let out a gusty sigh.

"What a fuss! The boy would be better off if everyone left him alone."

"Now, Emerson, you know that is nonsense. He seemed brighter, but he has a long way to go. Sennia was good for him, I think."

Sennia had carried on like a small tragedienne when we denied her request to accompany the Vandergelts. She was reluctant to give up her self-appointed role as Bertie's nurse, but her real reason for wanting to go to Luxor was that she missed Ramses.

"We'll take her with us to the dig tomorrow," Emerson said. "That will cheer her up."

"I do not believe in rewarding children for bad behavior, Emerson."

"She is only six. What do you expect her to do, sit in the house all day while we are at Giza? There is no school on Sunday."

"I ought to take her to church. Her religious training has been sadly neglected since we got here."

"Be damned to that," said Emerson. "I need you on the dig. We have lost several days, and with Daoud gone we are even more shorthanded."

"Do you intend to begin on the queen's pyramid tomorrow?"

Emerson gave me a severe look. "That sounds like blackmail, Peabody."

He was just making one of his little jokes. We had already decided that the queen's pyramid should be our next project. At least I had, and Emerson had not said we would not.

Since Friday was the day of rest for our Moslem friends, we had become accustomed to working on the Sabbath. It was a frightful nuisance to dress and drive all the way into Cairo to attend services, so I conducted a brief service of my own, with prayer and reading aloud from Scripture. At Gargery's request we also sang a few hymns. He favored the militant or the lugubrious of these. I had no objection to a rousing chorus of "Onward, Christian Soldiers," but to hear Gargery bellowing out verses like "Dark was the night, Sin warred against us, Heavy the load of sorrow we bore" was somewhat alarming. Sennia, who was unacquainted with sin in any form, enjoyed it very much. Emerson did not attend.

After this we all set out for Giza. Sennia had apologized very sweetly for her behavior, and we were all in a cheerful frame of mind, except for Horus, who was never in a cheerful frame of mind and who hated riding in his basket. Emerson complained, of course, about Daoud's absence and a number of other things, but I could tell he was looking forward to investigating the pyramid.

I had given the place only a cursory inspection before. A closer examination indicated that the task before us was not going to be easy. The pyramid itself was the best-preserved of the three that had been built for Khufu's queens. The names of several such ladies were known from other sources, but the precise ownership of the small pyramids was yet to be determined. Like the other tombs at Giza, all three had been cased with fine limestone, which had been stripped off, leaving the steplike core.

The entrance to the substructure was on the north side. Sand had drifted high around the base, burying the opening and the remains of the funerary chapel on the south side. If, as we had cause to suspect, it was the latest of several similar shrines, disentangling the various levels would be a daunting task. However, that was all to the good. It would keep Emerson busily occupied for some time. So we rolled up our sleeves, metaphorically speaking, and got to work. The first order of business was a meticulous survey of the area. Emerson and I set about this while Selim arranged the photographic equipment. I saw Sennia starting to scramble up a slope of sand and was about to call out a sharp warning when Gargery, close on her heels as always, pulled her away.

"Go and look for bones, Sennia," I ordered.

Her lower lip protruded. "I am bored with bones. Aunt Nefret is the only one who likes them, and she isn't here."

"Potsherds, then. Ramses likes them very much. You can have a collection ready for him when he comes back."

"He likes things with writing on them better."

"Look for them, then," I said in exasperation. "We are all going to be busy for a while, so amuse yourself like a good girl."

I watched the trio depart. First Sennia, trotting along at a brisk pace, then Horus, then Gargery, remaining a safe distance from the cat, who would not allow anyone to come between him and Sennia. Gargery was still limping a little. I did not waste my sympathy on him, however; it had been his choice to come with us and he would not have relinquished his post as guard for Sennia if he had had to crawl after her.

I cannot help blaming myself for the suggestion that she find something interesting for Ramses, though in the end the result would probably have been the same. They would have found their opportunity sooner or later. It was sooner than they could have hoped, for the child, remembering the inscribed stela, had headed straight for the dump site where that object had been. It was a considerable distance away and the terrain was uneven, with hollows and heaps of sand between.

Her high-pitched scream cut across the distance like a train whistle. Before it stopped, with shocking suddenness, Emerson was off and running. Selim dropped the camera. "Sitt! What—"

"Follow me!" I cried, and went after Emerson.

He had to cast about a bit before he found them, so I was on the scene almost as soon as he. Gargery lay flat on the ground struggling with a man who was dressed like one of the gaffirs. After the first horrified look I realized my unfortunate butler was not really fighting; he was only trying to hold on to the fellow, who was kicking and pounding him with his fists. Arms locked around the man's leg, Gargery hung on like grim death and it was not until Emerson dragged his captive away from him that he raised his head. Spitting out a mouthful of sand, he gasped, "The other one took her. It was that same chap—the one that showed her the stela, sir—he said he had something else for her, and then he took hold of her, sir and madam, and that one there knocked me down, and, and . . . I 'ave failed in me duty, sir and madam."

"No, you have not," said Emerson, who was holding his prisoner by the throat. The man was no longer struggling. His terrified eyes were fixed on Emerson.

Gargery was almost as wild-eyed as the prisoner. He kept flailing around, trying to stand, and would, I expect, have gone running off in frantic and futile pursuit had I not restrained him. I was, of course, intensely concerned, but I knew haste would accomplish nothing. It was too late to follow the other villain. I said as much to Gargery, adding, "This fellow knows where his companion has taken her. How you managed to hang on to him I do not know, but when we find her—as we will—it will be because of your courage and loyalty."

"Not just mine, madam," said Gargery.

He got to his hands and knees and crawled painfully toward an object that lay motionless on the ground, its tawny fur almost indistinguishable from the sand that surrounded it. Gargery gathered the cat's body in his arms and sat down, holding it on his lap.

"He kept biting and scratching until that barstard kicked him, madam, square in the ribs. Excuse me, madam. He's a hero, madam, poor old fellow."

He bowed his head. Two tears dropped down onto the ruffled fur.

"You are both heroes," said Emerson. "Selim, get this fellow to the house and lock him up. He has told me where they were to take her."

The rest of our men, including Amherst, had gathered round. A dozen eager hands reached for the quaking villain, and Emerson added, "He is not to be harmed. Is that understood?"

"Let me go with you, sir," William begged. Emerson shook his head. "Mrs. Emerson and I will deal with the matter. Selim, I leave you in charge, we must go at once. Look after Gargery—and the cat."

"I will carry him, sir," said Gargery, getting to his feet with Selim's assistance. "It's the least I can do for the poor, brave . . . Aaah!"

He dropped his burden and clutched at his arm. Horus gave him a malevolent yellow stare, rolled over, and began licking his side.

A hasty and necessarily cursory examination assured me that Gargery had no broken bones, though his bruises were extensive. I knew better than to try to examine Horus, but the energy with which he fought my attempt to wrap him in Emerson's coat suggested his injuries were less severe than I had feared. I handed the squirming bundle to William, who took it with the same look of terrified disgust with which an elderly bachelor might receive a wet, howling baby.

"Hold him tightly," I instructed. "He will try to follow us if you let him go."

"Yes, ma'am," said William. "Whatever you say."

Emerson kept patting Gargery mechanically on the shoulder, but every muscle in his body was tensed, and I knew I could not keep him from pursuit much longer. Not that I wanted to. I was as frantic as he.

"Now, Emerson," I began, and got no further. He caught my hand and set off with long strides toward Mena House, where we had left the horses. His pace was so rapid I could not find breath enough to speak until after we had reached the stable. Emerson's curses inspired the stableman to quick action, and it was Emerson's hands that saddled and bridled his own steed.

"Where are we going?" I asked breathlessly.

"Kafr el Barud. It's a hamlet due east of here." He tossed me into the saddle and mounted.

The grounds of the hotel were crowded with people and vehicles; we were unable to go quickly at first, and Emerson took advantage of the enforced delay to utter a few sentences of explanation.

"They had horses and a rug or cloak to wrap round her. The first man fled with Sennia while the other one was struggling with Gargery. They hadn't expected him to put up such a fight." He swallowed noisily, and then said, "They won't hurt her, Peabody."

"She has already been hurt—frightened, and roughly handled, and perhaps struck. How else could they keep her quiet? Good Gad, Emerson, can't we go faster?"

Emerson's lips curled back, baring his teeth. "Stay close."

I do not believe we actually knocked anyone down. The persons who fell to the ground tripped over their own feet in their haste to get out of our way.

How Emerson found the place I do not know; "hamlet" was too grandiose a word for the scattering of huts, not more than half a dozen of them, nestled in a hollow at the foot of the escarpment. It was one of the poorest, most miserable-looking collection of dwellings I have ever seen, even in Egypt. The inhabitants must have had to carry drinking water from the river or the nearest irrigation canal, for there was no well nor tree nor green plant. The crumbling mud-bricks of the houses were the same drab color as the surrounding soil. Emerson had galloped straight into what would have been the village square if the place had boasted such an amenity. There was no sign of life except for a dog sleeping in the dust, and a few chickens. Our approach had not been silent or inconspicuous; the inhabitants had had time to flee or conceal themselves.

"The place looks deserted," I said. "Are you sure he wasn't lying?"

"To me? I think not." Emerson, who had, of course, lost his hat, shaded his eyes with his hand and studied the dismal scene. "That seems the most likely place."

My own eyes had told me there was only one possible place where a prisoner might be held. It stood a little apart from the other houses and it was more stoutly built. Bolted wooden shutters covered the single small window and the door was also barred, from the outside. As we approached, the dog got up and stood watching us with feral yellow eyes. I knew the temper of these vicious half-wild beasts, so I was not surprised when it bared its teeth and began to growl. Emerson ignored it; he had no thought at that moment for anything except the child; but I picked up a stone and held it ready. My heart was pounding so hard it hurt my chest. Except for the dog's low growls the place was ut-

terly silent. It was like a Moslem cemetery, dusty
and deserted and baking under the hot sun. Was the
child unconscious, or bound and gagged, or in the
grasp of the villain who had carried her off? I could
not imagine Sennia failing to protest her captivity
if she was able to articulate.

We were almost at the door before I heard a
voice, and astonishment stopped me in my tracks.
It was not Sennia's unmistakable, high-pitched voice;
it was not the gruff voice of a man. The crooning,
quavering tones were a woman's, repeating soft en-
dearments.

"Little one, sit down and rest. Here is water, darling; will you drink? Or honey cakes, eat them,
they are good."

"La, shukran," said Sennia.

My knees almost gave way. It was such a relief to
hear her, sounding quite cool and unhurt, politely
declining the offering. I looked at Emerson. "What
on earth—" I mouthed.

He put his finger to his lips. I knew why he hesitated; he wanted to be certain there was no one else
in the room.

Sennia went on, in the same gentle voice. "I want
to go home, Mother. Please let me out."

"Sweet one, I cannot. He locked us in. You aren't
afraid, are you? Don't be afraid. You are safe with
me."

She had been very brave, but now she began to
cry, and when Emerson heard her sobs he lifted the
heavy wooden bar and wrenched the door open.

There was some light in the room from small
ventilation holes high under the eaves; I made out

dim shapes that were, as I later discovered, a low bed or couch, a brazier, and a few pots and baskets. In the first moment I had eyes only for Sennia. Her face was dirty and smeared with tears and her clothing was crumpled. That was all I saw before she hurled herself at Emerson. He caught her up in his arms and held her close.

"It's all right, Little Bird, we are here. Did they hurt you?"

"Not very much." She wiped her wet eyes with her fingers. "Did they hurt Gargery? And Horus? The man kicked him, the beast!"

"They are both all right," I said, deciding this was not the time to enter into detail. "Emerson, let's go."

"Not just yet," said Emerson. He set Sennia on her feet. "I have a few questions to put to this woman."

"Don't frighten her," Sennia cried. She ran to the woman, who was crouched by the brazier, and put her small arms around the shaking form. "She was kind. She only did what he told her. It wasn't her fault."

She wore the single garment characteristic of the poorest women of Upper Egypt, a square of dark brown woolen fabric wrapped round the body like the stola of the Greeks. It exposed her stringy arms and wrinkled throat. Her withered hands fumbled with the folds of the garment, trying to draw it over her head and face, but she was so frightened she could not manage it. My vision had become accustomed to the dim light; when she raised her head I saw her eyes were white with cataracts. She was blind.

"Who are you?" she quavered. "What do you want with me?"

Pity replaced the wrath that had darkened Emerson's countenance. He spoke to the woman in Arabic, softening his gruff voice as much as was possible. "We mean you no harm, Mother. I am the Father of Curses, and this is my wife, the Sitt Hakim. Only tell us who brought the child here and what he meant to do with her."

It took a while—and a number of caresses from Sennia—to win the poor thing's confidence. She said she knew nothing of the business except that her son had told her she must keep Sennia hidden for a few hours. He would return after darkness had fallen to take her away. He had not explained why; she had not asked. I believed her. The woman's role was to hear and obey, and she was too frightened and too frail to lie.

"We are going to take the child with us," Emerson said. "We are her family. Will he harm you, Mother, when he finds she is gone?"

"No, no. He is a good son. He takes care of me. He would not have hurt the child. I think . . ." She hesitated. "I think someone gave him money. We have very little."

She had a little more when we left. Emerson is extremely soft-hearted. I only hoped she had been telling the truth when she claimed her son would not blame her for the loss of his prisoner. There was no way she could have prevented it, but some men will vent their anger on the nearest object, especially if it is weaker than they are.

Emerson took Sennia up in front of him and she settled in the curve of his arm with a sigh. "Can we go home now? I want to see Gargery and Horus and I am very thirsty; she offered me water, but you told me not to drink water unless it was boiled."

I unhooked my canteen and handed it to Emerson. "You are a good girl, to remember that when you were so frightened."

"I wasn't frightened. Not very. I knew you would come."

Over her head Emerson's eyes met mine. I knew he was remembering another child who had said something of the sort to us many years before. Honesty compels me to remark that in Ramses's case the innumerable mishaps from which we had rescued him were usually his own fault, but this was not true of Sennia; we had failed her and it was only due to the mercy of God and the courage of Gargery that matters had turned out as well as they had.

Sennia handed the canteen back to me. "Can we go home now, please?"

When we reached the house we found a large crowd assembled—all our skilled men, all the female servants, and half a dozen of the gaffirs. Ali the doorman was not at the door; he was with the others, brandishing a heavy stick and shouting at the top of his lungs. His demands and those of the others were directed at Selim; they wanted action and they wanted it now, and poor Selim's attempts to be heard over the bedlam were in vain. He was the first to see us. The change in his expression made the others turn, and then we were the center of the shouting mob.

It took quite some time to quiet them. Kadija carried Sennia off to see Gargery and Fatima ran to the kitchen to cook Sennia's favorite dishes. The rest of them began an animated discussion. Should they celebrate the child's return with a huge fantasia first, or wait until after they had punished her abductors?

"Sir?" William edged up to us. I hadn't noticed him; he was so confounded self-effacing. "What can I do, sir?"

"Nothing," Emerson said, cruelly but correctly. Seeing the young man's face fall, I added, "Thank you, William, but as you see, the matter is under control."

"Yes, ma'am. I—I am very glad the child is safe."

Emerson had already turned away; I patted William's arm and followed my husband and Selim into the study.

"What have you done with him?" was Emerson's first question.

"He is locked in the garden shed, with Hassan on guard. They would have torn him limb from limb, Father of Curses, if I had allowed it. What happened? Where was she? Did you find the other man?"

We gave him a brief account of what had transpired. "Ah," said Selim, brightening. "So we will go there and wait for him to come back tonight!"

"That is a step we must take," Emerson agreed. "Though there is a chance someone will warn him.

It couldn't be helped, Selim, we had to get the child home at once. Fortunately we have another source of information."

I persuaded Emerson to wait a bit before beginning the interrogation of our prisoner, since I wanted to be present, and there were other duties I needed to carry out first. They did not take long. Gargery had been put to bed by Selim and smeared with green ointment by Kadija. He was a sight to behold, but his cheerful if distorted smile and air of self-satisfaction told me that he considered his bruises a small price to pay for his new role as hero—which, I feared, he intended to milk to the full. Sennia had been to see him; she was now in the bath, attended like a small Sultaness by Kadija and Basima and several other women—and Horus, who lay stretched out on a cushion watching.

The cat and I studied one another with mutual distaste. Now was when we missed Nefret. Veterinary medicine is not one of my specialities, but I knew that an animal in pain may attack even a friend. However, I have never been known to shirk my duty. I advanced upon Horus with a firm stride.

"Peabody, don't," Emerson exclaimed in alarm. "Not without gloves—not without several people holding him down—not without a stout stick . . ." His voice trailed off into silence. Horus had rolled over, and we saw that his entire underbelly was bright green.

"Oh," I said. "Kadija, how did you—"

Kadija glanced at me over her shoulder. "He has no broken bones, Sitt Hakim, and I think nothing inside is hurt. He has eaten a great deal of chicken and clawed halfway through the door of Sennia's room."

"But how did you—"

"I talked to him."

In what language? I wondered. I decided not to ask. Horus sneered at me.

The storage shed had no windows. The interior was as hot as an oven. The prisoner's sweating face shone like glass. He was a young man, dark skinned and heavily bearded. The men had not handled him gently. His head was bare and his robe was torn.

If there had been any fight left in him, the sight of Emerson's stalwart form filling the narrow doorway would have ended it. He had been sitting on the floor; he wriggled back as far as he could go and raised his hands in appeal.

"It is said that the Father of Curses does not torture prisoners," he croaked.

"Only when they refuse to answer my questions," Emerson said. "That has never happened. I hope you will not be the first. What is your name?"

The first few questions were answered without hesitation. His name was Mohammed, his profession camel driver, he lived in Giza village, where he had met Saleh Ibrahim, who had hired him for a little job. "The child was in no danger, Father of Curses, I swear. Saleh said she must be taken alive and unhurt or he would not be paid. He said—"

"Paid," Emerson repeated. "By whom?"

"I do not know, Father of Curses. I have done wrong, but do not send me to prison; beat me, and let me go. It was Saleh who planned it. He took her to his house. That is all I know. I swear I will never again—"

"Oh, be quiet," Emerson said in disgust. He turned to me and spoke in English. "I know his kind. He is a petty criminal, who will turn his hand to any job that does not require great courage or intelligence. What surprises me is that he had the intestinal fortitude to take on *this* job. He knew who the victim was; he knows who we are; he knew her relationship to us."

"He may have been promised a large sum of money."

"It would have to be a very large sum," said Emerson, with unconscious—and justifiable— egotism. "No. There is something he has not told us. Look at the miserable creature."

Sweat was pouring down the man's face, which had turned a peculiar shade of muddy gray. His hand had gone to his throat, and I saw that he was fingering an amulet of some sort.

"That won't help you," said Emerson. "Do you think God listens to the prayers of sinners and liars and tormentors of little children? You know who hired Saleh. If you do not speak . . ." He paused for effect. Mohammed's teeth began to chatter. "If you do not tell us the truth, the Sitt Hakim will fetch her parasol."

The fellow's eyes rolled back into his head, and he slumped over in a faint. "Now you've done it, Emerson," I remarked.

"I hope so," said Emerson. "Hassan, give him some water."

I had Daoud to thank for the legends that surrounded my parasol. He was a fine raconteur, and the tales he had told about us had spread throughout the length of Egypt. I had never been sure how much he believed in the magical powers of the parasol, but he had certainly managed to convince a number of other people. We revived Mohammed and found him pitiably willing to confess, but he was in such a state of terror, Emerson had to shake him a few times before he could speak intelligibly.

Only one thing could have persuaded him to brave the wrath of the Father of Curses and the terrible parasol of the Sitt Hakim. It was not money. It was the knowledge that the act had been ordered by a man he feared even more—and the hope of becoming one of his trusted men. I think I knew what he was going to say even before Emerson shook it out of him. "The Master. It was the Master! Who dares refuse his commands?"

My fertile pen falters when I attempt to describe the impact of Mohammed's statement. He would not have dared to lie. He was telling the truth—as he believed. Even Emerson was momentarily struck dumb.

Recovering, I said, "The Master is dead."

Mohammed looked like a cornered rat, terror and cunning mingled on his sweating face. "So they said of him once before. But he was not dead, Sitt, or else he came back from Gehenna, where the very afreets cower before him, and he punished those who had been disloyal. I have not seen him, but Saleh has. He gave Saleh money. He will give him more tonight, when he knows his orders have been carried out."

"Tonight," Emerson repeated, in a voice like the rumble of thunder.

"Obviously someone has used his name, Emerson," I exclaimed.

"Obviously." Visibly troubled, Emerson fingered the cleft in his chin. "Since none of his hirelings knew what he really looked like, it would not be difficult to convince them that he had returned. He has as many personalities as hairs on his head."

We had spoken in English, but Mohammed understood enough to give him new hope. "You believe me, Father of Curses! I can tell you no more. Let me go and I swear I will never again—"

"Shall we turn him over to Mr. Russell?" I asked.

"No, what purpose would that serve? Russell couldn't get any more out of him than we have. I want him here, at my disposal. I cannot think how he could be of further use to us, but one never knows."

Mohammed's howls of woe followed us as we went back to the house. I had instructed Hassan to get him food and water and make him as comfortable as circumstances allowed. He was a contemptible creature, but one must live up to one's standards.

We planned our expedition with care, confiding only in Selim. Though I did not suppose we would require his help, it would have been cruel to refuse his demand that he be allowed to accompany us. He was aching to get in a few blows on his own account.

It was late afternoon before we got off. Mohammed had been vague about the precise time of the meeting between the impostor and his hireling, probably because he did not know himself. "After nightfall" might be any hour between dusk and dawn, so we needed to be in position before sunset. We had a little less than a mile to walk from the place where we left the horses, and there we assumed Arab dress. Emerson enjoyed this part of the business, since in my guise of a Moslem female I was obliged to follow him at a proper distance. We approached the village from the south, where ridges of rock offered concealment. The sun was low in the west by then. He and Selim settled down to wait. I went on.

Emerson had not given in to this part of the scheme without argument, but in my opinion it was imperative that we have someone actually inside the house, and I was the only one who could approach it without arousing suspicion. Many of the poorer local women went unveiled, and so did I, but the head scarf shadowed my face, which I had darkened with one of the concoctions Ramses kept for that purpose.

I met no one as I shuffled toward the house. Even the dog had disappeared. During our earlier visit the inhabitants had hidden in their houses; now they appeared to have made a hasty exodus. They might be uneducated and ignorant but they were not stupid. "When the Father of Curses appears, trouble follows," as Daoud was wont to say. They must have known the trouble was not over—that the Father of Curses would hold someone accountable for Sennia's abduction—that he would return, breathing fire and summoning all the demons of Egypt to his aid. I did not believe any of the others had been directly involved, but it is not only the guilty who flee when no man pursueth.

I doubted they would have taken the old woman with them. She would have been an encumbrance, and would serve as a scapegoat. Sure enough, she was there, huddled in the corner by the brazier, looking as if she had not moved since we last saw her. She raised her head when I entered and closed the door after me.

"Do not be afraid," I said softly. "It is the Sitt Hakim."

She nodded. "I knew you would come back. The others knew too. They have run away."

"Your son has not returned?"

"No." In the same lifeless voice she went on, "He will not return. The story of your coming here has spread now, and if he hears of it he will go far away and never come back, and I will be alone, with no one to care for me. Is the child safe?"

"Yes. Safe and happy."

"She is a good child, kind and gentle. He swore he would not harm her. She would not eat the honey cakes . . ."

Her voice trailed off into mumbles and she began rocking back and forth, her arms folded across her breast as if she were nursing an infant. She had spent some of her windfall on opium. I recognized the smell. Well, who could blame her for wanting to escape from a life of blindness, poverty, and loneliness?

I looked round the room, trying to decide what

to do. The sky outside was darkening, and soon the interior would be pitch-black. The only place to sit was the floor, which was crawling with insect life; my ankles were already under attack. I decided to stand on one side of the room, where I would be concealed by the door when it opened. The old woman paid no attention. She was lost in memories of a happier past, when she had cradled a child.

It was entirely possible that our attempted ambush was doomed from the start. The villagers, dispersed across the landscape by now, would report the exciting events of the morning to everyone they met. One of them might even take the risk of heading Saleh off and warning him that his plot had failed. If he did not hear of it beforehand, he would certainly realize something was amiss when he found the door unbarred.

In my opinion, these possibilities did not justify abandoning our plan. They were possibilities, not certainties, and I felt sure Emerson would agree that we ought not miss even a remote chance of capturing the kidnapper, whom we would force to lead us to the man who had hired him. Was it the same individual who had murdered Asad and attacked us? It hardly seemed likely that we had more than one enemy after us (though I had known it to happen), but try as I might, I had not been able to think of a single underlying motive that would explain all the events. However, a new and intriguing idea had occurred to me after Mohammed's astonishing announcement that afternoon. Could our adversary be a lieutenant of the Master Criminal, bent on revenge for his master's death? Few if any of them could have known of his work for the War Office, and his demise might well have been blamed on us.

I had encountered several of these individuals, and since I had nothing better to do, I passed them in review. The sophisticated, charming Sir Edward? The gallant young Frenchman I had known as René d'Arcy? The amiable American lad, Charles Holly? Surely not any of them. They had all been perfect gentlemen, even if they were criminals. The only one of Sethos's immediate entourage who might have concocted such a diabolical scheme was dead. There could be no doubt of it, for I had seen her corpse. Of course I had not known all his people personally . . .

Such speculation got me nowhere, but at least it helped to pass the time.

Darkness had fallen. The old woman was asleep; I could see nothing, but I heard her thin whistling breaths. I had prepared myself for a long wait. The sound that shook me out of my half-doze was so unexpected and so uncanny, I almost lost my balance. It was the high-pitched, mournful howling of a dog.

The crack of a weapon, pistol or rifle, ended the dog's lament. I waited, holding my breath. What the sound betokened I could not tell; how far away it had been I did not know. But someone was out there in the hills, armed with a modern weapon. Once, in the days of my impetuous youth, I might have rushed out of the hut firing my own little gun. I knew better now. Whatever occurred, I must stick to my post until I was relieved. Grasping my pistol in one hand and my torch in the other, I pointed both at the door and stood ready.

I suppose the interval did not last more than half an hour, but I thought I would burst from frustration and worry before I finally heard a voice. "Peabody, it's me. Don't shoot! Is it safe to come in?"

My throat was parched, but I managed to croak a response. "Certainly it is safe. Do you suppose I would shoot blindly at an opening door?"

"I have known it to happen," said Emerson. The door creaked open and I saw his form outlined against the starlight. He had spoken in his normal tones and his torch was lighted, though he was considerate enough not to shine it directly into my eyes. Stiff with long standing, I stumbled toward him. He removed the pistol from my numbed grasp before he lent me the support of his arm.

"What happened?" I demanded. "I heard the dog howl—and the pistol shot."

"And you stayed in position? Good girl." He gave me a quick kiss. "Now if you can only get out of the habit of waving that damned gun at people . . . You aren't hurt, are you?"

"No, but I've been standing in one position for hours! Where is Selim? What happened, curse it?"

"Gone to fetch the horses." Emerson shone his torch round the interior of the hut. "Opium," he muttered. "Poor creature. We will have to make arrangements for her tomorrow, Peabody. Her son won't be coming back."

"Dead?"

"Yes. The dog must have been his; it was lying

beside his body. Strange, the loyalty the beasts feel even for masters who abuse and neglect them."

After the noisome dark of the hut the night air was as refreshing as cool water against my hot cheeks. I refreshed myself with actual water from my canteen, which I had been unable to do earlier since both my hands were occupied, and while we waited for Selim, Emerson answered my urgent questions.

"The tragedy, if you want to call it that, occurred not far from where we had concealed ourselves. As I reconstruct the affair, Saleh was to meet his employer in the hills above the village. The bastard may have meant to take Sennia away with him. He may have wanted proof that Saleh had her before he paid over the rest of the money. However— this is only a guess, but it makes sense—Saleh kept the assignation because he was too greedy to abandon the rest of the reward. His attempt to deceive his employer failed; he was forced to admit he had lost his captive."

"Or," I suggested, "the impostor may have heard of our visit. As you yourself pointed out, it would have been a subject of gossip all day, all over the area."

"Hmmm." Emerson fingered the dent in his chin. "Yes, that makes even better sense. Saleh hoped his employer was still unaware of the latest turn of events, and believed he could trick him into handing over the money. Or, it may be, he meant to overpower and rob him. The—er—impostor took the risk of meeting Saleh because the risk of leaving him on the loose was even greater; he might have been able to tell us something that would give us a clue as to the identity of the man who had hired him. I expect he meant from the first to kill Saleh, once the deed was done. The dog was the only thing he had not anticipated. It began to howl, and the bastard shot it."

"There was no trace of him, I suppose."

"No. It took us awhile, in the dark, to find the spot. He had plenty of time to knife Saleh, kill the dog, and make himself scarce."

"Foiled again!" I cried, shaking my fists at the dark, unheeding heavens.

Had I been allowed to follow proper procedures, I would have returned to the murder scene, searched for clues, and examined the body. This suggestion affected Emerson adversely. He assured me, with considerable vehemence, that he had done the job himself at least as thoroughly as I could have done. I doubted this, but his indignation rose to such a pitch, I deemed it advisable to abandon the idea.

"So what clues did you discover?" I inquired, as we rode back toward the house. Nodding graciously at Selim, I included him in the question. However, he was wise enough to remain silent.

"Nothing," said Emerson. "Did you suppose he would leave his card?"

"No footprints, no scraps of clothing?"

"Not even a bit of paper clutched in the stiffening fingers of the corpse," said Emerson, with awful sarcasm. "There was no struggle, not even an argument; the fellow came at Saleh from behind, put one arm round his throat to prevent an outcry, and drove the knife into his body with the other hand."

"It is an ingenious reconstruction, Emerson, but how can you be sure?"

"Elementary, my dear Peabody. Saleh would not have stood still and silent without making some attempt to defend himself if he had faced a man with a knife. His own knife was still in his belt. Anyhow, that appears to be our friend's approved method. He is as efficient as he is ruthless. One would prefer," said Emerson didactically, "to avoid being spattered with blood. The victim's own body would protect the murderer from that, except for his arm and sleeve."

"Have you anything to add, Selim?" I asked.

"No, Sitt Hakim. Except that I am sorry he died so quickly."

Such proved to be the general consensus. A number of our loyal men were still at the house; in lieu of a fantasia, they had decided to celebrate on a smaller scale. Food and drink (of a nonalcoholic variety) were flowing freely, and in the center of the room, like a monarch on his throne, was Gargery, excessively bandaged and smiling. The beverage in his glass appeared to be beer.

As soon as I could make myself heard over the questions and cries of welcome, I said, "I am pleased to observe, Gargery, that your injuries were not as painful as I had believed."

"I felt obliged to join in the celebration, madam,"

said Gargery self-righteously. "These good fellows insisted."

"Ha," said Emerson—but he said no more. Gargery's current status as hero still held. I had a feeling it would not hold much longer if he took too much advantage of it.

We were both quite hungry, so we sat down on the settee and accepted plates of spiced chicken and stewed lentils, and Emerson told the audience what had happened. Groans of disappointment followed the announcement of Saleh's death.

"What shall we do now, Father of Curses?" Hassan asked.

"Await my orders," said Emerson. "The Sitt Hakim and I will determine what is to be done."

They went willingly after that promise, and Gargery staggered off to bed, leaning on Fatima. Neither of us felt inclined to lend him a hand, since the staggers were somewhat exaggerated. At last we were alone!

"What shall we do now, Father of Curses?" I inquired.

"I took it for granted that you already had a plan," said my husband. "Whiskey and soda, Peabody?"

"Yes, thank you. As a matter of fact, I have been thinking."

"Hell and damnation," Emerson said mildly. "Well, my dear?"

It had been a rather tiring day, what with one thing and another, but a sip of the genial beverage had the usual inspiring effect.

"We must go to Luxor, Emerson."

Emerson began muttering to himself. It had once been a habit of his, though he had not done it lately. "Never get accustomed to it. How does she . . . Must?" He sat down with a thump and stared at me. His heavy brows formed a straight line across his manly brow.

"I will explain."

"Pray do."

"One of the unsolved mysteries about this business is Mr. Asad's role. The people who freed him could not possibly have supposed he would succeed in killing Ramses; he hadn't the strength or the skill to do it. I believe the episode was designed to arouse our interest—"

"It certainly did that," said Emerson, reaching for his pipe.

"Please, Emerson, do not be sarcastic. I am endeavoring to discuss this in a logical manner. I . . . Curse it, you have made me lose track of what I was saying. In short, Ramses and we were meant to search for Mr. Asad—here, in Cairo. Is that not what we would have done under normal circumstances? Instead, parental affection overcame our sense of duty and we did precisely the opposite of what our opponent had expected. Sending Ramses to Luxor was a serious error. The succeeding incidents, including Sennia's abduction, were designed to get him back to Cairo."

"He will certainly come back when he hears about Sennia," Emerson muttered round the stem of his pipe. "If you had not insisted on keeping the other incidents from him—"

"He would have returned before this. I sometimes think the boy has not much confidence in our ability to take care of ourselves."

"I cannot imagine how he could have got that impression."

"Emerson—"

"I beg your pardon, my dear. Well, well. I am not entirely convinced by your reasoning, Peabody, but," said Emerson, in a refreshing burst of candor, "I am always more comfortable in my mind when we are all of us together. Why can't we just tell—er—persuade the children to come home?"

"Because the scene of action is in Luxor! I am convinced of it. You were right—"

"I was?" Emerson gave me a look of exaggerated astonishment.

"Emerson, please don't do that. You were right in suspecting that there is something sinister behind the increase in antiquities theft. It is just like the old days, when Sethos controlled the business. What we learned today proves it: someone is masquerading as the Master. Has it occurred to you that this person may be one of his former lieutenants?"

Emerson shook his head. He appeared to be a trifle dazed.

"That assumption would explain the attacks on us, you see," I continued. "Revenge for the death of his leader! Furthermore, it would be to the advantage of this individual to keep us away from Luxor. That is why we must go there."

"Q.E.D.," muttered Emerson.

"I have it all worked out," I assured him. "The

school holidays begin shortly. We will stay with Cyrus and Katherine. They will be delighted to have us. You and I and Sennia, Gargery and Fatima and Daoud and Selim and Kadija and—"

"Good Gad, Peabody, you can't expect the Vandergelts to take in a mob like that."

"—and Basima and—"

"The damned cat? Peabody!"

"The Castle is a very large house, Emerson, and I expect Daoud and Selim may prefer to stay with their kin in Gurneh. We can be ready to leave day after tomorrow. I will wire Cyrus first thing in the morning. And now, my dear, I believe we should retire. I am a trifle weary and there will be a great deal to do tomorrow."

I put my empty glass on the table and stood up. Emerson remained seated. ". . . like an avalanche," he muttered, staring into space. "Get out of the way . . . only chance . . . nine people and the cat . . ."

I sat down again and put my hand over his clenched fists. "We must find the man who is behind this, Emerson. Family honor demands it."

"Family *what*?" Emerson's eyes came back into focus.

"The impostor is using your—" Not even in the privacy of our own home did we use that word. I started again. "He is using Sethos's name and besmirching his reputation."

"His reputation isn't exactly lily-white, my dear. However . . ." His noble brow furrowed. "It's beginning to add up," he said, as if to himself.

"Precisely, Emerson. I am glad you see it my way."

"I rather doubt it, Peabody. But we will go to Luxor. Just tell me one thing." He took me by the shoulders and turned me to face him. "Please tell me your decision was not affected by that damned dream about Abdullah, when instead of speaking to you he waved you to follow him."

"Why, Emerson," I said. "How could you possibly think that?"

TWELVE

When Ramses and Nefret arrived at the station, the train had just pulled in. They had to push through a throng of people, all waving their arms and shouting with excitement. Ramses was not surprised that the whole town had turned out; Cyrus was well known and well liked and his wife's numerous charitable activities had made her equally popular. It would have been cynical to suspect that they had a selfish motive—the hope that Vandergelt Effendi had returned to resume the excavations that had given employment to so many men of Luxor.

No such thought occurred to Cyrus; he was visibly moved as he stood in the open door of the car, clasping the hands thrust out to him and returning the cries of greeting and welcome. Finally Ramses put an end to the demonstration, which was threatening to pour into the compartment, and by dint of shouts and some shoving, cleared a path along the platform to the waiting carriages. Cyrus helped his wife down the steps and handed her over to Ramses before embracing Nefret. She kissed him back with hearty good-will, and then hurried to offer an arm to Bertie. He didn't need it; Daoud lifted him clean off his feet and lowered him gently to the platform.

"I will carry him to the carriage," Daoud announced, holding the young man in a fond grip.

"No—please—I'd rather walk. Really. Tell him," Bertie insisted.

He was laughing and a trifle flushed. Katherine—and probably Daoud—had muffled him in coats and mufflers and capes, but the bones in his face and in the thin hand that reached for that of Ramses were painfully prominent. Ramses distracted Daoud with a request that he see to the luggage, and put an unobtrusive arm round Bertie's shoulders. "Let's get you to the carriage. It's not far."

"Yes, right. It's just the excitement, you know. I'm glad to be here. Been looking forward to it. I hated to leave that little witch Sennia, though. I must warn you, Ramses—I'm in love. Do you think I'm too old for her?"

The brief walk to the carriage left him breathless, and he was talking too fast, putting up a valiant pretense at normalcy.

"We're all too old for Sennia," Ramses said lightly. "She wears me out, and even Father requires an extra whiskey after a day with her. Can you stick it for a few more minutes? Yusuf considers himself the official representative of the family and wants to welcome you personally. I'll see that he keeps it short."

After a whispered conference, Yusuf agreed not

to make a speech, which would have been lost on Bertie anyhow, since he had only a few words of Arabic. Several brothers and cousins had to be introduced, however, along with his pride and joy, Jamil.

Yusuf launched into an encomium on Jamil's intelligence and beauty and all-round virtue, while Jamil postured and smirked. If Vandergelt Effendi should decide to resume his excavations, there was no one better to serve as his reis. This last was aimed directly at Cyrus, who gave Ramses a knowing grin and a wink.

"Make our excuses, Ramses, your Arabic is better than mine."

"Yes, sir, certainly. We must go now, Yusuf."

"Wait." Bertie caught at his sleeve. "Who's that?"

Ramses turned. He hadn't recognized her before; she was wearing European clothing—a divided skirt belted tight around her narrow waist, a neat flannel coat, and a pith helmet that fit much better than the other. It was an old one of Nefret's, he supposed, like the rest of the outfit. Her black hair had been coiled and knotted at the back of her neck. Ramses wondered if Yusuf had seen her, improperly attired and in the middle of a crowd. Maybe not. She had kept in the background until then, and the clothes made quite a difference in her appearance.

Catching his eye, she drew herself up to her full five feet and gave him a dazzling smile before melting back into the mob.

"Who is she?" Bertie demanded. He had caught

only the fringe of the smile, but he looked as if he had been hit over the head with a brick.

"You'll meet her later," Nefret said.

"That's certain," Ramses muttered. Nefret turned her laugh into a cough, and began issuing orders. "Katherine, you and Cyrus ride with Bertie. We'll catch you up at the ferry landing. Daoud will bring the luggage on later."

The carriage drove away. Bertie had twisted round to look back. Lips compressed, Ramses handed his bride into the second carriage. "You gave her the clothes?"

"Yes, why not? I got tired of seeing that pathetic old pith helmet slide down over her eyes. She's much tinier than I am, of course, but I showed her how to—"

"Did you anticipate this?"

"I expected she'd turn up today, if that's what you mean. As for Bertie . . . well, Mother told us he needed a new interest, didn't she? I think he may have found it."

One of the graceful feluccas took them across the river, to the dock where Cyrus's carriage was waiting. Nefret firmly declined Cyrus's pressing invitation to return with them to the house.

"You'll want to settle in and have a little rest. We'll see you this evening."

"Come early and stay late," Cyrus said. "We've got a lot to talk about, I reckon." He drew a long breath. "It sure is good to be back."

Daoud turned up at the *Amelia* a short while later, bursting with conversation and questions.

They had a good long gossip, mostly about domestic and professional matters.

"When are you coming back to Cairo?" Daoud asked, somewhat accusingly. "The Father of Curses will not finish the excavation of the last mastaba until you return, and the Little Bird misses you. She wept very loudly when they said she could not come to Luxor with us."

Ramses smiled at that only too accurate adverb, but Nefret said, "You might at least write her a personal message, Ramses. Sit down and do it right now, and Daoud can take it with him. Must you go back tonight, Daoud?"

"Oh, yes. The Father of Curses cannot get on without me. I will spend a little time with Yusuf in Gurneh before I take the train. Is there something I can do for you before I go? Letters to carry back? News to tell?"

There was plenty of news. The question was, how much to tell Daoud? She had posted her letter the day before, but they probably would not receive it until the following week.

"Yes," she said. "There is news. Important news."

Ramses looked up from the sheet of paper over which he was frowning. (Why did men find it so difficult to write a chatty, informal note?)

"First," she said, "Miss Minton is asking questions of everyone in Luxor about illegal antiquities dealings. Second . . ."

"Nefret," Ramses said apprehensively. He had mistaken the reason for her hesitation. She frowned back at him. Did he really suppose she would inform the parents of Sethos's reappearance without consulting him? The news about the accident would have to wait too; Daoud would make it sound more alarming than it was. He might even insist on staying in Luxor to watch over them.

"Second, there is a letter on the way," she said smoothly. "Third, Mr. Bertie has found a new interest. Her name is Jumana."

"Three things," Daoud said happily.

"Can you remember them?"

"Oh, yes." Daoud was a trifle slow, but there was nothing wrong with his wits, or his memory, and he was delighted to be the bearer of important information. He ticked the points off on his fingers. "The lady Minton is asking about antiquities thieves. A letter is coming. Mr. Bertie has a new interest, Jumana. Who is she?"

"Yusuf's daughter. You will meet her this afternoon; she is a very intelligent young woman and we hope to train her as an Egyptologist. I know the Sitt Hakim will want to hear your opinion of the girl."

"Ah," Daoud said thoughtfully. "A girl. Hmmm."

Nefret waited for the idea to penetrate. Glancing at Ramses, she said impatiently, "Just write a few words. She doesn't really care what you say, she just wants to hear from you."

"So," said Daoud. "A girl." His pensive face brightened as the obvious answer occurred to him. "It will be as Allah and the Sitt Hakim decide."

"He's got that right," Ramses said, after Daoud had taken an affectionate leave of them. "What a devious woman you are. Daoud will break the news of our intentions to Yusuf, and if poor old Yusuf objects, he will be sat upon by Daoud, who considers Allah and the Sitt Hakim, not necessarily in that order, as infallible."

Nefret looked demure. "That had occurred to me."

Cyrus's carriage came for them at five. They hadn't expected it to be so early, and Nefret hurried to complete her toilette. She was fastening on her earrings when Ramses came back from the bath chamber. His face fell. He was no more observant about women's clothing than his father, but he could tell the difference between work clothes and an evening frock.

"I didn't know we were supposed to dress. They surely won't force Bertie into a boiled shirt and all the rest."

"What were you planning to wear?"

"Oh . . ." He looked vaguely around the room. "The usual, I suppose. Clothes."

"Wear whatever you like," Nefret said. "It's just the Vandergelts. They won't care."

Cyrus had dressed formally; he was a bit of a dandy and had a wardrobe almost as extensive as that of his wife. Being accustomed to the Emersons' habits, he made no comment about Ramses's flannels and the low-heeled, sensible slippers Nefret had substituted for the satin shoes she had intended to wear. They had bundled Bertie up like a mummy and ensconced him in a chair, but he swept the coverings aside and got to his feet when Nefret entered the room. She hastily sat down so that he could do the same.

"So what's your family up to now?" Cyrus inquired, while servants passed round the tea-things.

"Why do you ask that?" Ramses said. "Did anything happen while you were there?"

"Well, no. Not that I know of. But they were sure in a durned hurry to get us out of Cairo."

"They were probably afraid you'd try to run off and fight the Senussi," Nefret said.

Cyrus enjoyed her teasing, but he remained serious. "Well, I wouldn't mind taking a hand in something. I'm getting kind of bored. Any chance of catching a few tomb robbers?"

Katherine murmured protestingly and Nefret laughed. "I'm sorry, Cyrus. There've been a few incidents, but only the sort of thing you might expect, with supervision so lax. Alain Kuentz caught one of the Gurnawis investigating a cliff tomb near Deir el Bahri, but there was nothing in it."

"Kuentz is in Luxor? Nice young fellow. We'll have to have him to dinner." Cyrus tugged thoughtfully at his goatee. "Maybe the man he caught knows about more tombs."

"Now get that out of your head, Cyrus," his wife said firmly. "I will not have you chasing after thieves. If you're bored, hire some men and find your own tombs."

"Are you planning to excavate in Thebes this winter?" Ramses asked.

"Been thinking about it," Cyrus admitted. "Question is, where? Carnarvon's got the concession for the Valley . . ."

They discussed possibilities until dinner was

announced and Katherine said, "No more shop-talk this evening, if you please. Bertie and I can't get a word in edgewise while you three are going at it."

"Oh, I don't mind," Bertie said quickly. "I'd like to take a hand myself as soon as I'm feeling a bit stronger. Er—was that young woman at the station one of your people, Ramses?"

"No. Well—yes, I suppose she is. In a way."

Nefret gave him an amused look and explained.

"I remember her," Katherine said. "Miss Pinch said she was one of the most capable students she had ever taught, but of course there was no future for the girl. I'm surprised Yusuf hasn't married her off by now."

"She's trying to make her own future," Nefret said. "You should have heard her, Katherine, insisting that she could be just as good a reis as Jamil."

"She didn't say as good," Ramses corrected. "She said she'd be better. That wouldn't be difficult. Jamil is lazy and disinterested. Don't even think of hiring him, Cyrus."

Cyrus grinned. "I could tell by the look on your face what you thought of him. Maybe I'd better hire the girl."

"Don't make fun of her," Nefret said, dividing a frown between Cyrus and Ramses. "Why can't she be trained as an Egyptologist, as David was? Would you be willing to help, Katherine?"

"Of course she will," Bertie said. "Won't you, Mother? I mean to say, just because she's a girl—"

His mother fixed him with a curious stare and

he stuttered to a stop. "She was a pretty child," Katherine said. "I expect she's turned into quite an attractive young woman."

"She's a stunner," Cyrus said enthusiastically.

His wife turned the stare on him. "You saw her?"

"I didn't know who she was, but I couldn't help noticing her. Any man would."

Nefret decided it would be advisable to change the subject. "How is Anna getting on? I believe Mother said she had finished her V.A.D. training."

Before the meal was over Bertie showed signs of fatigue, and Ramses offered to help him upstairs, an offer Bertie accepted. The others had finished dinner and had retired to the drawing room before Ramses came back. He accepted a cup of coffee and responded to Katherine's anxious look with a reassuring smile.

"He wanted to talk. Got a few things off his chest, I think."

"I'm so glad," Katherine murmured. "Thank you, Ramses."

"I didn't do anything. Just listened. And," Ramses went on, "I assured him that it wasn't too late to begin a career in Egyptology."

"Really?" Cyrus leaned forward, his eyes bright. "Holy Jehoshaphat, but that's wonderful! D'you think he means it?"

"It seems to have given him a new incentive to recover. He was gulping down pills and drinking some noxious brew that's supposed to build him up."

"I'll see Yusuf tomorrow," Cyrus declared. "Get

a crew together. Do some preliminary surveying. Talk to MacKay about permits. The Valley of the Queens, maybe."

Nefret had been watching her husband. He was doing his best to enter into Cyrus's enthusiastic plans, but his eyes were half veiled by lowered lashes and he looked tired. She made their excuses as soon as she could. Cyrus ordered his carriage, but they had gone less than a mile when Ramses ordered the driver to stop and got out of the vehicle. "I feel like walking. Go on, I'll see you in a bit."

"I'd like a walk too." He stood looking down at her, his face in shadow, and she added uncertainly, "Unless you'd rather be alone?"

"No." He lifted her down and they started off arm in arm. The road was pale in the moonlight.

"Was it bad?"

"About what you might expect. Mud, pain, vermin, fear, loneliness, disillusionment. You don't want to hear the details. The worst of it was realizing that the enemy weren't demons but men like himself—just as lonely for their homes and families, just as frightened."

"I think he'll be all right," Nefret said gently.

"I hope so." He laughed, suddenly and unexpectedly. "He's certainly found a new interest in life. Peppered me with ingenuous questions about excavating—as if I couldn't tell what was really on his mind. God help me, I heard myself offering to give him a few lessons in hieroglyphs and Egyptian history."

"With Jumana?"

"That was definitely implied."

"Poor darling. We'll see if we can't find him another tutor."

Ahead the ruined walls of the temple of Seti I shone in the starlight. Remembering the night she and "the parents" had searched the crumbling precincts for Ramses and David, and the long hours of waiting before they found out what had become of them, Nefret clung more tightly to her husband's arm. Ramses appeared unaffected by painful memories—after all, she reminded herself, there was hardly a site on the west bank that didn't hold them.

"Am I going too fast for you?" he asked, slowing his steps.

"A little. Let's not hurry, it's a lovely night."

The road to the public ferry landing turned south. Leaving it, they struck off across the cultivation, following the raised pathway Cyrus had built so that he could reach his private dock by carriage. The original owners of the land were still living off the generous price he had paid.

They went on in silence for a while. Ramses began to whistle softly. Recognizing the melody, Nefret smiled to herself. They had waltzed to that song once. For the moment at least he had put aside his worries and was simply enjoying the night air and her company.

The lights of the *Amelia* were visible when a dark form burst out of a grove of palm trees and ran toward them. Ramses whipped around. Fortunately the moon was bright; he was able to stop himself before his raised hand caught her across the throat.

"Don't, it's Miss—it's Margaret," Nefret exclaimed. "What on earth are you doing here?"

Gasping for breath, the journalist took her arm in a hard grip and tugged at her. "Come with me. I've been waiting for hours."

"Come where?" Ramses asked, holding tightly to Nefret's other arm. "What's wrong?"

"Oh, don't ask questions, just hurry. I had to leave him—I don't think he can move, but if he can, he will . . ."

A feeling his mother would have described as a hideous foreboding came over Ramses. His fingers relaxed their hold on Nefret. She didn't have to ask who "he" was either. "Of course we'll come," she said, in her dispassionate, reassuring physician's voice. "Where is he?"

He was lying on the ground under one of the trees, flat on his back and unmoving. Trunk and branches diffused the moonlight; shadows hid his face and blurred his form, but there was no mistaking his identity.

"I can't see," Nefret said, dropping to her knees. "It's too dark. Is he injured?"

"I don't think so." Margaret leaned against one of the trees. "He's ill. At first it was chills, he was shaking and his teeth were chattering, but he could still walk, and I got him this far, but he wouldn't go to the dahabeeyah, and I did, and they told me you were out for the evening, and when I came back he was like this, and—"

"Slap her," Nefret said curtly. "She's hysterical."

"You slap her. I'm not awfully keen on hitting women."

"Delighted to hear it." Margaret took a deep breath. "I'm not hysterical, I was just trying to tell you everything at once. What's wrong with him, Nefret?"

"Damned beard," Nefret muttered. "How the hell can I make a diagnosis when I can't see him, and most of his face is covered with hair? He's not shivering now, his skin is dry and hot and he's comatose. It could be . . . Let's take him to the boat."

"Yes, right," Ramses said resignedly. "Nefret, go on ahead and get the crew out of the way."

She obeyed without hesitation or question. Ramses lifted his uncle and heaved him over one shoulder.

The gangplank was down and the man who usually kept guard was not there. So far, so good, Ramses thought. As he turned into the corridor leading to the sleeping quarters, he heard Nefret's voice in the saloon. She was chattering cheerfully in Arabic, presumably to Nasir. None of the cabins was occupied except theirs; he had a choice of rooms. He chose the nearest, edged in, dumped the unconscious man onto the bed, and rubbed his back. Sethos wasn't as heavy as Emerson, but he was a big man and at the moment, a deadweight.

Margaret had followed him in. "What can I do?" she asked.

"Draw the curtains." By the time she had done so he had found the oil lamp and lit it.

Nefret soon joined them, carrying her medical bag. She hadn't taken the time to change, and her filmy frock contrasted oddly with her brisk, professional manner. "Get some water," she ordered. "Margaret, sit over there and keep out of the way."

When Ramses came back from the bathroom she looked up. "Temperature a hundred and three, pulse rapid. Lift him up, Ramses, and let's see if we can get these pills down him."

"What are they?" Margaret asked.

"Quinine. I think he's got malaria."

"You think? Can't you tell?"

"Oh, certainly," Nefret said sarcastically. "Just give me a microscope and a few slides and the chemicals to fix them, and I'll give *you* a firm diagnosis—assuming I can remember from my lectures on tropical medicine what the bloody parasite looks like. Damn it, he's dribbling into his beard. Hang on a minute."

She got her fingers under one corner of the beard and ripped it off with ruthless efficiency. Her patient reacted with a querulous mutter and a louder comment. "Damned women."

"Open your mouth," Nefret ordered. "Now swallow. Well done! He can lie back now, Ramses."

Ramses lowered him down onto the pillow. With those curiously colored eyes closed and the mocking mouth relaxed, the resemblance to his brother was even stronger.

"That's all we can do now," Nefret said. "Except make him comfortable. When the fever breaks he'll start to sweat and then he'll sleep till morning."

"And then?" Margaret demanded.

"Then he'll feel reasonably well and we'll have to keep him here, by force if necessary, because if it is the commonest form of malaria the apyrexia will only last for a few hours. The next paroxysm will hit tomorrow—the same pattern, chills and fever. In other forms of the disease the interval is forty-eight hours or seventy-two."

"You keep quinine on hand?"

"Yes. Thanks to Mother, we have a well-stocked medicine chest, including laudanum and arsenic." Margaret's expression seemed to amuse her. She went on, "Some researchers believe that prophylactic doses of arsenic prevent malaria. I don't. He'll get a grain of quinine three times a day for three days, and half a grain for another five days. Have I convinced you that I know what I'm talking about, Margaret, or would you care to question me further?"

"I'm sorry. I didn't mean—"

"Never mind." Nefret inspected her. "Ramses, take her to the saloon and give her a glass of brandy."

"I want to stay here with—"

"You can relieve me later. Do as I say."

"What about Nasir?" Ramses asked.

"I sent him to bed. You'll have to wait on yourselves. Now get out of here, both of you."

She wrung out a cloth and began wiping away the perspiration that was now running freely down Sethos's face. Margaret accepted Ramses's hand and let him lead her out.

"Your wife is a remarkable woman," she said. "I had underestimated her. People do, don't they? She's so young and pretty."

"They seldom make that mistake twice."

The lamps in the saloon were still lit. He settled Margaret onto the divan and got out the brandy. He had intended to question her, but when he got his first good look at her he decided he had better give her a little time to recover. Her face was streaked with dirt and pinched with strain, and her stockings were in shreds. She wasn't wearing a coat. The once white shirtwaist was the color of mud.

"Were you hurt?" he asked.

She shook her head. A few sips of brandy brought some of the color back to her face. "I suppose you want to know what happened."

"Well, yes, I do. Take your time."

"But not too much time?" Her mouth curved and widened. "I won't lie or equivocate. Just tell me one thing before I begin. You knew he was still alive, didn't you? You weren't surprised, or uncertain as to his identity."

"Yes." After a moment he added, "Mother doesn't know. She told you what she honestly believed to be the truth."

"Ah." She leaned back against the cushions. "It would appear I did her an injustice. I hope you won't think me rude if I say that I think your mother capable of lying if it would serve her ends."

"Wouldn't most people?"

"I certainly would." She sounded quite her old self. "She had told me his name, or rather, his sobriquet, so I spent several days finding out everything I could about him. You'd be surprised how many sources I uncovered. And of course I remembered that outrageous letter he wrote, and the subsequent investigation; Kevin O'Connell gloated over me unmercifully because he got the story first."

She took another sip of brandy. "So?" Ramses prompted impatiently.

"So I began to wonder whether your mother had lied to me. Her attempt to discourage me from coming on to Luxor was also suspicious. I decided to investigate. At worst I'd get the material for an interesting feature story. I did, too!" she added, with almost her old complacency. "I had little difficulty in extracting information. People like to see their names in the newspaper. The police weren't very forthcoming, but your Egyptological friends saw no reason why they shouldn't tell me what they knew. Howard Carter was a mine of information, after I had plied him with drinks and convinced him that his friends the Emersons wouldn't mind his talking to me. They hadn't sworn him to silence, had they? Everybody who was anybody already knew the stories, didn't they?

"Well, yes, they did, he admitted. The Emersons had spoken freely about their bête noire. Had I heard about the time he took on the identity of a Coptic priest while his men were excavating illegally at a nearby site? I also got an earful about the recent increase in illegal excavations and theft. Most of it centered around the Luxor area, and Amelia's attempt to dissuade me from coming here made me all the more determined to investigate. What did I have to lose, after all?

"It was Sayid who gave me the final clue. Ninety percent of what he told me was pure fabrication, and I had to spend a long tedious day listening to his fantastic stories about the Master—whose right-hand man he claimed to have been—before I got what I wanted out of him. Is there anything that man won't sell?"

"No one's found it yet," Ramses said. "That's why those who know his habits make certain he won't be tempted to betray them. He told you where to find Sethos? How did he know?"

"It is known in Luxor that the Master has returned." She sounded as if she were quoting. "His whereabouts no man knows. His true appearance no man knows. He has a thousand faces and ten thousand names."

The night was very silent. There was no sign of life, no sound of movement outside, on the deck or on the dock. Nevertheless, Ramses's scalp was prickling.

"Never mind the picturesque details," he said somewhat brusquely. "Just tell me what happened."

FROM MANUSCRIPT COLLECTION M

(The Editor has determined to substitute for the hurried account given Ramses by Miss Minton, and repeated by him, one must suppose, in even more abbreviated form, the version written by Miss Minton herself at a somewhat later time. It is much more interesting.)

I might have known that when I encountered *him* again, it would be under circumstances as wildly theatrical as before. This time he didn't do it deliberately. Like certain other people of my acquaintance, he moves in melodrama, drawing it about him like a villain's black cloak.

I looked up Ramses and Nefret Emerson as soon as I got to Luxor. They weren't awfully pleased to see me. I couldn't take that as confirmation of my suspicions (or hopes), but I could tell I wasn't going to get any help from them. I went the rounds of the Egyptologists in Luxor. M. Legrain amiably admitted that it would have taken a lot of skill and knowledge to loot his storage magazines; Mr. MacKay informed me that the whole thing was poppycock and that the Emersons were known for inventing wild stories; Kuentz had a wonderful time telling me even wilder stories. He thought he was being clever, but the things he told me confirmed my suspicions. Someone was behind the recent rash of thefts here in Luxor. Someone had been using the German House for illegal purposes. I carefully wrote it all down, lies and all.

I had been besieged by hopeful dragomen ever since I arrived. I can't remember who it was who suggested Sayid; he'd been there from the first, and one couldn't help noticing him. He is one of the ugliest human beings I have ever seen and as persistent as a fly. I spent a long tedious day listening to the old rascal's lies about the Master, whose trusted lieutenant he claimed to have been, before I got what I wanted out of him. I'll never forget the look on the poor devil's face when I offered him a hundred English pounds if he would tell me where I could find the Master. It was an outrageous amount, more than he could earn in a lifetime. He didn't hesitate long.

Not until later did it occur to me that it had been too easy.

I waited until late afternoon next day before I set out. The house Sayid had told me about was on the west bank. It was only one of several places the Master used, but Sayid considered it to be the most likely.

"It is the largest house in the village and the others do not approach it, because they believe he is a holy man, a Haggi and a descendant of the Prophet. When you knock on the door, Sitt, make sure he knows it is you. He is always on guard, and quick with a knife. I would not want you to be harmed, Sitt."

I believed that. I still owed him fifty pounds.

Knowing that a tourist would be besieged and harassed by hopeful guides the moment she set foot on the west bank, I acquired women's clothing from Sayid (he charged me an extra pound) and put it on in the boat while he took me across. (Five pounds.) He landed me as close as he could, but I had a walk of almost two miles ahead of me. I had taken the risk of wearing my own clothes, including my shoes, under the robe. Authenticity is all very well, but I knew I couldn't walk that far barefoot, or in the clumsy sandals some of the locals wore.

I felt somewhat self-conscious at first, and very awkward in all those layers of cloth. It is not only demanded of women to conceal their faces; heads, bodies, and even hands are covered whenever they walk abroad. Sayid had informed me that my costume, which included a voluminous outer garment of black cotton, was what would be worn by a rigidly respectable, somewhat old-fashioned female of moderate means, but I'm sure he enjoyed watching me stumble and trip over my skirts. Sayid had quite a sense of humor.

Apparently I did look respectable, for no one accosted me or even gave me a second glance. My progress was slow, but I was in no hurry. I didn't want to approach the house until dusk.

I had no trouble finding it. Larger and more pretentious than the others, it stood a little apart from them, backed by a low undulating ridge of rock. I squatted down, knowing I was invisible in the twilight, and waited until most of the lighted windows in the houses of the village had gone dark. No lights showed in the house I wanted, and I began to wonder, not for the first time, if Sayid had sent me on a wild-goose chase. He had already squeezed fifty pounds out of me. He would probably consider it a fine joke if I found myself trying to explain to a genuine holy man, a Haggi and a descendant of the Prophet, who the devil I was and what I wanted.

Having come this far, I had to go on. Followed by two of the village dogs growling and snapping at my heels, I went to the door and knocked.

"It's me," I said. "Margaret Minton. Please let me in."

At first there was no answer. Then I heard a scrape of wood against metal, and the door opened onto darkness. "By God, it is," said a voice I knew. "Are you out of your mind? Get the hell away from here."

"Don't worry. I'm alone."

"So you think. Oh, Christ, it's probably too late. Come in and bar the door."

His voice sounded strange.

"Are you all right?" I asked.

"No. But I'll be in far worse shape shortly if I don't—". A match flared and wavered wildly before it went out. "Here," he said, thrusting something into my hand. "Light the candle. It's on the table."

In the brief flare of the match I had managed to close and bar the door. My hands were almost as unsteady as his; I spilled several matches onto the floor when I opened the box, but I managed to get the candle lighted.

I'm rather proud of my literary skills, but I find it almost impossible to describe my feelings. Start with disbelief, excitement, triumph, confusion . . . and now, as the import of his words sank in, mounting apprehension.

I wouldn't have known him. He was wearing the ubiquitous and usefully enveloping Egyptian dress; his galabeeyah was of fine quality and his beard was grizzled, and he wore the green turban restricted to descendants of the Prophet. He was the picture of the dignified holy man Sayid had described, except for his pale face and shaking hands.

"You *are* ill," I said, moving toward him. "Let me—"

"Shut up." He dropped to his knees and tugged at something on the floor. "We've got a few seconds. Maybe a minute. Damn, I can't do this. Give me a hand."

There had been no attempt to conceal the trap-door; it covered the entrance to a small underground room that was used for storage. Between us we got it up, and I saw the top of a rough wooden ladder.

"You first," he said. "Hurry."

"But it's a dead end!"

"You don't take orders well, do you?" He was still on his knees. A violent fit of trembling seized him and his teeth began to chatter, and at that strategic moment the door shuddered under the impact of a heavy object.

I got down the ladder without touching more than three of the rungs and reached up to steady him as he followed me down. He pushed my hands away. I couldn't see what he was doing, it was too dark; I heard scraping noises and a few muffled oaths, and then he fumbled for my hand.

"Through there. Get rid of your tob and habarah, you'll have to crawl. Hands and knees. Keep moving. It's about ten yards. When you can't go any farther, wait for me."

It was a tunnel, and I didn't like it one bit. Though walls and ceiling had been braced with pieces of wood, sand kept trickling through them. It inspired me to move more quickly than I might otherwise have done, but I hadn't gone more than a few yards before I heard his hard breathing and felt his hands pushing on the soles of my shoes.

"Forty-one, forty-two—can't you move any faster?"

I said, "Ouch." My head had just come into painful contact with a solid surface.

"Right-angle turn," said my invisible companion. "Forty-six . . . Faster."

He went on counting. When he reached sixty he grabbed hold of my ankles and pulled. I fell hard, flat on my stomach, and he fell on top of me.

I had once been in an air raid in London, when a shell landed within a hundred yards of the Underground station. It felt and sounded like that: a muffled blast and a horrible vibration. The slow dribble of earth increased to a steady rain.

"The ceiling's coming down," I said, through a mouthful of sand.

"Not just yet, I hope. Go on, we're almost out."

When I raised my head I saw starlight. The opening was only a few feet away. I squeezed through, encouraged by an occasional shove and a stream of muttered expletives, and found myself in the open air behind a tumble of mud-bricks that had once been a house or storage shed. Sethos followed me out. He was bareheaded; either he'd discarded the distinctive green turban or it had been pulled off. He sat down and wrapped his arms around his raised knees. "Go on."

"Where?"

"Anyplace where there are bright lights and hordes of people. Or you might cast yourself on the tender mercies of my . . . of the Emersons. Their dahabeeyah is a mile away. In that direction."

"What about you?"

"I'll be all right here."

Dancing lights, the flames of candles or lamps, surrounded the pile of rubble where the house had stood, and a cloud of dust was still settling. People were shouting. The sound of the explosion would have brought the villagers out of their houses, and I had an unpleasant suspicion that they weren't the only spectators.

"The devil you will," I said. "Blowing up the tunnel will only delay them. They'll spread out in all directions. Stand up."

A mile isn't really a great distance. It is very long when one is encumbered with an unwilling, increasingly helpless companion, and when every sound makes one's heart stop. We had not been far from the edge of the cultivated fields, a line as sharp as if it had been drawn by a straight edge, and there was some cover in the form of trees and irrigation ditches and fields of growing crops. I took advantage of it when I could. I can't deny that I was frightened for myself as well as for him. If they meant to kill him or take him prisoner they could not leave witnesses. Who were they? A gang of rival thieves? Surely not local men. They were pretty sure of getting off if they were caught stealing antiquities; nobody was going to make a fuss about that except a few narrow-minded Egyptologists. Murder was something else.

No, not local men. They wouldn't have the guile to use me as a means of getting at Sethos. They had used Sayid too. He must have been laughing in his ragged sleeve while he bargained with me. He'd been paid to give me that information, and I thought I knew why. They must have tried to trap him before. They had failed because he was too quick for them, and too well-prepared. But if I turned up at his door, innocent and stupid and incompetent—a woman, in other words—I might delay him just long enough.

We were lying flat in one of the muddier irrigation ditches at the time, while footsteps passed slowly along the raised embankment and faded. I hated to leave that ditch. For a few minutes I didn't believe I could, but I finally managed to get him to his feet and moving.

He hadn't spoken for quite a while. He didn't speak again until I finally saw the lights of the dahabeeyah ahead and made the mistake of offering what I thought was a word of encouragement.

"There it is. Just a little farther."

The violence of his reaction caught me off guard. He pulled away from me and staggered back. "Where are we?"

I told him. He wrapped one arm round a tree trunk and fended me off with the other hand. "No."

"You need a doctor. Would you rather I found a boatman to take us across to Luxor?"

"You would, wouldn't you?"

"Yes. Make up your mind. It seems to me this is the lesser of two evils."

He let out an odd, choked laugh. "Lesser of . . . three evils. No, that's wrong. Least of three. Staying here . . . the worst . . ."

He slid through my outstretched hands and fell heavily to the ground. I knew I'd never get him up again; except for the spasms of shivering that shook his body, he lay unmoving and unresponsive. I took off my coat and put it over him. He'd been thinking more clearly than I; with the goal I had sought so close, I might have made the mistake of trying to drag him across the dock and up to the gangplank, and then everyone in Luxor would be gossiping about it next day. A visit from me, even at this hour, would not arouse surprise, though. I had already acquired a local sobriquet: "the woman who looks for secrets."

Though I tidied myself as best I could, brushing the dried mud off my skirt and coat and tucking straggling locks of hair into what remained of my once neatly coiled chignon, the man on watch by the gangplank was visibly taken aback by my appearance.

"Was there an accident, Sitt?"

"Oh, good, you speak English," I said gratefully. "I lost my way and fell into an irrigation ditch. Will you tell Mr. and Mrs. Emerson I would like to see them?"

"They are not here."

The fact that the gangplank was still out should have warned me, but I felt as if I had been hit a hard blow in the stomach. "When will they be back?"

"I do not know, Sitt. They are at the Castle of Vandergelt Effendi," he added somewhat doubtfully. My appearance clearly had not inspired confidence.

I thanked him and turned away. I hadn't realized how I had looked forward to thrusting my responsibility on someone else; it was like a heavy burden settling back onto my shoulders. There was nothing I could do but wait. The Vandergelts were old friends of theirs, they might not come back for hours.

It seemed like days.

Ramses said, with grudging respect, "You got him all the way from the Tarif? No wonder you look as if you'd been dragged behind a cart. Sorry—I didn't mean—"

"Don't apologize." Margaret finished her brandy. "I know I look like the wrath of God, and I don't care. May I—may I go back to him?"

"One or two more questions."

She sank back onto the settee, her lips curving in a sardonic smile. "Is that all?"

"For the moment. Why did you bring him here?"

She hadn't expected that. Ramses realized she hadn't even thought about it. Her forehead wrinkled in puzzlement. "Where else could we go? He needed a doctor and I could never have got him across the river . . . I suppose it ought to have occurred to me that I might be putting you and your wife in danger. I'm sorry about that."

Ramses shook his head. "If you had been followed this far, they had ample time to dispose of him while you were waiting for us to return. Perhaps I ought to have expressed myself differently. What made you suppose we would take him in?"

"Another interesting question," Margaret said thoughtfully. "Bear in mind I wasn't thinking too clearly. I simply assumed you would do the decent thing."

"Yes, of course," Ramses said wryly. "Noblesse oblige and all that."

"Your mother said he had saved her life. You wouldn't—you aren't going to turn him over to the police?"

"I haven't decided what the devil I'm going to do with him. Don't worry," he added, less forcibly. "So long as he's ill he's safe with us."

Abbreviated though her account had been, it had taken longer than he had realized. He held the door for her, wondering how they were going to account for her presence. She wouldn't leave unless he dragged her away kicking and screaming. It would be even more difficult to explain the presence of a strange man.

His uncle was deeply asleep and Nefret was arranging a blanket that covered him to the chin. She must have changed the sheets; a pile of crumpled linen lay by the bed.

"You should have waited for me to help you," he said.

"Any halfway competent nurse can shove a two-hundred-pound man around, even when he's a deadweight. The sheets were soaked. The fever has broken, and he'll sleep through till morning now."

"I'll stay with him," Margaret said. "You must be tired."

"I'm used to this, but I'll accept the offer. Go wash your face and hands and take off those filthy clothes. I'll get you one of my dressing gowns. The minute he stirs, wake me. We're next door."

As soon as they were in their room Nefret kicked off her shoes and began unfastening buckles and buttons.

"Are we going to bed?" Ramses asked, without much hope.

"Not yet, we've a lot to discuss. Hand me my dressing gown, will you please? The crew will be up at dawn. How are we going to account for them being here?"

"She was here earlier, looking for us."

"Yes." Nefret tied the sash of her dressing gown. "So she came back later . . . and he with her . . . and they both had a bit too much to drink." She chuckled. "They had better be Mr. and Mrs., hadn't they."

"But she's known in Luxor," Ramses protested.

Nefret waved a dismissive hand. "Men have no imagination. He's her estranged husband, who followed her here hoping for a reconciliation. Which duly took place. That's why they were celebrating tonight."

"Your imagination is as outrageous as Mother's," Ramses said. "There are so many holes in that plot, it resembles a sieve. What if he's ill again tomorrow?"

"He will be ill again." She curled up on the bed. "You've got him right where you wanted him. Before the next attack he'll be weak but coherent."

Ramses tossed his coat over a chair and began unbuttoning his shirt. "Taking advantage of a sick man? Well, why not? It's in the best traditions of the Game."

"Ramses, you have to. This is a very unpleasant development. You don't understand the implications."

"I don't understand what you're getting at, no."

He finished undressing and put on a galabeeyah, knowing he might be rousted out of bed early in the morning by a hysterical woman. Nefret sat up, tucking her feet under her.

"If he'd had an attack before, he'd have recognized the symptoms. With most types of malaria there are inevitable relapses; we've not learned how to cure it, only control it, and one never knows when the next attack will come on. A farsighted man, as I believe him to be, would be damned good and sure he had quinine with him at all times."

"So?"

"So, if this is the first attack, he was infected approximately ten days ago, through a mosquito bite. There are malarial areas in the Delta and the Canal Zone, but public health methods have reduced the incidence of the disease. There is only one other area near here," Nefret concluded, "where malaria is endemic."

"The oases?"

"That's right."

"Kharga," Ramses muttered. "It's been more than ten days since Asad was freed."

"So he's been back since, on other business. As you pointed out, it's only a few hours away by train." She leaned forward, her smooth brow furrowing. "Remember it was he who asked you if you suspected him of setting Asad on your trail. The idea had never occurred to you, or to me, before he brought it up. Guilt?"

"I can't believe it."

"I don't like the idea any better than you do, but we'd be fools to ignore the possibility. He knew you took Wardani's place last winter; he knew Wardani's lieutenants had been sent to the oases, and he's certainly clever enough to realize that an emotional fellow like Asad could be egged on to seek revenge. You said it yourself—he's after something big, something for which he needs time and privacy. What better way of keeping us in Cairo, out of his way, than to set a dedicated assassin on your trail? Unfortunately for him, we didn't react as he had hoped. Everything that's happened since has been designed to get us to leave Luxor."

"Including the attack on Mother?" Ramses demanded incredulously.

"His henchmen—I love that word—may have misunderstood his instructions."

"Now look here, Nefret—"

"It was just a thought," Nefret murmured. "No, darling, there is another alternative. He was telling the truth when he spoke of a rival. Someone else is after his big discovery."

"So it would appear." He blew out the lamp before he went to her. "Sayid was bribed to tell her where she might find Sethos. It's the only possible explanation; Sayid is the last man on earth Sethos would have trusted with that information. They must have tried to trap him before and failed. They hoped her presence would slow him down enough for them to move in."

"Sayid must know who 'they' are, then."

"Not with everyone trotting about in disguise," Ramses said disgustedly. "He's not the keenest of observers. Oh, we'll have a chat with him, but I expect he'll claim it was just a jolly little joke on the Sitt."

"We're in too deep to pull out now, aren't we?" she asked in a small voice. He took her in his arms.

"I'm afraid so. Get some sleep, it's late. We'll worry about our next move tomorrow."

The proximity of his wife had the usual effect, but the damnable sense of duty his mother had pounded into him made him say, "Perhaps I ought to stay with him tonight. If he's feeling fit enough by morning, he'll try to get away."

"No, he won't. I took his clothes."

THIRTEEN

Emerson was determined to go on working until the last possible moment—leaving all the domestic and travel arrangements to me. That suited me admirably, since he would only have been in the way, so I sent him off to Giza after breakfast, with every intention of joining him once I had completed my tasks.

We had announced our intentions at breakfast, arousing some mild surprise and a great deal of pleasure, especially from Sennia. There had been no question of her attending school that day. Not only was she entitled to a rest after her frightening experiences, but I didn't want to let her out of my sight—or at least, out of the house. After her cries of delight had subsided and she had been persuaded to resume her chair, I said, "We have a great deal to do if we are to be ready to leave tomorrow evening. You must help Basima pack your clothes and the other things you want to take."

"My presents." Her juvenile brow wrinkled. "I don't have all my Christmas presents. Can we go to the Khan el Khalili, Aunt Amelia?"

"No!" I moderated my sharp tone. "There won't be time. You can finish your shopping in Luxor."

"Supposing I bring back a few bones from Giza," Emerson offered. "You can wrap them up for Aunt Nefret."

"I would rather pick my own bones," said Sennia. "Can't I go with you?"

"No! Er . . . there will not be time. Fatima will need your help too."

"Amazing," Emerson said to me, after she had gone dancing off to visit Gargery and begin her packing. "I had expected she would be timid about returning to Giza."

"It is a testimonial to her strong character and, I would like to believe, to her trust in us. A trust," I added firmly, "that will not again be misplaced. We must make certain she is guarded at all times without arousing new apprehensions in her. This was really a very good idea of mine, Emerson. With all the excitement she won't have time to brood about her experiences."

As soon as Emerson had taken his leave, I wrote out several telegrams and sent one of the men to the telegraph office, instructing him to stop at the railroad station afterward and purchase our tickets. A consultation with Fatima came next; I felt a slight touch of uneasiness when I found her in the kitchen gathering the ingredients for her famous plum pudding. For such a self-effacing, soft-spoken little woman she could be extremely stubborn about what she considered to be her duties and privileges, and preparing Christmas dinner was one of them.

Cyrus's chef might not take kindly to having another cook underfoot.

By midday matters were well in hand at the house, so I took a picnic basket and set out for Giza, after warning everyone in the house to make certain Sennia had someone with her at all times. I placed my greatest trust in Kadija; she was as strong as a man and as dependable as one could wish.

I found Emerson with William Amherst finishing the survey of the site and persuaded them to stop for a bite of lunch.

"The Professor has told you of our plans?" I inquired of the young man.

"Yes, ma'am. Do you mean me to go with you? I wouldn't want to be in the way . . ."

In fact, William had been the furthest person from my thoughts, but his wide, moist eyes held a look of appeal I could not resist. To leave such a friendless individual alone over the holiday seemed cruel in the extreme. He would be of no use here, since Emerson would not allow anyone to shift a single basket of sand without his supervision. He was well acquainted with the Vandergelts and Cyrus had always spoken well of him . . .

I weighed these factors with my customary quickness, and I believe there was scarcely a moment's pause before I replied. "Naturally I had counted on your joining us, William. Cyrus will be glad to have you."

"You are too good," the young man exclaimed.

Emerson had been muttering over his cucumber sandwich. It usually takes him awhile to get his mind off the work he has been doing. The exchange caught his attention. He looked up, scowling. "In her own characteristic fashion. Curse it, Peabody, did you come alone?"

"Certainly. I have my parasol."

Emerson did not pursue the subject. He had found another that gave him an excuse to complain. "You ought not have left Sennia."

"Emerson, there are eight people in the house, not counting the cat. I do think you ought to stop work for the day, though. We have a number of minor matters to clear up."

"Yes, and one of them is here at Giza," Emerson said. "I want to have a closer look at the scene of yesterday's crime."

"What, the murder scene?"

"I was thinking of the crime of abducting our ward. But you are in the right; we had better see what, if anything, is left of Saleh."

He gave me a challenging smile. Needless to say I remained unperturbed. It was William who turned pale. "Left of . . ."

"The jackals and wild dogs will have been at him," Emerson said cheerfully.

"I am surprised you haven't already attended to that," I said, watching William's countenance take on a greenish hue. What the devil was wrong with the man? He ought not be so squeamish after so many years in Egypt.

"I was waiting for you, my dear. Not for all the world would I deprive you of the pleasure of examining a dismembered corpse. Come along, Amherst, you won't want to miss this."

I honestly do not believe Emerson was motivated

by malice. He is of the school that believes the best way to conquer a weakness is to face it head-on.

An examination of the spot where Sennia had been seized gave us no new information. Returning to the hotel, we collected our horses and hired one for William, overruling his feeble excuses.

However, only a person of excessively delicate sensibilities would have been overcome by what we found. Predators had been at the body of the dog. The remains were somewhat scattered about, but enough remained to identify it. Of the body of its owner there was no trace, except for a copious quantity of dried blood, already blurred by blowing sand.

"Someone must have collected whatever the jackals left, and buried it," said Emerson. "Touching consideration. I suppose even a swine like Saleh might have a friend. Let us see if we can locate him."

With William trailing reluctantly after us, we made our way down the ridge into the village. Since we had to assume we had been seen, Emerson announced our approach in the loudest possible voice and in terms designed to reassure the hearers. "We mean no harm to the innocent. You know us, you know that when our word is given it is not broken. We will pay well for information. Baksheesh!"

The seemingly empty houses disgorged a trickle of people, fewer than twenty in all, ranging in age from naked toddlers to a toothless, bent old man, who proclaimed himself the sheikh of this wretched place.

"We have your word, O Father of Curses?" he

mumbled. "We are innocent. We have done no wrong."

Emerson reached into his pocket. Coins jingled. The audience edged closer.

We got very little in the way of useful information, though Emerson dispensed baksheesh with a lavish hand. All in the village knew that Saleh was a bad man, but always before he had done his evil deeds elsewhere. They had known nothing of his latest venture into crime until he came to the village carrying a child whose struggles and complaints made it clear that she had not come willingly. They had been too afraid of him to interfere. He had not been seen with a stranger, in the village or elsewhere. In short, they were ignorant and innocent, and they were relieved he was dead. But they had buried his remains because that was their religious duty.

"And because they didn't want his ghost coming back to haunt them," said Emerson to me in English. "Do you want to dig him up, Peabody? Most probably he's buried deep."

"I see no point in doing that, Emerson. I wonder what he did with the first payment he had been given."

"It wasn't on his body." Emerson fingered the cleft in his chin. "Hmph. Let's have a look."

Emerson and Amherst—who had regained his nerve now that there were no dismembered corpses to be inspected—found the little bundle tucked into a crevice in the crumbling wall of the hut. While they searched I did what I could for the old woman. She was in pitiable condition. Opium destroys the appetite of the user, and it was evident that she had not even had the will or the energy to drink water. She sucked greedily at the canteen I held to her lips and then sank back with a sigh.

"My son is dead, Sitt Hakim. Soon I will die too. I have no wish to live."

"There are others who will care for you," Emerson said. "We will make sure they do."

"Ah?" She raised her head. "Then I will live. The Father of Curses has said it!"

"How does it feel to be a demigod, with the power of life and death?" I inquired, as we left the nasty place.

"Splendid," said Emerson with a grin. He had removed the rag that had been wrapped round the money, and I recognized the notes issued by the National Bank of Egypt. "Fifty Egyptian pounds," said Emerson, counting. "He paid well, the swine. This should keep the old lady in lentils and opium for a while."

He gave the money to the mayor, whose rheumy eyes popped when he saw the amount, and whose wrinkled face fell when he heard Emerson's instructions. I did not doubt they would be followed to the letter, since Emerson announced his intention of sending round from time to time to make certain. He added in an offhand tone that if one of them *remembered* something of interest, he would pay well for information.

"Do you think someone is concealing something?" I inquired as we mounted and started back to Giza.

"I rather doubt it, but should that be the case he

wouldn't speak up in front of the others. We will have to wait and see."

Fatima had tea ready when we reached the house, where we found Daoud making serious inroads on a plate of sandwiches. Fatima had fed him the latest gossip along with the sandwiches, and he was fairly bursting with outrage at the effrontery of the man who had dared lay hands on the Little Bird. Naturally he was convinced he could have prevented it if he had not been in Luxor. We let him get it out of his system and then Emerson said, "You could not be in two places at once, Daoud. We sent you to Luxor to find out how matters are proceeding there. Make your report. Fatima, more sandwiches, if you please."

Daoud held up his hand. "One," he said, raising a finger twice the length and breadth of mine.

Without pausing for breath he proceeded to reel off the facts which, he added, Nur Misur had told him to relate. He had just finished the second of them when Sennia burst into the room, embraced us all, and settled herself comfortably on Daoud's large lap. "How are they all?" she demanded. "Is Bertie better? Do they know we are coming?"

"Are we?" Daoud asked.

"Oh, yes, didn't the Professor tell you? All of us, on the train tomorrow. Tell me how they are, Daoud. Do they miss me?"

"Very much," Daoud assured her. "Mr. Bertie is better. Three. He has found a new interest. Her name is Jumana."

I did not doubt he had repeated the message word for word. It was not at all what I had had in mind for Bertie, but Emerson's well-shaped lips curved in one of those masculine smiles.

"The girl Nefret mentioned? Well, well, there is nothing like a pretty woman to—"

"Emerson, please!" With a gesture, I reminded him that there was an innocent child present. "Did you meet the young woman, Daoud?"

"Oh, yes. Nur Misur said you would want to know what I thought of her. She is very, very pretty."

He took another sandwich.

"Is that all?" I demanded.

Daoud pondered the question. "She talks in a loud voice and says what she thinks. So it is likely Yusuf will not find a husband for her, though she is very, very—"

"Yes, I see. Oh, dear. Emerson, I foresee complications."

"So long as it does not turn out to be another pair of confounded young lovers," Emerson grunted. "We used to be infested with them, and a damn—er—deuced nuisance they were."

"There is a more important thing," said Daoud, who had no interest in young lovers. He added punctiliously, "It was not Nur Misur who told me of it."

"Something about tomb robbing?" Emerson inquired.

Daoud cleared his throat. With the instincts of a master storyteller he had saved this bit of news for the last, and his solemn voice made it evident he was quoting. "It is known in Luxor that the Master has returned. His whereabouts no man knows. His true appearance no man knows. He has a thousand faces and ten thousand names."

The silence that followed was broken by the crash of shattering china. Mr. Amherst had dropped his cup.

FROM MANUSCRIPT H

The soft sound brought Ramses instantly awake. The curtains at the window fluttered in the morning breeze. He had just enough time to swing his feet to the floor and make sure he was decently covered before the door opened.

Nefret sat up with a start. The candle Margaret held cast ugly shadows over her face, shaping black hollows under her cheekbones and lengthening her nose. "Come at once," she ordered. "He's awake."

The window of the room where they had installed their guest faced east. It wasn't quite as early as Ramses had thought; the sky over the eastern cliffs was pale with the approach of dawn. He had expected to find Sethos on his feet and in a combative frame of mind, but the light from Margaret's candle showed a motionless form lying on the bed. The face above the blanket that covered him from feet to chin was unshaven and sunken, with a scowl almost as forbidding as one of Emerson's.

"Clever," he said. "I suppose there's no use asking you to give me back my clothes?"

"That's open to negotiation," Nefret said. She looked and sounded a good deal brighter than Ramses felt. Stifling a yawn that threatened to crack his jaws, he leaned against the wall and folded his arms. Nefret opened her medical bag. The expression on Sethos's face when he saw the thermometer cheered Ramses quite a lot.

"No," he said firmly.

"Yes," said Nefret. "Shall I have Ramses hold you down?"

His uncle considered the question. Ramses, who was beginning to enjoy himself, watched the struggle between common sense and an unreasonable but understandable desire to hit out at someone.

"At least get her out of here before you rob me of what remains of my dignity," Sethos said, glancing obliquely at Margaret. It was the first time he had deigned to acknowledge her presence.

"That's reasonable," Nefret conceded. "Margaret, go and get dressed. Use the room next to this one."

Sethos submitted to Nefret's examination in tight-lipped silence. "Temperature and pulse normal," she announced. "But you know what's going to happen, don't you?"

He responded with another question. "Malaria?"

"It looks like it. What time did the last attack begin?"

Sethos brushed this aside with a wave of his hand. "You needn't stand over me like a prison guard, Nefret. I haven't the strength to fight *you* off, much less the pair of you, and I'm not foolhardy enough to risk falling ill before I can find a safe hiding place. We need to come up with an explanation for my being here. Any ideas?"

The force of his personality was strong as ever, even though he was flat on his back looking like death warmed over, but this time his attempt to distract them failed.

"Have I your word you won't try to leave?" Nefret asked.

"For what it's worth." His lips twisted. "Would a cup of coffee be asking too much?"

"I'll see what I can do."

Sethos's eyes followed her as she went to the door, her white gown falling in graceful folds.

"Is there any chance of concealing my presence from your crew?" he asked.

"Not likely. However—"

The door opened again. Nefret thrust a bundle of clothes at Ramses. "You may as well get dressed too."

"Bolt the door," Sethos suggested. "Unless you want an audience."

"She got you here, all the way from the Tarif," Ramses said. He stood up, stamped his feet into his boots, and fastened his belt. "At considerable risk to herself and without anyone seeing you. Give the woman credit."

"Never mind that. I presume you know that there are several unpleasant persons looking for me? You might put yourself and your wife in danger if I remain."

"You can't leave now without being seen, unless you mean to swim across the river. I have an idea . . ."

Ramses waited until the women had joined them before he explained his plan. The coffee Nefret brought finished clearing his head and he flattered himself that he managed to produce a clear, lucid argument, despite his uncle's frequent attempts to interrupt.

"We can't conceal indefinitely the fact that we have a guest. Misdirection is our only hope. They know Margaret was with you last night. They know, or will learn, that she came here earlier in the evening, alone. Ashraf saw her leave; he will swear she did not return. If we can get her over to Luxor unobserved, no one will know where she was for the rest of the night. I'll have to take her across myself. She can borrow Nefret's tob and veil. It will be a bit tricky, but I think we can manage it if we get the crew out of the way."

"If she has any sense, which I doubt, she'll refuse," Sethos drawled. "D'you suppose they won't want a chat with the last person known to be with me?"

"She only has to walk from the dock to the hotel," Ramses said. "Once there, she stays—is that clear, Margaret? Don't set foot outside the hotel until you hear from us. And don't respond to any written messages."

Margaret nodded brusquely.

"As for you," Ramses went on, returning his gaze to his uncle, who stared back at him without blinking, "we met you at the Vandergelts' last night and brought you here when it was apparent you were coming down with malaria. You don't trust these 'native' hospitals and you refused to be examined by a male physician."

Nefret let out a gurgle of laughter. She was always quick. Sethos wasn't far behind her. Ramses had expected—had, in fact, rather hoped for—an outraged protest. "A woman," he said flatly. "You'll tell the crew I'm—"

"Cyrus's spinster sister. Very proper, very modest. First trip to Egypt. Hates everything about it."

"Don't tell me how to play a role," Sethos grunted. There was a glint in his eyes that Ramses didn't like at all.

"Control your histrionic urges," he said sharply. "No one will set eyes on you. Our steward wouldn't venture to intrude on a maiden lady."

"But I ought to have a wig or a nightcap," Sethos insisted. "Just in case. And a flannel gown."

Nefret's laughter shook her whole body. Margaret's face grew even grimmer. She got to her feet.

"Is he feeling better?" she asked Nefret.

"Obviously," Nefret gasped.

One long step brought Margaret to the side of the bed. She raised her hand and brought it down with stinging force across Sethos's unshaven cheek.

"That," she said, "is for making a fool of me in Hayil. And this—"

He caught her hand before it connected a second time. Margaret called him a name that made Ramses blink. She was choking with rage. "For being a supercilious, ungrateful, selfish pig!"

She pulled her hand free and flung herself out of the room. The door of the adjoining room slammed.

"That's got rid of her anyhow," said Sethos. "Now—"

"You are a pig," Nefret snapped.

"The sentiment seems to be unanimous," Sethos said, meeting Ramses's hostile stare. "As I was about to say, your plan is admirable as far as it goes, but it doesn't go far enough."

"I know. I'll take care of the rest tonight."

"No," Sethos said. "I think I know what you have in mind, and it makes a certain amount of sense, but I'll see to it myself."

"With a temperature of a hundred and three? By nightfall you'll be burning with fever or shaking with chills. There's just one little thing. Before I mount my fiery steed and ride out to challenge your enemies, I'd rather like to know who they are, and what they are after."

His uncle's expression made his palms itch; he was in complete sympathy with Margaret's desire to slap that supercilious smile off his face. Sethos knew it was not concern for him that had prompted Ramses's plan. If word got out that they were harboring a stranger on the *Amelia*, someone might hear of Margaret's visit earlier that same evening and put two and two together. "The Master" must be seen and recognized after that visit, so that his enemies would not come looking for him here.

"This hasn't anything to do with the Senussi or Sahin Bey or the damned Department, has it?" Ramses demanded. "It's the same old antiquities game. You let things slip for a time, and a new player has jumped in. Who?"

"If I knew, don't you suppose I'd have dealt with him? You had better believe me, Ramses, reluctant though you may be to do so. I've been trying for weeks to identify the fellow. If he's an Egyptian, he's an unusual specimen, because he's utterly ruthless. He's killed at least three people. I don't want you to be the fourth. Amelia would take it badly."

"You aren't going to evade the issue again," Ramses snapped.

He sat down on the side of the bed and took his exasperating kinsman by the shoulders. "What's he after?"

The muscles under his hands contracted in a series of shivers. "What?" Ramses demanded. "Queen Tiy's jewels?"

"Sorry," Sethos muttered. "I'm feeling a bit . . . The jewels? There weren't any. That entertaining episode, and the rumors I spread about, were just my way of announcing my return." He closed his eyes.

Ramses's hands tightened involuntarily. Sethos moaned.

"Leave him alone, Ramses," Nefret said. She leaned over the bed. "I want you to take another dose of quinine. Then I'll get you a nice frilly nightcap and we'll let you sleep."

Where she had obtained the cap Ramses could not imagine. He had never seen her wear it. It had pink bows and rows of lace ruffles.

"Surely not even Mother wears those?" he asked.

"It's what they call a boudoir cap," Nefret explained. "To cover one's untidy hair while one drinks one's morning tea, before one's maid attends to one's toilette. It came with the negligee—a set. I intended to give it to Sennia."

"I'm going to kill him," Ramses said.

"You can kill him after breakfast, darling. Go on up; I'll be along after I've had a word with Margaret."

As he made his way up the stairs to the upper deck, Ramses considered his plan again. It had a number of weak spots, but he had been unable to think of anything better. Cyrus would have to be warned, and another lie concocted for him and Katherine; not even to Cyrus could they reveal the true identity of Nefret's patient. Ramses swore under his breath. Inventing wild fictions was more along his mother's lines than his—but he could only thank God she wasn't here, adding further complications to a situation that was already getting out of hand. He'd have to wait until afternoon, when the men were sleeping, to take Margaret across the river, and by one means or another force Sethos to divulge the secret he was determined to keep to himself, and . . .

And get rid of Jumana and Jamil. He had no sooner seated himself than they turned up. With another muttered oath he went to the rail. When she saw him Jumana began waving and calling out. She looked like an animated doll in Nefret's clothes.

"Don't swear," Nefret said, joining him at the rail.

"Was I? Tell them they won't be needed today, Nefret."

"Eat your breakfast before it gets cold," Nefret said, and went back down the stairs. Nasir was standing at attention, a napkin over his arm as she had taught him, ready to serve the food, but Ramses stayed at the rail, watching as Nefret talked with Jumana. It was a task he ought to have tackled himself, instead of leaving it to her, but that infuriating conversation with Sethos had left him so angry he wasn't sure he could trust himself to behave normally.

The loan of a few books satisfied Jumana. Jamil lingered, exchanging witticisms and boasts with Ashraf, before he followed his sister. Nefret came upstairs. She declined Nasir's offer to warm the food, told him they would wait on themselves, and began eating tepid eggs and soggy toast.

"I'm sorry," Ramses said. "I ought to have sent them away myself instead of—"

"Stop it." She looked up. Her eyes were blazing. "You're always sorry about the wrong things. What sort of idiotic stunt have you planned for tonight? If you're determined to go through with it, I'm going with you."

"Someone has to stay with him."

"Someone! Why is someone always me?" Her eyes were brimming with tears—probably of rage.

"In this case—"

"I know." She wiped her eyes. "But I insist on knowing where you are going and what you mean to do."

"The obvious move is to go back to the house where he was staying and pretend to look for something he'd been forced to leave behind. I'll show myself to some of the villagers, indicate guilt and alarm, and beat a hasty retreat."

"I thought that was it. Damnation, Ramses, what if some of the—the others are watching the place?"

"I'll retreat even more hastily." It was a fairly feeble attempt at humor and Nefret was not amused. He took her hand in his. "I doubt they have the manpower to waste on surveillance, Nefret. But it would certainly help if I knew who they are and how many of them there are and what they want from him."

Her unsmiling lips tightened. "I'll find out."

"You'd take advantage of a sick man?"

She pushed her chair back. "One more insouciant remark, Ramses Emerson, and you *will* be sorry. He was faking that attack. If it follows the usual pattern, it won't hit again until later this afternoon, and at this moment I wouldn't give a damn if he were about to breathe his last. Do you want to come with me?"

"I wouldn't miss it for the world."

Sethos was lying with his back to the door. When it opened he turned over. The ruffles framing his bristly face should have been mirth-provoking, but he carried it off as only Sethos could.

"Now what?" he demanded.

Nefret sat down beside him and began to speak softly. After only a few sentences Sethos threw up his hands. "I know better than to argue with a woman when she's in that frame of mind. You'd dismember me without hesitation if it would help him, wouldn't you?"

"Yes."

"Hmmm. There's nothing like devoted love to bring out the finest qualities in . . . All right, all right. I was going to tell you anyhow." His eyes turned to Ramses. "So far as I know, there are only three of them in addition to their anonymous leader. One's a Syrian named Mubashir, who worked for me in Cairo in '08. He probably thinks he's still working for me. Short, stocky, scars on both cheeks . . ."

He gave brief descriptions of the other two, adding, "Mubashir's the most dangerous. One of the best men with a knife I've ever employed, and quick as a snake. You'll go armed?"

"He will," Nefret said, before Ramses could answer. "Do you think they'll be waiting for you to come back?"

"Not if they know my habits. One of the reasons for my long, successful career is that I never return to a place once it's known to the other side, even if it means abandoning useful items." He gave Ramses an insolent grin. "You made good use of the items I had to leave behind once before. You'll find that skill useful tonight, but don't be tempted to show off. It's a family failing. All you need do is make sure some of the villagers see and identify you. You're about my height and build. The green turban should dispel any doubts; I lost mine somewhere along the way, but you can probably come up with—"

"He's doing it again," Ramses said to his wife.

"Right. I am willing to believe," said Nefret, articulating with precision, "that you haven't learned the identity of the leader. Why haven't you questioned that man Mubashir?"

"Go after Mubashir?" Sethos shuddered, or pretended to. "Thank you, no; I would rather my liver, lungs, and intestines remained intact. I wouldn't get anything useful out of him anyhow. If my wily opponent has the wits for which I give him credit, he'll be playing the game as I did, skulking about by night, keeping conversation to a minimum, and never letting any of them get a good look at him.

You'd be surprised how effective that sort of child-ish playacting can be with people who—"

"I don't want a lecture," Ramses said, trying to keep his voice level. "I want to know what started this game. What's the prize and where is it?"

"It's rather a long story . . ."

"Quiet." Nefret raised her hand. "Is that Nasir calling us?"

"Nasir can go to the devil," Ramses said. "I want answers, Sethos."

"They can wait," Nefret said. "No, really, dar-ling; he's going to ramble on and on until *you* hit him or *I* hit him, or Nasir comes bursting in here. The only thing that matters now . . ." She leaned over Sethos, her face so close to his that their noses were almost touching. "If anything—anything at all!—happens to Ramses tonight," she said in a voice as sweet as a chime of golden bells, "and it happens because you concealed information that might— might!—have made a difference . . ."

For a long second he stared as if mesmerized into her blue eyes. Then he swallowed, with difficulty, and turned his head away. "There's nothing. You have my word. For what it's worth."

Nasir's hails were becoming peremptory. Ramses left Sethos to his wife's tender mercies; she looked like a ministering angel as she lifted his head and held a cup of water to his lips, her hair a halo of gold.

He got past the door of their room before Nasir appeared, still shouting his name. So far they had managed to keep the staff in the dark about their visitor. The longer they could do so the better; the word would be all over the boat and then all over Luxor. So preoccupied was he that it took a little time for the import of Nasir's announcement to sink in.

"Vandergelt Effendi?" he repeated hollowly. "Here?"

Cyrus was waiting in the saloon, impeccably garbed in his favorite snowy linen, radiating good humor. He gave his disheveled host a long look, and his eyes twinkled.

"Hope I'm not disturbing you. Figured you'd be up and about by now."

"We were. We are." Ramses tried to smooth his hair and focus his brain. He still hadn't thought of a story to tell Cyrus. "Always glad to see you. How is Bertie getting on?"

"Real well." The twinkle intensified. "Even better since our little visitor dropped by."

"Good Lord." Ramses dropped into a chair. "Jumana?"

Nefret arrived in time to hear the last word. "What's she done now?"

"Paid a call on Katherine, proper as you please. Presented her with a pretty bouquet. Got the flowers out of my garden, I think," Cyrus added with a grin. "That's quite a girl. She said you had promised to teach her everything she needs to know to become an Egyptologist."

"What else did she say?" Ramses asked apprehensively.

"Quite a lot. She was trying to impress us with how much she already knew about the subject."

"I do apologize, Cyrus," Nefret said.

"What for? No reason why she shouldn't pay her respects, even if she did have an ax to grind. It's a refreshing change to find someone who wants books instead of baksheesh. And I'll tell you something else. Bertie perked up like you wouldn't believe." Cyrus chuckled. "He didn't make much headway with the young lady; once he'd admitted he wasn't an Egyptologist she ignored him as if he were a block of wood. As soon as she left he went off to his room with a stack of books."

Nefret looked at her husband. There was no meaningful exchange of glances this time; his face had gone courteously blank and she knew he had stopped listening to Cyrus. There was enough on his mind, heaven knew, but Nefret had a feeling he wasn't taking this latest development seriously enough. Katherine would certainly disapprove of Bertie's attachment to an Egyptian girl, however innocent the relationship.

I'll make damned good and sure it is innocent, Nefret thought—for Jumana's sake if not for Bertie's.

She brought her attention back to Cyrus, who had launched into an animated discussion of his future plans. Bertie wasn't the only one who had "perked up" since they arrived in Luxor.

"I thought maybe you two would like to go around with me looking for possible sites."

Ramses looked as if he had been poleaxed. "Today?"

"I'm anxious to get started. But if you folks have something else to do—"

"I'm afraid we are busy today," Nefret said. "What about tomorrow—or the day after?"

"Why, sure." Cyrus rose and picked up his hat. "You'll have to excuse me. I got so carried away I forgot you might have other plans."

"Not at all," Nefret said. "We'd love to go with you. Soon."

"There's no hurry," Cyrus said amiably. "Lots of other things I can do. I might have a word with Yusuf, ask if he has any suggestions."

"Excellent idea," Ramses said.

As soon as Cyrus had gone he turned on Nefret. "Tomorrow? He won't be recovered by then, will he?"

"Probably not. We'll just have to put Cyrus off again. You didn't tell him about his ailing sister."

"I couldn't think of any explanation that made sense," Ramses admitted. "My brain seems to have gone dead."

"Small wonder. Why don't you get a few hours' sleep?"

He went to her and took her hands in his. "You didn't get much sleep last night either."

"I don't have the kind of day ahead that you do." She freed her hands and put them on his shoulders. "Go and lie down. I'll wake you in time for lunch."

He hadn't supposed he would sleep but he did, waking of his own accord after a dream so outrageously horrific that he smiled drowsily as he remembered it. The boat capsizing and Margaret calling him names as she sank, while he trod water and made no move to rescue her; Cyrus riding up and down the west bank, bellowing, "That's not my sister Emmeline!"; Sethos telling Nefret that he would turn back into a prince if she kissed him; Sethos again, perched on the tumbled ruins of his house, watching with a smile while Mubashir neatly removed Ramses's lungs, liver, and intestines and put them into canopic jars. The carved human heads on the lids of the jars did not have the royal uraeus on their brows, and Ramses had been about to object to this omission when he woke up.

When he joined Nefret for luncheon he told her about the first part of the dream, thinking it might amuse her. The last two episodes almost certainly would not.

"You know what the Freudians would say about your letting Margaret drown," she said gravely.

"They'd be wrong. God knows I wish she hadn't complicated our lives, but I have a great deal of admiration for her. As soon as he's fully recovered I'll hold his arms while she hits him as often as she likes. You don't suppose Cyrus does have a sister named Emmeline?"

"I don't think he has a sister by any name." She did smile then. "How did your unconscious come up with Emmeline? Someone I missed?"

"The only Emmeline I've met was Mrs. Pankhurst, and I assure you I never got within ten feet of her. Nor wanted to."

They made conversation until Nasir had cleared the table and taken himself off. Ramses lit a cigarette. "Is she ready?"

Nefret nodded. "What about the dinghy?"

"It might be recognized. I'll steal or hire a boat. See you in a bit."

The first part of the plan went off without a hitch. By the time he got back to the *Amelia* in the small sailing boat he had hired, after the usual intensive bargaining, the crewmen had settled down for their afternoon rest and the only traffic on the river was a few commercial steamers and barges. With Nefret's assistance he got the black-robed woman out the window and into the boat. Neither of them spoke much during the voyage. He was busy with the tiller and the sails and she didn't seem inclined toward conversation.

As they neared the east bank she raised her bowed head. The veil hid all of her face except for her eyes. They were sunken and shadowed, but when she spoke it was in her usual brisk voice.

"You'll let me know?"

"Yes. In person, sometime tomorrow, if we can manage it. Remember what I said about sticking close to the hotel. It would make my life much more difficult if you were abducted."

"Or killed."

"That's the only positive aspect to the situation. If they do come after you they will want you alive."

"Do you call that positive?"

"It's much harder to carry off a healthy, hearty woman than to slit her throat." He didn't give her time to comment on that. "I'm going to put you ashore as close to the hotel as I can. You'll have something of a scramble climbing the bank, but after what you did last night I expect you can manage it."

She managed, with a certain amount of slipping and swearing. Ramses waited until she had reached the top of the embankment before he followed, in time to see her dart across the road and start up the long curving arm of the staircase that led to the door of the Winter Palace. She'd be all right now—if she remembered to divest herself of her Egyptian dress before she tried to go in.

The wind had died down, and it took him twice as long to get back across, using the oars a good part of the way. He returned his hired vessel, removed beard, turban, and aba behind a tree, and headed for the *Amelia*, scratching absently at his jaw. He'd been trying to develop an adhesive that didn't itch, without success thus far.

The sun was sinking westward and cool gray shadows stretched across his path. As soon as darkness had fallen he could finish the rest of the program. He was rather looking forward to it. Action of any kind was easier than waiting, and he didn't really anticipate any trouble. Nefret's part was the hardest. She wouldn't whine or cry, but she would be sick with apprehension until he came back.

It had gone well so far. He wondered, with a complacency he was soon to regret, why he had let himself get worked up. This situation was no more complicated than the messes his parents got into all the time.

It must be an unknown tomb Sethos and his rival were after. There were plenty of them in Thebes. In the past half-century alone, over fifty had been discovered, more than two dozen in the Valley of the Kings itself, three—or more?—by the indefatigable Abd er Rassul family. To be sure, the majority had been unfinished or thoroughly plundered, and the rare exceptions to the latter condition had been those of officials, not royalty. But there were a number of pharaohs still missing: Horemhab, several of the Ramses, Tutankhamen . . . Golden visions swam about in his mind.

Ashraf was sitting at the foot of the gangplank, smoking and staring placidly into space. He sprang to his feet when he saw Ramses.

"Nur Misur is looking for you, Brother of Demons."

The golden visions were replaced by what his mother would have called a hideous foreboding. "What has happened, Ashraf?"

"Nothing, nothing. But she said—"

Ramses hurried up the gangplank, leaving Ashraf talking to himself. Nefret must have heard their voices. She came running to meet him, eyes wide, face strained. He caught her in his arms.

"Darling, what's wrong? Did he—"

She pushed him away. "He didn't do anything. The next paroxysm has started, I've got to get back to him. But, oh, Ramses—you won't believe this— it's too awful—"

"What? For God's sake, Nefret!"

There was a crumpled piece of paper in her hand. A telegram. He snatched it from her.

"Arriving Luxor Wednesday A.M. with Sennia, Selim, and others. Staying with Cyrus, no need for you to do anything." She had even paid for another extra word. "Love, Mother."

R amses drew the curtain aside and looked out the window. The night sky was brilliant with stars, and moonlight streaked the rippling dark water. He had stripped to shirt and drawers and removed his shoes. "It's time I was going. Are you sure you can handle him?"

The ghost of a smile touched Nefret's lips. "Look at him."

The first stage of the attack had passed, and fever reddened the sick man's face. Though his eyes were open, he did not seem to be aware of his surroundings, and he hadn't spoken, except for incoherent murmurs.

Nefret extinguished the lamp before she joined him at the window. Ramses felt as if he ought to say something, but he couldn't think what. Don't worry? But she would. I love you? That sounded as if he never expected to see her again. What was there to say, after all? He kissed her upturned face, a hard, quick kiss, and slid out the window. Reaching up, he took the bundle she handed him.

"Don't be tempted to show off," she whispered, and withdrew from the window.

Once ashore, he wrung out his dripping undergarments and put them on again. The fabric was uncomfortably clammy but there was a chance he'd want to discard the robe, and he didn't fancy running about in his bare skin. The waterproof wrappings had kept the clothing dry. He put them on—robe, beard, turban, sandals, knife belt—and started walking.

Though he kept a wary eye out, he had ample time for what his mother would have called ratiocination during the mile-long hike. Unfortunately he still couldn't think of any way of averting the catastrophe that would soon be upon them. He and Nefret had discussed alternatives that afternoon, once he'd recovered from the shock of the telegram.

"Tell them they mustn't come" had been her first suggestion.

"Tell Mother not to do something?"

"You're right, that would only make her more determined. What do you suppose brought this on?"

"Why speculate? It could be anything from wanting to share a jolly Christmas celebration to . . . I'm afraid to think."

"They can't know about him. Uh—can they?"

"Anything's possible where my mother is concerned, but I don't see how that fascinating bit of information can have reached her. We've got to get him off the *Amelia* before they arrive, Nefret."

"Yes." They stared blankly at one another. "How?" Nefret asked. "Where to?"

A rustle in the vegetation brought Ramses's attention back to his surroundings. He was almost at the edge of the cultivation; to his right, the broken columns of Seti's temple glowed pale in the moonlight. Time to concentrate on the job ahead. One crisis at a time, he told himself.

He was familiar with the village, though he'd never had any reason to linger there; it was one of several small settlements between the southern end of Drah Abu'l Naga and the Seti I temple. He circled the place, fingering the torch in his pouch and wondering whether he would have to use it. The moonlight should be bright enough if he could attract someone's attention.

From the ridge he selected as his vantage point, the small huddle of huts looked deserted. Most of the villagers went to bed as soon as it was dark; lamp oil was costly. A pile of rubble indicated the site of Sethos's house. He'd done a thorough job. Not a wall had been left standing. The locals had probably added their bit, rooting in the ruins in search of some object they could use, or, if one was charitably inclined, for a body dead or alive.

Ramses picked up a handful of stones and began pitching them in the general direction of the village, spacing them so that the sounds would suggest they had been set rolling by approaching feet. He waited for a bit, listening. He threw one more stone, and was rewarded with the first response, a loud canine yelp. The stone must have struck a sleeping dog.

He headed down the slope, impatient to get the business over. Several other dogs had added their comments to the original complaint. A light showed at the window of one of the houses and a voice shouted imprecations in Arabic. All perfectly normal and harmless, just as Sethos had predicted.

The aroused sleeper had his head out the window, cursing the dogs. They were now following Ramses, snarling and barking. He stopped a few feet from the house, full in the moonlight. A halt in the curses, followed by a cry of surprise, assured him he had been seen, so he turned and trotted back the way he had come.

The dark form seemed to rise up out of the ground directly in his path. He flung himself to one side and flipped over, landing on his feet as a knife drove into the ground on the spot where he had just been. He caught one glimpse of a scarred, distorted face before he broke into a run, hurtling obstacles in his path and resisting the temptation to look back. Footsteps pounded after him, but he didn't doubt he could keep ahead, and if he didn't lose the fellow before he reached the edge of the cultivation, there were a number of handy bolt-holes in the temple ruins, with which he was thoroughly familiar . . .

Mubashir—it had to be Mubashir—was as familiar with the terrain as he was. He avoided several pitfalls Ramses had hoped he'd fall into, and came doggedly on. Finally, though, the sound of footsteps stopped. Ramses was about to risk a glance back when something slid past his ear and sliced through the shoulder of his borrowed garment before thudding into the ground ahead of him. He ran faster.

When he reached the back of the temple he collapsed, panting, onto the ground behind a tumble of fallen blocks and took stock. There was no sign of his pursuer. The Syrian had thrown the knife only when he realized he was going to lose the race. It had been an incredible throw, in moonlight and at a rapidly moving target, and Ramses was glad he hadn't looked over his shoulder. He might be missing the end of his nose instead of a bit of his earlobe. It had stopped bleeding, but the gash on his shoulder was still oozing.

After removing his extraneous garments and beard, he entered the water, and before long he was pulling himself up to the open window. Nefret was there. She took the bundle from him and stood back while he climbed in.

"Go and change those wet clothes," she ordered. Then her eyes widened. "Goddamn it, Ramses, what happened?"

The cuts had opened up and he was dripping blood as well as water on the floor.

"I told you not to show off," his uncle remarked. He was sitting up in bed. The fever had passed. Fresh sheets were tucked neatly around him, and he was wearing a nice clean nightshirt. Except for his heavy growth of beard and a certain hollowness around his eyes, he looked reasonably healthy and extremely comfortable.

"You didn't tell me your Syrian friend could throw a knife," Ramses snapped.

"I thought that was implicit in my description of his skills."

Nefret's jaw was set. "Shirt off," she said.

"It's nothing. Honestly."

"Take it off." Her medical bag was on the floor by the bed. Fumbling a little, she took out various items while Ramses tugged the wet fabric over his head and tossed it into a corner.

"You got off lightly," said Sethos, inspecting him.

"I was running like hell."

"Wise move. Well?"

Ramses sat down, rather squashily, and recounted his adventures while Nefret splashed antiseptic all over him. Her hands were still shaking.

"It seems to have been an effective performance," Sethos conceded. "You were somewhat careless—"

A wordless snarl from Nefret stopped him. She slapped a final bit of sticking plaster onto Ramses's shoulder, reached into her bag, and took out a hypodermic needle and a small bottle.

"Hold out your arm," she ordered, advancing on Sethos.

"What's that?"

"Something to help you sleep."

"I don't need—"

"But I," said Nefret, "need to stick something sharp into you. If I hadn't taken the Hippocratic oath this would be a knife. Ramses, go to bed, you must be absolutely exhausted."

"I want to watch," Ramses said.

As he knew from personal experience, Nefret had a light hand with a hypodermic needle. She jabbed this one into Sethos's arm with almost as much force as if it had been a knife.

She had left a lamp burning in their room. He had barely time to close the door before she flung herself at him, winding her arms tightly round his neck and hiding her face against his breast. "I'm going to kill him," she mumbled. "Not you, me. After what you went through today . . . He didn't even thank you!"

Watching his uncle cringe away from Nefret and her needle had made Ramses feel more tolerant. "He resents accepting favors. I expect he hasn't had much practice at it."

"Don't try to make me feel sorry for him."

"Nothing you could do would annoy him more." He slid his fingers into her hair and tilted her head back, and was about to kiss her when his jaws parted in a huge, involuntary yawn. "Sorry, darling."

"Bed," Nefret ordered. "This instant."

He hadn't realized how tired he was until his aching body came to rest on the mattress, but his mind wouldn't stop churning. "I hope we aren't shopping for sites with Cyrus tomorrow."

"I put him off." Nefret removed the pins and combs from her hair and began brushing it. "The arrival of the family was a sufficient excuse."

"Oh, God, yes. What are we going to do about them?"

The long waving locks fell over her shoulders in a golden shower. She smiled at him and extinguished the lamp. "Don't worry about it tonight, darling. I've got a plan."

FOURTEEN

Tell them everything?" Ramses said doubtfully.

"Tell everyone everything!" Nefret gestured extravagantly with a slice of buttered toast. Her eyes were bluer than the morning sky and bright as the sun over the eastern cliffs.

The knowledge that his exasperating kinsman was deep in drugged slumber had allowed Ramses to have the best night's sleep he had enjoyed for days. What with one thing and another, he had been in an excellent mood when they went up to breakfast. Until then.

"That's your famous plan?"

"It solves the major difficulties, doesn't it? We're getting so tangled up in lies and omissions, we won't be able to keep track of what we've told whom." She planted her elbows firmly on the table and leaned forward. "We agreed last year that we would stop playing these games because it's caused a lot of trouble in the past. And here we are, at it again! The parents have been hiding things from us and we've been hiding things from them. I say we put an end to it once and for all."

She bit into her toast, and watched him think it over, weighing all the pros and cons in his methodical fashion. At least he was thinking, not raising indignant objections. To her the argument was logical and sensible, but there were several things to which her eminently logical husband did not respond sensibly.

"It's Mother, isn't it?" she asked.

"What?" His eyebrows tilted.

"She's the one you don't trust to behave. For heaven's sake, Ramses, your mother has passed unscathed through more hair-raising adventures than any woman in fact or fiction, and she's enjoyed every second of it! It's time you began treating her like an equal."

For a moment she was afraid she had pushed him too far. Then his tight lips relaxed into a sheepish smile. "I will if she will."

Nefret laughed. "I'll have a word with her. You gave her a bad fright last winter, darling. Until then she hadn't been able to admit how much she cared for you, and now she's making up for lost time. So you agree?"

"Yes. It's amazing," he added ingenuously. "I feel the way one of those poor overburdened donkeys must feel when the last load is lifted off his back. What have I done to deserve you?"

The return of Nasir with a fresh pot of coffee prevented Nefret from telling him, in considerable detail and with appropriate gestures. She pushed the toast rack toward him.

"We need to work out a few of the details," she admitted.

"Quite a few. 'Everything to everybody' is going a bit far. Are you planning to confess all to—er—Emmeline?"

"She'll do the confessing," Nefret said grimly. "If it takes me all morning. I'm against mentioning the arrival of the family, though. He—she—would take a chance on trying to swim the river rather than face Mother."

"When do you propose to break it to Mother and Father?"

After all his resistance, he had finally accepted the inevitable. Nefret smiled fondly at him. "As soon as we can get them to ourselves. Then we can decide how much to tell Cyrus, and what to do with Emmeline, and . . . Now what's the matter?"

"I was picturing how they'd react—Father heading straight for the *Amelia*, by the first means of transport he can steal or borrow, and Mother right behind him. We could take him somewhere else, give them time to cool off before they confront him. I've had an idea—"

"Let him go before we've forced him to confess?"

"Certainly not."

Nasir loaded a tray with food for "the poor sick lady." They had managed to get Margaret away unseen and unsuspected, but it would have been impossible to account for Nefret's frequent visits to the guest room without explaining that she had a patient. Nasir had been very sympathetic.

Sethos was at the window. He had draped a sheet

round him in a fair imitation of a toga, and with his three days' growth of beard and hostile eyes he reminded Nefret of one of the wickeder Roman emperors—Nero or Caracalla.

"Get back in bed," she ordered, as Ramses put the tray on the table.

"I never want to see another bed as long as I live."

"Sit down and eat your breakfast, then." She shook two tablets from the bottle of quinine and held them out. He swallowed them with a grimace.

"Look here, you two, this has gone far enough. Does Vandergelt know he has an ailing sister?"

"No," Ramses admitted.

"So he hasn't come round to see how she's getting on? Disgraceful. You can't keep this up much longer. It's becoming too complicated."

You don't know the half of it, Ramses thought.

"If you are thinking of leaving us," said Nefret, arms folded, "you had better reconsider. You aren't over this yet."

"I'm recovering nicely, thank you, Doctor. All I need is enough quinine to get me through the next few days. I can swallow pills with no help from anyone."

"Where?" Ramses asked.

"A hotel."

"That's absurd," Nefret exclaimed.

"Explain it to her, Ramses." Sethos returned to his eggs and toast.

It was the same scheme that had occurred to Ramses. He gave his fuming wife a reassuring nod. "It's the only possible alternative. He'll need a few more days of rest and creature comforts, which would be hard to come by in a cave in the hills. There's safety in numbers and a certain anonymity in the role of a tourist."

And if Sethos's enemies caught up with him, it wouldn't be here. Ramses did not underestimate them; they had already managed to discover several of his hiding places, and the longer he remained, the greater the chance of discovery. His epiphany as Haggi Sethos the night before would put them off for a while, but the story about Emmeline wouldn't hold up for long. He didn't want to wake up in the middle of the night to see Mubashir climbing in their window.

"Exactly." Sethos had been eating with the grim determination of someone performing a necessary duty. He pushed his empty plate away. "If I may have the loan of a suit of your clothes, and a razor, and a few other objects designed to add verisimilitude—"

"What hotel did you have in mind?" Nefret interrupted. A new and pleasing idea had replaced her indignation. "It wouldn't be the Winter Palace, by any chance?"

"It's a matter of complete indifference to me" was the curt reply.

"Oh, really? She got there all right, but we haven't had a chance to communicate with her since yesterday afternoon."

The briefest flicker of emotion passed over Sethos's face before it resumed its habitual blandness. "If you agree, we'd better get started. It will take a while to transform me into a debonair world traveler."

"Quite a while." Nefret was clearly enjoying herself. "You'll need our cooperation to carry this off, and you won't get it until you've told us everything we want to know."

"Is blackmail allowed by the Hippocratic oath?"

"I can't recall its being mentioned. There's no hurry," Nefret added sweetly. "You can't leave today in any case."

"But—"

"Explain it to him, Ramses."

"You'll probably have another attack this afternoon," Ramses said. "Right, Nefret? We can't complete the necessary arrangements and get you into the hotel before that."

"Right," Nefret said. "Start talking."

It was Nefret's idea that they lunch at the Winter Palace. "We ought to make certain she's all right. And she'll want to hear about him."

"I did promise we would let her know, but I should think she'd have recovered from her romantic fantasies. He's behaved like a brute."

"Ah, well," said Nefret enigmatically.

"What's that supposed to mean?"

"Nothing of importance." She adjusted her hat and straightened her skirt. "There, I'm ready."

The tourist ferry appeared to be suitable for their purposes. At that time of day there were hordes of people returning to their hotels after a morning of sightseeing. If they could get their unwilling and unwanted guest to the quay, he would blend in perfectly. After that he would be on his own, and if he didn't have sense enough to stick to the plan, it would serve him right if his enemies caught up with him.

He claimed he had told them everything he knew. Having declared himself resigned to the inevitable, he had produced a glib but—when you got right down to it—uninformative story. The devil of it was there was no way of checking on its accuracy, though Ramses meant to ask a few questions of a few people.

One of them was not available. Sayid must have found a tourist to victimize, for he was not at his usual spot in front of the Winter Palace. They asked at the desk for Miss Minton and were informed that she was in the dining salon.

One would have supposed from her appearance—smartly dressed, carefree and smiling—that she had not a worry in the world. She must have been watching the door, though, for the moment they made their appearance she stood up and waved, motioning them to join her. At the sight of her companion, Nefret stopped short.

"What the devil is he doing here?"

The headwaiter gave her a startled look. Ramses took her arm. "Control your homicidal impulses and try to act like a lady."

"Why didn't she tell us she knew the bastard?"

"Because she had no reason to suppose we would be interested," Ramses said. It was sometimes necessary to belabor the obvious when Nefret's indignation got the better of her. "Remember that we've never been properly introduced. Smile. Or at least stop grinding your teeth."

"Smith" was on his feet when they reached the table. After asking whether they were acquainted and receiving a prompt denial from Smith, Margaret introduced them, adding, "Algie is with the Department of Public Works in Cairo. Mr. and Mrs. Emerson are—"

"I have heard of them, of course," Smith said smoothly. "This is indeed a pleasure. Won't you sit down?"

It was a table for four, and the waiter was holding a chair for Nefret. She remained standing. "We wouldn't want to intrude."

"Not at all," Smith said. "I was about to leave in any case. An appointment."

"Aren't you on holiday?" Ramses asked, avoiding the use of that preposterous name. The faintly sinister commonality of "Smith" suited the fellow better.

"The appointment is with a mummy." He looked quite different from the tight-lipped, hard-eyed man they had met in London. Instead of the stark black and white of evening dress, he wore clothing suited to the climate and his announced program. The suit showed signs of wear, and the pith helmet he had politely removed from a chair was somewhat battered. He'd spent some time in the East. India?

"Mr. MacKay most kindly offered to show me round the Valley of the Kings this afternoon," Smith went on. "One of the pharaohs is still in his sarcophagus, I believe?"

"Amenhotep the Second," Ramses said. "So you are a friend of MacKay's?"

"Never met him. Friends in Cairo gave me letters of introduction to a number of people." He summoned the waiter and asked for his bill before continuing, "I've met most of the archaeologists in Luxor. Very agreeable chaps."

Nefret appeared to be studying her menu. Margaret was listening politely, but Ramses noticed she was pleating her napkin into fold after fold.

"How much longer are you staying in Luxor?" he asked.

It was the sort of casual question anyone might have asked of a stranger, but the lines in Smith's cheeks deepened. "A few more days. I'm finding Luxor much more interesting than I had expected."

He took his leave of them. Nefret barely gave him time to get out of earshot before she turned on Margaret and demanded, "Is that man a friend of yours?" Margaret spoke at the same time. "How is he?"

"He's much better," Ramses said. "There's been no sign of trouble. What about you?"

Nefret subsided, looking as if she regretted her impulsive question—as well she might. Excessive interest in Smith might make Margaret wonder what had prompted that interest.

Margaret shrugged. "Except for an invitation to join you for dinner last night at the Savoy, nothing has occurred."

"They didn't waste any time," Ramses said. "How did they know you'd got back?"

"My entrance was somewhat conspicuous," Margaret said with a wry smile. "I had to disrobe—or should I say unrobe?—in front of the doorman, he wasn't going to let me in, and I made something of a spectacle of myself dashing through the lobby in my less than impeccable clothing. Everyone stared." She reached into her handbag and took out a folded piece of paper. "You'd made me nervous," she added accusingly. "I made the safragi slip the note under the door."

"Very sensible." Ramses examined the brief message. "It's not my handwriting."

"I wouldn't have known that."

"But he couldn't be sure you wouldn't. The handwriting is obviously disguised." He passed the note on to Nefret.

"It's written in English," Nefret said thoughtfully. "Good English."

"What there is of it. Only one sentence, without embellishment. Still, it does raise provocative ideas. I'll keep this, if I may, Margaret. Congratulations on refusing the invitation."

"I found it insulting. How could they suppose I'd be dim enough to respond to a disingenuous attempt like that one?"

"It was worth a try." Ramses slipped the note into his breast pocket. "They'll try again—something less obvious next time. You are the only person who knows where he went that night. Be on your guard. You ought to have stayed in your room and not come down to the dining salon."

"I was about to start climbing the walls," Margaret said sullenly. "If I hadn't run into Algie—"

"How long have you known him?" Nefret asked.

"I met him ten years ago, when I was in India

doing a series of articles on the Northwest Frontier problem. I didn't know he'd been posted to Egypt... Has he told you why those men were after him?"

The second "he" obviously did not refer to Smith. Margaret's dismissal of him suggested that she had no suspicion of his real role; she'd have been quick to exploit their earlier acquaintance if she had known he was involved with intelligence. Ramses didn't believe in the Public Works Department any more than he believed Smith was on holiday.

The expected letter from Nefret arrived the day of our departure. Emerson was in a fairly lively mood that morning since Gargery had refused to give up his turn to serve breakfast and went staggering round the room groaning, softly but persistently, until my afflicted spouse ushered him, gently but firmly, out of the room. I had been about to do so myself. I did not begrudge Gargery his groans or limps, but the hands smeared with green ointment did put one off a bit.

Refreshed and alert, Emerson resumed his seat and asked if there was anything of interest in the post. I handed him the letter, which I had already perused, and awaited his comments.

"Hmph," said Emerson.

"What do you make of it?" I asked, after a long pause.

"You refer, I presume, to the precipitation of sundry objects on Ramses," said Emerson, buttering another piece of toast. "I don't know what to make of it and neither do you."

"Nefret is still concealing something from me," I mused. "I sense that, very strongly. You are quite right, Emerson; conjecture is futile until we have all the facts. How glad I am that I had already made up our minds to go to Luxor!"

Everything was in order; the only matter yet to be resolved was the disposition of Mohammed, who was still languishing in the garden shed. It would not have been expedient or humane to leave him there during our absence, which might extend to several weeks. (I could not suppose it would take longer than that to put an end to the tomb robberies, identify the individual who had taken Sethos's place, and tidy up a few other little details.) Since he had been left alone to commune with his conscience (such as it was) and his fear of punishment, I expected to find him in a receptive mood when we visited him on Tuesday morning. His first words indicated that like all persons of low intelligence and little imagination, he had only room in his head for a single idea.

"You will let me go, Father of Curses?"

"If I were in your shoes," said Emerson, "I would prefer to remain in custody. Saleh is dead—murdered by the man you know as the Master."

Neither by word nor look did the wretched man indicate regret for his associate's demise, or fear for himself. "Is it true?"

"The Father of Curses does not lie," said Emerson grandly.

"No. Let me go, then. I swear I will never—"

Emerson cut him short with a blistering Arabic oath. "Repeat, word for word, every conversation you had with Saleh regarding the—er—Master."

"Word for word" would have been beyond the fellow, of course. Even after insistent interrogation Emerson succeeded in getting little more out of him than he had admitted earlier. He had never been in the presence of "the Master," never seen him or heard him speak. Saleh had not described him. Why should he? He was the Master. "He has a thousand faces and ten thousand names!"

When we left, we were still undecided as to what to do with him. "I think he was telling the truth," Emerson remarked. "Saleh would not have shared his favored position with an underling like Mohammed. Shall we let him go?"

"We could ask Mr. Russell to take charge of him while we are in Luxor."

"What would be the purpose of that? All Russell has done so far is complain. We present him with a perfectly good murder, and leave him to investigate it, and what has he discovered? Nothing. I see no sense at all in telling him about Sennia."

"I would not be surprised to discover that he has already heard of it."

And so it proved. Shortly thereafter we were in receipt of an extremely stiff note from Mr. Russell, demanding our presence in his office that afternoon concerning a matter of importance.

"No time," said Emerson, tearing the note to shreds and tossing the scraps onto the floor.

"He may have news about Asad's murder," I suggested.

"Bah," said Emerson.

And with this I was inclined to agree.

The remainder of the day was spent in rearranging everyone's luggage. Fatima had packed all her cooking utensils, Sennia all her toys, and Emerson every book in his study, despite the fact, as I was careful to point out to him, that Cyrus had one of the best Egyptological libraries in the country. Just before we left for the station, while I was counting heads and bundles, Emerson slipped out. He was back almost at once. I gave him a look of inquiry, to which he responded with a shrug and a nod. He had freed Mohammed. I hoped we would not live to regret it, but reminded myself of one of my favorite aphorisms: "What's done is done."

It required all my considerable energy and talents of organization to get our extensive entourage and their boxes onto the train. Sennia was so excited her feet seemed hardly to touch the ground. Even Kadija could not keep hold of her, so Daoud lifted her onto his broad shoulders. William met us at the station. He had only one sadly battered suitcase.

The train was late in leaving; it usually was. As a rule I sleep well on trains, but Emerson's grumbles about the narrowness of the berths, and an occasional howl from Horus, in the next compartment with Sennia and Basima, kept me from repose. I finally gave it up at sunrise and wakened Emerson, who had, in his provoking fashion, succumbed to sweet slumber at about the time I realized I was wide-awake and would remain so. He did not like it, but we were all up and dressed when the train finally pulled into the station, only three hours late.

I was gratified to see a large crowd assembled, though I had expected no less. The return of the Father of Curses to the scene of his many triumphs was an event, an occasion, a homecoming. They were all there—Yusuf and his family, Katherine in a particularly becoming green frock, Cyrus, who swept his fine Panama hat from his head when he saw us at the window.

"I don't see Ramses and Nefret," I said to Emerson.

Emerson took a tighter grip on Sennia, who was bouncing up and down and waving both arms. "Don't begin fretting and fussing, Peabody. They will be here. Hallo, Yusuf! (How fat he's become!) Salaam alcikhum, Omar (you old villain). Feisal— Ali—"

Sennia's shriek hurt my eardrums. "Ramses! Here I am, Ramses! Aunt Nefret!"

Then I saw them making their way toward the door of our carriage, Ramses bareheaded as usual, Nefret holding his arm. Emerson caught Sennia, who had squirmed away from him and was making for the door. "You had better carry her, Daoud, or she'll be trampled underfoot. Good Gad, what a crush! Let me help you down, Peabody."

But when I put my foot on the step I was seized, firmly and respectfully, and drawn into a hearty embrace—the heartiest and most heartfelt I had ever received from that particular individual. I looked up into the smiling, sun-browned face of my son. "It's good to see you, Mother," he said, and kissed me on both cheeks.

A good deal of hugging and kissing went on, accompanied by the wringing of hands and slaps on the back that represent exchanges of masculine regard. Bertie had not accompanied the others; his mother had felt he should not tire himself. Cyrus's boundless goodwill extended even to William, whom he had not expected, and who hung back until his former employer seized his hand and welcomed him.

Naturally I was pleased by the warmth of Ramses's greeting. I wondered what he was up to now.

It was not until much later in the day that I found out. Emerson and I had agreed we would consult Ramses and Nefret before deciding how much to tell the Vandergelts, but one cannot dismiss one's host and hostess immediately upon one's arrival. We had to eat a hearty breakfast, congratulate Bertie on his improved looks, and listen to Cyrus's animated schemes for excavating. Emerson joined in with almost as much enthusiasm, and while they discussed the relative merits of Drah Abu'l Naga and the Valley of the Queens, Katherine told me about Jumana. I informed her that Nefret had already mentioned the girl to me, and that she sounded like a worthy candidate for further education. Katherine was quick to agree.

"It seemed to me that the best scheme—subject of course to your approval, dear Amelia—would be for you to take her back to Cairo with you. None of the schools here can teach her anything more. Cyrus and I would be delighted to bear the cost of her education."

I felt sure they would be. For Katherine, at least, no sum would be too great if it would remove the girl from her beloved and susceptible son.

"I see no objection," I replied. "I would want to meet her first, of course."

"There will be no difficulty about that," Katherine replied somewhat snappishly. "She has been here almost every afternoon. Bertie has begun studying hieroglyphs with Mr. Barton, and he suggested she join the class."

Cyrus had overheard. "Well, now, Amelia, doesn't that make sense to you? A little competition spurs a student to work harder, don't you think? He'll have to spread himself to keep up with her."

It was clear, from his appeal, that he and Katherine had had words on the subject. Naturally I agreed with Cyrus. In my opinion there was not the slightest possibility that a serious attachment could develop—the girl was only sixteen, and once Bertie was back in the world again he would undoubtedly find other young women to whom he was attracted. In the meantime, anything that encouraged the boy to perk up was all to the good. Only time would tell whether his interest in Egyptology would last. I sincerely hoped so. It would be just the thing for him, and would please Cyrus a great deal.

Before I could express my views—more tactfully than I have done in this private journal—Sennia interrupted. Tearing her attention away from Ramses, she announced, "I can teach Bertie hieroglyphs. He doesn't need another teacher."

"I'm sure you could," Bertie said, with an affectionate grin. "But we didn't know you were coming, Sennia, and you will be going back to Cairo before long. I'd invite you to attend the class, but I'm afraid it wouldn't be advanced enough for you."

This left Sennia in something of a quandary, for though she obviously agreed with Bertie's assessment of her skills, she was loath to abandon her role as mentor.

While she was thinking it over, Albert announced that luncheon was served, and we had to force down more food. I had been watching Ramses closely, and as the meal went on I began to see signs of fidgeting—not easy to observe in an individual so controlled, but clearly perceptible to his mother. My burgeoning suspicions were strengthened when he and Nefret declined Katherine's thoughtful suggestion that we four might like a little time together.

"You'll want to rest for a while, surely," Nefret said to me. "One doesn't sleep well on a train, and you must have been frightfully busy getting ready to leave on such short notice."

"Who needs to rest?" Emerson demanded. "Cyrus and I are going to Gurneh to talk with Yusuf about hiring a crew."

A general outcry from everyone except Cyrus—and William, who had not ventured to express an opinion on any subject whatever—put an end to this idea. I reminded Emerson that we had yet to unpack and settle in. "And," I added, with a meaningful look at my son, "there is still a great deal of news to be imparted."

"Quite," said Ramses, rising in haste. "After you've had a good long rest. We will come back for tea, if we may."

"Supposing Emerson and I come to you," I said. "I yearn to see the dear old *Amelia* again."

Nefret's countenance was a good deal easier to read than that of Ramses, but she rallied quickly. "Of course. What a good idea."

I managed to nag and prod Emerson into leaving earlier than he had intended, not because I hoped to catch my dear children doing something of which I would not approve . . . Ah well, if I must be honest, that was exactly what I hoped. That they had some private and secret activity planned for the afternoon was manifest from their behavior. That they counted on completing it before teatime was equally obvious.

We were at least half an hour before our time, but the untroubled countenances of my children informed me that I was too late. Whatever they had been up to, it had been accomplished. At Nefret's invitation I made a tour of inspection—solely to renew fond memories, as I assured her—and then we returned to the saloon, which was filled with the golden light of late afternoon. Accepting a cup of tea from Nefret, I gazed about with considerable emotion. How many happy hours had I spent in that room with those I loved, engaged in amiable conversation or, upon occasion, in equally pleasurable arguments with Emerson. Except for new curtains and coverings, Nefret had made few changes, but I observed with some surprise that my portrait had been replaced with a copy of one of the scenes from Tetisheri's tomb.

"Did you tire of having me glare down at you from the wall?" I inquired, laughing to indicate it was just one of my little jokes.

Ramses came at once to sit beside me. He put his arm round my shoulders. "What is it?" I cried in alarm. "Why are you doing that?"

"Because he loves you and is happy to see you," Nefret said. Ramses had gone a trifle red in the face.

"Oh," I said. "Well, my dear boy, I am happy to see you too."

"We are all happy to see one another," declared Emerson. "Why is it necessary to say so? What the devil have you done with your mother's portrait, Ramses?"

"That's rather a long story," Ramses said.

"Then I will tell mine first," I declared. "I believe you are au courant about our adventures in Cairo, except for the latest, which occurred this past Sunday."

I was informed that they knew all about that too, since Sennia had treated Ramses to a highly colored account of her adventure. I had asked her not to speak of it for fear of worrying Bertie, thinking that that admonition would prevent premature disclosure to all parties; nor had she. She had only told Ramses, during a brief interlude when she had got him off by himself. I allowed Emerson to relate the results of our investigation while I indulged in a few cucumber sandwiches.

"He called himself the Master," Ramses said in an odd flat voice.

"Apparently that is the case," said Emerson, in the same sort of voice. His eyes locked with those of Ramses. I have never believed that complex messages can be exchanged by means of glances—except in the case of Emerson and myself—but Ramses's pensive face broke into a smile.

"It's all right, Father. He's got a perfect alibi."

It would be impossible to convey in a few sentences the effect of that simple statement, or the incoherence of the succeeding exchange. As Ramses later admitted, he had been racking his brains to think of a tactful means of breaking the news. I cannot say that it came as a complete surprise. Naturally, the possibility had already occurred to me. What hurt most of all was not the duplicity of my children but that of Emerson.

"You knew!" I cried in poignant reproach. "You have known from the first! Emerson, how could you have kept it from me?"

Emerson began, "General Maxwell—"

"Swore you to secrecy? Such oaths do not, should not, cannot, apply to the relations between husband and wife."

My attempt to put him on the defensive did not

succeed, I am happy to say. I do not care for meek-
ness in a husband, and Emerson is particularly
handsome when he is in a rage. His cheeks turned a
becoming shade of brick-red and the cleft in his
chin vibrated.

"Be damned to that," he said hotly. "His survival
was a military secret, and furthermore, Amelia, it
was none of your confounded business."

I was about to reply, in equally heated terms,
when Ramses cleared his throat. "Forgive me for
interrupting, but that is beside the point now. You
haven't heard the worst of it. We need your advice."

The reminder was well-timed. I had not finished
with Emerson by any means, but that discussion
was best conducted in private. And when I heard
"the worst of it," I could only agree that a council
of war was badly needed.

It had obviously come as a considerable relief to
Emerson to learn that Sethos could not have been
the man behind Sennia's abduction. I would never
have believed him capable of such a thing, but evidently I had greater faith in Emerson's brother
than he did. The knowledge that Sethos had resumed his criminal activities was disappointing
but not wholly unexpected. The news that he was
threatened by a ruthless new competitor aroused
some concern, but was of interest primarily because it explained much that had been a mystery
thus far.

"The attacks on us in Cairo were meant to keep
us there and induce Ramses to return," I said. "You
remember, Emerson, that I remarked upon how ineffectual they were—"

"We both remarked upon that," said Emerson, with a sour look at me. "I had begun to suspect—"

"As had I, my dear. Poor Mr. Asad's death was the only real tragedy, and now we know why the body was brought to us. The killer obviously expected that when Ramses heard of it he would come rushing back to Cairo in order to wreak revenge— and defend us from danger."

We had settled ourselves comfortably by then, Emerson smoking his pipe and Nefret curled up on the settee next to him. I smiled pleasantly at my son, who began to protest. "Now, Mother—"

"You would have, you know. That is why I tried to keep the facts from you. But," I went on quickly, "I was wrong to do so. We were also wrong to divide our forces. Now that we are together again and in perfect confidence with one another, I do not doubt we can deal expeditiously with the remaining difficulties." Emerson opened his mouth, but his expression warned me that I had better go on talking. "I presume that before you removed your—er—guest you persuaded him to confide in you?"

"Precisely what I was about to say," Emerson grunted. "What is it they are after? A new tomb, I suppose? It must be located in some relatively populous area or this fellow wouldn't be so determined to get you out of the way. Surely not the East Valley?"

"Well reasoned, Father," Ramses said. "We had arrived at the same conclusion. It can't be anything but a tomb, and if the site were remote they could clear it without fear of interruption. This fellow—"

"What do you call him?" I asked.

Ramses looked blank. "We don't call him anything, Mother. We don't know who he is."

"References to him would be simpler if we gave him a nom de guerre," I explained.

Nefret chuckled. "Quite right. Would you consider 'X' too trite?"

"We ought to be able to come up with something more inventive. One of the more unpleasant pharaohs, perhaps? Or el-Hakim, the cruelest and most fanatical ruler of the Fatimite Dynasty?"

"It is just like you, Amelia, to waste time on something so trivial," Emerson exclaimed. "Where is the damned tomb? The sooner we get at it and clear it—"

"That's just the trouble," Nefret said. "Sethos claimed he doesn't know."

Emerson jumped to his feet. "He lied. Just give me ten minutes with the bas—um—with him!"

"I think he was speaking the truth, Father," Ramses said, glancing at his wife. "If you will allow me to continue, I'll tell you what he said."

Sethos had admitted that when he returned to Egypt in September it was with every intention of resuming his former business activities. He had not been in communication with his old associates for several years, so he was surprised to learn from one of them that they had been expecting to hear from him since the previous spring. All the Cairo underworld knew that "the Master" had returned; one of the most notorious, a man named Mubashir, had boasted of having spoken with him.

It was apparent that someone had taken advantage of his formidable reputation and habit of anonymity, for reasons which were not difficult to deduce. He was reluctant to approach Mubashir directly, so he decided to throw down the gauntlet, so to speak, by carrying out several thefts, including the robbery of Legrain's storage magazines and the removal of the statue of Ramses II. This had the desired effect of informing the impostor that a rival had appeared on the scene. It had the unfortunate effect of inspiring the impostor to violent attempts to remove the said rival.

One could almost feel sorry for the bewildered criminals of Luxor. It did not take them long to realize there was not one Master, but two, since each of them was attempting to identify the other and claiming to be the true and original Master Criminal. Some had spoken with Sethos, some with the impostor, and they had no way of knowing which of the two was genuine. Recruitment suffered; the more cautious of the fellows refused to have anything to do with either.

"It is still a mystery to me why, if this—er—whatever—hopes to become the new head of the illegal antiquities game, he hasn't stolen anything," Emerson said. "Apparently Sethos was responsible for the thefts of which we heard. Nothing of interest has come on the market recently. Why hasn't he begun removing smaller objects from the tomb, as the Abd er Rassuls did at Deir el Bahri?"

"That is how the authorities caught up with the Rassuls," Ramses pointed out. "This fellow has probably learned from their mistake. If he can make a clean sweep of the place over a period of only a few days, he can be well away from here before the objects appear on the market, and leave no trail the police could follow. But at this point the very existence of such a tomb is pure conjecture. Sethos arrived at the same conclusions we did, on the basis of the same clues—or so he claims. If there is such a place, its location is known only to its discoverer. He'll need assistance when he removes the contents, but it is only common sense to confide in no one until that day comes."

"Hmph," said Emerson round the stem of his pipe.

A hail from Ashraf, standing guard at the gangplank, made me realize how much time had passed. "There is Cyrus's carriage come for us," I said. "We mustn't keep him waiting. Emerson, put your coat on. Ramses, are you ready, my dear?"

Nefret ran off to get a wrap, and while the men collected their scattered garments I considered Sethos's story. It made perfectly good sense, but then I would have expected nothing less from my old adversary and present brother-in-law. Believing him dead, I had not had sufficient opportunity to adjust to that relationship. It would take some doing. The thought of seeing him again, as I meant to do next day, induced confused emotions—memories of long years of aggravation and impertinent advances, equally strong memories of his noble sacrifices for us and for his country.

Apparently the latter sacrifice had been only a temporary arrangement. Mentally I added a new task to the list I had composed. Sethos would have to be reformed, and made to remain reformed. He could not be allowed to return to his old ways.

There was one other little matter that was of equal importance, and I brought it up after we were on our way to the Castle. "It should not be difficult to identify el-Hakim. He is an archaeologist, not an Egyptian, and since there are only a few remaining in Luxor—"

"Curse it, Amelia, there you go again!" Emerson shouted. "Stating as fact what is as yet only an unproved theory."

I knew why he was in such an acrimonious frame of mind, so I replied calmly, "All the evidence points to that conclusion, my dear. This fellow would not be able to masquerade successfully as the Master had he not many of the latter's skills and attributes— including his ruthlessness. He has committed three murders "

"And tried to commit a fourth," said Nefret.

"Yes." I turned to Ramses, who immediately assumed an expression of wary expectation. "I am not going to criticize you, my dear," I assured him. "I understand why you felt it necessary to divert attention from the presence of a guest aboard the *Amelia*, but—"

"Speaking of that," Nefret said quickly. "We've been unable to think how to break it to Cyrus that he has an ailing sister."

"Oh, dear," I murmured. "He's bound to hear of it sooner or later, I suppose."

"We were counting on you, Mother," said my son, "to come up with a convincing explanation."

"Lie, you mean," grunted Emerson. "That is your forte, Peabody. Well?"

"Not now, Emerson, we have arrived. Just leave it to me."

I was guilty of a slight amount of hubris when I implied that I had, on the spur of the moment, invented an explanation for a particularly inexplicable situation. However, I am accustomed to having such tasks thrust upon me and I did not doubt that, given sufficient time, a solution would come to me. Unfortunately, I was not given any time at all. Cyrus was waiting at the door to greet us, as was his hospitable habit. Hospitality was not his only aim, however; as the others passed on into the drawing room, he drew me aside.

"All right, Amelia, what's going on?"

Hoping he did not mean what I feared he meant, I attempted to equivocate. "I beg your pardon, Cyrus?"

"How is Emmeline?"

A grin spread across his lined countenance as he waited for an answer. None was immediately forthcoming. I defy any reader to produce one.

"Selim was kind enough to ask after her," Cyrus went on. "He had heard from his Uncle Yusuf, who had heard from Jamil, who had heard from your steward about my poor sister. Sure came as a surprise to me that I had one."

"What did you say to Selim?" I asked, still sparring for time.

"Why, I thanked him for his interest. Who is the lady?"

"Bless you, Cyrus! It is a somewhat—er—

complicated story. I will explain it to you later. Katherine will be wondering what is keeping us, and Emerson—"

"Tonight," Cyrus said firmly.

"Yes, of course. Tonight."

I hope I may not be accused of braggadocio when I say that by the time we joined the others I had arrived at the obvious solution. Having cleared my mind of that matter, I was able to concentrate on my suspects.

We were quite a large party in ourselves, but Cyrus enjoyed nothing more than seeing every seat at his dining table occupied. He had only managed to collect two other guests that evening: Mr. Barton, who had been persuaded (without difficulty) to stay to dine after giving Bertie his lesson in hieroglyphs, and Mr. MacKay, whom Cyrus had caught on his way home from the Valley.

Owing to the impromptu nature of the gathering (and Emerson's well-known aversion to evening dress), attire was casual and so was conversation. Emerson did most of the talking, so I was able to study my suspects—three of them, including William. I was acquainted with MacKay, but I had not met Mr. Barton.

The poor lad was not prepossessing. His features were rough-hewn and his movements awkward. Some of the awkwardness might have been occasioned by the fact that he never took his eyes off Nefret, which rendered the neat consumption of food and drink difficult. Sentimentality and youth were irrelevant, of course; I had known a number of criminals with those characteristics. His relative lack of experience in the field might suggest that he was unlikely to have discovered a new tomb, but such discoveries are often serendipitous. It was safe to assume that he was familiar with the name and career of Sethos; that gentleman's exploits (along with our own) had become part of the legendry of Egyptology.

Mr. Barton appeared to have a solid alibi for at least one incident. He had been with Nefret and Ramses when the body fell from the cliff, so it could not have been he who pushed it off. However, I was not prepared to accept unquestioningly Ramses's belief that the man had been deliberately murdered. I respect my son's acumen, but he is sometimes mistaken. In fact, I could think of no sensible reason why anyone—Bedouin, Senussi, Turk, or tomb robber—would drop a rock and then a body on Ramses. It could not have anything to do with the matter of the missing tomb. It must have been an accident. And therefore Mr. Barton was still a suspect.

I transferred my attention to Mr. MacKay, who was talking to Cyrus about the Valley of the Kings.

He had been in Egypt longer than Barton and was reputed to know every square foot of the Valley. If the tomb was there, he was the most likely person to have come upon it. The other considerations I have mentioned applied equally well to him. I knew nothing to his discredit—indeed, his reputation was of the best—but even the most honest scholar might be seduced by a discovery as rich as this one could be.

William Amherst—shy, harmless William—had

been in Cairo when the attacks on us took place. To be sure, he had not been in Luxor when Sethos and Ramses were attacked. The reverse was true of the others . . . but was it? I would have to find out. Another possibility was that there were two people involved, one in Luxor, one in Cairo. The more I thought about that, the more likely it seemed. William had come to us seeking a position on our staff after Ramses left for Luxor. He had been in Egypt for many years and had worked with Cyrus in the Valley and at other sites. His career had not been particularly successful; his self-confidence had been eroded and his means were limited. He admitted to having been in Luxor, among other places, the previous year. Was his seemingly candid admission of moral collapse following his alleged attempt to enlist a way of concealing his true activities?

William began to squirm and look nervously at me, so I turned to Bertie, who was on my left, and asked him how he was getting on with his studies. The conversation had already taken an archaeological turn; poor Katherine was the only one present who had not a consuming interest in the subject, but she had become accustomed to enduring such discussions with a courteous appearance of interest, and she was anxious to encourage Bertie. I joined in at appropriate intervals, but never believe, Reader, that I had lost sight of what must be, for a time, my primary consideration. Deduction alone might lead us to discovering the identity of our unknown opponent, but if we could induce him to seek us out it would save time and trouble. I was considering ways of doing this when a chance question from

Mr. MacKay gave me the opportunity. It was only a courteous inquiry as to how long we meant to remain in Luxor, but I immediately took advantage, catching Emerson with his mouth open.

"We are giving serious thought to spending the rest of the winter in Luxor. We have almost finished the task with which Herr Junker was good enough to entrust us, so there is nothing more for us to do at Giza, and Emerson believes that a detailed survey of the Luxor sites would prove useful."

Emerson closed his mouth with an audible click of teeth; Cyrus expressed his delight and approval; and Mr. MacKay frowned. "Not that you have not done your best," I added graciously. "But it is too large a task for one man."

The young fellow's troubled brow cleared. "Candidly, Mrs. Emerson, it would be a great relief to me. For some time I have been torn between my duty to my profession and my duty to my country. Were you and your family here, I could leave with a clear conscience."

He sounded sincere. Was he?

Ramses had spoken very little. Observing his enigmatic look at MacKay, I realized his thoughts had been running along the same lines as mine.

MacKay and Barton did not linger over coffee, and both declined a postprandial libation. Their working day began at dawn. Soon thereafter Katherine took Bertie up to bed, and Cyrus suggested she retire as well. I was about to administer a tactful hint to William when he murmured something about being tired from the trip, and effaced himself. They were scarcely out of the room when all eyes focused on me, some in hopeful inquiry, some—Cyrus's—in stern expectation.

"You aren't going to wiggle out of it this time, Amelia," he remarked. "I'll sit here all night if I have to."

"So you've heard," Emerson said resignedly.

"About Emmeline? Yep. Now I've kept mum, folks, didn't deny or admit anything. Seems to me I'm entitled to hear the whole story. Who is the mysterious lady?"

"That is no lady," I said, unable to resist a touch of humor. "That is the Master Criminal."

Cyrus's jaw dropped and Emerson let out a strangled oath. Nefret's face rounded in a smile. Ramses said nothing.

"Now, Emerson, don't roar," I said. "I realized immediately that we have no choice but to confide wholly in Cyrus. Why should we not? He has been our staunchest ally and dearest friend."

Cyrus let out a choked gurgle and cleared his throat. "Thank you, Amelia. I—uh—I thought I was used to your shenanigans, but you knocked the breath clean out of me with that one. Why are you folks sheltering your worst enemy? Or are you holding him prisoner? Why? Holy Jehoshaphat, I thought the fellow was dead."

"Ramses will explain," I said.

Ramses started violently and so forgot himself as to scowl at me. It seemed to me only fair that since he and Nefret had initiated the deception, they should render the necessary explanations, but I gave him a brief breathing space by remarking,

"Cyrus, I believe that instead of brandy I would like a whiskey and soda, if you would be so good."

Ramses then launched into his narrative, to which I listened with as much interest as Cyrus, since I was curious to know how Ramses was going to avoid certain matters which could not be divulged even to Cyrus: namely and to wit, Sethos's relationship to Emerson, which was a private family matter, and the former's career as a secret agent, which was a private government matter.

I must say that after a somewhat faltering start Ramses did credit to my training. His mention of a "lost tomb" fascinated Cyrus to such an extent that his critical faculties were dulled, and our friend readily accepted Ramses's explanation that he had come to Sethos's aid because he was, in a sense, the lesser of two evils.

"His rival is completely ruthless—a killer," Ramses said. "And I am sure I need not remind you of the numerous occasions upon which Sethos risked his life to protect the lady he loves devotedly . . ."

He proceeded to remind them of those occasions, at unnecessary length, and in a prose style that was reminiscent of Miss Minton's more romantic passages. Ah well, I thought, as Emerson chewed fiercely on the stem of his pipe and my son pretended to look apologetic, I suppose I had it coming. I did not doubt that Ramses enjoyed getting back at me for "putting him on the spot." Our relationship was developing in quite an interesting fashion.

Ramses was able to tell the truth, the whole truth, and nothing but the truth about Miss Minton's involvement, which explained to everyone's satisfaction how Sethos had ended up at the *Amelia*. He ended with an apology for involving Cyrus, which the latter, now bright-eyed as an adventurous boy, brushed aside.

"I understand. Had to keep those thugs away from the *Amelia* and your lady. Getting him off the boat was a good idea too, but you'd better make sure the word spreads that you no longer have a guest. How about if I tell the world that poor old Emmeline's decided she wants nothing more to do with this unsanitary sickly country? Packed her traps and gone off in a huff. I could take you to the train tomorrow, Amelia, bid you a brotherly farewell, you can get off at Hammadi and catch the next train back . . . What's so funny, Nefret?"

"You," Nefret sputtered. "We ought to have taken you into our confidence from the start. You're almost as good at invention as Mother."

"Quite," said Ramses, giving Cyrus a look of alarm. "It won't wash, Cyrus. We can't prove Emmeline was ever here at the Castle, because she wasn't. All we can do is add another lie to the rest and say she's gone—and the sooner the better. I'll tell Nasir and Ashraf tomorrow, and if they wonder how the bloody hell—excuse me—how we got 'her' away unseen, they can speculate to their hearts' content."

Cyrus was obviously disappointed. "Well, if you say so. Now how are we going to go about finding that gol-durned royal tomb?"

A thump and a click brought us all to our feet. It sounded as if someone had slammed a door which had been slightly ajar; yet I had made certain both doors to the sitting room were tightly closed before I began to speak. Emerson dashed toward one door and Ramses, whose hearing was slightly more acute, for the other. He flung the panel wide; and there, blinking and emitting little bleats of alarm, was William Amherst.

FIFTEEN

William stuttered out a series of incoherent phrases—"Couldn't sleep—came down to get a book from the library—fell against the door—frightfully sorry . . ." He *was* holding a book, and he was attired in pajamas and dressing gown, but no sensible conspirator would neglect such obvious precautions. We did not bother asking whether he had overheard all or part of our conversation, since he would not have told the truth anyhow. It might have been only idle curiosity that had prompted him to ease the door open—or someone else might have opened it before he came along.

Cyrus was loath to admit that his former protégé could be guilty of wrongdoing. "He sure has changed, though. Used to be a swell young fellow who would look you straight in the eye. He's a different man."

"Hmmm," I said.

"No!" Emerson's shout rattled the crystal. "No, Amelia. We already have two experts in disguise in this—er—group. I refuse to admit even the slightest possibility of a third!"

We did not linger long after that. I persuaded Cyrus that since Sethos's murderous rival was (presumably) the only one who knew the location of the (hypothetical) tomb, our first priority should be identifying him—which would have the additional advantage of preventing further violence. I also felt obliged to scold Cyrus a little, for his own good.

"There is absolutely no reason to suppose that the tomb is that of a royal personage, Cyrus. I know that it has been your greatest ambition to find such a tomb, but the greater your expectations, the greater will be your disappointment should those expectations fail to materialize. Let imagination flourish freely, my friend, but do not pin your hopes—"

"You have made your point, Amelia," said Emerson. "I hope that *you* will take it to heart."

I rose before my spouse, as I usually do, filled with ambition and energy. I had believed, before we arrived in Luxor, that life had become somewhat complicated. Little had I known! Stimulated though I was by the tasks that awaited me, I admitted the necessity of organizing them in order of priority and feasibility. I therefore slipped out of bed without wakening Emerson, assumed a dressing gown, and went into the sitting room that adjoined our bedchamber.

We had, of course, been given Cyrus's best suite of rooms. They were even more elegant and comfortable than when I had stayed in them before.

The same fine Oriental rugs covered the floors and the light of early morning filtered through the beautifully carved mashrabiya screens that covered the windows. Katherine's thoughtful hand was visible in the new draperies, the luxurious appointments of the adjoining bath chamber, and the nice little desk in the sitting room. Nothing had been overlooked: notepaper and envelopes, writing materials and blotting paper. I settled myself into the comfortable chair and drew a sheet of paper toward me.

"Interview the other archaeological suspects," was the first item of business. Despite Emerson's jeers I felt certain that I had been right in believing that the man behind the mystery was an Egyptologist. I was acquainted with all of them, but never before had I had occasion to study them as possible murderers and criminals. I wanted to interview the ones who had not been present the previous evening.

Under this heading I added: Alibis. I doubted anything would come of this; it is only in fiction that detectives are able to extract verifiable statements from their suspects. Memories are faulty, and witnesses, particularly to nocturnal activities, are often lacking. Still, it was worth a try, and a "Timetable of Attacks" might be useful. I wrote this phrase under "Alibis."

"Find the Tomb" was my second heading. Two methods of inquiry suggested themselves, aside from the obvious one of catching the villain and forcing him to confess. Yusuf and the other members of the family in Gurneh might know something. I did not suppose they would deliberately conceal information, but they might consider it unimportant. Emerson and Selim were the best persons to ask such questions. The other line of inquiry was to search for the place ourselves. This was not such a hopeless endeavor as it might sound, since logical analysis had limited the number of likely areas, and the villain might have left signs of his presence that would be visible to expert eyes like ours. A further advantage to this procedure was that if we came anywhere near the actual location it might inspire our adversary to attack us.

I had got this far when I heard a rustle of bed linen and a querulous oath from the adjoining room and Emerson abruptly appeared in the open doorway.

"So there you are," he exclaimed.

"Where did you think I would be?"

"With you, one never knows." Emerson leaned against the doorframe and rubbed his eyes. He is not at his best in the morning, physically or mentally, but even his present state of dishevelment—hair tousled, eyes half closed, chin bristling—did not detract from his splendid looks. Since we were not in the comfort of our own home, he had agreed to wear a minimal amount of sleeping attire—pajama trousers, to be precise—which exposed to my fond eyes the admirable musculature of his chest and shoulders.

I was a trifle out of temper with him, however. My attempts the previous night to carry on a conversation had failed. All he would do was grunt.

"Since you are awake, I will ring for tea," I said. "I could do with a cup; I have been working for over half an hour."

Emerson stumbled across the room and leaned over my shoulder. "Another of your confounded lists," he said disagreeably. "'Find the Tomb'? Good Gad, you make it sound as simple as scrubbing a floor or—"

But at that point the sitting room door opened—the service at the Castle was always first-rate—and Emerson retreated, mumbling irritably. "Your dressing gown is in the wardrobe," I called after him.

He was wearing it when he returned, and his expression was a trifle less forbidding. "I hate it when you creep away like that," he said. "When I reach out for you and you aren't there—"

"Drink your tea," I said. That might have been meant as an apology, but it had sounded more like criticism.

A cup of the genial beverage, heavily loaded with sugar, restored Emerson. Reaching out a long arm, he took my list from the writing desk and studied it. "I don't see any mention of your favorite method of identifying an enemy," he remarked. "Something along the lines of 'Wait to be attacked,' or 'Instigate an attack,' or—"

"I have already taken care of that," I replied.

"Hmmm, yes. Your announcement last evening that we intended to remain in Luxor for the rest of the winter. Really, Amelia, I wish you would warn me of these little schemes of yours; if I were not so accustomed to your methods I might have blurted out a denial. You do realize, I hope, that your entire theory and methodology are based on pure surmise? We don't know that there is a tomb; we don't know that the discoverer is an Egyptologist; we don't know why, assuming that the first two premises are correct, he has refrained from removing the artifacts. He may—note the word 'may'—have attempted to keep us from coming here, but now that we are here he may simply wait until we leave, however long it takes. He doesn't appear to be in any particular hurry."

"Anything is possible, my dear. However, he went to considerable lengths to induce us to remain in Cairo, and he is now aware that Sethos is also after his treasure. Were I in his position—"

"Yes, yes, I know what you would do," Emerson muttered. "Speaking of my—of Sethos, I don't see his name on your list. I expected your first move would be to head for the Winter Palace."

The idea had, of course, passed through my mind. But greatly as I yearned to come face-to-face with the remarkable individual who had returned—again!—from the dead, I knew that we must avoid drawing undue attention to the hotel. It was well known in Luxor that Emerson never went to such places if he could get out of it, and our appearance at an early hour would be so unusual as to arouse curiosity.

I explained this to Emerson. "I will pen a brief missive to Miss Minton, asking her to join us for luncheon at two."

"Ah, yes, Miss Minton," said Emerson thoughtfully. "You haven't put her on your list either."

"I had not finished the list. Rest assured I am well aware that we owe her a debt of gratitude for rescuing your—er—Sethos. I have it all worked out. Now hurry and dress, Emerson, we must get an early start."

When we went down to breakfast we found the Vandergelts already at table. I had expected Cyrus would be "raring to go," as he quaintly expressed it, but I was somewhat surprised to see Bertie also dressed for riding.

On second thought, I was not surprised.

Our appearance had interrupted a rather brisk discussion between mother and son. Katherine turned to me in appeal. "I have been trying to dissuade Bertie from going, Amelia. He isn't fit enough yet."

Rapidly I considered what advice I ought to give. Bertie's presence would inhibit our conversation to some extent, since we had agreed that for the time being at least Katherine should be spared the knowledge that we were involved with not one but two groups of criminals. She had seen the advantages of Egyptology as a profession for Bertie, but she would most probably consider that a distinct disadvantage.

The young man was too well-bred to say more than, "I assure you, Mother, I am up to it," but his mutinous expression made it clear he meant to have his way, so I patted her hand and reassured her.

"We will only be out for a few hours, Katherine, and in the coolest part of the day. Nefret and I will make sure he doesn't overdo."

"Quite right," said Emerson, pausing in his brisk intake of nourishment. "You can't keep the lad wrapped in cotton wool forever, Katherine. Let him have his head. We will look after him."

Having mixed his metaphors and thoroughly vexed his hostess, he returned to his eggs and toast with the complacent air of a man who has been the soul of tact. Unconvinced but outvoted, Katherine said no more.

We had arranged the night before that Nefret and Ramses should meet us at the Castle. When they turned up they were accompanied by two youthful Egyptians, whom I had no difficulty in identifying as Jumana and her brother.

Daoud's description of the girl had not done her justice. What made her remarkable was not only her pretty face but the vivacity that animated every feature. Her brother bore a strong resemblance to her, but that morning his handsome face was disfigured by a swelling that had almost closed one of his eyes.

As soon as we set off, Jumana attached herself to Emerson, so I joined Bertie, whose attempt to ride beside her she had coolly ignored. His eyes fixed on the slim little figure of the girl, who was gesticulating so vigorously she appeared to be in danger of falling off the horse, he did not respond to my innocuous if pointless remark that it was a fine morning. I nudged him gently with my parasol.

"I beg your pardon?" he said, starting.

"Well?" Nefret had joined us. "What do you think of her?"

"I have not had time to formulate an opinion," I replied. "If she is as intelligent as she is—er—enthusiastic . . ."

"She is also a conniving little minx," said Nefret with a smile. "You see how she is making up to Father. Before you got here, Ramses was the object of her attentions."

"Oh, I say," Bertie exclaimed. "She's not a . . . she's not like that. Really, she's not."

"Her interest is purely professional," Nefret explained. "She's a Moslem female; she assumes that the men in the family make the decisions, and she is dead set on becoming an Egyptologist."

Bertie's ingenuous face brightened. "Well, so am I." He drew himself up, straightened his shoulders, and looked about with an air of great interest. "Cyrus mentioned we were going to Deir el Bahri. That's Queen Hatshepsut, isn't it?"

"Very good," I commended, and launched into a little lecture on the career of that illustrious woman. Nefret, who of course knew all about it, fell back to where she had wanted to be all along—with Ramses, that is.

The queen's mortuary temple was one of the favored sites on the west bank and one of the most conspicuous. As we approached I explained the architectural features to Bertie and attempted to conjure up a picture of how it must have looked in Hatshepsut's time, with flowering trees lining the causeway and huge statues adorning the columned terraces. He was listening attentively and had asked several intelligent questions when Emerson took it upon himself to interrupt.

"Don't let her give you too much at one time," he advised. "She'll drown you in facts if you allow it."

Bertie insisted that he had enjoyed every word,

but Emerson obviously wanted a private conversation with me. He suggested that Bertie join Jumana, which pleased everyone except possibly Jumana.

"'Find the tomb,'" said Emerson in a low growl. "Rather a formidable task, isn't it, even for you?"

His gesture took in the long curve of the cliffs that enclosed Hatshepsut's temple and the ruins of the one next to it. Even in that limited area there were a hundred possible hiding places. It fit one of our criteria, however. It was certainly public enough. There were not as many tourists as there had been in past years, but they were all over the place, in clumps and pairs. (The second member of the pair being in all cases a dragoman or guide. It required force majeure to be left alone.)

"Ah well, we can only do our best," I replied. "No one can succeed unless he tries. Life—"

"One more aphorism—particularly one beginning 'life'—and I will divorce you, Peabody," said Emerson. But he smiled as he said it. "It's not going to be easy exploring with this entourage trailing us. What the devil are we looking for anyhow? A signpost, labeled 'THIS WAY TO THE LOST TOMB'?"

I always allow Emerson his little touches of sarcasm, which give him the illusion that he is being witty. Smiling back at him, I said, "We are supposed to be looking for a site for Cyrus. That provides us with a reasonable excuse to go anywhere we like. We can't allow Bertie to clamber about the cliffs, though. Leave it to me."

"I always do," said Emerson.

Jumana had left Bertie and was trotting briskly toward us. I told Emerson to go on and summoned the girl to my side. We had a little chat. I do not believe in beating about the bush, particularly with young persons. Subtle hints pass right over their heads, and this young person appeared to be even more determined and self-centered than most. I reminded her that Cyrus was extremely wealthy, dedicated to archaeology, and devoted to his stepson, and added, "I want you to stay with Bertie today, and on future occasions, while the rest of us engage in activities that would be too strenuous for him."

"Ah," said Jumana, her smooth brow wrinkling as she thought it over. It did not take her long to catch my drift. "If I do that, you and Mr. Vandergelt will like me very much?"

I assured her that we would. At least she had not demanded a direct quid pro quo! Leaving her and Bertie to stroll slowly about, we set off in a southerly direction, trailed by Jamil, who was carrying the water bottles. He fell farther and farther behind as we followed the steep path toward the base of the cliffs.

"He is certainly a reluctant assistant," I remarked to Ramses. "How did he get those bruises?"

"According to Jumana, he got into a fight at one of the Luxor coffee shops. In her opinion—she has a good many opinions," Ramses interpolated, with a sidelong glance at me—"he spends too much time in such places, with companions who are of questionable reputation. He's the apple of Yusuf's eye, though, and the old rascal refuses to discipline him. Watch where you step—it's rather rough going here."

He caught hold of my arm. I could have recovered from my stumble without assistance, but I thanked him and explained, "I am quite familiar with the terrain, my dear. I was scanning the cliffs for tomb entrances."

They—the cliffs, not the entrances—hung over us. Countless years of weathering by wind and water had shaped the stone into bizarre formations, some roughly columnar, some reminiscent of molten stone that had flowed over the top and then hardened. I did not need Emerson—or Ramses—to tell me that looking for an opening in that broken surface was almost certainly futile. Ramses felt obliged to tell me, though.

"One never knows," I replied. "Your father must believe there is some purpose in this expedition. Has he confided in you?"

"No. However, I think he wants to have a look at the place Kuentz showed us."

"Where someone dropped various objects on you? Hmmm. I had forgotten to put that on my list. Wait just a minute."

I removed the list from my pocket and opened the pencil case attached to my belt while Ramses watched with unconcealed amusement. "Why don't you join Cyrus and rest for a bit?" he suggested.

Emerson and Nefret had forged ahead, leaving Cyrus seated on the ground with his back against a boulder. When we came up to him he was mopping his flushed, sweating face with a handkerchief.

"Are you all right, Cyrus?" I asked.

"Never been happier," said Cyrus, between

wheezes. "Take me a day . . . or two . . . to get back in shape . . ."

I told Ramses to go on and beckoned at Jamil. After handing each of us a water bottle, he seated himself on the ground a little distance away.

"You don't appear to be enjoying yourself, Jamil," I remarked.

Jamil shrugged. "This is not work for a man, Sitt Hakim."

"What kind of work would you like to do?"

Another shrug.

"You must have some idea," I persisted. "Some of your cousins and your uncles work for us. They earn good money and are respected."

A slight curl of the boy's lip indicated his view of that idea. "If archaeology does not interest you, there are other worthwhile careers," I went on. "Cook, police officer—"

"Waiter, house servant," said Cyrus, whose Arabic was good enough to enable him to follow the conversation. "His opportunities are limited, my dear. It isn't right or just, but that's the way the world is."

"Ambition can o'erleap limitations," I said. "Look at David. And at Selim and Abdullah, for that matter." Jamil did not respond, even with a curl of the lip, so I poked him with my parasol to get his attention, and went on in Arabic, "You come of an honored family, Jamil. You too can be honored and respected if you work hard and study. There are those who will gladly help."

"Yes, Sitt Hakim." His smile would have been as charming as his sister's if it had had her warmth.

"I am surprised to find such lack of ambition in a member of that family," I remarked, as we continued on our way. "Perhaps my kindly little lecture will have some effect. He appeared to take it to heart."

"Huh," said Cyrus. "You'd better concentrate on Jumana. She's got enough ambition for both of them."

It was not long before we caught the others up. They had found the place without difficulty. The body had been removed, by predators or the police—probably the latter, since there were no indigestible bits scattered about.

"Has the fellow been identified?" I inquired.

"I asked to be notified should that occur," Ramses replied. "But I don't expect they will go to much trouble, unless someone reports a son or husband missing. He was a poor man. Worn, cheap garments. Not even a pair of sandals."

Emerson looked up. "Confound it, Ramses, there must be something there or the fellow wouldn't have attempted to prevent you from finding it."

"Kuentz must have been mistaken about the location. I didn't see any sign of an opening, and anyhow, he says the place contained nothing of interest."

"Hmph," said Emerson, fingering his chin. "I need to have a talk with Kuentz." And off he went with his long stride.

"Emerson, come back here!" I shouted. "You can't walk all the way to Deir el Medina."

He could have and would have had I not prevented him. I was also forced to forbid him to climb the cliff in search of Mr. Kuentz's purported tomb. In my opinion, it would have been both dangerous and unproductive, and we had to return in time to keep our luncheon engagement.

The going was easier on the way back, since it was downhill most of the way; but by the time we had collected Bertie and Jumana, both of whom looked very pleased with themselves—for, I sincerely hoped, different reasons—we decided that Emerson and I would go to the *Amelia* with the children and freshen up a bit there before proceeding to our appointment. Cyrus's face fell. The arrangement left him no choice but to escort Bertie back to the Castle. I had never intended to take him along anyhow; I had a number of things to say to my brother-in-law that could not be said in Cyrus's presence.

FROM MANUSCRIPT H

As they got ready for their visit to the Winter Palace, Ramses's nerves began to twitch. The interview with Sethos promised to be awkward, if not actually explosive, and he was worried about Margaret. Smith's presence added another disturbing element. He wondered if his mother had him on her list, and what she had written under "What to do about it."

She was the coolest of them all, inspecting them to make certain they were tidy enough to meet her standards, and giving Emerson's dusty coat an extra brushing. Ramses half-expected her to demand he hold out his hands as she had done when he was a child. When they were in the dinghy and under way, she whipped out her list and Emerson, who had been scowling and rubbing his chin, snarled, "Did you overlook something, Amelia? 'Reform Sethos,' for example? I see you have your parasol, but—"

"Sssh." She indicated the boatman. "Leave it to me, Emerson."

"Curse it," said Emerson. "Ramses, I presume you know what he looks like. At the moment, I mean."

"He was wearing Ramses's clothes," Nefret said. "The brown-and-gray tweed he bought in London last summer. Ramses also supplied him with a mustache and a sunburn. In return, he supplied us with the name under which he intended to register." She put her hand over Emerson's clenched fist. "Father, promise you won't start shouting at him. And Mother, you won't be rude to Margaret, will you?"

Both of them looked at her in shocked surprise. "I am never rude," said his mother stiffly. "I never shout," his father shouted.

For once Emerson did not linger in front of the hotel exchanging witticisms with dragomen, beggars, and vendors. He marched straight to the reception desk, where he was greeted effusively by the assistant manager. "Welcome back to Luxor, Professor and Mrs. Emerson. We heard of your arrival and were hoping you would honor us with a visit. Are you lunching? I will have a table prepared."

"Yes, very good," said Emerson. "You have a guest who registered yesterday, a Mr.—er—"

"The Honorable Edmund Whitbread," Ramses supplied.

"Oh, Honorable, of course," Emerson muttered. "What's his room number?"

"The gentleman left us this morning. He was on his way to Assuan, I believe. Oh, dear. I am very sorry, Professor, you appear a trifle—er—put out. Had he expected you to call?"

"Evidently," said Emerson in a choked voice.

"He said he would be back in a few days, he asked us to keep his room for him . . ."

"Key," said Emerson, holding out his hand.

It was strictly against the rules, but the fellow didn't even hesitate before he produced the key. How does he do it? Ramses wondered enviously. He doesn't threaten, he doesn't even raise his voice.

Emerson maintained a simmering silence as they proceeded to the lift. His wife was the first one who had the courage to break it. "Bad luck," she said. "It wasn't your fault, Ramses."

Ramses realized, to his surprise, that he had no intention of apologizing. Perhaps letting Sethos go had not been a wise move, but he didn't regret it. "It was the news of your arrival that made him bolt," he said. "What do you expect to find in his room, Father? D'you suppose he's had the common decency to return my best suit, or leave us a note of apology?"

"One never knows," his father said with a grudging smile. "We'll have a look later. First we will collect the lady—assuming she hasn't taken herself off too—and have lunch. I'm hungry."

Ramses knocked and announced himself, but

Margaret refused to open the door until Nefret had spoken to her. The room was in disorder—the bed unmade, the furniture shifted around—and Margaret was equally disheveled. Her clothes looked as if she had slept in them.

"Thank heaven!" she exclaimed, clutching at Emerson's arm like a drowning woman who has found a lifeline. "I haven't been out of this room since yesterday afternoon, I didn't dare even open the door for the waiter, and I wasn't sure the invitation was from you, and . . . and I'm ravenous!"

"Now, now," said Emerson, glancing uneasily at his wife, who remarked, "There is no excuse for hysteria, Miss Minton. We will go down to luncheon at once. First smooth your hair and put on your hat."

"Of course. It wouldn't do to appear in public without a hat, would it?" She pressed her hands to her flushed cheeks. "I beg your pardon. I have been under something of a strain."

Their table was ready, and Emerson insisted she eat something and have a glass of wine before she explained. A lady in distress always brought out the chivalrous side of his nature. He even called her Margaret. His wife did not.

"If you are yourself again, Miss Minton, we would appreciate a brief, coherent narrative."

Half a glass of wine and a roll had restored Margaret's self-possession and her sense of humor. "Are you sure you wouldn't rather wait and *borrow* my written account?"

"Just tell us," Ramses said quickly.

"By all means," said his mother.

"You may wonder why I asked Nefret to speak before I opened the door. Yesterday afternoon, just as I was about to go down for tea, there was a knock at my door, and a voice. Your voice, Ramses."

Ramses bit off an oath. His father didn't.

"Bloody hell and damnation! What did he say?"

"'It's me, Margaret. All right, are you?' It sounded exactly like you, Ramses."

"It would," Ramses said between his teeth.

"So of course I unlocked the door, and started to open it. He slammed it, practically in my face, and ordered me to lock it and keep it locked. He didn't sound like you then! He went on to tell me what a bloody idiot I was, and that there were at least three people in the hotel, including himself, who would lay violent hands on me if I put my nose outside that door, and that he wasn't the only one who could imitate your voice, and . . ." She smiled wryly. "If he meant to frighten me, he succeeded. When he stopped listing all the things that could happen to me, I asked several questions—you can imagine what about—but there was no answer."

The waiter brought their soup, and with a murmured apology, she began to eat.

"Two other people," Emerson muttered. "Who the devil . . ."

"It may not have been true," Ramses said.

"I couldn't take the chance, could I?" Margaret demanded. "And later that night, after I'd gone to bed, someone rattled the doorknob. I'd just got up nerve enough to turn out the light and I was half asleep. I yelled, 'Who's there?' Nobody answered. Then, just before dawn—"

"Good Gad," Emerson exclaimed. "Again?"

"He said he was the safragi, with my breakfast. I hadn't ordered breakfast."

"Three in all," Nefret murmured. "I wonder how many of them were Sethos?"

"I'm glad you find this amusing, Nefret," Margaret said.

Nefret hastily wiped the smile off her face. Ramses didn't understand her amusement either; Sethos's intentions might have been honorable, but his methods were deplorable.

"He'd have had time to pop by just before he went to catch the Assuan train," Nefret went on.

Margaret dropped her soup spoon. "He's gone to Assuan?"

"Not bloo— not likely," said Emerson. "But he has left the hotel, the bas— the ungrateful wretch. Ramses got him over here yesterday, since the presence of a stranger on board the *Amelia* had become known. Good idea, really. Confuse the trail."

"Thank you, Father," Ramses said.

"Hmm, yes. You can't stay here either, Margaret— Miss Minton—"

"Please use my given name, Professor. Formality is somewhat absurd under the circumstances."

"Er—thank you. As I was saying, we need to get you away from here. Peabody?"

"Quite right, Emerson. She is going back to the Castle with us. I have already spoken to Cyrus about it."

Of course she had, Ramses thought. She had probably put it on her list: "Move Miss Minton." Neither of the Vandergelts would have had a word to say about it.

She and Nefret went with Margaret to help her pack while Ramses and his father investigated the room Sethos had occupied. It was on the same floor as Margaret's, a few doors down the hall. The servants had been there that morning; the bed had been made and fresh towels placed on the table by the washstand. The wardrobe was empty. The only sign of occupancy, past or future, was a book on the bedside table—a popular guide to the antiquities of Upper Egypt. When Ramses picked it up, an envelope fell from between the pages. It was addressed, in a bold, black scrawl, to Professor Radcliffe Emerson.

Emerson read the enclosed letter and handed it to Ramses. "'Sorry to have missed you. I had business elsewhere. Be good enough, I beg, to present my compliments to the ladies of your family, and to Miss Minton, who, I understand, will be leaving Luxor immediately. Sincere regards . . .' It's signed 'Whitbread.'"

His father's unnatural calm augured poorly for someone—probably Sethos. "The ladies of your family," Emerson said, in the same cool voice. "Good of him to include Nefret."

"It is, rather, considering how she bullied him. Father, he had to be careful what he wrote. The chance of anyone other than you finding the message was remote, but he doesn't take chances, even remote ones."

"What annoys me most," said Emerson reflectively, "is his ability to anticipate our movements.

He could have left this at the desk. How did he know I'd search his room?"

"Anyone who was familiar with your habits could anticipate that, sir."

"Oh? Hmph. It was certainly the safest method of communicating with us. That's a fairly pointed hint about Miss Minton. Well, well. Let us join the ladies and pass on his compliments. Bring the book along."

"Yes, sir," said Ramses. "I had intended to do so."

They looked into Margaret's room, where the three women and two safragis had almost completed packing her bags. "We'll meet you in the lobby," Emerson said, retreating in haste as his wife fixed him with an inquiring stare.

"You are going to tell her, aren't you?" Ramses asked, lengthening his stride to keep up with his father. Emerson rang the bell for the lift, waited two seconds, and plunged down the stairs.

"Yes, certainly. It is a waste of time trying to keep things from your mother, she always finds out anyhow, and then she . . . Er—I've been meaning to ask . . . not that it's any of my affair . . . but you and Nefret . . . Er?"

"The same," Ramses said with a smile.

"Ah. And the two of you—er—getting on well, are you?"

"Yes, sir." He couldn't leave it at that; he knew what his father wanted to hear, even if he was unable to ask a direct question. "We are exceedingly happy."

"Ah." Emerson's hand rested briefly on his shoulder. "Good. Let's see if we can locate that rascal Sayid."

He charged across the lobby, pausing only long enough to toss the key and its massive brass tag onto the desk. "Hurry, before your mother catches us up."

"I meant to interview Sayid earlier," Ramses admitted. "He wasn't here yesterday."

The usual assemblage of putative guides and hopeful dragomen had gathered at the foot of the stairs, which was as close as they were allowed to get. They surged forward when the doors opened, and stopped, with a certain amount of shoving and jostling, when they recognized Emerson and Ramses.

"Nor is he present today," Emerson said, scanning the upturned faces. "Salaam aleikhum, Mahmud—Ali—Abdul Hadi. Where is Sayid?"

An eager chorus replied, not only from the ones he had addressed, but from the entire group. "Not here, Father of Curses—I can serve you as well—what is it the Father of Curses desires?"

"Sayid." Emerson descended the stairs. "When did you last see him?"

It took them awhile to compare notes, but Ramses was conscious of a sinking sensation at the pit of his stomach even before they reached a consensus. Sayid had not been seen for at least three days.

"He has been murdered," I remarked, drawing a somewhat wobbly line—occasioned by the motion of the boat—through one of the items on my list.

For once not even Emerson objected to what

some might consider a premature conclusion. Miss Minton had gone pale. The only face that did not reflect some degree of distress was that of Ramses. The stony mask did not deceive me or Nefret, but it was Emerson who uttered the words I had intended to say.

"You couldn't have got to him in time, Ramses, even if you had not had more pressing matters to deal with. He must have been killed the night of the failed raid."

"But you haven't even looked for him," Miss Minton exclaimed. "He may have gone off with a party of tourists."

Ever courteous, Emerson gave her the explanation the rest of us did not need. "Sayid is always at the Winter Palace. If he had been hired by a visitor, his associates would know of it."

"They would know of his death, surely," Miss Minton persisted.

"His body will probably never be found," Ramses said. "If I had arranged the business, I'd have carried him, dead or alive, to the gebel and tossed him into one of the more remote wadis. By the time he is found, if he ever is, there won't be enough left to identify."

I decided it was time to change the subject. I was sorry about poor Sayid, who had been annoying but harmless, but there was nothing more we could do for or about him.

"Did you find anything in Sethos's room?" I inquired.

Emerson produced the letter and read it aloud. It was a singularly uninformative document, as we all agreed. The reference to Miss Minton was not well received by that lady, but she said only, "What about the book? Are any of the words underlined or any of the sites marked?"

"Feel free to look through it," Ramses said, handing her the volume in question. "I doubt Sethos would do anything so trite, however."

Cyrus's carriage was waiting for us at the dock. When she saw it, Miss Minton hung back.

"I feel awkward imposing on Mr. and Mrs. Vandergelt."

"Would you prefer to return to the hotel?"

My tone was somewhat sharp. Instead of snapping back at me, she lowered her eyes and murmured, "I wish you didn't dislike me so much, Mrs. Emerson. What more can I do to win your acceptance, if not your goodwill?"

"The most sensible course would be for you to leave Luxor at once."

"I can't do that!"

"You can, but I didn't suppose you would. A journalist in pursuit of a story—"

"Do me the credit to believe that is not my primary motive. I want—I want to help."

"No, you want to find our elusive acquaintance. Didn't your latest encounter with him destroy your romantic fantasies?"

A dark flush mantled her cheeks. "You are a merciless opponent, Mrs. Emerson. I do want to know what became of him. Is that so surprising? Whether he liked it or not—and he made it clear that he did not!—we shared a terrifying experience." She hesitated briefly, and then burst out, "I may have been the innocent cause of his betrayal, but I was also his salvation, and by God, before I'm through with him he's going to admit it, and thank me!"

I said no more, since the men had finished putting her luggage into the carriage, and Emerson was calling us to come along, but her outburst, whose genuineness I did not doubt, had made me think better of her. A woman who would accept meekly the rudeness to which he had subjected her was not a woman I could admire. In fact, she had a number of admirable qualities. If only she had not been a confounded journalist!

Nefret and Ramses refused Emerson's suggestion that we leave them off at the *Amelia*. The carriage would have been uncomfortably crowded with five persons, but it was clear to my sympathetic imagination that they preferred to be alone. As they walked away I saw his arm go round her waist and her head come to rest against his shoulder. Miss Minton was watching them too. She sighed.

Instead of standing hospitably open as they usually did when the Vandergelts were in residence, the gates of the compound were closed and the aged gatekeeper had been replaced by a sturdy youth whom I recognized as one of Yusuf and Daoud's kinsmen.

Cyrus and Katherine came out to greet us, and I knew at once from Cyrus's self-conscious look and Katherine's stiff smile that he had confessed some, if not all, the truth. No one else noticed anything amiss, I believe; Katherine was always a lady and her reception of Miss Minton was perfectly cordial. She announced that tea would be served in an hour, sent Miss Minton off with one of the maids, and then turned to me.

I anticipated her. "Yes, Katherine, I owe you an explanation and an apology. Shall we retire to the library? Where is William?"

"In the library," Cyrus said, tugging at his goatee. "At least that's where he was last time I saw him."

"The sitting room, then," I said, and led the way.

"I had to tell her," Cyrus burst out.

"Of course," I replied graciously. "There should be perfect confidence between husband and wife. We only wanted to spare you worry, Katherine."

"I know. Amelia, I would willingly—gladly— risk myself, and even Cyrus, to help you, but—"

"But not Bertie. My dear, I understand and I don't blame you one particle. If I believed there were the slightest possibility he could come to harm I would leave at once. In fact, I had already considered moving our inconvenient ménage to our old quarters."

Emerson's countenance brightened. I had thought the idea would appeal to him; when he is a guest in someone else's home he has to mind his manners. "Excellent thought, Peabody. Yusuf won't mind doubling up."

A flush of shame, as I took it to be, warmed Katherine's cheeks. "No, you mustn't even consider it. You would be much more open to attack there, and I would never forgive myself if anything happened to one of you, especially to the child. I mean it, Amelia, I really do. Cyrus, I am sorry for the horrid things I said to you. I behaved like a shrew and a miserable coward. I won't do it again."

He took her hand. "Quite all right, my dear. Bertie will be fine, you'll see. Matter of fact, Amelia, I was kind of disappointed you didn't bring *him* along too. I've been curious to meet the fellow after that trick he pulled on me some years back. What did you do with him?"

"Nothing," Emerson growled. "He'd gone."

At my suggestion he elaborated, working himself up into a state of considerable indignation as he described the way Sethos had played on Miss Minton's nerves. He ended by reading the note that had been left for him. I was pleased to observe that Katherine appeared more intrigued than fearful; as for Cyrus, he made no secret of his amusement.

"Fellow has a certain style, hasn't he? Kind of a mean stunt he played on the lady—"

"But necessary," Katherine interrupted. "From what you have told me of her, Amelia, she wouldn't have been deterred by a courteous warning."

"Quite right, Katherine."

"Well, I guess maybe he was trying to keep her out of trouble," Cyrus conceded. "Doggone it, it's a shame he got away from you, he must know more than he's telling. Any chance of tracking him down?"

"I can't think how," Emerson admitted. "He must have prepared a number of hiding places when he was in Luxor in the old days. Some, if not all, are known to his adversary; after that near miss the other night he won't be foolish enough to use them again. I am at a loss as to where to look for him."

Naturally I was not. I was on the verge of saying so when Miss Minton entered the room, hoping she was not too early for tea, and Katherine immediately took up her duties as hostess. After tea, when Emerson and I were in our room changing for dinner, he exclaimed, "Damnation! We forgot to ask about that fellow—er—Smith when we were at the Winter Palace."

"You could not have done so if you were unable to remember his real name," I replied.

"Well, whose fault is that? You were the one who kept referring to him as Smith. Did you make inquiries?"

I saw no reason to admit that I had also forgotten that ridiculous appellation. "I could hardly have done so, Emerson, while Miss Minton was with me. We don't want her to know of our interest in the fellow. But I will inquire as soon as I can."

I meant to inquire about someone else as well. The interval had given me time to reconsider my first impulse, and I determined to keep my own counsel until I could confirm my hunch. Emerson had no self-control. Our quarry would have to be approached cautiously, as one stalks a wild animal. I was undoubtedly the proper person to do it.

SIXTEEN

He was waiting for me at the top of the cliff as I climbed, moving with the effortless ease found only in dreams. I took the hand he extended, and he drew me up to stand beside him.

"I came," I said.

"You were slow in coming," said Abdullah.

I sat down on the ground and wrapped my arms around my raised knees. The morning air was as refreshing as cool water against the skin, but it was still a little chilly, and I was not wearing a coat. "I had some difficulty convincing Emerson," I explained. "You know how stubborn he is."

"No, that is not the reason."

Tall and straight, black-bearded and finely dressed as he always was in these visions, he towered over me. He had covered his mouth with his hand to conceal a smile.

"No," I admitted, smiling back at him. "I was on the wrong track, wasn't I?"

"Yes. If you had come before, you would have saved yourself and those you love trouble and danger."

"Not more of your enigmatic hints, Abdullah!" I exclaimed.

"Trouble and danger are your constant companions, Sitt. It would serve no purpose to warn you of what lies in store, even if I were allowed; in avoiding one peril, you would run straight into another."

"Hmph," I said. "What about the tomb, then? You must know where it is."

"Tomb? Which tomb? I know them all—three more in the Biban el Moluk, six in the Queens' Valley, seventeen—"

"Three in the Valley of the Kings?"

"Two of a richness hitherto unknown," Abdullah said meditatively. He sat down beside me. "But they are not what you seek now."

"Never mind that!" I exclaimed. "Two rich tombs in the Valley of the Kings! Where?"

This time he did not bother to hide his smile. "They will be found in the fullness of time, by those who are destined to find them. Do you know why I summoned you to Luxor?"

"Obviously it was not to help me find lost tombs," I muttered. "Why, then?"

"Because this is your place. Look about you." He gestured.

The rim of the sun showed above the eastern cliffs, a crescent of fiery red. The valley lay in shadow, from the dim outlines of the Theban temples across the river to the pale porticoes of Hatshepsut's temples, directly below us. Slowly the crescent widened into a glowing orb, and the light spread, sparkling on the water, brightening the luxuriant greenery of the fields, turning the silvery sand to

ELIZABETH PETERS

pale gold. The world had wakened to life after the sleep of darkness.

"How beautiful is your rising," I murmured. "The living Aten who—"

"The lord Amon-Re," Abdullah corrected somewhat snappishly. "Your Aten was a short-lived god, invented by a heretic."

I had always suspected Abdullah was a pagan at heart. Since I did not care to engage in a discussion about religion with a man who was presumably in a position to know more about it than I, I said mildly, "They were both sun gods. Aspects of the same divine force."

"Bah," said Abdullah. "Amon-Re was the great god of Egypt. Ruler of Heaven, Lord of the Silent."

"Yes," I said dreamily. "Abdullah, you were right to bring me back. I wonder if I could persuade Lord Carnarvon to give up his concession in the—"

Abdullah interrupted me with a shout of laughter. "I should not have spoken of rich tombs," he said, rising and taking my hand to lift me to my feet. "I was boasting, Sitt; but there is no danger that you will break the thread of the future, for the lord will not let you have the Valley. I must go now. Think on what I have told you."

"You haven't told me anything useful," I grumbled.

He turned my face up and kissed me on the brow, as a father might have done. "God go with you, Sitt. May all the gods go with you."

The dream was clear in my mind when I woke in the morning, and I am sure I need not tell the

Reader what part of it was clearest. Emerson was still asleep, flat on his back with his arms folded across his chest, like a mummified pharaoh. I leaned over him.

"Emerson! There are two rich undiscovered tombs in the Valley of the Kings!"

Emerson said, "Hrmph," and rolled over, turning his back to me.

His recalcitrance, which I ought to have expected, gave me time to have second thoughts. Prudence overcame archaeological fever. I returned to a supine position and proceeded to have them.

Emerson would not consider a dream a sufficient guide to excavation. It was impossible to explain to someone who had not experienced them how vivid and real those visions were. I could still feel the pressure of Abdullah's lips on my brow; had I been gifted with artistic talents, I could have reproduced every line and every whisker on his face.

What the devil had been the point of that particular dream? Surely those tantalizing hints of tombs in the Valley had only been meant to tease me. Hints were of no use if I couldn't get the confounded firman. He must have said something else. I was going over that conversation in my mind when Emerson turned and flung out his arm.

As he later admitted he had been dreaming too, of fighting with an opponent whose identity he claimed not to remember; the blow he directed at this phantom landed squarely across my ribs, evoking a cry of indignation and pain which was loud enough to rouse Emerson.

He was still apologizing and looking for bruises when the servant brought our tea. I sent my spouse off to bathe and dress, and consulted my list. In fact, I had already determined on a course of action which did not include describing my dream to Emerson. There was only one other person who might give credence to it, and she was the very individual I had meant to consult about an equally important matter.

She and Ramses arrived at the Castle as we were finishing breakfast, and joined us on the veranda with their little entourage. It was a pretty, shaded spot, curtained with vines, a place conducive to friendly social intercourse. One would never have supposed that the smiling faces hid so many dark secrets! Jumana pounced on Emerson; she had been reading his *History*, and showered him with questions which were not so much designed to obtain information as demonstrate how clever she was. The innocent man, bemused by fluttering lashes and wide dark eyes, nodded and smiled, while Bertie tried to get a word in. My tall son was holding his wife's hand under the table (he thought no one noticed, but of course I did) and chatting with Sennia, who had pulled her chair next to his. It occurred to me that I might have some difficulty getting Nefret to myself. And how were we to elude Miss Minton, whose cool black eyes moved from face to face as if trying to read the thoughts those countenances concealed?

Finally Cyrus pointed out that they had yet to decide where they would go that day. Many of the most promising sites, including the East and West Valleys and the Asasif had already been allocated to other excavators. There were a number of pleasant ruins scattered about, but Cyrus was only interested in tombs. They finally settled on the Valley of the Queens.

Six unknown tombs in the Valley of the Queens . . . Remembering Abdullah's words I was gripped by a brief spasm of archaeological fever. But no, I told myself, duty before pleasure. It wasn't likely that they would find any of the missing tombs that morning. I informed Emerson that I would not accompany him since I had other tasks, including some necessary shopping in Luxor.

My remark fell into one of those silences that sometimes occur (though not often with us, I admit), and a number of heads turned in my direction. I had expected Emerson would be suspicious, but since he could not force me to go with him and since he would rather have been hanged than go to the shops with me, he would have no choice but to acquiesce. Suspicious he unquestionably was. His sapphirine eyes narrowed. Then they opened wide, in an unconvincing display of affability, and he said, "Very well, my dear. Whatever you say."

This was an extremely disconcerting development. Emerson must be up to something. Ah well, I thought, I cannot be in two places at once. I had hoped Nefret would offer to accompany me, but she did not, so I had to ask her point-blank. Needless to say, she agreed.

Ramses was even more suspicious than his father.

As we left the table, he took me by the arm and drew me aside. "Now see here, Mother," he began, his eyebrows forming an alarming angle.

"Ramses," I said, just as firmly. "Do you suppose I would do anything to endanger Nefret?"

"Not intentionally. But you—"

"It is high time you got over treating her—and me!—like children."

His finely cut lips relaxed into a half-smile. "That's what she said. I'm trying, Mother. It isn't easy."

"I know, dear boy. We feel the same about you and your Father."

"About us? But we aren't—"

"Feeble, helpless women?"

Ramses threw up his hands. "All right, Mother, you win. Try not to—oh, confound it, you know what I mean to say. Nefret isn't—er—she isn't the only one I care about."

One of his hands had come to rest on my shoulder. I patted it affectionately. "And your father is not the only one I care about. Look after one another, and don't let him do anything foolish. I know the signs. He is up to something,"

"Unlike you?"

I decided to ignore this.

We finally got them off, including Bertie. Katherine tried to prevent him, but I felt obliged to oppose her wishes. The boy had improved amazingly in the past few days, and in my opinion maternal fussing is deleterious to young persons.

"I never fussed over Ramses," I pointed out to her. "And see how well he has turned out!"

There were several domestic matters to be dealt with before we could leave for Luxor. I had always envied male police officers and detectives their freedom from such distractions; Mr. Sherlock Holmes, for example, never had to concern himself with ordering meals, settling disputes with contentious servants, or coping with small sulky children and large sulky cats. Then there was Christmas, now less than a week away. It had to be celebrated in proper fashion, for all our sakes, but especially for Sennia's. She had been happily occupied with nursing Gargery and Bertie, but with both her patients on the way to recovery she had begun to complain—about being forced to remain inside the stout walls of the Castle, about seeing too little of Ramses. It was hard on the child; but I could hardly tell her why we dared not let her go abroad.

Then there was Fatima, who was baking Christmas cakes and biscuits in Cyrus's kitchen, to the extreme exasperation of Cyrus's chef. And Horus, who had taken to prowling up and down in front of the door where the Vandergelts' cat Sekhmet dwelled in more than Oriental splendor. Sekhmet had belonged to us before Cyrus and Katherine adopted her; she had only been bred once—to Horus himself, in point of fact—and I had my suspicions about Horus's present interest . . .

With my usual tact, I soothed the chef, set Sennia to making paper ornaments for the tree (wondering where the devil I was to find one), instructed Gargery to keep her amused, and asked Nefret to remove Horus long enough so that the terrified servant who was supposed to look after Sekhmet could get into the room. Unfortunately, Sekhmet whizzed through the door as soon as it opened—thus confirming my diagnosis of her condition—and Nefret was rather badly scratched before we managed to capture both animals.

Nefret laughed, though. "Life is never so interesting without you, Mother," she said affectionately, while I painted her scratches with iodine. "When are you going to tell me what scheme you have formed? I don't believe for an instant that you really mean to shop today."

"I will tell you all about it as soon as we are alone, my dear. It is certainly a nuisance to keep track of what various persons know and what must be kept from them! I was forced to give Katherine some idea of my plan, to prevent her from accompanying us, so all that remains is to get away without Miss Minton. Mark my words, she will be lying in wait for us."

In fact, the cursed woman was seated in the carriage when we came out of the house, elegantly attired in a shepherd's check suit and wearing a jaunty little hat tipped over one eye.

"I hope you don't mind my accompanying you," she said, baring her teeth at me. Her black eyes looked like jet beads.

"Out of the question," I said.

I won my point, naturally, but not without an argument. She tried every underhanded trick she could think of, from threats and promises of assistance, to pleading. She was forced to give way at last; when she pushed past me, on her way to the door, I saw there were tears in her eyes.

"She really cares for him," Nefret said, as I joined her in the carriage.

"Those were tears of rage, I expect," I replied. "But I have no sympathy for bathetic sentimentality. She ought to have more pride. So you have discovered my little scheme?"

"It wasn't difficult," Nefret said, with a knowing smile. "You are aching to confront him. Do you know where he is?"

"At one of the other hotels, I expect. One would not expect such a devious man to do anything so obvious, but that is why it is so clever. One is reminded, is one not, of Mr. Poe's 'Purloined Letter' trick."

"I wasn't," Nefret said. "But the same idea had occurred to me. It has only been five days since he fell ill and he knows there is danger of a recurrence if he doesn't take proper care of himself."

"Have you mentioned your idea to Ramses?"

"No, not yet. But I will, Mother, and if we locate Sethos I will tell him that as well. I can't lie to him. So if you would rather leave me off at the *Amelia*—"

"Good gracious, no. I will tell them all about it myself, this evening. I just didn't want them along, shouting and cursing and confusing the issue."

The line between Nefret's brows smoothed out. "What are you going to do with him if you find him?"

"That is one of the matters I wanted to discuss with you. I mean to question him intensively, of course. I feel certain he knows more than he admitted. So far we are at an impasse. Oh, I expect that eventually I can work it out, but my investigations may take a little time and I would like to settle the business before Christmas."

"Christmas, of course," Nefret murmured. The corners of her mouth twitched.

"We may want to bring him back to the Castle with us," I continued.

"Good Lord, Mother, you can't do that to poor Katherine! Hasn't she enough to contend with already?" Her face underwent a series of strange alterations. In some alarm I reached for her. She waved me away, sank back into the corner, and laughed so hard tears filled her eyes. I handed her my handkerchief.

"I do apologize," she gurgled. "I was picturing Christmas at the Castle, with Horus trying to get at Sekhmet, and Bertie trying to get Jumana off in a dark corner, and Katherine trying to keep him away from her, and the chef storming out of the house because Fatima won't let him use the ovens, and—and—and in the middle of it all, Uncle Sethos, disguised as Father Christmas!"

I allowed the dear girl to enjoy her moments of merriment. Far be it from me to mar those moments by reminding her that if we did not succeed in identifying the villain he might be among the guests.

We took the ferry across and as we leaned against the rail, holding firmly to our hats, I told Nefret about my dream, and the one that had preceded it.

"But how unkind!" she exclaimed, her eyes twinkling. "To tell you of rich tombs and not disclose their location—"

"He was teasing me. He enjoys doing that. Never mind the unknown tombs, Nefret, I have been haunted by the feeling that I missed something of importance—one of those confounded mysterious clues Abdullah is so fond of dropping."

"Tell me again what he said."

I repeated the conversation. She shook her head. "I can't think what it might be."

"You don't really believe in my dreams, do you? It is good of you to pretend to take them seriously."

"How could I be arrogant enough to deny the possibility? Even if they are the product of your sleeping mind, they cannot be dismissed as meaningless."

"I do not believe in the libido," I warned her.

Nefret's face dissolved into laughter. "Of course not, Mother, darling. Anyhow, Abdullah would never be vulgar. We're about to dock; where are we going first?"

There were at that time eight European-style hotels on the east bank. Two of them were clean but inexpensive; the other six offered greater amenities along with higher rates.

"Again, I would welcome your advice," I replied. "He might have doubled back to the Winter Palace under another name—"

"Not in the same suit of clothes," Nefret said.

"And not on the same day," I agreed, thinking what a pleasure it was to deal with an intelligent, intuitive (female) mind. "The closest hotel to the Winter Palace is the Luxor . . . Watch your step, my dear, the quay is very slippery."

"So we are going to the Luxor?"

"No. Sethos told the clerk at the Winter Palace he was going to the railroad station. I believe that is exactly what he did. If he had taken a carriage to any other destination, the driver might remember him, and that he would avoid at all costs. It is easy to lose oneself in the crowd waiting for the train, and slip away. The Hotel de la Gare is within easy walking distance of the station."

"That is very ingenious, Mother," Nefret said.

I smiled modestly in acknowledgment of the compliment and waved my parasol at a passing carriage.

We went first to the Winter Palace, where I learned that Mr. Bracedragon-Boisgirdle (whose eminently forgettable name I had, fortunately, noted in my diary) had taken his departure two days earlier. This was most satisfactory news, for it confirmed one of my theories (not that I had ever doubted its accuracy). I then directed the driver to take us to the Hotel de la Gare.

The best Baedeker could say about the station hotel was that it was clean. It certainly did not measure up to my standards; the threadbare carpet in the lobby was gritty with sand and the desk clerk had obviously been wearing the same collar for several days. His jaw dropped when he saw us; it was not the sort of place where ladies of our distinction were likely to come.

"Good morning," I said pleasantly, placing my parasol on the desk. "I am looking for a gentleman who arrived yesterday morning."

The clerk looked from me to the parasol, to Nefret, and back to me. It took him several seconds to get his jaw into operation.

"Yes, Sitt. There were several—"

"Let me see the register, please."

Seven persons had checked into the hotel the previous day. Two were man and wife—or claimed to be—and there had been a party of three gentlemen. That left two possibilities. It was not necessary for me to elicit descriptions from the clerk; one man had given the name of Rudolf Rassendyll.

"His bizarre sense of humor will prove to be his downfall one day," I remarked to Nefret, as we started up the stairs to the third floor. The lift was out of order, of course.

"How many people have read *The Prisoner of Zenda*?"

"Quite a lot, I should think. It was careless of him."

The door was at the end of a dismal corridor lit only by a nearby window. The advantages of the location were manifest; no one could get at him via his windows, of which there were probably two, since his was a corner room, and they provided convenient exits. No doubt he had already knotted one of the bedsheets into a makeshift rope.

"Are you going to pretend to be a servant?" Nefret whispered.

I looked at her in surprise. "No, why should I do that?" I removed one of my gloves and knocked emphatically on the door. "It is I, Amelia. Let me in at once."

Utter silence followed. I knocked again. "I have

no other appointments today," I said in a louder voice. "You may as well open the door."

The portal was flung wide, and there he stood.

I thought I had prepared myself mentally for the meeting. I had been mistaken. The last time I had seen him he had been lying on a litter, dead or dying, as I believed, drenched in blood and wearing an auburn wig and mustache. It might have been Emerson who confronted me now—ruffled black hair, prominent chin, squared shoulders. Even the scowl was familiar. He was wearing a dressing gown I recognized as one of Ramses's, and his feet were bare. I found myself somewhat short of breath.

"Quite right," he said. "You would stand there all day, shouting."

He stood back and beckoned us in. "Is that all?" he inquired. "Where are the rest of them? Radcliffe, Ramses, Miss Minton—"

"Let us not waste time in irony," I said.

"How did you find me?"

"That is also irrelevant." The room did have two windows. It also had a narrow bed, a wardrobe, a small table, a single chair, and a set of chipped bathroom utensils, blatantly displayed, without so much as a curtain to conceal them. "Goodness, how unpleasant," I said. "You can't stay here."

"Not any longer, no."

My knees were a trifle unsteady. I sank into the chair. It wobbled, but held. "Sit down," I ordered, removing a bundle of cloth from my bag. "You don't look at all well."

"For God's sake, don't cry," Sethos exclaimed.

He began to back away. "You never cry. You didn't shed a tear when I died in your arms. You—"

The room was too small for him to retreat far. He fetched up against the edge of the bed and collapsed onto it.

Nefret had closed and bolted the door. Since there was not another chair, she sat down next to Sethos.

"I have no intention of crying," I said, shaking out the bundle.

"What the devil—" Sethos began.

"Don't swear," I said automatically. "It is, as you have no doubt observed, a galabeeyah. I took the liberty of borrowing a long scarf from Katherine. It will serve as a turban. You must leave here this evening. I doubt we were followed—your adversary cannot be everywhere—but he may be clever enough to investigate the other hotels. It was foolish of you to use that pseudonym."

"I—" said Sethos, trying to pull Nefret's hand away from his forehead.

"No fever," she announced.

"How much quinine did you give him?"

"Enough for five days. Half a grain per day."

"Hmmm. I would have recommended more. How many days has it been?"

"I've rather lost track," Nefret admitted. She began counting on her fingers. "Sunday, Monday—"

Sethos said, "Why—"

"Never mind. We will have to risk it. He should be over the worst by now."

Sethos said, "How—"

"Through the window, of course," I said impatiently. "Mr. Rassendyll will renege on his bill. No doubt they are accustomed to that sort of thing at the Hotel de la Gare. Go straight to the landing and take the ferry across. Someone will be waiting for you on the west bank."

"Where—"

"The Castle?" Nefret inquired. Sethos gave her a look of abject horror.

"No, Selim will take him to our old house. Daoud is staying there too. That should be ample protection. I do not see any dirty crockery, so I assume he has not eaten today. It is necessary to keep one's strength up. Nefret, would you be good enough to go down and order food?"

She did not demur by so much as a raised eyebrow; her sympathetic imagination told her that I wished to be alone with him. After she had departed I locked the door and returned to my chair. I had believed my thoughts were in perfect order, but strangely, I found myself mute. We contemplated one another for a few moments. His eyes were the first to fall.

"You shouldn't have come here," he said. "I swore never to see you again, and I meant to keep my promise this time."

" 'There is a fatality that shapes our ends,' " I remarked. "Or is it the War Office that has shaped them? Don't bother to deny that you are still working for British intelligence. You deceived Ramses and Nefret, but you cannot deceive me. It was on your account that Mr.—er—Smith came to Luxor. You were to report to him, and that is one of the reasons why you were so anxious to get to the Winter Palace. He left the day after you arrived. You had been to Kharga. Why would you go there unless it was to spy on the Senussi?"

Much of what I had said was pure surmise—logical, but unproved. He remained silent, head bowed, until I added, "You accepted the assignment Ramses refused."

I had been sure that would stir him up. He stiffened and scowled at me. "If you think I did it on his account, you are mistaken."

"I would never accuse you of being guided by altruism or affection," I assured him.

"He couldn't have carried it off. If he had dropped out of sight, Sidi Ahmed's men would have tried to rip the beard off every stranger who approached the camp."

"Your official job is a side issue now. The interesting attentions we have recently received are directly related to the matter of the missing tomb. What do you know that we do not?"

He had recovered his composure. He rubbed his bristly chin and gave me a cynical smile. "You do go straight to the point, Amelia dear. I am ignorant of the answers to the two most important questions: the location of the tomb, and the identity of my rival."

There was a knock at the door. "Curse it, I didn't suppose she would be so quick," I said. "We must have a council of war. There isn't time for it now. Give me your word—"

The rapping became louder and more peremptory. Sethos leaped to his feet. "That isn't Nefret. Amelia, don't open the door."

He was too slow to stop me. Ramses had taught

me a rather nice little trick of letting an adversary start into the room and then slamming the door hard against his face. I was anxious to try it, and hopeful of capturing one of our foes. Unfortunately, the person in the hall was not a foe. It was Margaret Minton.

"Confound it!" I said.

"Hell and damnation!" said Sethos.

I seized Margaret's sleeve and pulled her into the room. "How did you find us?"

"I hired a boat and then located the driver who brought you here. Didn't you realize you were leaving a trail anyone could follow? And you—" She turned furious eyes on Sethos. "Rudolf Rassendyll!"

"I will not tolerate criticism from you, Miss Minton," I said coldly.

"Forgive me. Accept my abject apologies." She stamped her foot. "I always say the wrong thing, and I'm sorry, I truly am, but it doesn't matter; we've got to get him away from here as soon as possible."

"I was about to make those arrangements when you—"

Another knock at the door. We were all a trifle tense; I started, Miss Minton let out a little scream, and Sethos swore.

"Nefret?" I called.

The answer was in the affirmative. Nefret, the waiter, and the tray crowded into the room. After some complex maneuvering we got the tray on the table, the waiter out, and the door locked.

Perched on the side of the bed, arms folded, Sethos said, "This is becoming positively farcical. Are we expecting any other guests?"

The question was addressed to the company in general, not to Miss Minton. He had not spoken to her or looked directly at her. "Eat your breakfast," I said thoughtfully.

"Lunch," said my brother-in-law, inspecting his plate. The vegetables had been stewed into gray ambiguity and the chunks of meat were burned. "I may as well. I won't be allowed to say anything."

"Please, Amelia." Margaret clasped her hands and looked at me imploringly. "Don't be angry. I only want—"

"What the devil is she doing here?" Nefret demanded.

"He must leave now," Margaret insisted.

I had arrived at the same conclusion. The advantage of darkness, which had affected my first plan, was now outweighed by several disadvantages. Luxor would soon be gossiping about the procession of well-dressed females who had come calling on the amazing Mr. Rassendyll. Anyhow, it had been naive of me to assume Sethos would go where I told him to go and stay where I ordered him to stay. He was eating the horrible mess with more appreciation than it deserved. The placidity of his countenance aroused the direst of suspicions.

"You are correct," I said.

Sethos choked. His countenance was no longer placid.

The enthusiastic cooperation of two other sensible persons (i.e., women) made the arrangements much easier. In fact, I doubt I could have managed them by myself. Nefret was the first to leave. We gave her ten minutes' start and then proceeded to the next stage of the plan. I left Miss Minton to stand guard outside the door while I hurried down and went round the hotel to wait under the window. Sethos had not objected. He appeared to be somewhat stupefied.

The back of the hotel bordered on an empty space occupied only by weeds and mangy dogs. An obscenely fat rat sauntered across the dusty ground, giving me and the dogs an insolent look. I didn't blame the dogs for not wanting to tackle it.

I was beginning to fear Sethos had found some way of getting past Miss Minton when the rope of twisted sheets (it had been under the mattress) tumbled out of the window with a suitcase tied to the end. Sethos came down hand over hand. He was wearing the turban and galabeeyah, but his face was too pale. I scooped up a handful of dirt.

"Amelia, don't," he said, fending me off. "Let me go out of your life. I'm no good to you or anyone else now."

"Dear me, how tragic," I remarked. "You left out the part about returning to your gutter."

"I was saving that," said Sethos. His smile lessened his resemblance to Emerson; it had a quality of mockery that was never to be found on the candid countenance of my spouse. "Very well, Amelia—"

Miss Minton came trotting round the corner of the building, her hat tipped over one eye. "Good, you've got him," she gasped.

"As I was about to say," remarked my brother-in-law, "I can deal with one domineering female, possibly with two, but not with three. Do me one small favor, if you will. Don't dash about looking for our killer. I'll take care of him myself."

"Ah," I said. "I thought so. You mean to make a target of yourself in the hope that he will attack you. That's all well and good, and we may yet have to resort to some such expedient, but what, may I ask, is the point of going through the performance unless we are on hand to catch the fellow? Stop arguing and come along, before someone sees us."

Nefret was waiting at the dock with the boat she had hired, and a pile of parcels. She shoved them into Sethos's arms. The boatman gave him a critical look, wondering no doubt why we employed such a dirty fellow. I had accidentally got some of the dirt into his eyes; but that was all to the good, since they now had the red-rimmed look of the infection from which many unfortunate Egyptians suffer.

"What did you purchase?" I asked, once we were under way. Some of the boatmen understand a bit of English.

"The first large objects I could lay my hands on," Nefret said. "Including a perfectly hideous model of the facade of Abu Simbel."

"We'll give it to Gargery for Christmas," I said.

Our unkempt servant, squatting in the bows, let out a strangled cough.

He made one more attempt to dissuade me as he put our parcels into the carriage. "Aren't you being rather cold-blooded about the risk to Selim and Daoud and the rest of the clan? My enemies will track us eventually."

"But not immediately. It may take them a day or two. By then we will be prepared."

We drove straight to the house. Had I not been preoccupied with more serious matters my heart would have swelled with nostalgia at the sight of our old home, which held so many memories. The climbing roses were dead, of course. Abdullah had never watered them either. But what did that matter? He had been right; this was where I was meant to be.

My spirits received a slight check when I learned that the only men in the house were Yusuf and his youngest son. They were both in the parlor smoking and drinking coffee, and before I could get down to business I had to refuse refreshments and apologize to Yusuf for not coming to call earlier. The house was in perfect order and the parlor looked much as we had left it, even to the ornaments on the whatnot.

"I thought you had gone to the Queens' Valley," I said to Jamil.

"The young Effendi was weary," Jamil replied, staring curiously at Sethos. "We took him back to the Castle."

"Selim and Daoud?"

"Are with the Father of Curses. But we are at your service, Sitt Hakim, my father and I."

And about as much use as Sennia, I thought.

"Is Kadija here?" Nefret asked.

She had been waiting for a summons. Nefret's question was enough; when she appeared in the doorway, black-robed but unveiled, I could have kissed her. Nefret did. Kadija folded her in arms almost as brawny as those of her husband Daoud and then looked inquiringly at me.

"Thank goodness," I exclaimed. "Listen carefully, Kadija. This man—" I indicated Sethos. "This man is my prisoner. He must be kept hidden and secure."

"Ah," said Jamil eagerly. "I will guard him, Sitt Hakim. With my father's gun."

A suitable occupation for a man, I thought. I said firmly, "No gun, Jamil. He is to be well-treated and unharmed."

"May God bless you, Sitt," Sethos whined. "You are merciful. You are kind. You are—"

"I leave him in your charge, Kadija," I went on. "This is the most important thing. No one outside the family must know he is here. The Father of Curses and I will return tonight, to question him." Studying the boy's weak, handsome face, I decided I had better reinforce my warning. "Jamil—Yusuf—no one is to leave the house until I give permission, except, of course, for Daoud and Selim. They will take the horses to the dahabeeyah tomorrow morning. Is that clearly understood? If either of you mentions the presence of our—er—prisoner . . ."

I did not finish the threat. The parasol and the invocation of Emerson should suffice.

Sethos slunk off with Kadija and we returned to the carriage. "The skulking and whining were rather overdone," I said. "I hope he won't be carried away by the role; it is one of his weaknesses."

"The role of prisoner," Margaret murmured. "How did you think of that? It would never have occurred to me."

"I could hardly have described him as an honored guest, or a new servant, now could I? Besides, I wanted him locked up. I don't trust him."

"It was a brilliant idea, Mrs. Emerson," Margaret said sincerely.

I smiled at her. "You may call me Amelia." I consulted my lapel watch. "I hope we are not too late for luncheon. It has been a busy morning!"

FROM MANUSCRIPT H

Ramses found it difficult to concentrate on archaeology when his wife and his mother were off somewhere, bent on mischief. He consoled himself with the thought that they couldn't get in too much trouble on the streets of Luxor. Perhaps his mother meant to perch on a bench somewhere, examining the faces of passersby. She had always claimed she would recognize Sethos anywhere, in any disguise. Perhaps she really intended to shop. Christmas was approaching, and he had never known his mother to be distracted from those festivities by anything as unimportant as a murderer. Perhaps . . .

Bertie had to speak to him twice before he took note of his surroundings. "I beg your pardon?" he said.

"I only wanted to ask a few questions, if you don't mind. I didn't want to interrupt Cyrus and the Professor."

"I doubt you could have," Ramses said. His father and Cyrus were some distance ahead, with Selim and Jamil in close attendance. Somewhat guiltily he turned his attention to his companion. He ought to have been looking after Bertie. But Jumana was riding close on Bertie's other side, and Daoud was behind him, and although Bertie was flushed and perspiring he seemed to be all right.

They had taken the road from Medinet Habu into the cliff-enclosed valley. Few tourists came that way; the Cook's tours allowed only enough time for the major sights: the east bank temples, the Ramesseum and Medinet Habu, the royal tombs, and a few selected tombs of the nobles.

It was likely that Sethos had maintained his role of tourist. He wouldn't risk—

"Is this where Cyrus wants to dig?" Bertie asked.

"What? Oh, sorry. It's one possibility. There've been over seventy tombs found already, but most are unfinished and undecorated—more like caves, really. They date from the Nineteenth and Twentieth Dynasties, and include tombs of royal princes as well as queens."

"Are we going to see any of them?" Bertie passed his sleeve over his forehead.

"It looks that way." His father and Cyrus were talking with an Egyptian who had emerged from a rough shelter. "The most important tombs are closed. The custodian has the keys."

They inspected three of the tombs, finishing with that of Queen Nefertari Merenmut, where Emerson fulminated about the damage to the exquisitely painted reliefs.

"There's a worthwhile project for you," he declared. "You should be spending your money on repairing scenes like these, instead of exposing more antiquities to be looted and damaged."

"I haven't exposed anything yet," Cyrus retorted. "Jumping Jehoshaphat, Emerson, all I want is one tomb—one good tomb. That's not asking much."

The sun was high overhead when they settled down in the mouth of an unfinished tomb and opened the basket of food.

"That's enough for you today, Bertie," Emerson announced.

"I feel perfectly fit, sir," Bertie protested.

"Of course you do." Emerson smiled paternally. "It's a long ride back, though, and you mustn't overdo. Tomorrow is another day."

Daoud wanted to take Bertie home, but Emerson had other ideas. As soon as they had finished eating, he sent Bertie off with Jamil and Jumana.

"That's got rid of them," he announced, taking out his pipe. "Now we can get down to business."

"Will he be all right?" Ramses asked, watching the little cortege wind its way along the valley floor toward the entrance.

"She'll look after him," Emerson said. "Pack up, Selim, and let's be off."

"Where?" Ramses asked.

"Where do you think?"

"Deir el Medina?"

"Very good," Emerson said.

"Is it the man Kuentz you suspect?" Selim asked, jumbling crockery and leftover food into the basket. Apparently Cyrus and Emerson had not been talking archaeology with him.

"I think he's our man, yes," said Emerson.

"The broken stela Sennia found," Ramses said.

"Well done," said his father.

"I don't get it," Cyrus said blankly.

"The bottom part had been knocked off," Ramses explained. "It was a fresh break. The name and titles of the owner were missing. That's why it took me awhile to remember where I had seen others like it. In those cases, the owners were described as workers in the Place of Truth—the Valley of the Kings, that is. The men who cut and decorated the royal tombs lived at Deir el Medina."

Emerson's pipe had gone out. He gave Ramses an encouraging smile and struck a match.

"The stela was planted," Ramses said. "Not only to capture our interest—Father might well have insisted on excavating the entire damned rubbish dump, which would have taken the rest of the season—"

"Your mother wouldn't let me," said Emerson, grinning.

"If I may finish, Father? It also got Sennia interested in the dump site and made it easier for the kidnapper to approach her. But it's not proof of Kuentz's guilt."

"Bah," said Emerson.

"He's the one who sent you to the spot where the rock fell," Cyrus pointed out.

"And the body. I think I've figured out why—"

"So do I," said Emerson. "The poor devil was an innocent bystander who happened to be in the wrong place at the wrong time."

"Yes, sir, I agree. But even if we are right, it doesn't necessarily incriminate Kuentz."

"So let us go and make him confess," said Daoud. "He tried to hurt the Little Bird."

"Well said, Daoud." Emerson knocked out his pipe and rose.

"We don't know that he's guilty," Ramses insisted. "Leave the questions to us, Daoud."

"Of course," said Daoud.

After handing over the keys and tipping the custodian, they rode back between the rugged, sun-bleached cliffs to the road and took the turning that led to the workmen's village.

"A word with you, Ramses." said Emerson. The others obediently fell back.

"Yes, sir?" said Ramses.

"Did I sound patronizing?"

"Yes, sir."

"Habit, my boy. Didn't intend to."

"That's all right, sir." It was more of an apology than he had counted upon, and perhaps more than he deserved. He added, "I shouldn't have been so defensive."

"You are leaning over backward to be fair. Wasn't Kuentz one of Nefret's swains a few years ago?"

"Yes, sir."

"Is he still?"

"Damn it, Father—"

"Jealousy," said Emerson, "takes people differently. I, for example, shout and threaten. It's the best method. Get it out of one's system. Women are—er—they don't think the way we do."

My God, Ramses thought, I'm about to get that kindly lecture fathers are supposed to deliver before their sons marry. He's a little late. More than a little. I don't think I can stand it if he starts telling me how . . .

"I agree, sir," he said quickly.

"You," said his father, carefully not looking at him, "try to be fair and reasonable. I don't recommend that approach. Your mother, for one, doesn't like it at all."

Ramses was at a loss for words. After a moment Emerson went on, "Don't keep your thoughts to yourself. I never do, and neither does your mother, and so we—well, we thrash it out, you see, and that's all to the good."

"I expect you're right, sir. I appreciate your advice."

"Hmph," said Emerson, who was brick-red with embarrassment. "One more bit of advice, then. Don't always give the other fellow the benefit of the doubt. Your instincts are good enough guides."

"What do you suggest? Instead of shaking hands with Kuentz, I should walk up to him and punch him in the face?"

Emerson grinned. "It might not be such a bad idea. Well. That's all I wanted to say."

He loosened the reins and urged his horse into a trot.

Ramses followed more slowly. He had been touched and amused by that exchange; it wasn't easy for Emerson to talk about personal matters, but when he did he went straight to the point and hit the nail square on the head. Now all I have to do is follow his advice, Ramses thought. If I can.

Had he been too inclined to give Kuentz the benefit of the doubt? The evidence was mounting up. Another point against Kuentz which no one had mentioned was the fact that he had not always been at the dig at times when most excavators would be working. Their opponent must be busy these days, trying to find Sethos, keeping track of their activities, guarding his find. If he wasn't there today . . .

He was, though. He had a crew of ten or twelve men at work, and a good twenty square meters had been cleared since Ramses had last seen the site.

He greeted them with his usual exuberance and shook the hands of everyone except Daoud, who folded his arms and fixed Kuentz with an intimidating frown. Emerson explained that Cyrus was looking for a site.

"What about you, Professor?" Kuentz asked.

"Possibly, possibly. We have decided to stay on in Luxor for a while."

Kuentz was full of suggestions. They included almost every site in Luxor. Were the omissions significant? Damned if I know, Ramses thought, watching in growing distaste as Kuentz slapped people on the back and emitted genial roars of laughter and finally turned the conversation from professional advice to general gossip. How was Miss Minton getting on with her story about tomb robbers? He owed her a dinner invitation, though he wouldn't be able to match her generosity; the Winter Palace was too expensive for a poor hard-working archaeologist. The Vandergelts must excuse his failure to call on them, as courtesy demanded; he would come by one day soon, if he might. How was Mrs. Emerson? Had Nefret recovered from her shocking experience the other day?

"I feel responsibility," he explained to Emerson.

"No reason why you should," Emerson said, stroking his chin. "The tomb you mentioned was empty anyhow, I believe."

"Except for broken pieces of Roman mummies. They looked as if someone had danced on them," Kuentz said with another guffaw. "Teeth and bones and scraps of linen." He turned abruptly. "What are you doing?" he shouted at one of the workmen, who was holding up an object that appeared to be a broken pot. "I told you not to remove anything. Damn these people, they have to be watched every second."

"We are keeping you from your work," Emerson said. "Time we were getting back anyhow."

"Time for tea?" Another hearty laugh. "You English must have your tea. I will see you soon again, I hope."

"Sure," said Cyrus "We'll have a little dinner party. You and Barton and Lansing and a few others."

"It will be an honor." Kuentz shook hands all round again and hastened back to his crew. They heard him shouting Arabic curses as they mounted and started off.

"Did he confess?" Daoud asked hopefully.

"No," Emerson said. "But there were a few points of interest, eh, Ramses?"

"Yes, sir."

"Roman mummies. Disgusting objects. All in pieces, too."

"Yes, sir."

"Not the right place. Don't say 'yes, sir' again," he added.

"No, sir."

"Excuse me—" Cyrus began.

"Later, Vandergelt, later. I am anxious to get back. If Amelia isn't there I will be forced to take steps. She was up to no good."

"She went looking for Sethos," Ramses said. His father nodded. "D'you suppose he found him?"

"I wouldn't be at all surprised," Emerson said gloomily.

SEVENTEEN

W hen Emerson burst into the sitting room and found me placidly drinking tea, his expressions of pleasure and relief took a predictable form.

"Well, what the devil have you been doing?"

"Good afternoon to you, too," I replied. "Close the door, Emerson, and make sure there is no one lurking in the corridor."

Cyrus kissed his wife and joined her on the settee. Ramses did not kiss his wife. However, he took the hand she extended and continued to hold it as he stood beside her.

"And how was your day?" I inquired. "Speak up, Emerson, Bertie is resting, but he will be down soon, and so will Sennia, and William may take it into his head to do more reading."

"I beg," said Emerson, slamming the door, "that you will not provoke me, Peabody. You first. I presume you found the—you found him, you are looking particularly smug. Where is he?"

"It was really very clever of her," Margaret said. "The way she deduced where he had gone—"

"I don't give a damn where he was, I want to know where he is now," said Emerson.

"At our house. Locked up and guarded."

"By Jamil and Yusuf? Good Gad, Peabody—"

"And Kadija."

"Oh. That's all right, then. Selim and Daoud will be there by now. What did he tell you?"

"He maintained he does not know the identity of his rival or the location of the tomb."

"He lied," said Emerson, starting for the door.

"For pity's sake, Emerson, sit down! I told Kadija we would come round this evening. It is all arranged. Now tell me what you did this afternoon. Did you find the tomb and capture the villain?"

"We are getting closer to a solution, I think," Ramses said, over Emerson's growls. "Father and I agree that Kuentz is the most likely suspect. There are several circumstances—"

"You needn't explain," I interrupted. "I had come to the same conclusion. He must have had a confederate in Cairo. William Amherst?"

Emerson rolled his eyes, in that way he has, and Ramses said, "Not necessarily. We haven't made out a timetable—unless you have, Mother?"

"I haven't got round to it yet."

"I believe you will find, when you do, that Kuentz could have been in Cairo on the significant dates. He maintains two residences, if they can be called that; it's a useful device, since people would assume that if he's not in one place he is at the other, whereas in reality he could be somewhere else—on the train to Cairo, for instance."

"William has been behaving suspiciously," I said.

"Whether he is involved or not," said Ramses, somewhat impatiently, "Kuentz is the man we must watch."

"You intend to follow him?" Nefret asked.

"It's the only way, Nefret," Emerson said. "With Daoud and Selim we should be able to keep him under surveillance, at least during the hours of the night. He's got to do something soon. The longer he waits, the greater the chance someone will find his prize, and the word has got about that we are engaged in a survey of the Western Valley sites."

"Perhaps he will attack one of us," I said, giving Katherine my cup.

"Don't get your hopes up, Peabody," Emerson said amiably. A cup of the genial beverage had refreshed him, and I knew he was looking forward to trailing Kuentz. Emerson loves disguises, though he is not very good at them.

"An attack on us would be futile," Emerson went on. Katherine, who had been watching Cyrus anxiously, let out a sigh of relief. Emerson gave her a reassuring smile. "He can't wipe out the lot of us. By descending on Luxor en masse, we have left him with only one viable alternative. He's got to clear that tomb before we find it."

"Christmas Eve," I murmured.

Even Emerson, who ought to know me better, stared at me in surprise. Strangely enough, my son was the first to comprehend.

"Of course. He'll expect us to be absorbed with holiday merriment that night—decorating the tree and eating Fatima's plum pudding. Well done, Mother."

I heard voices outside—Sennia's high, birdlike chirps and Bertie's laughing responses.

"There is only one person who is in danger now," I said hurriedly. "We must . . . Ah, Bertie. How are you feeling, dear boy?"

Naturally I did not intend to wait until Christmas Eve to apprehend our suspect, nor did I believe it would be practical to follow Kuentz. He might not be our man after all, in which case the real culprit could go about his business unseen and undetected. A much easier method, one I had always favored, was to make him come to us—or, in this case, to Sethos. His attempts to track Sethos down and murder him strongly suggested that either, (a) Sethos did know where the tomb was located, and el-Hakim (I preferred my nom de guerre to the anonymous X the others used) was aware of this; or (b) Sethos did not know, but el-Hakim believed he did. In either case, Kuentz, or whoever he was, would try to dispose of Sethos before he emptied the tomb.

I explained this to Emerson while we were changing after tea.

"Hmmm," said Emerson. "Aside from the fact that some might consider it callous to stake my— to stake him out like a goat for a tiger—"

"It was his idea."

"So you say. Hurry and dress, we had better get over there."

"He is in no danger as yet," I assured my husband. "The gossip mills in Luxor work quickly but not instantaneously, and no one except the family knows there is a stranger in the house. We will see to it that the word gets out tomorrow afternoon. That will give us time to arrange for protection."

"I don't like this," Emerson muttered, lacing his boots.

"It is an eminently logical, practical plan."

"All your plans are," said Emerson. "Until they fall apart."

I had thought Margaret would insist on accompanying us, but she did not so much as ask. I had some trouble dissuading Cyrus, who was understandably curious about the man who had once taken his place, and even more with Sennia, who declared she was bored and was only prevented from throwing a tantrum by Bertie, who requested another story and a lesson in hieroglyphs. In the end the party consisted of Emerson and me, Ramses and Nefret, just as I had planned.

Emerson set the pace, which was rapid enough to make conversation difficult. At one point, when we were slowed by a heavily loaded camel, I said to Nefret, "Touching, is it not, how concerned Emerson is for his brother? I wonder how they will greet one another."

"So do I," said Nefret.

The men of the family were on the veranda, watching for us. "Everyone here?" Emerson asked, counting heads. "Selim, has Yusuf explained to you and Daoud—"

"I explained," said Jamil, caressing his mustache.

"Where is Jumana?" Nefret asked.

"In her room, reading a book. We do not want women involved in men's business."

"It's a pity he has to be involved," Nefret said angrily, as we hastened down the corridor. "I don't trust him to hold his tongue."

"We will let him loosen it tomorrow," I said. "By that time—Ah, Kadija. How is our—er—guest?"

"I was about to take him food, Sitt Hakim. You will stay and eat with us? There is plenty."

"Yes, thank you. After we have talked with him."

The room—it had once been David's—was lit by the soft glow of oil lamps. There was only one window, and the shutters opening onto the courtyard were closed and barred. Sethos had been lying down (the sheets were wrinkled), but he was on his feet when we entered, shoulders braced and jaw tight. Kadija had cleaned him up, possibly by force; she would not have tolerated such a filthy person in the house. His black head was bare.

Emerson tried to enter first, but I slipped past him. Clenched fists and a dark scowl are not evidences of brotherly concern. I took Sethos by the shoulders and pushed him back onto the bed. He was unable to offer much resistance.

"Lie down," I ordered. "You are having another paroxysm, aren't you?"

Sethos looked at Emerson. "Can't you stop her?"

"No," said Emerson. "Never could. Er—are you—um . . ."

"Having another paroxysm," Sethos admitted. "This one's not so bad."

"When did it start?" Nefret asked. I reminded myself that she was the doctor, and stepped away as she approached. She made a quick examination and asked a few more questions, and then said, "He's better. The first stage lasted less than an hour and the fever isn't as high. I'll stay with him tonight."

"No, you will not," said Sethos, galvanized into speech. "I refuse to go through another session with you and your Hippocratic oath. What the devil is this—a medical consultation, or a council of war, or possibly a social gathering? Do sit down, all of you, and make yourselves comfortable. I'm sure Kadija will serve coffee."

So much for the brotherly greetings, I thought. The atmosphere was marginally more cordial, however. Emerson's fists had unclenched and Ramses was smiling.

"I'll keep Nefret away from you," he offered. "If you tell us what we want to know."

"Yes, let's get down to business," said Emerson gruffly. "No more beating about the bush. We believe Kuentz is the man we're after. We intend to follow him until he leads us to the tomb."

"There's a simpler way," Sethos said. "Pass the word that I'm here. He thinks I know the location of the tomb, that's why he has been so hell-bent on killing me."

"Ha," I exclaimed. "I thought so."

Emerson gave me a forbidding scowl. "Where is the damned tomb, then?"

"I don't know. That," said Sethos, with a fair imitation of his infuriating smile, "is what comes of having a reputation for omniscience. 'The Master knows all.' But I've wondered lately whether he has firmer grounds for his suspicions. He may not be the only one who knows the location. If the original finder was a local man—a man who once worked for me—old loyalties or higher baksheesh might induce him to seek me out."

"No such devoted former follower has approached you, I take it," Emerson said.

"There aren't that many of them left, and the Luxor lads are so bloody confused they run for cover at the very mention of the Master."

"Then Kuentz—if it is Kuentz—has only three men on whom he can rely," Ramses said.

"Yes, well, even if it's true that's not such good news. You encountered one of them. The other two are almost as deadly."

Kadija knocked and entered, to announce that the meal was ready. "Shall I bring his food here?" she asked.

"Later," I said. "He's not feeling well enough now. We will be with you shortly, Kadija. Let us finish making our plans. Tomorrow we will allow the word to get out that there is a mysterious prisoner in the house. *He* will attack tomorrow night, or at the latest, the night following. We will be ready for him."

"Them," Sethos corrected. "If he's determined to make an end of me he won't come alone. And who the hell do you mean by 'we'?"

"The four of us and Daoud and Selim," I said. "That should be sufficient."

"Not Margaret and the Vandergelts?" Sethos demanded. His face was slick with perspiration. "For the love of God, Radcliffe, you can't let her—"

"Er—yes," said Emerson. "Leave it to me."

"The fever is breaking," I announced, wiping Sethos's brow with my kerchief. "That's good. Rest now, you will be perfectly safe tonight. It might be a good idea, though—just as a precaution—if you were armed. Take my pistol."

"I don't want your damned pistol," Sethos said violently. "Shoot someone yourself. Radcliffe—"

"Yes, yes," said Emerson. "Er—it will be all right." He came toward the bed, his feet dragging, and stood looking down at his brother. "Well. Uh—good night."

"You might at least say you are glad to see one another," I said with a sniff.

"I'm not glad to see him," Sethos declared. "I meant never to see him again."

Emerson's tight lips relaxed. "That is probably the kindest thing you've ever said to me." He took Sethos's hand and shook it. "À demain," he said, in his execrable French accent.

"Dieu aidant," said Sethos. His accent was perfect.

"Men!" I said.

FROM MANUSCRIPT H

With a flourish, Nasir placed a plate of boiled eggs in front of Nefret. The plate was flat and the eggs rolled wildly from side to side. One of them must have fallen off while he was carrying it up the stairs. It was cracked and leaking.

"Thank you, Nasir," Nefret said. "Do you remember what I told you about egg cups?"

Nasir scuttled off and Ramses said, "He forgot them on purpose. I refuse to eat the cracked one."

"No one expects you to, darling." She gave him a bright smile. "It's a lovely day."

They had had another argument the night before. Ramses had lost. The aftermath had been even better than usual, but he was still uneasy.

"So far," he said. "I hate these complicated schemes of Mother's. Something's bound to go wrong."

"No, it's not. And if it does you can't blame her; we all agreed. Can you think of anything we overlooked?"

"Well . . ." Sensing his mood, Nasir timidly proffered an egg cup, rather in the manner of a supplicant offering to a notoriously temperamental god. Ramses took it and grunted a thank-you.

"Mother and I," Nefret said patiently, "will stand guard with Daoud while you and Father and Selim climb all over the damned cliffs looking for Alain's tomb of Roman mummies. I think Father's theory about that is somewhat far-fetched, but never mind. In the meantime, Kadija will make sure no one leaves the house until after midday. At which time Jamil will head straight for the nearest coffee shop and Yusuf will tell everyone in Gurneh, in strictest confidence. Jumana thinks she is helping Kadija and Jamil thinks he is mounting guard over a dangerous prisoner. What could go wrong there?"

"If I knew, it wouldn't go wrong." He stood up and looked over the rail. "Selim and Daoud have left the horses and gone on."

"Father wanted to get an early start. But we needn't rush; we're to meet them at Deir el Bahri, and you know Father, he'll be perfectly happy inspecting the Metropolitan's excavations and criticizing Mr. Lansing."

"You're determined to cheer me up," Ramses grumbled. "You could, very easily, if you would agree to stay at the Castle tonight. Mubashir is a killer, Nefret. Even Sethos has avoided him."

"I thought we'd settled that." She went to him and he turned, his back against the rail, and put his hands on her waist, enclosing the delicate bones and soft curves in the cage of his fingers.

"I love you," he said.

"That's no excuse." She laughed and stood on tiptoe, face lifted. He was about to make the obvious response when the muscles under his hands went rigid, and her eyes widened. "Good Lord. Is that "

The person approaching the boat looked like an old woman, stooped and stumbling. By the time Ramses realized who it was Nefret was racing down the stairs. When he caught her up she had reached Jumana. The girl had fallen, but she was still conscious. She raised a face smeared with dried tears. Dust coated her long lashes.

"It was Jamil. He—"

The sense of vague apprehension that had bothered Ramses all morning coalesced into a tight knot. Nefret had removed Jumana's head cloth. The hair on her temple was clotted and stiff with blood.

"You must listen," Jumana gasped.

"Later. You can pick her up, Ramses, nothing seems to be broken."

The little body was as light as a child's and trembling with pain and fear, but she kept trying to talk as he carried her to the saloon.

"He locked me in my room. I was not asleep. I heard the key turn. But I had another key, he had done it to me before, and when I opened the door I saw him going to the stables, and I thought, He has disobeyed the Sitt Hakim, he is going to the dahabeeyah without me and—ah!"

"I'm sorry," Ramses said. He lowered her gently onto the divan. "Is her leg broken?"

"Just a sprained ankle, I think," Nefret said. "Get me some water. And a napkin."

"You must listen! I followed, I was angry. But he did not come here, he went to Naga el-Tod, to the hotel—"

"Kuentz," Ramses said, handing Nefret the dampened napkin.

"Yes, it was he. I saw them talk together and I knew I must tell you . . . What has he done? Has he done wrong?" Fresh tears slid over her dirty little face.

"Did Jamil hit you?" Ramses asked. I'll strangle the young swine, he thought.

"No. I ran away, and I was afraid they had seen me, so I ran very fast, and I fell and hit my head and I fainted and . . ."

"Get me my medical bag," Nefret said.

"No time." Ramses lifted the girl and went down the gangplank at a run, with Nefret following.

"Take the stallion," he said. "He'll carry two. You can hold her, can't you?"

"Yes. But you—"

"If Jamil told Kuentz about their 'guest,' he may decide to act now, when there's no one at the house but women and children and poor old Yusuf."

Nefret had scrambled into the saddle. Ramses handed Jumana up to her and began shortening the stirrups. "Go straight to the Castle. Don't let anyone or anything stop you. If they did catch a glimpse of her they may come here."

"I understand." She gathered Jumana into a firm grip and smiled down at him. She did understand—not only what she must do and why, but how much it cost him to let her go off alone, encumbered with a half-conscious child. Events had conspired to force him into a decision he had not had the courage to make before. She was braver than he; she had not tried to dissuade him or told him to take care. All she said was, "I'll join you at the house as soon as I can."

"Yes," Ramses said, and saw her blue eyes flash with pride. "Send Mother and Father too, if you can find them. I may need all the help I can get."

Ramses mounted the mare without bothering to adjust the stirrups and urged her into a trot. It was impossible to go faster, there were too many people, donkeys, camels, carts, carriages on the road. He hoped and prayed he was worrying unnecessarily, but Jamil had deliberately disobeyed orders and gone straight to their chief suspect. They had never suspected Jamil; the members of that family were above suspicion, almost by definition, but the clues were there. Hadn't Jumana boasted of her brother's knowledge of the west bank mountains? Looking for tombs was a popular amusement. If Jamil had found the tomb and Kuentz had caught him in the act and had proposed an alliance . . .

Once he left the main road he made better time. How long had Jumana been unconscious before she woke and dragged herself, with a sprained ankle and a possible concussion, to warn them? She'd get her chance, all right—and anything else she wanted, including Bertie.

Yusuf's two youngest children were playing on the veranda. Ramses let out a long breath of relief. Nothing had happened. Yet. He left the mare standing and took the children into the sitting room where Yusuf was enthroned on the settee. Leaving Yusuf in the middle of one of his long-winded greetings, he ran along the corridor. Better safe than sorry, his mother would say. The older children and the women were in the courtyard, busy with domestic chores. He cut their greetings short too.

"There may be trouble," he said, addressing Kadija. "Get everyone into the sitting room and keep them there."

She didn't waste time asking questions, not Kadija. Herding Yusuf's assorted wives and descendants ahead of her, like a flock of bewildered sheep, she disappeared into the house.

They came over the wall, agile as weasels—three of them. Only one of the faces was familiar, and it wasn't that of Kuentz or Mubashir. Ramses had seen the man somewhere, on the street in Luxor, or outside the hotel.

The sight of him stopped them for a moment. They had expected only women and children.

Then he realized that Kadija was behind him, silent and solid as a rock, holding a granite statue of a centaur by the neck, like a club. She had snatched up the first heavy object that came to hand.

"Go in," he said urgently. "Stay with the children. Lock yourselves in."

He pushed her into the house, slammed the door, and put his back against it. After a whispered conference, the three men drew apart, one on either side of the courtyard, the other in the center. Rudimentary tactics, but effective, considering the odds. One was as dark-skinned as a Nubian, the other two had the sharp features and long limbs of the Western Desert peoples. Their robes had been pulled up and tucked into their belts, and the blades of the knives they held were a good eight inches long. He drew his own knife.

The shutters of the room on his right opened and his uncle climbed out the window. He had discarded his galabeeyah and was wearing only a pair of loose drawers—probably Yusuf's, since they were bunched up around his narrow waist.

"Get back inside," Ramses ordered.

"Can't let them in the house, can we? I don't suppose you had sense enough to accept that gun."

"You gave it to Nefret, not me. Where did you get the knife?"

"Kadija. Here they come. You weren't planning to fight fair, I hope."

"No. We'll take the one on the right."

That would put him between Sethos and the other two. He wasn't counting on much help from his uncle, whose lean body showed the debilitating effects of his illness, but he felt his spirits lift. Fighting side by side with a man of his own blood, as his mother might put it . . . On the whole, a stranger with a pair of revolvers would have been preferable.

"Now," he said.

Faced with two opponents heading for him at a dead run, their quarry hesitated for a brief but vital second. Sethos slashed at his face, Ramses struck his arm up and plunged his own knife into the man's belly. Spurting blood weakened his grasp on the hilt and when the man fell, his weight pulled the knife out of Ramses's hand.

He felt the tip of a blade slice across his back as he bent over, trying to free his knife. It was stuck, caught on a rib, and the hilt was slippery with blood. He snatched up the knife the dead man had dropped, rolled to his feet and kicked out, deflecting the blade that was aimed at Sethos's back. Sethos was on his knees, streaming blood from hands and face. Ramses parried a slash at his knife hand and chopped at an arm with the flat of his other hand.

The explosion sounded like a charge of dynamite, freezing all four of them for an instant. Christ Almighty, Ramses thought, it must have been that antique Martini of Yusuf's. I hope it didn't blow up in his hands. He stood over his uncle, trying to watch both men at once. They had got over their momentary paralysis and were coming at him again, from different directions. Ramses's ears were still ringing, but he thought he heard . . .

The back gate gave way with a crash almost as loud as that of the gun. Hands on his hips, black hair wildly windblown, Emerson took in the scene in a single glance. His lips curled back, baring his teeth.

It was over in less than ten seconds. One of the two men was sprawled on the ground, with his neck bent at an impossible angle. Emerson had hit him in the throat. The other writhed in Ramses's grasp, his arm twisted painfully behind his back.

"Thank you, Father," Ramses said. "Again."

"Just saving you a little time," said Emerson with what his son could only regard as a wildly optimistic assessment of the situation. He wasn't even breathing hard. "Er—all right, are you?"

It was his usual question, but Ramses knew it was not directed at him. Sethos, now sitting up, raised his head. "Just a few scratches. Nothing serious. Flesh wounds."

"You aren't very good with a knife," Ramses said. He didn't want thanks, and he was pretty sure he was not going to get any.

His uncle's blood-streaked face broadened in a grin. "I've always preferred to hire other people to do the fighting."

"Except on certain occasions," said Emerson. "I still have a scar . . . Well, well. Shall we tie that fellow up, or kill him?"

"We might want to ask him a few questions before we kill him," Ramses remarked dryly.

"Only one of my little jokes," Emerson said with a chuckle.

He lifted the prisoner with one hand and held him on tiptoe. "Where is your Master?"

Answers to his questions were quickly forthcoming but not as informative as they had hoped. "The Master" had had other urgent business that morning; no, he had not explained what it was, he had sent the trio to rid him of Sethos and was to have met them later to settle their accounts before he left Luxor. Now, the prisoner admitted with refreshing candor, he would as soon not keep that appointment. The Master did not accept excuses or tolerate failure.

"He may be telling the truth," Emerson mused. "These lads are killers and criminals. Kuentz wouldn't tell them anything more than they needed to know. Damnation! He's probably looting the tomb at this very instant! We'll tie this fellow up and toss him into a shed. Kadija!"

It had been Kadija who fired the gun. The recoil would have broken the shoulder of a normal person; Kadija admitted that hers felt a little sore. The others arrived before long, and while his mother was sorting things out in her usual brisk manner, Ramses asked, "Didn't Nefret come with you?"

His mother was slapping bandages on Sethos. He'd been lucky, or very, very agile; none of the cuts were deep. "She felt obliged to stay with Jumana. The poor little thing had lost consciousness and Nefret is afraid of concussion. But do you run along, my dear; she will be worrying about you. We can take care of Mr. Kuentz and the tomb."

Ramses knew she would be worrying and he was anxious to reassure her, but his mother's bland self-confidence was somewhat alarming. It was possible—probable, in fact—that Kuentz was already at work, frantically trying to clear the tomb, hoping his other men could keep them occupied.

"Kuentz won't be alone," he warned.

"The more the merrier," said his father, flexing his hands.

"He may be armed."

"So are we," said his mother. The implements hanging from her belt jangled as she stood up.

He couldn't leave Nefret wondering and fretting. He'd done it too often. "Wait half an hour," he said urgently. "I'll meet you at Deir el Bahri."

"No, no, my boy," Emerson said. "He'll be in a hurry. He may damage some of the artifacts." His eyes were shining. If there was anything he enjoyed more than a fight, it was a new find. He fully expected to get both.

"I'll come as soon as I can," Ramses said. His mother's peremptory voice followed him as he hurried along the corridor. "Ramses, come back here this instant. You need—"

The mare was where he had left her, browsing on the petunias in the flower boxes. He hadn't gone far when he heard hoofbeats behind him and glanced over his shoulder. He reined the mare in and waited for the other man to come up to him.

"Why didn't you go with them? With luck you could have rescued Mother again."

Sethos shook his head. "She'd have ended up rescuing me. In either case, Radcliffe wouldn't like it. I stole his horse. That should slow them down a bit."

Ramses knew that if he asked any of the questions that bubbled in his brain they'd end up in one of those interminable discussions. It was a family failing. Without replying, he set the mare to a gallop. Sethos wasn't much good with a knife, but he rode well, guiding the big gelding with expert hands. God help Margaret, Ramses thought. When she sees him romantically bloody and bandaged . . . Is that what he wants? What does he want? Why didn't he stay at the house?

The gates of the Castle were open when they arrived, and Cyrus was in the courtyard, about to mount his placid mare. "Well, thank goodness," he exclaimed. "Everybody all right? Is this—"

"Mr. Cyrus Vandergelt, allow me to introduce Sethos," Ramses said. "Alias quite a number of other people."

"Including me," said Cyrus, his leathery cheeks wrinkling in a smile. "Come on in. You look as if you could use a drink."

"I can't stay," Ramses said. "I only stopped long enough to tell Nefret . . . Where is she?"

"She left—can't have been more than half an hour ago, maybe less. The little girl is going to be fine, so Nefret and Miss Minton went charging out of here, heading for the house. They wouldn't wait for me." His smile faded. "You didn't run into them?"

"No." Ramses turned on his uncle. "You expected this!"

"I was afraid of it. Your wife's impulsive habits are well known, and if Kuentz could get hold of a hostage he'd have us right where he wants us. He's obviously got more manpower than we thought. One of them must have been watching the dahabeeyah—"

Ramses snatched the mare's reins from the groom and swung himself into the saddle. Tight-lipped and no longer loquacious, his uncle mounted the gelding.

"Wait for me," Cyrus shouted.

"No, you can't help with this. If you want action, go after Mother and Father. Somewhere along the cliff south of Deir el Bahri. Take a weapon."

As he turned the mare toward the gate he saw Cyrus run back into the house.

"Are we going to ride furiously off into the sunset, or have you any bright ideas about where to look for them?" Sethos inquired.

"Goddamn you," Ramses said.

"I expect He already has. Half an hour or less . . . they must have been intercepted before they left the Valley. Plenty of cover near the entrance. There may be signs of a struggle."

What there was was a dead horse and the motionless body of Margaret Minton and a puddle of blood that shone wetly in the sunlight.

The place was only ten feet from the road, a miniature wadi walled in by boulders. There was no sign of Nefret or her horse. Sethos was out of his saddle before Ramses could move. Kneeling beside the body, he said, "Margaret," in a whisper with almost no breath behind it. He didn't touch her.

There was no room in Ramses's mind for sympathy. He went to them and pushed his uncle roughly out of the way.

"She's not dead. Get the canteen off my saddle."

She stirred when he bathed her bruised face and then she tried to sit up.

"Easy," Ramses said, bracing her shoulders. Her eyes opened. They passed uninterestedly over him and Sethos, and focused in a concentrated glare.

"Nefret. He took her. I tried . . . He killed my horse."

"Who?"

She rubbed her eyes. "The boy—Jamil. He called her, begging for help, and she went to him—you know Nefret—there was another man, hiding behind the rocks—ugly scarred face . . ."

He cut her short. How the business had been managed was unimportant now. "Any idea where they might have taken her?"

"No. I'm sorry, Ramses, I tried—"

"It's all right." He couldn't reproach her, she had done her best. Fortunately there was another scapegoat close at hand. Sethos was still on his knees, motionless as a statue. "A hell of a lot of help you are," Ramses said. "Get her back to the Castle."

Sethos edged closer. "What are you going to do?"

"I can only think of one place. If she's not there . . ." He pushed Margaret at Sethos. He had to catch hold of her or let her fall, but it would have been hard to say who was supporting whom. Shock and loss of blood had drained the color from Sethos's unshaven face. Margaret glared at him.

"Go with Ramses. He needs—"

"No, he doesn't," Sethos said. He looked up at Ramses. The gray-green eyes were sunken but clear. "I'd only be in his way. Kuentz didn't blow up the German House. I did. You can guess why. Good luck."

The War Office had nothing on Sethos when it came to dribbling out information only as it was needed. That bit of news strengthened Ramses's hopes. Kuentz had been using the German House as his base for antiquities dealing, and perhaps for other purposes. He couldn't have many hideaways left.

Anyhow, secrecy was no longer an issue. With Nefret in his hands he could clear the tomb in broad daylight while they looked on, helpless to interfere.

How had they got her away? She'd have fought them tooth and nail. Maybe the blood wasn't hers. Dead, she would be of no use to Kuentz. Mubashir wouldn't dare kill her. He could do other things, though. Remembering the distorted face he had glimpsed in the moonlight, Ramses felt his throat contract. He couldn't swallow, his mouth was too dry.

At least he knew he was on the right track. Forcing himself to stop long enough to question a woman working in the fields, he heard of a rider carrying something before him on the saddle. He had been heading for the river.

The run-down hotel appeared to be uninhabited. A few scrawny chickens scattered, flapping their wings and squawking, as he rode into the courtyard. The place had a disheveled sort of charm—picturesque, as Baedeker might say—with vines sprawling over the baked mud walls and partially veiling the famous bathtub. Apparently the chickens were the only creatures that hadn't had sense enough to run from a man with a knife and a prisoner. Ramses dismounted and forced himself to stand still while he got his breathing back to normal and considered his next move. He was unfamiliar with the layout of the hotel. The back of his hand was still bleeding. He wiped it on his shirt and eased his knife out of the sheath. He'd got most of the blood off, but he couldn't risk it sticking. Half a second might make all the difference.

The vines along the wall rustled. Ramses spun round and saw a face, wide-eyed with terror, peering out from among the leaves. It was the proprietor, Hussein Ali. Ramses dragged him out by the collar and broke into his protestations of ignorance and innocence.

"Where are they? Which room?"

"He threatened me with his long knife. How was I to know he had offended the great and powerful—"

"*Which room?*"

It was at the back—the best room in the hotel, Hussein Ali explained. A suite, in fact! Two adjoining rooms, one for sleeping, the other—

Obviously not for bathing. Ramses left him salaaming and explaining, and went to the door. It had once been quite beautiful, painted with bright designs like so many of the doors of Gurneh houses, before time and neglect had taken their toll. It stood ajar. There was no point in reconnoitering, he knew what places like this were like; the windows at the back would be high and narrow, to keep thieves out.

The Syrian must know he was here. He hadn't bothered to lower his voice, and Hussein Ali had yelled even louder.

He kicked the door back against the wall. No one there. The doors lining the narrow hallway were closed, except for one at the far end. The need to see her, to know she was alive, was so strong it pulled him like a cable, straight down the hall to the open door.

Sunlight streamed in through the windows high under the eaves. It shone on her hair. She was lying on the filthy divan, her feet and hands bound. Her eyes were open, blue as cornflowers and limpid with relief. She had been afraid for *him*.

Mubashir sat beside her. "Welcome, Brother of Demons," he said. "Come in and drop your knife." His own blade rested on her cheek.

I cannot imagine how I could have been so careless as to let both of them get away from me. I had not seen the blood on the back of Ramses's shirt till he turned, but he pretended not to hear my call. When we found Sethos had slipped away too, and that he had taken Emerson's gelding, my indignation could not be restrained.

"The foolish man is in no condition to ride," I exclaimed. "And if he were, he ought to have come with us and offered what assistance he can. After all we did for him—"

"Get me a horse," said Emerson, as single-minded as Richard III.

"Perhaps we don't require further assistance," I conceded, as Selim ran toward the stable. "Selim and Daoud and you and I should suffice. Supposing we find him, that is. We have disposed of three of his followers; he can't have many left."

"The devil with the horses," said Emerson, who obviously had not heard a word I said. "We may as well go on foot."

"Go where?" I demanded. "You don't know the precise location."

Emerson fingered the cleft in his chin. "It has to be somewhere between Deir el Bahri and Deir el Medina—probably less than a hundred yards beyond the place where the accident occurred. Kuentz was afraid they might notice something if they went any farther. It's less than half a mile as the crow flies."

"We are not crows, and it's all up- and downhill! For pity's sake, Emerson, use your head. Ramses said he would meet us at Deir el Bahri. If we start there and follow the cliff south—"

"Then where is my damned horse?" Emerson demanded. "Selim!"

"Here, Father of Curses."

Emerson's jaw dropped and Selim, anticipating his protest, explained, defensively, "There are no others." He was leading Yusuf's fat mare.

"I can't ride that!"

"If she can carry Yusuf she can bear your weight," I remarked. It was all to the good, really. Gripped by intense archaeological fever, Emerson would have outstripped the rest of us had he been properly mounted. Before he could propose a change of horses, I ordered Selim and Daoud to follow me.

It took Emerson awhile to catch us up, though I expect the mare, encouraged by Emerson's pleas and curses, had not moved so quickly in years. We went on at as rapid a pace as the placid beast could manage. Even in the extremity of passion Emerson would never mistreat an animal, but he was livid with annoyance when we reached Deir el Bahri, and he started up the path toward the cliff without waiting for the rest of us.

Ramses was not there. It had not been very long since he left, I told myself. Nevertheless I felt a faint quiver of uneasiness. Our best-laid plans had already gone agley (to quote Mr. Burns). Had some other unforeseen catastrophe occurred?

Vague forebodings should not be a guide to action, I reminded myself. Ramses would come when he was able, and he was aware of the path we meant to follow. My first duty was to my impetuous spouse. We left the horses with one of the gaffirs and hastened after him.

I had to stop occasionally to catch my breath, for it was all uphill and over rocky terrain. The hour was still early but the shadows were shortening and the morning chill had left the air. I had braced myself for a long exhausting walk—or climb, rather—with no promise of success at the end of it, but soon after we had passed the spot where the body had fallen, I heard voices and the sounds of activity ahead.

"Hurry!" I cried, for one of the voices had been Emerson's, raised in a vehement curse. Scrambling over loose scree, we made our way around a rocky spur and stopped, thunderstruck at what we beheld.

It was no wonder Kuentz had been reluctant to

open the tomb. The place was within a few hundred yards of the busy bay of Deir el Bahri and only a short distance from one of the paths that crossed this part of the gebel. It lay in a shallow declivity; from where Kuentz stood, his rifle aimed at Emerson, he was protected on three sides. Behind him, half a dozen men were at work, furiously digging away a heap of stony debris. We had indeed underestimated his manpower. We had also been wrong about the location of the tomb. It was not high in the cliff, but at its base, like the royal cache.

I was too short of breath to speak, so Emerson got in first. "Go back, Peabody."

"I'm afraid I cannot allow that," Kuentz said jovially. "Come ahead, Mrs. Emerson, and stand by your husband. Daoud and Selim too."

Daoud looked hopefully at me. I took hold of his arm. "We must do as he says, Daoud. He would kill Emerson first."

"Ah." Daoud nodded sagely. "It is true. You will make a plan, Sitt, and tell us what to do."

I sincerely hoped I could. At the moment nothing occurred to me.

"You may as well make yourselves comfortable," Kuentz remarked as we joined Emerson. "This will take awhile. Sit down."

Seated, we presented less of a threat. I was afraid I would have to lecture Emerson about the advisability of obeying the orders of a man with a rifle, but he had got over his annoyance and was watching Kuentz with cold calculation.

Shakespeare notwithstanding, a lean and hungry-looking villain is no more dangerous than one who laughs too much. Kuentz's broad smile and easy stance aroused the direst of forebodings. The brown hair that covered his hands and forearms, and showed at the neckline of his shirt, gave him the look of a loup-garou halfway through the transformation.

"You cannot hope to succeed in this endeavor, Mr. Kuentz," I said. "Reinforcements are on the way. Your rival lives, and the three men you sent to murder him are dead or prisoners."

He was not as cool as he pretended. His smile lengthened into a snarl and the barrel of the rifle shifted toward me. Then he shrugged. "You are probably lying. Even if you are not, it is of no consequence. Your reinforcements, if they exist, wouldn't dare attack while I hold you at gunpoint."

"No doubt, but how long can you do that?" I asked. "Clearing an entire tomb will take—"

"Tomb?" Kuentz let out a guffaw. "You are in for a surprise, my friends."

"Not a tomb? What is it, then?" I asked. Emerson gave me a sour look. He was also burning with curiosity, but he was too proud to ask questions.

"Speculate." Kuentz chuckled. "It will help to pass the time."

"Be quiet, Peabody," Emerson growled. "Don't give him the satisfaction."

So we sat in silence. The temperature rose as the sun did the same, and the surface under me was hard as stone and lumpy with pebbles. The ambience was not conducive to ratiocination, but I do not allow physical discomfort to distract me. I had been correct in believing that the body (the most recent body, I should say) was that of an innocent bystander, whom Kuentz had cold-bloodedly murdered when the poor fellow came upon him while he was levering out a section of rock. Emerson's original theory had been incorrect (though I doubted he would ever admit it). He had suspected the great find lay concealed behind the nasty bits of mummy. Nonsense, of course; Kuentz must have known that a minor inconvenience of that sort would not prevent us from investigating. That there was such a tomb of Roman mummies seemed probable. Kuentz would not have admitted its existence had that fact not been generally known.

Putting aside these now irrelevant facts, and my raging curiosity about Kuentz's discovery, I considered various options. There were not many. Ramses and Nefret would walk into the same trap, since we could not warn them. Kuentz could not let us go. Most probably he would force us to enter the hole in the ground once he had emptied it of its contents (what the devil could they be?) and shovel the debris back into place, sealing the entrance.

I was about to ask our jolly adversary whether I might drink from my canteen when I heard the rattle of rock. Someone was coming. Surely not Ramses, he never moved so clumsily. Unless his injuries had been more severe than I believed them to be . . .

Emerson let out a muffled swearword when Cyrus came into view, puffing and sweating and—I beheld with considerable alarm—with a rifle slung over his shoulder.

"Don't shoot, Cyrus," I shrieked. "He has the drop on us!"

I had never admired my old friend more. A single glance informed him of the futility of resistance, and the danger of failing to respond instantly to my order. He let the gun slip to the ground, and raised his hands.

Kuentz let out another of those infuriating guffaws. "So this is your reinforcement? You are a sensible man, Mr. Vandergelt. Go and sit by the others. We are getting to be quite a nice little party."

Cyrus dropped heavily to the ground and passed his sleeve across his wet face. "Guess I better not risk reaching for a handkerchief," he remarked coolly. "What's going on?"

"He says it isn't a tomb, Cyrus."

"Well, right now I couldn't care less." But his eyes moved past Kuentz to the back of the little bay. We could see the opening now, black against the pallor of the rock. How deep was the shaft, and how much longer would it take to empty it?

One of the diggers called out. I could not make out the words, but Kuentz's response made the question clear. "Coming. Wait."

He was not laughing now. His eyes moved over us, one by one. We are within seconds of death, I thought.

As it turned out, I was wrong. Seeing my hand move toward my pocket, Kuentz said, "Don't be foolish, Mrs. Emerson. There is an alternative to violence on either side. I have a card up my sleeve, you see. Nefret."

Emerson went rigid. "What do you mean?"

"Mubashir is holding her prisoner. You've heard of him, I expect. A very unpleasant man. If anyone except myself approaches, he will kill her. I would hate to have that happen."

"You are bluffing," I said.

"My little scheme may not have succeeded," Kuentz admitted. "But if it did, the charming lady is now with one of the most accomplished killers in Egypt. Are you willing to take the chance? Discuss it among yourselves," he added, grinning like an ape. "But don't move."

He backed slowly away. The little bay was not deep; he could keep us in his sights even when he was at its far end.

"Let me kill him, Sitt," Daoud begged.

"He would kill you first," I said, watching Kuentz. "Wait. Cyrus, where is Ramses?"

"I don't know." Cyrus's face was grim. "He's not bluffing, Amelia. I was on my way here when I met Margaret and your old pal Sethos coming back to the Castle. That young devil Jamil helped ambush the ladies; the other fellow knocked Margaret unconscious and carried Nefret off. Ramses has gone after them."

"Alone?" I gasped.

"Sethos wasn't in any condition to help him," Cyrus said heavily. "He fell out of the saddle as soon as we got to the Castle. Anyhow, if she's where Ramses thinks she is, he'll have to sneak into the place and pull some cute stunt to get to her without being spotted. If she's not there . . . Well, folks, there's only one alternative that I can see."

"Quite," I agreed. "We must capture Kuentz alive—alive, Daoud, did you hear—and force him to tell us where she is. How shall we go about it? I have my knife and my pistol, and Daoud and Selim are armed, and there is Cyrus's rifle, and—"

Emerson had not spoken. His broad forehead was furrowed, his eyes glittered like sapphires. "Control yourself, Peabody," he said, in the purring voice that betokened the Wrath of the Father of Curses (to quote Daoud). "Let me talk to the bastard."

He rose slowly to his feet, hands spread and empty. "Kuentz!" he shouted.

The risk of movement was not as great as it seemed. Our vile opponent knew that a fusillade of gunfire would draw attention, and if he killed one of us, the others—especially Daoud—would run amok. Kuentz came back to the mouth of the bay.

"Don't try anything, Professor."

"Just stretching a bit," said Emerson, suiting the action to the words. "The cards are all in your hands, to continue your unimaginative metaphor. You will release Nefret after you have got your prize safely away?"

"Of course. I bear her no ill will. I loved her once, you know."

"Then the sooner your aim is accomplished, the sooner we will have her back," Emerson said. "How can we help you?"

"A rather disingenuous offer, Professor," Kuentz said.

"Your life is dearer to me than my own at this moment," Emerson assured him. "You are the only one who can save her from the Syrian."

"True." Kuentz stroked his beard. "I am tempted to let you have a look. It's a sight you have never seen, and will never see again, and you are among the few who can appreciate it. I will let Selim and Daoud help my workmen finish clearing the shaft. Then you can go down, one by one, before I have it out."

"Agreed," Emerson said.

Kuentz made me unfasten my belt of tools, and told Cyrus and me to remove our coats before he let us proceed in single file, Daoud and Selim first. The workmen stopped and stared when we entered the bay. Quickly I assessed them. They were local men, some of whom had worked for us at various times, and I had the distinct impression that they were not at all happy. Kuentz had hired them for what appeared to be an ordinary excavation, but when he pointed a gun at the Father of Curses and the Sitt Hakim, the unfortunate fellows realized something unpleasant was about to happen. I knew we could not expect help from them, however; if they got the chance they would run like rabbits, and none of them was courageous enough to attack an armed man.

Kuentz ordered Cyrus and Emerson and me to stand against the rock face and took up a position far enough away so that even Emerson could not have reached him in a single bound. "All right, Selim," he said. "Get to work. One false move and I fire."

Selim's tight lips parted. "I obey the Father of Curses. We will clear the shaft for *him*. Come, Daoud."

"Yes. Get out of my way," Daoud added, pushing assorted Gurnawis back from the opening.

There was not much left to do. They must have started work before daylight, and the shaft was not deep. I could see the top of Daoud's head when he stood at the bottom. Lying flat on the ground beside the opening, Selim shone his torch down while Daoud filled one basket after another and handed them up. It took two of the workers to lift the basket he had raised with one hand.

"It is open." His voice echoed up the shaft. "There is a chamber beyond—"

"Come up," Kuentz ordered. His face was aglow, and for a moment I saw the ardent young scholar he had been before he was corrupted by greed and—as I was beginning to suspect—something else. "Ladies first, eh, Mrs. Emerson? Daoud, lower her down. The rest of you stand still."

Emerson mumbled a protest, but wild horses could not have kept me away. As he had done so often before, Daoud took my wrists in his big hands and let me down, slowly and carefully, till my feet rested on the rough stone that floored the shaft. The opening at the bottom, on the right side, was less than five feet high. I could see nothing of what lay beyond.

"Mr. Kuentz, I require a source of illumination," I called. "You made me discard my torch."

"Yes, to be sure. Selim, give her yours."

Daoud handed it down. I had to bend over to traverse the short passage. When it ended I rose cautiously to my feet.

It was not a tomb. It was a shrine. Against the far wall, wrapped in folds of time-browned linen, stood the god. The light of the torch reflected in the subtle golden curves of the face; eyes inlaid with crystal and obsidian returned my unbelieving stare with calm indifference. He was crowned with twin plumes of gold, and lapis lazuli outlined his brows, and at his feet lay a tumble of golden vessels containing the dried remains of his last offering: Amon-Re, Ruler of Karnak, King of the Gods, Lord of the Silent.

EIGHTEEN

It is difficult to think clearly when you are hanging head down across a surface that is in jarring motion, with a rough cloth covering your face. Nefret made the mistake of trying to struggle. She knew it was a mistake even before her head was seized and slammed against a hard object.

When she came back to consciousness the second time, she was still dangling head down, still muffled in fabric from head to foot. Not a horse this time, a man's shoulder. After a few steps he lowered her onto a lumpy surface that smelled of mildew, and unwound the cloth.

She had no idea where she was, but she recognized her captor from Sethos's description. His mouth drew up in a grotesque smile, distorted by the scars that had slit his cheeks. The smile and the hand that stroked the hair away from her face made her skin crawl. "Lie still," he said softly. "I will come back." He went out the door, leaving it open.

Her wrists and ankles were tied, and a gag covered her mouth. She began twisting her hands, trying to loosen the ropes as Ramses had taught her. Please let him be alive, she prayed. God, Allah, Amon-Re, who hears the words of the silent, anyone . . . Please.

Remembered images flashed through her mind, recapitulating the events that had led up to the disaster. Jumana's deadweight numbing her arm, the horrified faces of the family when she rode into the courtyard, Emerson snatching the girl from her, her mother-in-law's crisp orders . . . watching them ride off, knowing she couldn't leave until she was sure Jumana didn't need her . . . Margaret Minton's fixed, white face. Margaret understood the danger but she didn't feel the sickening terror that had seized Nefret. She knew what it meant, she had felt it before: the knowledge, inexplicable but sure as sight, that he was at that very moment in deadly peril. As soon as she was at ease about Jumana she had left the Castle, driven by the need to go to him, unable to wait another moment. She had eluded Cyrus, but not Margaret; they had been together when Jamil appeared from behind a pile of rocks, waving and calling piteously for help. His galabeeyah was ripped off one shoulder and there was blood on his face.

She only hesitated for a moment. They might have been wrong about the boy; he might have had an innocent reason for seeking Kuentz out, or he might have failed to realize how dangerous his ally was. If he had tried to remonstrate or had threatened to confess . . .

It was not blood on Jamil's face, only dirt, but by the time she realized that, it was too late. She managed to draw her pistol and heard Jamil yowl as she fired, blindly, but the other man, the man with the scars, struck it out of her hand and took her by the throat. She couldn't scream for help, she couldn't see Margaret or the horses or, in the end, anything but blackness.

What had happened to Margaret? She raised her head and looked around the room. It had a pathetic, faded look, as if someone had been trying to imitate the ambience of a proper hotel without the money or the knowledge to do it right—worn matting on the floor, tattered curtains at the window, a set of chipped, soiled bathroom utensils, and slung carelessly over the back of a chair, a man's shirt. A European shirt. The pieces weren't hard to put together. It was Alain, then. She had liked him, she had hoped they were wrong. He had killed at least three people. And Ramses had gone alone to face him and his accomplices, and Margaret might be dead, and the ropes weren't any looser. Please, God.

Mubashir came back carrying a bottle of water and a glass smeared with greasy fingerprints. He sat down beside her, too close, his hip against her thigh, and in spite of herself she cringed away. He smiled again.

"Are you afraid? I could hurt you. I would like to. But my master has said not, unless someone comes looking for you. You are hoping it will be your husband, yes? You should hope he will not come. I have heard of the Brother of Demons, but he cannot get the better of me." His fingers fumbled at her face, pulling the gag down. "Do you want water? The Master said you could have it, and food, if you wish."

"No." She was dry-mouthed with fear and her throat hurt, but she couldn't bear the thought of his arm raising her, the filthy glass against her lips. "Untie me. The ropes are too tight. The Master said not to hurt me."

"Ah, but then I would have to hurt you, because you would try to get away." His callused fingers stroked her cheek. "You fought hard for a woman. I liked that. Do you want the water?"

Nefret shook her head.

"If you change your mind, you will have to ask," he said, with another of his grotesque smiles. He filled the glass and drank, and then he began talking—stories of all the men he had killed and how he had killed them, in loving detail. He doesn't realize he is speaking to a woman who has probably disemboweled more people than he has, Nefret thought. A lot more neatly, though . . .

She would have to persuade him to untie her feet, at least. Knees up while he was bending over her, catching him under his chin, hoping she had strength enough to knock him out or even down, then a dash for the door. Had he left it open in order to tantalize her with a glimpse of freedom?

He must be safe, she told herself. I always know when he isn't. The agonizing, irrational terror had faded, but cold reason told her there was more than sufficient cause for worry. He wouldn't rest until he had found her and she did not doubt he would—someway—somehow. But what could he or anyone else do?

The hateful voice droned on. The sunlight paled. It was midday or later. She would have to beg. She hated the idea, but she had to do it, soon, before her legs were too numb to function.

Then she heard the hoofbeats. That was why the door had been left open; the Syrian was taking no chances on being caught by surprise. She knew who it was even before she heard his voice. He had come alone, had not even tried to conceal his presence. She tugged at the ropes binding her wrists, and the Syrian grinned at her and drew his knife.

Ramses stopped in the doorway, his feet slightly apart, his own knife held low and loose. When he saw her, some of the color came back to his face, and he let out a long, controlled breath.

"I'm all right," she said. The blade of the Syrian's knife was cold against her skin.

"Yes." His mouth softened into a smile.

"Marhaba, Brother of Demons," Mubashir said. "Come in and drop your knife, or I will cut her face open before I kill you."

Ramses glanced at his weapon, and tossed it carelessly away. It struck the floor point down and quivering, ten feet from him. "Are the odds more to your liking now?" he asked. "Or do you only fight with women?"

The arrogant challenge had the desired effect. The Syrian's nostrils flared. He leaped up and lunged.

Later, when Nefret tried to describe the encounter to a fascinated audience she failed. They were both so quick, the Syrian's bulky body almost as agile as her husband's taller, slimmer frame. Ramses moved with the efficiency of a machine and the grace of a cat, twisting and dodging and turning so that time after time the long blade slipped past his body or left only a superficial cut, using his hands and knees for defense since attack was impossible. He kept retreating, but gradually he maneuvered the heavier man around until he was between him and Nefret. Both were breathing quickly but Mubashir was livid with mounting fury. He hadn't expected any trouble with an unarmed opponent. "Stand and fight," he shouted, adding an unprintable epithet.

Ramses planted his feet. Both hands locked round the other man's wrist, halting the descent of the knife inches from his face. For an instant they stood braced in matching strength. There was a blur of movement, so fast she couldn't make it out; Ramses's left hand lost its grip and he dropped to one knee, ducking his head to avoid the wild swing of the Syrian's fist.

Then Nefret understood that every move, even the last, had been part of a deliberate and desperate plan, calculated as precisely as the steps of an intricate dance. Ramses's free hand closed over the hilt of the knife that stood upright and ready, as he had placed it. His long arm swung under and up and around, in a close, deadly embrace, and the blade entered Mubashir's back, under the left shoulder blade. The wound was not mortal, the penetration not deep enough to kill; the Syrian jerked away, breaking Ramses's hold, and Ramses, on his feet, lashed out with his fist. The Syrian's blade slashed his sleeve from shoulder to elbow, but the blow landed square on Mubashir's face, toppling him over backward. The impact and the man's own weight plunged the knife home.

Ramses stood staring down at the twitching body. "Second time today," he said obscurely, and stooped to take the Syrian's knife from his lax hand.

Knowing that the slightest sound or movement might break his concentration, Nefret had forced herself to remain mute and rigid. Now that it was over she was too short of breath to speak. As he came toward her she turned, offering her bound wrists. He cut the ropes, and then he caught her to him in a grip that made her ribs ache. She lay still, content to be in his arms, to feel under her cheek the rapid beat of his heart. It was some time before it slowed to normal and he relaxed his hold.

"Sorry," Nefret said, trying to speak steadily. "I was careless."

"Pure bad luck. Happens to me all the time," he added, with a smile that faded into a frown of concern as his eyes examined her. "Did he hurt you? There's blood on your dress."

"It's your blood." The sleeves and breast of his shirt were slashed into strips and stained red from a dozen cuts. She couldn't control her voice any longer. "Tell me again that you're a coward!"

"What? Oh. But—"

"No one else could have done it, not even Father! I've never seen anything so—so wonderful and so brave and so—so breathtaking! I was absolutely terrified."

"So was I. Don't look at me like that, or I'll lose

what is left of my wits and kiss you, and . . . and this isn't an appropriate venue."

"I can't walk when my feet are tied," she pointed out. "Is Margaret safe? And Sethos?"

"Yes, but God knows what the rest of them have got themselves into by now." He freed her ankles, but when she started to stand he picked her up and carried her toward the door, stepping unconcernedly over the fallen man's sprawled legs. The Syrian looked as formidable in death as he had in life; his eyes were open and staring, his scarred face distorted in a snarl.

"My beloved coward," she said softly.

It was unbelievable, preposterous, incredible. No cult statue had ever been found, in situ or anywhere else, and this one had to have come from one of the great temples. Seated, it was over three feet high, and it appeared to be of solid gold, as were the vessels scattered at its feet. No wonder Kuentz had not dared to remove them; the appearance of such objects on the market would have started alarm bells ringing throughout the scholarly world. Nor could he move the statue until he was ready to take it away, out of Egypt and to a buyer who had already agreed to pay extravagantly for it.

But do not suppose, Reader, that the stupendous sight distracted me for more than a few seconds. I would have exchanged the statue and everything else in the small shrine for Nefret, or any one of those dear to me. When I turned away and went back through the low passage I was trying to think how we could use this to our advantage.

Kuentz was waiting, near the opening, when Daoud pulled me up. "Well?" he demanded. "Incredible, isn't it?"

"Incredible," I agreed. "Words fail me. Emerson, you will not believe—"

"Don't tell him. Let him see for himself." He sounded like an enthusiastic boy. Emerson, the greatest Egyptologist of this or any other age, dominated the field like a colossus; no youthful scholar, however villainous, could remain indifferent to his approval.

Despite his excitement Kuentz had sense enough to step back when Emerson approached. My husband's eyes locked with mine. "Be ready," they said. I inclined my head slightly. Obeying Kuentz's gesture, I returned to my place beside Cyrus. Emerson needed no one's assistance to descend. He lowered himself by his hands and disappeared from sight.

He remained below for a long time. Not a sound issued from the pit. Torn between suspicion and anticipation, Kuentz edged closer to the opening. "What are you doing, Professor?" he called.

Emerson's untidy black head appeared. His hands resting lightly on the edge of the pit, he looked up. "It's a fake," he said.

Instantly I dropped to the ground, pulling Cyrus down with me. It was a sensible but unnecessary precaution; Kuentz lost his grip on the gun when Emerson's hands closed round his ankles and pulled his feet out from under him. Selim snatched the weapon up and Emerson seated himself on Kuentz's chest, and the reluctant Gurnawis pelted out of the place, scattering in all directions.

"Ah," said Daoud, who had watched the performance interestedly. "Soon I can kill him, is it not so? Where is Nur Misur?"

"I expect Ramses has her safe by now," Emerson said calmly. "Selim, find me some rope."

I was sorry Ramses had not heard that splendid tribute. I was unable to share Emerson's confidence, but there were a few things to tidy up before we could search for our missing children. I always carry a coil of rope on my belt, in case I find it necessary to tie up a prisoner; with this and strips of cloth torn from various articles of clothing, we bound Kuentz hand and foot, despite his struggles. While we were doing this, Cyrus edged up to the opening of the shaft.

"I can't stand it," he said suddenly. "You folks are going to think I'm a selfish, cold-blooded viper, and I won't take more than a minute, but if I don't see what's down there I'm going to burst."

"Go right ahead," Emerson said amiably. "It may take us a minute or two to find out where that scum of a Syrian took Nefret. Give Vandergelt Effendi a hand, Daoud. Now then, Kuentz, what have you to say?"

Recognizing at last the futility of resistance, the Swiss lay still, breathing heavily. "It was a lie," he gasped. "The statue is genuine. You know it. You knew it!"

"He has still some of the instincts of a scholar," Emerson remarked to me. "If they had not been present in his mind, my little ruse would not have succeeded. Yes, it is genuine, and yes, I knew it, and yes indeed, I hoped the momentary relaxation of your guard would—"

A whoop like that of a banshee floated up the shaft. Emerson grinned. "Vandergelt has not my self-control. Perhaps we ought to leave him here to guard the statue. I wouldn't put it past those rascals from Gurneh to sneak back after we leave. Where are we going, Kuentz?"

"You cannot make me speak," Kuentz said sullenly.

"I wouldn't be so sure of that," Emerson said mildly. "I am known for my patience and forbearance, but where the safety of my daughter is concerned . . . You said you loved her once. I think you still do. You had no intention of giving her up, did you? And yet you left her in the hands of a murderous brute. If she has been harmed or even handled roughly, I will kill your Syrian friend and then come back and kill you."

Sweat poured down the man's face. "I am willing to strike a bargain. No, listen! You cannot get her away from Mubashir without my help, I am the only one he'll listen to. I will go with you and order him to release her if you promise to let me go."

Emerson is accustomed to get his own way, without compromise or bargaining. His eyes narrowed into slits of sapphirine fire.

"We must discuss it," I said. "Come with me, Emerson. Selim, watch him."

We went together out into the sunlight. Under my restraining hand Emerson's arm was hard as granite. "We must agree, Emerson," I said softly. "I share your admiration for Ramses's abilities, but even he has his limits. He may also be a prisoner, or . . . Kuentz has nothing to lose. He already faces the death penalty."

"So we let him get away with . . . how many? Three murders? Four?"

I remembered something Nefret had once said. "Is it wrong to care so much about someone that nothing else matters?" In the last extremity, when a loved one is at risk, nothing else matters. Certainly nothing so abstract as justice. It is, after all, a concept defined by men.

"Yes," I said.

Instead of replying, Emerson emitted a wordless shout and began to run. I turned and saw them coming, holding one another's hands, the sunlight bright on Nefret's golden hair. I started toward them, rather quickly, but not running . . . Not very fast, at any rate.

Emerson had enveloped his daughter in a close embrace. I looked at my son. He gave me a rather tentative smile.

"I apologize for my appearance, Mother. We came straight here, since we thought you might be . . . Mother?"

Arms, breast, face, side, hand . . . I gave up the attempt to tally his wounds. "Another shirt ruined," I said, and threw my arms around him.

The remainder of that day was something of a bustle, what with arranging for the shrine to be guarded and the prisoner removed, tending to the wounded, and bringing one another up-to-date.

Our celebratory preprandial gathering in the beautifully appointed sitting room of the Castle included only part of the group. Sennia was with Jumana, delighted to have another sick person to look after. Sethos was tucked up in bed with Margaret watching over him—or standing guard over him, to put it another way. What would transpire with those two I did not know, but it had been evident to me for some time that he had now, if he had not had before, a certain interest in her. I had sent William to relieve Daoud. My necessarily brief explanations confused him a great deal, I believe, but he was obviously pleased to have such responsibility rested upon him.

"He suffers from a lack of self-confidence," I explained, as Cyrus handed round the whiskey. "That is why he behaved so suspiciously. Self-doubt leads to paranoia and feelings of guilt. It is a well-known psychological fact—"

"I don't want to hear about it," said Emerson.

"Me neither," said Cyrus. "I'll give Amherst a job if he wants one; I can use him. But I don't want to talk about him. Well, what shall we drink to first?"

My eyes moved round the room—from Bertie, whose ingenuous countenance still displayed some perplexity; to his mother, relieved at last of her anxieties; to Ramses and Nefret, seated side by side on the sofa, their fingers entwined; to Cyrus's lined, smiling face; and to my dear Emerson, who was not even listening.

"What?" he said.

"To friends and loved ones," I said.

"To another miraculous escape," Cyrus amended.

"There was nothing miraculous about it," Emerson declared. "Good Gad, we have had considerable practice at this sort of thing; all that is required is courage and strength, superior intelligence, quick wits, the ability to respond instantly to unexpected emergencies—"

"And the help of our friends," I said modestly.

"Yes, ma'am," Bertie burst out. "And I take it most unkindly, if you will allow me to say so, that you wouldn't let me—"

"We will let you take a hand next time," I said.

"If there is a next time," Bertie exclaimed.

"There will be," said Emerson. "There always is."

"Not this year," I said, giving Katherine an encouraging nod.

"I trust not," Emerson said, giving *me* a hard stare—as if the whole thing had been my fault! "We have enough to do as it is. We will have to stay on for a few weeks, Peabody—but not here," he added hastily. "Wouldn't want to put Katherine and Cyrus out. Can we evict poor old Yusuf—find him another house?"

"Leave it to me," I said, waving aside Katherine's polite protestations.

Cyrus was lost in wistful speculation. "You'll let me help, won't you? Closest I'll ever come to a major find, I guess. I just don't seem to have the luck. How long do you suppose that statue has been there?"

"Since 663 B.C.," Ramses said.

"I say!" Bertie exclaimed. "That's deuced clever. How can you be so precise?"

Ramses looked at his father. Humming tune-lessly and off-key, Emerson reached for his pipe and returned his son's deferential glance with one of expectant interest.

"I may be mistaken," Ramses said, "but it is a reasonable guess. The rulership of Thebes changed many times over the years, from northern conquer-ers to Cushite kings to high priests, but they were all, even the Cushites—especially the Cushites—devout followers of the old gods. There was a cer-tain amount of looting, I daresay, but the shrines would have been sacrosanct. Conquerers boasted of having restored the statues and the offerings. Then, 'the Assyrians came down like a wolf on the fold.'"

"Poetry," I murmured.

"Not only poetry, but Byron," Ramses admitted. "That is how it must have been, though. 'The sheen of their spears was like stars on the sea.' For the first time in its long history, the city of Thebes was taken and sacked. 'From Thebes I carried away loot rich and beyond measure; two obelisks cast of shin-ing bronze . . .' The Assyrians cared nothing for the gods. Among their booty were the furnishings of the temples and the divine statues—except one. How the priests got it away we will never know—"

"Unless there's a papyrus or ostracon in there," Cyrus broke in.

"That would be a find, wouldn't it?" Ramses agreed. "Even more important than the statue in some ways. But it must have been a hurried, frantic job, with the Assyrians advancing—already on the east bank, perhaps—and they hoped to retrieve it one day. They must have been killed defending the city. All knowledge of the location was lost."

"Until Jamil found it," I said. "What will become of him?"

"What has become of him, you mean," Emerson said. "Nefret cannot have wounded him seriously, or he would not have been able to take her horse and get clean away. We still don't know how deeply he was involved. Kuentz isn't talking. In a way, I hope the boy doesn't come back. He would face a prison sentence at the very least, and that would bring disgrace on the whole family."

It did seem likely, as we all agreed, that Jamil had been the original discoverer of the shrine; otherwise Kuentz would never have enlisted him as an ally. He had worked for Kuentz, among others; either Kuentz had caught him in the act or Jamil had had enough sense to realize that he could not dispose of the incredible find by himself, and guided, perhaps, by the instinct that allows one morally corrupt individual to recognize another, he had approached Kuentz.

Speculation could carry us no further, so we abandoned it for the nonce. A few more congratulatory speeches and a trifle more whiskey concluded the evening.

It was not until the following morning that I was able to arrange a conference that would, I expected, answer my remaining questions. It took place in Sethos's sickroom. The only other persons present were our four selves, for the matters under discussion were of a nature that could not be disclosed to anyone else, not even our dearest friends—or Margaret Minton.

I had not informed my brother-in-law of my intentions; with most men, particularly the members of the Emerson family, advance warning is a tactical error. However, I paid him the courtesy of waiting until the servant informed me he had finished breakfast, and was up and dressed, before I knocked.

When he saw who it was he put down the book he had been reading, and sat in surly silence while the others filed in. I was pleased to see that he had shaved that morning and that he was looking quite respectable in a shirt and trousers borrowed from Ramses. The two of them were almost the same size. After I had locked the door I invited everyone to sit down.

"By all means," Sethos said. "A private little family conference, is it? Margaret told me about your activities yesterday, so you needn't go over them again. Congratulations on your discovery."

"Damnit, man, is that all you have to say?" Emerson demanded.

"I am somewhat curious about one thing."

"And what is that?" I asked.

He turned those strange gray-green eyes on Ramses. "How the devil did you get her away from Mubashir?"

"It wasn't very nice of you to let him go alone if you thought he couldn't," I said critically. "But I feel obliged to remark that from what little I have been allowed to hear of the affair, it would be impossible to praise too highly the courage and cleverness and skill and—"

"Mother, he's doing it again," Ramses interrupted. "Don't let him get you off the subject, or we'll be here all day."

"Quite," said Emerson. "You have an agenda, I believe, Peabody. I suggest you stick to it."

"Certainly, my dear." I unfolded the papers I had taken from my pocket, spread them out on the table, and cleared my throat.

"This won't take long. Assuming, of course, that our—er—kinsman does not continue to equivocate."

"Kinsman," Sethos repeated. "On the whole, Amelia, I would prefer—"

"Perhaps it would be better if I simply stated the facts." His lips parted, but long years of experience with Ramses, and to some extent, Emerson, had taught me how to turn a conversation into a monologue. Raising my voice slightly, I continued.

"You are still working for British intelligence. You were sent here to ascertain the intentions of the Senussi and the extent to which they had influenced the desert tribes. Mr. Bracedragon . . . Mr. Boisgirdle . . . Mr. *Smith* is the person to whom you report. You met with him the evening you went to the Winter Palace."

Up to this point I was on solid ground. The rest of it was somewhat problematic, and I hesitated, trying to think how to get the confirmation I needed before committing myself. One look at Sethos told me I was not going to get any help from him. He had tilted his chair back and was watching me with a mocking smile.

"What shall we do with Mr. Kuentz?" I inquired. The front legs of the chair thudded onto the floor. "Why are you asking me?" he demanded, with an unconvincing show of surprise.

"The matter is a trifle delicate, is it not? Our friends are under the impression that we arrested Mr. Kuentz because he was a murderer and tomb robber—which is good and sufficient cause. Your superiors may not wish it known that he is also a German spy."

"I might have known you would arrive at that conclusion," Sethos muttered.

"It was obvious," said Emerson, folding his arms and trying to look as if he had known it all along.

"Well, it was, rather," I admitted. "Ramses's encounter with poor Mr. Asad could only have been arranged by someone who knew the role Ramses had played the previous winter—in other words, an agent of Turkish or German intelligence—but I cannot blame myself for failing to give that interesting clue the importance it deserved, since the attacks on us continued even after Ramses had left Cairo. Everything that happened from then on was designed to keep us in Cairo and bring Ramses back. That was what confused me initially, the fact that our adversary had two roles and two motives. I even considered the possibility that there were two different people involved: an enemy spy, who had sent Mr. Asad to prevent Ramses from returning to his activities on behalf of the War Office, and an archaeologist, who had found something of value in Luxor which he had determined to exploit for his own gain. Of all people on earth we were the most likely to interfere with such a discovery, not only because of our expert knowledge of the area but because of the bonds of friendship and loyalty that unite us with the members of dear Abdullah's family. Emerson's influence with them is paramount, his reputation awe-inspiring. Kuentz feared that once in his presence, Jamil might break down and confess. He was mistaken about that, for the wretched boy's desire for power and wealth was stronger than loyalty; but he had good reason to be concerned."

"I'm surprised he didn't simply kill Jamil," Nefret said.

"The murder of a member of *our* family would have brought us here at once, Nefret. Besides, he needed Jamil to spy on you and Ramses and report your activities to him."

"Get on with it, Peabody," Emerson grunted.

"Where was I?" I consulted my notes. "Ah, yes. Mr. Kuentz is a German agent, but he is also an archaeologist, and a good one. He recognized that the statue was the discovery of a lifetime; and although he continued to carry out his original assignment, his primary motive from then on was to make himself rich. I daresay he is not the only man who would be seduced from duty by such a prize."

"I understand his point of view quite well," said Sethos meditatively.

Being accustomed to his attempts at provocation and distraction, I silenced him with a stern look and went on. "You knew or assumed that the Central Powers had a man in Luxor. I will not ask how you knew, since you wouldn't answer me, claiming that it is classified information—which it may be—but it would be logical for them to do so. Your role was to find out who he was and what he was doing. In pursuit of these aims you made several trips to Kharga Oasis—as Kuentz had done. The place is a hotbed of subversion, and readily accessible by rail, as the other oases are not. You learned that your counterpart had been there, but nothing more that would enable you to identify him."

I turned over another page. "It came as a considerable surprise to you, I expect, to find that someone was impersonating you. Why? you must have asked yourself. Could it be that this individual was the German spy you sought, making use of your notorious—er—well-known prestige to win adherents? Or"—I paused to catch my breath—"could it be that there was another player and that the prize was an archaeological discovery of great value?"

"I thought you were going to state facts," Sethos said.

"Those were rhetorical questions," I explained. "But if you would care to answer them . . ."

"Why not?" said my brother-in-law, with an appearance of candor that aroused the direst of suspicions. "You seem to have it all worked out anyhow.

"I hadn't been in Luxor for two days when I began hearing rumors about a great discovery. One hears such things frequently, of course; usually the rumors are false. The rumors about the return of the Master were more serious, and when I recognized one of my former hirelings I decided I had better move cautiously in reestablishing contact with my old organization. As you know, I wasn't cautious enough."

He paused to light a cigarette. "Continue, if you please," I said.

"Do you really want to hear all these tedious details?" He blew out a cloud of smoke.

"No," said Emerson. "I want to get back to the shrine."

"I believe I can summarize the main points," I said. "You wondered why, if the impostor meant to take over the antiquities business, he hadn't stolen anything. We know the reason now, of course; the magnitude of the find was such that he did not want to attract the attention of the authorities until he had made arrangements to remove and dispose of the statue. Suspecting something of the sort, you decided to challenge him—a typically reckless and ill-considered move, I might add—by carrying out several daring thefts. Was destroying the German House another such challenge?"

"In part. The locals avoided the place; they had been told it was haunted or cursed or something of the sort. That in itself suggested someone was using it, so I searched the place. He hadn't left anything incriminatory, not even a codebook, but the wireless was there. So I decided I might as well blow the bloody place up, cut his line of communication, and remove one of his hideaways.

"At this point I still didn't know whether I was dealing with one man or two, but when I was notified of Asad's death I felt certain the two were one. As you yourself so cogently remarked, only a man who knew of Ramses's role last winter would have realized that Asad might constitute a danger to him. We will never know for certain unless Kuentz decides to confide in us, but I expect Kuentz ran across Asad on one of his trips to Kharga, and heard his heated remarks on the subject of British oppression and the martyrdom of his beloved leader; which gave Kuentz the bright idea of turning him loose and encouraging him to seek revenge on a traitor. It was not such a bad scheme. All it cost Kuentz was a few pounds and a little time, and if it had succeeded it would have put Ramses out of commission, and seriously distracted the rest of you. He wanted to keep you away from Luxor, for the reasons you have indicated.

"What he failed to understand was that Asad's heart . . ." The corners of his mouth turned up in a particularly offensive smile. "His heart, shall we say, wasn't in it. Kuentz had arranged to meet Asad in Cairo, promising aid and comfort for the cause. When they met, Kuentz discovered that Asad had not only failed to kill or incapacitate Ramses, but that he was riddled with guilt and remorse. There was a reasonable chance he would go to his—er—friend and confess. So Kuentz killed him."

"My reasoning exactly," I said.

"Quite," said Sethos, nodding gravely in acknowledgment. "To sum it up, the Germans and Turks had planted a number of agents in various trouble spots, awaiting der Tag, and archaeology provides excellent cover. If my quarry was an Egyptologist who had come across a startling discovery in the course of his normal activities, a discovery rich enough to seduce him from his duty—well, that would account for what had happened."

"Good enough," said Emerson, bounding to his feet. Ordinarily he enjoys participating in our little deductive sessions, but archaeological fever had overcome him. "So you will take steps to get Kuentz off our hands?"

"I will wire Cairo today," was the reply.

"Just write out the telegram," I said. "You use some sort of code, I suppose. I will send it when I go to Luxor this afternoon. I have a great deal of shopping to do before—"

I have seldom heard such language, even from Emerson. Nor did Emerson object, as he usually did, to bad language from anyone except himself. I waited until Sethos had worn out his store of invective, and then said, "You aren't fit to go anywhere yet. Nefret, perhaps you had better take his temperature."

Sethos gave his brother a look like that of a caged animal. Emerson shook his head. "It's no use," he said gruffly. "She always gets her way. Anyhow, you aren't—you ought not—er—we cannot allow you to—"

"Disappear again into loneliness, danger, and despair," I said. "Not with Christmas only two days off."

Sethos covered his face with his hands. "Get me pen and paper."

FROM MANUSCRIPT H

The tree was bright with candles and hung with the little ornaments which David had made all those years ago and which had become a treasured part of their holiday celebration. Leaning against her husband, Nefret was so tired she couldn't have moved if her life depended on it. Her mother-in-law had had them all working round the clock to get things ready, and when she wasn't after Nefret to help with wrapping gifts and hanging decorations, Emerson was demanding photographs, sketches, and plans. There was one moment Nefret would never forget, when she stood in the underground chamber with Selim and the cameras, and realized she was still clutching the wreath she had been making when Emerson dragged her away from the Castle.

After they had finished taking photographs, she laid it at the feet of the god.

It had been worth it. Sennia was beside herself, fluttering from person to person like a ruffled white butterfly, tearing the wrappings off her gifts, shrieking with pleasure. A letter from Rose had arrived that morning, with the news that Seshat had had her kittens—four of them, all healthy and handsome and brindled like their parents—and Sennia was still puzzling over how to allocate them. One for herself, of course (Nefret wondered how Horus would react to that!), and one for Ramses; but should the others go to Gargery, or "the Professor," or Daoud, or Mr. Amherst, who was clearly in need of appreciation and affection, or Bertie? Bertie sat by his mother, holding her hand—or perhaps she was holding his hand, to prevent him from joining Jumana, who was sitting next to Emerson, her foot on a hassock, fluttering her lashes and talking nonstop. Emerson listened with an indulgent smile, but his eyes, like Nefret's, wandered round the room, lingering longest on the face of his wife.

Wearing a gown of her favorite crimson, she was bustling about, managing everything and everyone—persuading Gargery to rewrap his replica of Abu Simbel, which had an unforeseen tendency to shed sand all over the carpet, pausing for a moment to chat with Amherst and give him an encouraging pat on the back, helping Fatima pick up the ribbons and paper Sennia had scattered. She looked very handsome, her cheeks flushed and her hair twisted into a coil atop her head. (Nefret had certain suspicions about the unrelieved black of that handsome head of hair, but she would never have expressed them.)

All the Egyptologists Cyrus could collect were there, as well as several friends from Luxor. Marjorie Fisher and Cathy Flynn had not brought their cats, who were usually honored visitors; Horus was roaming free, at Sennia's insistence, and since he regarded all male felines as potential rivals and all females as potential prey Coco and Bes had been forced to miss the festivities. "The family" had sent their representatives—Daoud and Selim, Fatima and Kadija and Basima, graciously sharing in a festival that was not their own—though Daoud had remarked, in that innocently shrewd way of his, "The Lord Issa is one of the great prophets. Why should we not honor his birth?"

The occasion was certainly ecumenical. In the center of the room, on a plinth, sat Amon-Re, candlelight streaking his face and crown with gold. Emerson had been unwilling to leave him unguarded any longer and clearing the shrine had proved to be a disappointingly simple business.

There had been nothing in the chamber but the god and his offering vessels—no papyri, no final plea scratched on an ostracon or on the walls. Perhaps it had not been necessary. He heard the prayers of the silent, and no one deserved his mercy more than the devoted priests who had saved him from the invaders. Remembering her mother-in-law's account of Abdullah's enigmatic words, Nefret shivered a little. He had spoken of Amon . . .

I mustn't be superstitious and sentimental, she told herself firmly.

One look at Sethos was enough to dispel such fancies. She could not exactly call him a skeleton at the feast, but he bore no perceptible resemblance to Father Christmas, even with the beard he had insisted upon wearing. Bolt upright, in a particularly uncomfortable armchair, he watched the proceedings with a singular absence of expression. He did not look at Margaret, or she at him, though she was seated not far away. Catching Nefret's wandering eye, his lips curled in acknowledgment of the absurdity of his presence: the prodigal son, the black sheep. Not even her formidable mother-in-law, she thought, could bring that sheep back into the fold.

"What will happen to those two?" she asked.

"What two?" Ramses had been watching Sennia, when he wasn't looking at her. "Oh. The mind boggles. Aunt Margaret? God save us! He does care for her, though. If you had seen his face the other day—"

"I knew before that," Nefret said smugly.

"Because he behaved so abominably to her?"

"He was falling in love with her and he didn't want

to," Nefret explained. "Women are such nuisances, aren't they? Always hanging about demanding attention and complaining, and getting themselves captured."

"'White hands cling to the tightened rein,'" her husband agreed solemnly. "'Slipping the spur from the booted heel—'"

"Poetry!" Nefret said scornfully. She pulled his head down and kissed him. He responded without self-consciousness or restraint, and when they broke apart and saw that his mother was—of course!—watching them with an approving smile, he grinned at her and held Nefret closer.

"Kipling had never met you or Mother," he remarked, raising her hand to his face. "He wouldn't have written such rubbish if he had."

"She's gesturing at us," Nefret said, as his lips explored her palm and fingers. "I think she wants us to sing carols. Couldn't we slip away?"

"Away from Mother, when she's in a sentimental mood? Not bloody likely. Contain yourself a little longer, you shameless woman."

"I am entirely without shame," Nefret murmured. "But I don't think I can control myself if she tries to make the Master Criminal join in a rousing chorus of 'Deck the Halls'! Surely not even she would expect . . ."

She did expect it, and he was too cowed to protest. Or perhaps, Nefret thought, there was another reason. She was surprised to find that he knew all the words.

Sethos was gone next morning, and so was Margaret. Despite Emerson's indignant complaints,

Nefret suspected he had collaborated in his brother's disappearance. It would have been difficult for the pair to get away without help from someone.

The beard and Ramses's best suit were missing too. The only thing they found in Sethos's room was a small parcel, addressed to Nefret. It contained a bracelet of linked carnelian plaques, exquisitely carved with the figures of a king and queen enthroned.

"Amenhotep the Third and Queen Tiy," Ramses said, breathing hard. "He lied about that, too! He did find her jewelry."

"Good of him to share," his mother said coolly.

He had left nothing for her.

What do you suppose he's done with the rest of the jewelry?" Emerson asked.

We were in our room, collecting the articles we would need that day. I buckled my belt of tools round my waist.

"He will sell them to a wealthy collector—he has built up quite a clientele, I imagine—or a well-funded museum. Some of those institutions have no scruples about purchasing stolen artifacts."

"Hmph," Emerson agreed. He gave me a side-long look. "I was somewhat surprised that he—er—neglected to give you anything."

"It was a typically oblique and a typically graceful gesture, my dear. An acknowledgment of his altered feelings for me—and you—and his commitment to another lady."

"Hmmm," said Emerson. "You really think she—"

"Temporary commitment, perhaps I should say. How long the—er—arrangement will last one cannot predict, but she is a very determined woman and he is no longer an impetuous youth. It is time he settled down."

"I doubt he would agree, Peabody. Confound it, he as good as admitted he has not abandoned the antiquities game. Are we to be on opposite sides again?"

"He did add a certain spice to our lives, Emerson, admit it."

Emerson passed his hand over his mouth. "I will admit he was the only adversary worthy of our steel."

"You have forgiven him, then?"

"Oh, bah, forgive . . ." Emerson no longer attempted to conceal his smile. "I suppose I can hardly blame him for having the good taste to admire you. And he hasn't tried to murder me for years! I wish he would turn to a line of work that doesn't interfere with mine, but I can even put up with that, unless . . ."

"Unless what, Emerson?"

"Unless he has the damned audacity to die again!"

Turn the page for a sneak peek at

A RIVER IN THE SKY,

the all-new Amelia Peabody adventure
by Elizabeth Peters,
coming soon in hardcover from William Morrow.

Emerson looked up from the book he was reading. "The Old Testament," he remarked, "is a tissue of lies from start to finish."

As I have said before, and never tire of repeating, my husband is the greatest Egyptologist of this or any other century. It cannot be denied, however, that he holds somewhat unorthodox opinions on certain subjects. Prejudiced he is not; his critical comments are applied indiscriminately to all the major world religions, and not a few of the minor ones. Ordinarily I do not bother to protest, since contradiction only inspires him to more outrageous flights of rhetoric. However, I had become bored with my own reading material—an article on negative verb forms in the latest issue of the *Zeitshrift fur Aegyptische Sprache*—and considered what response was most likely to result in a refreshing discussion.

The weather was unusually warm even for August in Kent, and the roses in the garden outside Emerson's study drooped dustily. This chamber, the library in point of fact, is one of the most comfortable rooms in the house, a pleasant clutter of books and papers sprinkled with the ashes from Emerson's pipe and the hair shed by cats of various colors. We all tend to gather there; Emerson's attempts to claim it as his own are sporadic and ineffectual. He only does it to stir up an argument when other sources fail.

The only other member of the family present that morning was Nefret, our adopted daughter. My son was presently on an archaeological excavation in Palestine; his Egyptian friend David, whom we regarded as one of us, had betaken himself to Yorkshire in order to be with his affianced bride, my niece Lia.

If I had been looking for support—which I was not, since I do not require assistance in my discussions with Emerson—I would have known I could expect no agreement from Nefret.

To look at her, one would have assumed Nefret to be a classic English beauty, fair skinned and blue eyed, with a glorious crown of golden red hair. Yet her formative years had been spent in a remote spot in the western desert of Egypt, where the old gods were still worshipped, and she had served as high priestess of Isis before we rescued her and brought her back to the land of her ancestors. Though I had endeavored to instruct her in the faith of those ancestors, I harbored no illusions as to my success. Early impressions are difficult to erase and from time to time she would say or do something that indicated she was more in sympathy with Emerson's views than with mine. Her frequent visits to the little pyramid we had caused to be built in honor of a young man who had perished in her service might have been occasioned by respect and fond remembrance; but it would not have surprised me to learn that she sometimes addressed a prayer to one of the pagan dieties mentioned in the inscriptions. Curled up on the sofa, playing with one of the cats, she looked at me with an anticipatory smile.

I returned my attention to Emerson, whose smile was not so much anticipatory as provocative. I had decided on a flank attack rather than a direct assault.

"Good heavens, Emerson, are you reading the Bible? Are you feeling quite well?"

Emerson's smile broadened into a grin that displayed a set of large white teeth. "Nicely done, my dear. I assure you, my health has never been better."

As if to verify the statement he rose to his feet and stretched. Muscles rippled across the breadth of his chest and along his arms. They were admirably displayed by his costume; his shirt was open at the throat and his sleeves rolled above the elbows. His thick black hair was becomingly dishevelled and his blue eyes shone with sapphirine brilliance. The sight of Emerson's splendid physical endowments never fails to stir strong emotions, but on this occasion I resisted the distraction since I was genuinely curious.

"Why are you reading the Bible, Emerson?"

"The answer to that question will become evident in due course, Peabody. Have you no comment to make on my original statement?"

"Well, as to that," I replied, settling myself more comforably, "you know as well as I do that the statement is, to say the least, inaccurate and exaggerated.

Don't tell me you have read the entire Old Testament. How far had you got?"

Emerson glanced down at the volume open on his desk. "Genesis and Exodus," he admitted. "It gets damnably boring after that."

"One does not read the Bible to be entertained, Emerson," I said severely.

"Than why the devil does one read it?"

Before I could reply, an emphatic knock at the door preceded the appearance of Rose, who announced that luncheon was ready. Our very efficient housekeeper is allowed in Emerson's study only when it reaches a stage of questionable hygiene; she gave it a critical look, pursed her lips, and shook her head.

Emerson saw the look. Rising in haste, he said, "Coming, Rose, coming at once."

A formal meal, in such warm weather and when there were only three of us, was in my opinion a waste of time. Gargery, our butler, did not share this opinion, primarily because he seized every opportunity to listen and contribute to our conversation. (I do not encourage this, but Emerson has not the least notion of proper behavior with servants.) After serving cold ham and salad, Gargery inquired, "May I ask, sir and madam, whether you have had a letter from Master Ramses recently?"

As I had often told Gargery, our son had reached an age at which that childish title was inappropriate. The name was equally inappropriate, but Ramses had been given that appellation in infancy because of his imperious manner and the fact that his swarthy complexion and dark eyes and hair appeared more Egyptian than English. (I have sometimes been asked to account for this resemblance. I see no reason why I should.)

I replied with a rather curt negative, and Emerson, who had finished his ham and salad, asked, "What do you know about the Old Testament, Gargery?" he asked.

"It's been a while since I dipped into the Good Book, sir," Gargery admitted. "I remember David and Goliath, and the parting of the Red Sea, and a few other stories."

"Stories is the word," said Emerson. "There is not a jot of historical evidence for any of them."

This was aimed at me, not at Gargery, so of course I responded. "If it is history you want, you had better skip on to the books of Kings and Chronicles. The historical validity of the Exodus has been much debated—no, Emerson, I do not care to debate it now—but the lives of the kings of Israel and Judah are based on solid historical evidence."

Emerson pushed his plate away and planted his elbows on the table—a deplorable habit of which I have not succeeded in breaking him. "Is that so, Peabody? Perhaps you would care to cite a few examples."

Though I would never have admitted it to Emerson, it had been some time since I had dipped into the Old Testament. I promised myself I would do so immediately after luncheon. "Do your own research, Emerson. You wouldn't take my word anyhow. Nefret, my dear, you haven't eaten a thing. You seem a trifle out of sorts these days. Is something worrying you?"

The disingenuous attempt to change the subject succeeded. Emerson, who adores his adopted daughter, glanced at her in alarm.

"No. Well. . . . I miss the boys. Not that you and the professor aren't splendid company," she added quickly. "But with David in Yorkshire and Ramses off in the wilds of Palestine . . ."

"You have no one to play with," I suggested.

Nefret returned my smile. "I suppose that was how it sounded. Oh, it is perfectly understandable that David would rather be with Lia; they're madly in love and it will be some time before they can be married. But why did Ramses go haring off to Palestine? He might at least have the decency to write."

"Mr. Reisner's offer to work with him at Samaria was a splendid opportunity," I said. "And you know Ramses has never been a good correspondent."

"Well, sir and madam, I don't understand it either," Gargery declared, serving plates of custard. "Egypt is where we always work. Why did Master Ramses go off to that heathenish place?"

"The adjective is singularly inappropriate, Gargery, since we are speaking of the Holy Land, sacred to three great world religions. And," I added, "I cannot remember inviting your comments on the matter."

Unperturbed by my rebuke, for he had heard similar remarks so often they had ceased to make an impression, Gargery declared, "I worry about him, madam, and that's a fact. You know how he is."

I did know how he was. Ramses had a habit, a propensity, one might say, of getting in trouble. It would take too many pages of this journal to compile a list of his adventures, which included being kidnapped off the top of a pyramid, being temporarily entombed in another, stealing a lion . . . But as I have said, the list is long.

Candor compels me to admit that certain of Ramses's escapades were due in part to the activities of his father and myself, for our dedication to truth and justice had occasionally brought us into contact with various criminal elements—tomb robbers, forgers, a murderer or two, and even a Master Criminal. To do myself justice, I must add that I had done my best to protect him as only a mother can. Certain of his narrow escapes were unquestionably the result of his own recklessness and although he had settled down a bit as he approached the official age of maturity—which he had reached this past month—I had been forced to the conclusion that I was no longer in a position to control his actions. At least not when he was in a place where I could not get at him. It had occurred to me, upon occasion, to wonder whether Ramses had deliberately selected a place where I could not get at him.

"For your information, Gargery," I said, "the site of Samaria was once the capital of the kings of Israel, after the United Kingdom broke into two parts after the death of Solomon, Israel being the northern and Judah the southern. The city was subsequently conquered by—er—various conquerors, ending with the Romans. The Roman temple on the summit of the tell—as such sites are called, being the remains of one settlement atop another . . ."

As I had expected, my lecture succeeded in boring Gargery to such an extent that he cleared the table and removed himself. It also bored Nefret, who asked to be excused, and Emerson, who declared he knew that, Peabody, and left the room. I knew he was going to the library to look up the information I had given in the hope of finding me wrong. He would not. I had been careful to stick to generalities.

As a rule it is not difficult for me to read Emerson's mind. However, speculate as I might, I was unable to account for his sudden interest in a subject that had hitherto roused only derision. I found time that day to refresh my memory of the biblical books I had mentioned. I did not doubt Emerson was reading them too, and I intended to be ready for him.

He did not refer to the subject again. When he informed me, the following morning, that he had invited two guests to join us for tea, my attempts to ascertain more information about them were met with evasion and, when I persisted, a flat out refusal to say more. Rather than give him the satisfaction of demonstrating further interest I did not pursue the matter, but I felt a certain foreboding. Emerson's acquaintances include Arab sheikhs, Nubian brigands, thieves of various nationalities, and one or two forgers.

I was therefore pleasantly surprised when the guests proved to be unarmed and harmless. They were an odd pair, however. Major the Honorable George Morley appeared to be in his late thirties or early forties. Of medium height, with thinning brown hair, he carried himself like the soldier he had been, but his well-tailored clothes failed to conceal the fact that the life of a country gentleman had thickened his waistline and certain other parts of his anatomy.

In contrast to the solidity of Morley, the other man gave the impression that a strong gale would blow him off his feet and send him floating across the landscape. His hair might have been white or very fair. His beard was of the same indeterminate shade, so that his face looked as if it were framed by a halo that had slipped its moorings. His eyes were of that pale shade of blue that, if physiognomists are to be believed, are characteristic of mystics and fanatics.

His name was equally remarkable. Morley presented him as Reverend Plato Panagopolous. His garments were of somber black and he wore a clerical collar. I asked, with my usual tact, to which particular church or denomination he belonged. I had to repeat the question before he replied: "I serve the Lord God of hosts in all his manifestations."

He contributed little to the conversation after that, except for murmurs of vague agreement when someone commented on the beauty of the August weather or the prospect of rain, but from time to time his gaze focused on me or Nefret, and a singularly sweet smile warmed his thin face.

Pouring tea and offering plates of biscuits and cucumber sandwiches, I wondered what the devil Emerson was up to now. As a rule he avoided English squires and otherworldly eccentrics like the plague. Nefret, as puzzled as I—and as bored— gave me a questioning look. I smiled and gave my head a little shake. "Be patient," was my unspoken message. "Emerson is bound to burst out before long."

I confess, however, that I was not prepared for the precise nature of the outburst.

"The Old Testament," said Emerson, fixing Morley with a piercing stare, "is a tissue of lies from start to finish."

"Really, Emerson," I exclaimed. "That is very rude to our guests, who probably take quite a different view of Scripture."

Morley laughed and waved a plump pink hand. "Not at all, Mrs. Emerson. I fully expected some such view from the professor. I am here to change his views, if possible."

"Proceed," said Emerson, folding his arms.

But before Mr. Morley could do so, Panagopolous leaped to his feet and began speaking in tongues.

Genuine, actual languages, that is to say. I recognized Hebrew and Latin, and what sounded like Greek; but his speech was so disjointed and his voice so high pitched I understood only a few words. He might have been the reincarnation of one of the Old Testament prophets, eyes blazing, hair and beard bristling, arms flailing.

"What the devil," Emerson exclaimed. "He is about to have a seizure."

"Don't touch him," Morley said. "He is not ill. It will pass."

Sure enough, the spate of speech stopped as suddenly as it had come on. The reverend's bristling hair and beard settled back into place. He resumed his chair, and took a biscuit.

"Did you understand what he said?" Morley asked coolly.

"Gibberish," Emerson said, even more coolly.

I realized I was staring rudely (if understandably) at the reverend, who was placidly munching his chocolate biscuit.

"Languages are not my husband's specialty," I said, getting a grip on myself. "I recognized a few words—names, rather. He referred, I believe, to the city of David and the conquest of Jerusalem by Nebuchadnezzar of Babylon."

"Very good, Mrs. Emerson." Morley beamed at me and patted his hands together in applause.

Emerson glowered at the reverend, who was working his way through the plate of biscuits with calm concentration.

"And is this your evidence?" Emerson demanded. "The ravings of a religious fanatic?"

The parlor door opened a few inches. Expecting to find that Gargery, frustrated in his attempt to hear through a heavy wooden panel, had eased it open, I was disconcerted to see Horus squeeze through the opening.

We have a good many cats, too many, as some might say. They were all descendants of a pair of Egyptian felines we had brought back with us from Egypt, and they had bred true to type, being handsomely brindled animals with large ears and a high degree of intelligence. Horus was undoubtedly one cat too many. He was a bully and a philanderer, whose contempt for us was matched by our detestation of him. For some unaccountable reason Nefret doted on him.

Apparently he had learned how to open doors. After an insolent survey of the persons present he sauntered across the room and jumped up onto the sofa next to Nefret, shoving her aside so he could sprawl out.

"What a handsome cat," said the reverend, whose chair was beside the sofa. "Here, puss, puss, good puss. Would you like a biscuit?"

"Chocolate is not good for cats," I said. The comment came too late; with a sudden lunge, Horus snatched the biscuit from the reverend's fingers and crunched it up, sprinkling damp crumbs over the crimson velvet upholstery of the sofa.

Emerson had had enough. Breathing heavily through his nose, he fixed Morley with a hard stare. "I agreed to listen to your proposition, Mr. Morley—against my better judgment—because you claimed to have solid documentary evidence supporting it. Thus far that evidence has not been forthcoming."

"This prospectus," said Morley, removing a handsomely bound booklet from his breast pocket, "contains a photograph of the scroll I mentioned when we last—"

"Photograph, bah," said Emerson. "I would have to see the scroll itself."

"It is in·extremely fragile condition, professor, and cannot be carried about. Several learned authorities have inspected it and pronounced it genuine. You may communicate directly with them if you like."

"Well, I don't like," Emerson declared. "So-called experts can be hoodwinked as easily as other men. Anyhow, I have no interest whatsoever in biblical legends, or in the Israelites, who were treacherous, bloodthirsty sinners, turning on one another whenever they ran out of Amalekites, Jebusites, Philistines, and Moabites to slaughter. Furthermore, the scheme you propose is unacceptable on several grounds."

"What scheme?" I asked.

I might as well have saved my breath. Having regained his, after his long diatribe, Emerson continued. "You cannot be unaware of the unsettled state of the area in question. Your scheme may—almost certainly will—enflame conditions that endanger the peace of the entire region."

I got one word out—"What"—before Morley interrupted. The narrowing of his orbs indicated rising temper but—I do him credit—though his voice was a trifle loud his speech was measured.

"With all due respect, Professor Emerson, that is only your opinion. I have permission from the authorities to carry out my scheme." He sipped genteely at his tea.

"What scheme?" I demanded.

I can, when occasion demands, raise my voice to a pitch that is difficult to ignore. Morley started and burst into a fit of coughing—having, I deduced, swallowed the wrong way. Emerson, who knew the futility of ignoring it, replied in a tone almost as vehement as mine.

"The damned fool is mounting an expedition to Jerusalem, to look for the Ark of the Covenant."

The ensuing silence was broken by Nefret's melodious chuckle. "I do beg your pardon," she murmured, trying to keep a straight face.

"Your derision is justified," said Emerson. "People have been looking for the damned thing for centuries. They are welcome to keep on looking for it, insofar as I am concerned; it is a harmless enough fantasy. That is not my point. My point is—"

"You have made it, Professor." Morley placed his cup carefully on the table and rose to his feet. "I will take no more of your time."

Though as a rule I deplore Emerson's bad manners, I was as anxious as he to get our visitors out of the house. I had fully expected the reverend to fall writhing to the floor during his initial outburst. His present look was almost as disconcerting; looking up from his pensive contemplation of the (empty) biscuit plate he inquired, "Are we going now?"

I accompanied our guests into the hall. Morley took his hat from Gargery, who was hovering, and turned to me.

"If the Professor should change his mind—"

"He will be sure to inform you," I said. "Good afternoon."

We shook hands, and I offered mine to the reverend. He met it with a surprisingly firm grip and a sweet, childlike smile.

"Good afternoon, Mrs. Emerson. Those were excellent biscuits!"

Gargery followed me to the parlor, so closely he

was almost treading on my heels, and began clearing away the tea things, with glacial slowness.

Emerson went to the sideboard and poured the whiskey. "Here you are, Peabody. We both deserve it, I believe, after that interview."

"He can't have been serious," Nefret exclaimed. "Why on earth did you bother listening to such an absurd proposal?"

"I had my reasons," said Emerson. He gave me a sidelong glance. "They were excellent reasons. That is all I can tell you."

"Can, or will?" I inquired. A few sips of the genial beverage had restored my composure and a few ideas were simmering in my head.

"Can," said Emerson, with considerable emphasis.

"Sworn to secrecy, were you?"

"Quite," said Emerson, giving me a meaningful look.

"Ah," I said.

"What on earth are you two talking about?" Nefret asked.

"I am waiting for your Aunt Amelia to tell ME what I am talking about," said Emerson.

"Oh, very well," I said. "Far be it from me to make you break your sworn word. You will not be guilty of that error if I tell you."

"Precisely," said Emerson, no longer attempting to conceal his smile.

"Please do, madam," Gargery exclaimed. "I can't stand the suspense much longer."

There was no use ordering Gargery out of the room; he would only listen at the door.

"Confound it," I muttered. "Why can't they leave us alone? I suppose the meeting occurred last week, when you said you went up to London to work at the British Museum. What were you given this time? I don't want any more cursed emeralds."

"I was given nothing, Peabody. Not even the threat of a title. Apparently the royal family only pays on delivery."

"Royal family," said Gargery in dying tones. "Madam . . ."

I addressed Nefret instead of Gargery. She had been courteous enough to refrain from questions, though her wide blue eyes indicated her interest. "Some years ago we were able to be of service to her late Majesty in a delicate family matter. Upon its successful conclusion she summoned Emerson to Windsor and offered him a knighthood—which of course he refused."

I ignored the groan from that consummate snob Gargery and went on. "She then presented him with that vulgarly ostentatious emerald ring which you may have seen in my jewel box. Apparently she passed on the story to her heirs, in case another delicate situation arose. This delicate situation, one may deduce, inspired the otherwise inexplicable visit today from Mr. Morley. Now, Emerson, it is your turn. I hope His Majesty doesn't expect you to go looking for the Ark yourself."

One of the kittens wandered in and jumped onto Nefret's lap. Stroking it, she remarked, "Does it exist? As I recall, from my studies at the vicarage, the Ark contained the tablets given to Moses on Mt. Sinai."

"The Ten Commandments," I said helpfully.

"Yes, Aunt Amelia. But I thought the professor didn't believe in Moses. Or the Exodus. Or—"

"That doesn't mean the fabled Ark is pure fiction," Emerson replied, taking, as was his habit, the opposing side. "We know that Jerusalem was besieged and overrun by the Babylonians, who carried away its residents into captivity. There was time—"

"So you admit that not all the Old Testament is a tissue of lies," I said. "The fall of Jerusalem is mentioned in Second Kings, if my memory serves."

"It is also described in the Babylonian annals," Emerson retorted. "An historical source, Peabody. As I was saying, there was time during the siege for the inhabitants to conceal their greatest treasures. The Ark was only one of them, though the most important. There were vessels of gold—an altar, candelabra, incense vessels, and so on. Who is to say they may not still lie hidden under the ruins of the Temple?"

"Do you believe that, Emerson?"

"Certainly not," said Emerson, tiring of his teasing. "Jerusalem was taken and sacked many times. If the Bablyonians didn't seize the temple treasures somebody else did. The Arch of Titus in Rome shows Roman soldiers carrying away some of the treasures, including a menorah. The Ethiopians claim the Ark was taken there by the son of Solomon and the Queen of Sheba. People have looked for it in Ireland, at Mt. Sinai, and for all I know in Birmingham. Even if I believed there were the possibility of such a discovery, I would not countenance an expedition by an untrained amateur in a particularly sensitive part of the world."

"Gargery," I said in some exasperation. "Will you please finish clearing the tea things away? The kitten is about to knock over the cream jug."

Nefret removed the cat, and Gargery, who had abandoned all pretense of carrying out his duties, exclaimed, "Then why don't you and madam go looking for the treasure, sir? You'd do a proper job of it."

"Kindly stay out of this, Gargery," I said. "It is difficult enough to keep this family on track without your digressions. I cannot imagine what the Ark of the Covenant has to do with any of this, or why the British government should take an interest in the plans of an adventurer like Morley."

"Would you care to have me explain, Peabody?" Emerson inquired in a devastatingly mild voice.

"That is what I have been asking you to do, Emerson."

"Hmph," said Emerson. "I presume you are familiar with the present uneasy political situation in the Middle East?"

"I am not, sir," Gargery said eagerly.

"Nor am I," Nefret admitted.

"You really ought to make an attempt to keep up with modern history," I said. Emerson, who had opened his mouth, closed it. "Palestine is of course part of the once-mighty Ottoman Empire, which during the sixteenth century of the Christian era controlled the entire Middle East, North Africa, and parts of Eastern Europe. Like all empires founded on conquest and injustice it could not endure; gradually its territories were lost and at the present time only the support of Britain and France, who fear the collapse of the aging giant would open the doors of the East to Germany and Russia keeps the Sultan on his throne in Constantinople."

"Very poetically expressed," said Emerson, who had been waiting for my breath to give out. "To look at it another way, Nefret and Gargery, the aging giant is rotten at the core. Provinces like Syria and Palestine are racked with poverty and corruption. Britain and France don't give a curse about the misery of the people; what concerns them is that in the past decade or so German influence in the region has increased enormously. When Wilhelm the Second visited Istanbul and Jerusalem, he was greeted as a conquering hero. The Germans are constructing a railroad line from Damascus to Mecca, and one is entitled to assume that they aren't doing it for altruistic reasons. If war should break out—"

"War!" Nefret cried. "And Ramses is there, in the thick of it?"

"Stop worrying about your brother," Emerson said impatiently. "There won't be a war, not for a few more years. But it's coming, and Germany is already making preparations—such as that railroad. Very useful for moving troops and supplies." This speech was presumably an attempt to reassure Nefret. Not surprisingly it failed.

"War or no war, if there is any way Ramses can get in trouble, he will," she said vehemently. "If the situation is so unstable—"

"Nonsense," I said. "Samaria—the modern Sebaste—is nowhere near the area where the

Germans are working, and Mr. Reisner is a responsible individual. Emerson considers him one of the most qualified of the younger generation of Egyptologists."

"Hmph."

"Or would, if he considered any other Egyptologists qualified," I amended.

"He's not so bad," Emerson admitted. "Though one would suppose he had enough on his plate with his excavations at Giza and in the Sudan, without taking on another responsibility in an area he knows nothing about—"

"Reisner would argue that the basic techniques of excavation are the same in all parts of the world," I said.

"Well, well," said Emerson. "Hmph."

The ambiguity of this response ought to have raised alarm bells. It is not like Emerson to be ambiguous. In my defense I must say that I was more concerned with calming Nefret. "George Reisner is a mature, dedicated individual who lives only for his work. Not even Ramses can get in trouble while he is in Reisner's charge."

Spellbinding suspense featuring the indomitable

AMELIA PEABODY

from *New York Times* bestselling author

ELIZABETH PETERS

Don't miss these critically acclaimed bestselling tales
of suspense, romance, and intrigue in an
exotic and dangerous world

LORD OF THE SILENT
978-0-06-195166-4

For Amelia and her family, the allure of Egypt remains as powerful
as ever, even in this tense time of World War. But nowhere in this
desert world is safe, especially for Amelia's son Ramses and his
beautiful new wife Nefret.

And don't miss

LION IN THE VALLEY
978-0-380-73119-0

THE DEEDS OF THE DISTURBER
978-0-380-73195-4

THE APE WHO GUARDS THE BALANCE
978-0-06-195163-3

THE FALCON AT THE PORTAL
978-0-06-195164-0

HE SHALL THUNDER IN THE SKY
978-0-06-195165-7

Visit www.AuthorTracker.com for exclusive
information on your favorite HarperCollins authors.

Available wherever books are sold or please call 1-800-331-3761 to order.

EPP1 1209